# FAGIN'S BOY

# FAGIN'S BOY

*A Gay M/M Historical Romance*

# JACKIE NORTH

*Jackie North*

M M  R o m a n c e  A u t h o r

*This book is dedicated to...*

*Dear Old Dad, who introduced me to the spirit of
Christmas Present, oh, so long ago*

*And to all those orphans out there
--You know who you are*

*"Where have you been, this long, long while? Ah! The same sweet face, but not so pale; the same soft eye, but not so sad."*

--*OLIVER TWIST* BY CHARLES DICKENS

# CONTENTS

# THE FURTHER PARTICULARS OF
# A PARISH BOY'S PROGRESS

Oliver stood in front of the looking glass that rested, tipped back in its oval frame with curlicue ends, on top of the chest of drawers. He slowly took off the somber black top hat he was wearing and, with his fingertips, placed it on the chest of drawers.

The looking glass told him what he already knew: that his face was white with cold, his hair crushed by the hat's brim and sticking out from his ears, and his eyes looked as flat as the pieces of silver that had been pressed upon Uncle Brownlow's dead and forever-closed eyes. Oliver could not see, now or ever, the angelic beauty so many had told him he possessed. But what did that matter when everything in his world was no longer as it had been?

The small room around him was clean and warm and snug under the eaves, the baseboards and wooden floor shining with the particular brilliance of many scrubbings and hand-rubbed wood oil. The floor was covered with several patterned pieces of carpet; bright wallpaper along the inside walls brimmed with small country flowers. To one side of the window, on the single white wall, hung two small watercolors that Aunt Rose had done for him, depicting the small cottage in Chertsey; on the other side was a colored print of a map of England.

It was a pleasant room, all the way up at the top of the house, full of cloudless echoes of privacy, with only the maid and the cook to trouble him at the other end of the narrow passageway. Oliver had not minded being tucked away at the top of Uncle Brownlow's townhouse. It allowed him to be away from Mr. Grimwig, who had often said, regardless of who was listening, that Oliver was a bad seed, born to be bad, and likely to hang. Uncle Brownlow had often chided Mr. Grimwig about this, but he would chide him no more.

But the room did not belong to Oliver. Not the ornaments on the bookshelf, nor the white, scalloped drapes, not even the washbasin with the pitcher and the tiny, almost unnoticeable crack along the handle. None of it was his. Not anymore. Nothing was Oliver's except for his clothes, his books, and the miniature portrait of his mother, which was a painted copy of the large one that used to hang in the parlor. The original had been lost in one of the moves to or from the country, which had been made more often in recent years as Uncle Brownlow's illness had retreated or advanced.

The doctors, one of whom had been Mr. Grimwig's own, had called the illness consumption, but neither the good summers in the country nor all the plasters and blisters in the world had kept Uncle Brownlow from being taken home to God.

Oliver was yet too numb to cry; his body felt stiff against the onslaught of sorrow that battered against his breastbone. With a hard swallow, smoothing the placket on the fine black wool of his suitcoat, Oliver regarded the bookshelf under the window and concentrated on the row of books there.

He looked at his botany book, which was mostly about flowers that could be planted in churchyards. Then at the grey-bound collection of Dr. Johnson's poems. Then at the green geography book he'd studied from cover to cover so many times, the edges were frayed. And then at the much-loved *Cobwebs to*

*Catch Flies*, the first book Uncle Brownlow had ever given him. Oliver had practically memorized the book by now and sometimes still took it down to muse through the pages and pretend that everything was as it always had been.

With one last glance at his own tired expression, he turned away from the looking glass, away from the stark, stiff outline his mourning clothes made against the clean white walls. Away from the image of the sweet young man people thought him to be. Occasionally, the anger he carried inside flickered in his eyes, but mostly people saw what they wanted to see: young Oliver Twist, diligent in his studies, kind to all, extremely good, and wanting for nothing.

Looking down at himself, he touched his collar, slowly, feeling the last tingle of the dampness from the flakes of snow that had vanished in the relative warmth of the room, sensing the tug of threads beneath his fingers. He wanted to loosen his cravat, but he needed to remain respectably dressed. He also needed to go downstairs in a moment to join the somewhat solemn assembly that was now drinking cups of tea and partaking in whatever plates of cake Mr. Grimwig's housekeeper could press upon them to accept. And he wondered, when he got down to the parlor, whether Mr. Grimwig would throw him out now or later.

He knew that thought was an unintended result from his own dark musings and might never happen. Uncle Brownlow had asked Mr. Grimwig to look after Oliver, and look after him he would, until the world's final trumpets sounded. Mr. Grimwig was a gentleman and, as such, would keep his word. Of course, there was no telling in which way he would keep it, whether it would be with kindness or with hard looks and scolds and thumps of his cane. Probably the latter.

Oliver had read once about how chameleons could change their color, but Mr. Grimwig was no chameleon and would not, very likely, ever change. At least that made him predictable, which was something to be thankful for, as was the fact that Mr.

Grimwig had not cast Oliver out into the freezing winter streets. It was well within his right to do so, especially since, in Mr. Grimwig's opinion, Oliver had never been a trustworthy boy, nor worthy of Uncle Brownlow and his kindness.

Oliver thought about washing his face and hands in the basin at the washstand, but that would just delay what must come, and he wanted to have it over with.

"Oliver!"

The voice came from the ground floor. Mr. Grimwig, unable to mount the stairs most days, preferred instead to stand at the bottom and shout and pound his cane. Uncle Brownlow had found him and his pounding cane amusing, but then, they'd always been the best of friends.

"Oliver Twist!"

He needed to go down. He needed to be brave and walk down the steep staircase with his head high and look everyone in the face and take their kind words with the aplomb of the heroes in his favorite books. Besides being a gentleman, he knew how to behave at a funeral reception, for he'd attended enough of them from his employment, starting at the age of nine, at Mr. Sowerberry's undertaker's shop.

Oliver's welcome at the reception wasn't an aspiration completely doomed to failure even if, as was very likely, Mr. Grimwig would meet him with a pinch to the back of Oliver's arm. The pinching had replaced the head thunking that Uncle Brownlow had finally objected to, some years back. Either action, however, would be accompanied with a hissed warning about workhouse boys and how easily they tended to go astray.

Mr. Grimwig had never forgiven Oliver, even after these five years, for what he ostensibly felt was the outright theft of the new suit of clothes, the stack of expensive books, and the five-pound note, none of which had ever been returned to Uncle Brownlow. Mr. Grimwig had held Oliver absolutely at fault for this theft, even after his abduction back into Fagin's gang had been exposed as being completely out of the Oliver's control.

The theft only proved, in Mr. Grimwig's mind, that one couldn't take in a workhouse orphan without experiencing, at the very least, a heartache. Especially not after the boy had been in the company of a gang of pickpockets.

"Oliver *Twist!*"

Oliver did not want to give Mr. Grimwig a chance to upbraid him, in front of guests, no less. Though Mr. Grimwig might enjoy it, Oliver most certainly would not, so he opened the door and hurried down the stairs.

The carpet runner muffled his steps as he descended, stumbling down the risers in his haste. He paused a moment at the top of the last flight of stairs before continuing down, rubbing along the inside of his left arm, over the scar from the bullet that Giles had shot him with. Even though the scar didn't ache now as it sometimes did, it was a touchstone upon which he could place his fingers and take a deep breath and manage whatever Mr. Grimwig might have to say to him.

The parlor, the small library, and the shining landing before the front door were stifling, the air warm and close compared to the rooms above. From the many grates, Oliver could feel the warmth of the coal fires mixed with the press of people. Everyone was dressed in solemn black and brown, standing together, talking in low voices in a way that told him there would soon be animated chatter and a sense of liveliness.

The funeral of Mrs. Bedwin, the former housekeeper and his old nurse, had been like this. She had caught a chill two springs ago and left this world in her favorite grey silk dress, white pelerine, and black bonnet—her Sunday best. And after the mourners had come back from the graveyard, their exhaustion had put them at their ease. Being joined together in something commonly shared had relaxed their guard, and they were less inclined, it seemed, to stand on ceremony.

Funerals did that, and that was just the way of the world.

# TREATS OF A FUNERAL RECEPTION, WHEREUPON OLIVER'S FUTURE IS DETERMINED

"**O**liver, come here at once."

Oliver stopped on the bottom step and, ignoring his unhappy reflection in the looking glass that hung on the wall next to the front door, scanned the gathering to see where the call had come from.

Mr. Grimwig was waiting, having taken the spot nearest the fire in the parlor. Of course, he was always the one nearest the fire. He gestured, a scowl already in place, as though Oliver had spoken back to him in a disrespectful manner or, perhaps even more damning, had refused to approach altogether.

Oliver hurried over to him, but had Oliver complied even sooner than he was able, it would not have mattered. Mr. Grimwig was cross with him from the moment he got up in the morning to the second his cap-covered head hit the pillow at night.

He nodded at Mr. Grimwig and the two men who stood at his elbow, whom Oliver knew well. Parson Greaves had attended Uncle Brownlow in his last hours, and Mr. Beauchamp, who ran the Pear Tree Court Bookshop, had become a close friend of the family ever since he'd stood up for Oliver at the trial, so long ago. The two men had cake plates in hand, cups of tea balanced on the edges of the plates, and were dressed in black out of respect for Uncle Brownlow. It was good that the men were standing there, as they presented too much of an audience for Mr. Grimwig to do more than scold.

"We were waiting for you," said Parson Greaves kindly.

"We were just talking and enjoying some cake," said Mr. Beauchamp, idly rubbing his mismatched brown waistcoat. He was slightly bald and round, but pleasant for all that. He reached out to pat Oliver gently on the shoulder.

"I blame it on too much time alone with his books, gentlemen," said Mr. Grimwig. "It puts too many thoughts in that foolish head."

Mr. Grimwig often talked this way, about a boy in the abstract, as if Oliver wasn't even there. But in spite of the sudden anger that boiled behind his eyes at the explicitly untrue remark, a funeral reception was neither the time nor the place to say what he really thought, so he didn't say anything.

"Did you know, gentlemen," said Mr. Grimwig, going on, "that the number of workhouse boys turned criminal is shockingly high? Why, I have the numbers right here in my head, if you'd care to hear them."

The two men shook their heads, as if astonished by this fact, but the gestures seemed shallow at best. Both men eyed Oliver kindly, as they might look at someone who has lost a beloved guardian.

"I'm sure," said Parson Greaves, "that the numbers can be turned either this way or that, and that even an orphan can rise to do good works. What about Dick Whittington and his cat?"

"He wasn't an orphan," said Mr. Beauchamp.

"We are all orphans eventually," Parson Greaves said, nodding sagely.

If Oliver wasn't mistaken, Parson Greaves and Mr. Beauchamp looked a tad relieved when Grimwig nodded as well. But then Mr. Grimwig tapped his cane twice to bring everyone in their party to attention.

"There's many a man who has made his mark in the world," said Mr. Grimwig. He then spoiled any kindness that might have been lurking in his words by saying, "But I've yet to see any potential in young Twist here."

Oliver felt his jaw tighten even as he opened his mouth to protest, but closed it. It wouldn't matter, anyway; Mr. Grimwig had never liked him. And now that Uncle Brownlow was solidly buried in the frozen ground, Mr. Grimwig's distaste for Oliver and all that he was would be clearly shown, and probably daily, if not hourly.

"It's a sad day, Oliver," said Parson Greaves.

"Thank you," said Oliver, keeping his voice steady, as he watched Parson Greaves and Mr. Beauchamp look at him, which people tended to do, for a little, sometimes.

For years now, ever since he'd been sold to Mr. Sowerberry when he was nine, he'd experienced those stares and assessing expressions, sometimes imagining they must see a greasy spot on his lapel, or perhaps a stray hair, or a smut on his cheek. But that had never been the reason. It was Mr. Grimwig who'd finally explained it to him, in his way, some years ago, and several times since then, once when he and Uncle Brownlow were waiting for Oliver to adjust his cap in the slender looking glass that hung in the front hall.

"That boy is as prideful as a peacock!" Mr. Grimwig had said, exploding. "As in love with his own reflection as any Narcissus!" But before Oliver could gather his anger fast enough to deny it, Uncle Brownlow had ushered them both to the steps where they could hear church bells ringing and see the beautiful spring day beckoning.

Since then, Oliver had been attuned to such comments and the looks that went with them. It could be that he was wrong; the two gentlemen might be thinking something else altogether, or perhaps not. His only hope was that even if they saw him and admired his face, they would not think him vain.

"My dear friend Mr. Brownlow was not his real uncle, as you

know," said Mr. Grimwig. "The boy has relations in the country, a poor curate and his wife near Chertsey and, perhaps, some additional kin near Lyme Regis. But none that could take him in, or that would want to, I'll be bound."

Grimwig was talking to the gentlemen, as though Oliver wasn't standing *right* there. Oliver felt a flash of rage beneath his breastbone and a great, swamping desire to state, quite clearly, that Uncle Brownlow *had* been his real uncle, in every way that mattered.

But instead of protesting, Oliver turned his face away, feeling the heat there, to look at the paintings on the wall. At the red velvet atop the mantel. At the little stag made of Chinese porcelain. At the wreath made of dried flowers and hair that Uncle Brownlow had kept near him everywhere he went. Oliver liked to imagine the hair in the wreath had belonged to his mother, but he'd never asked, and now that Uncle Brownlow was gone, he'd never know. Certainly Mr. Grimwig wouldn't know, or even if he did, would never stoop to share that information with Oliver.

"Will you remain at home?" asked Mr. Beauchamp, in a hearty voice that was obviously an attempt to ease Oliver's discomfort. "Or will you go to university?"

Parson Greaves laughed. "Of course, Beauchamp, you would urge more education on the boy. Can't you see he's destined for the church?" The parson winked at Oliver in a friendly way because, of course, even the most angelic looks could not gain one entrance into the seminary, and Oliver was a poor religious scholar at best.

"Well, Oliver," said Mr. Beauchamp. "Do you have any dreams? But of course you do, for all young men have dreams."

"Oliver dreams of being waited on hand and foot for the rest of this life, don't you, Oliver. He is determined to live a life of leisure, I believe, always has his nose in a book, always reading. For all the good it does him. Are you listening, Oliver?" Mr.

Grimwig nudged him hard with a swing of his cane against Oliver's leg. "Mr. Beauchamp is speaking to you."

Oliver opened his mouth, ready to say something, anything, to make Mr. Grimwig stop.

"Now, I'm just a parson," said Parson Greaves, almost hurriedly, "but if you're looking for work, as Mr. Grimwig states, then you could do worse than to gain employment in a factory. They're hiring in factories, such as the mills up north, and perhaps a change of air would assist you on your way with your bereavement."

Oliver kept still, oddly struck by the sudden turn of the conversation. But he did not want to work in a factory and choke his lungs with chemicals and filth. No, he wanted to own a bookshop, pure and simple. It was going to be a nice little establishment, clean and quiet and full of books that he could read any time he cared to sit down and take one off the shelf.

Oliver stepped back a little and clasped his hands behind his back. "I want to own a bookshop," he said, feeling brave by sharing this out loud.

Mr. Grimwig knew this wish of Oliver's; in fact, he had heard it many times over the years. But he'd never supported it, saying that bookshop owners were leeches on society, selling dreams for a price and leading people astray when they should be applying themselves to good, honest work. He did not say this now, of course, because there was a bookshop owner present.

"You'd need to learn that from the ground up," said Mr. Beauchamp. "I'd take you on as an apprentice in my bookshop in an instant; however, I already have two and have no need of a third."

Oliver felt his body jerk as though someone had struck him. Working in someone else's bookshop was an idea he'd not considered before, but it was a good one. Of course, it wouldn't be seemly to ask Mr. Beauchamp if he might reconsider, for indeed, it might be for certain that he had no places available at his shop.

"But I say, Parson Greaves," said Mr. Beauchamp, patting the brown serge waistcoat over his belly. "Weren't you, in passing, discussing that acquaintance of yours? Surely it was just the other day when he said he needed a likely boy for an apprentice?"

Mr. Grimwig went still. Oliver likewise held himself still and pretended not to be the least bit interested in Parson Greaves's potential response. He examined his boots, looked at the backs of his hands, imagined how nice a cup of tea would be right about now, anything but think about the parson's friend's need for a likely boy.

"Oh, yes," said Parson Greaves. "I was at the church meeting, you know, the one regarding the broken windows in the narthex, and he was there. Mr. McCready. You remember."

"Mr. McCready?" asked Mr. Beauchamp, as if searching his memory. "Oh, yes, indeed, Mr. McCready. He owns a small haberdashery in Soho."

There were nods in their small circle, except for Mr. Grimwig, whose sour mouth turned down in a frown.

"I know no Mr. McCready," he said.

Oliver wanted to point out, explicitly, that simply because Mr. Grimwig did not know a man personally did not mean that the man did not exist. But he kept his mouth shut because, for some reason, these two men seemed as though they wanted to help him. At the very least, they were, at present, nodding and smiling, as though Oliver's apprenticeship to the shop owner was a foregone conclusion.

"He keeps a very nice shop," said Parson Greaves. "I've been in there several times in need of a shoelace or a packet of soap powder, a needle, or some such thing that you never would guess you'd need until you do. And then, there, in his shop, is the very item you were looking for."

"It's a good, clean shop," said Mr. Beauchamp. His tone was more serious and less playful than Parson Greaves'. The deeper and slower tones lent his words an air of gravitas. "And the boys he hires are well mannered and tidy. He learns them a trade, he does."

When he looked up, Oliver saw that Mr. Grimwig was looking at him, his brows all beetled down and a tightness narrowing his round face. Oliver knew the second he indicated a preference that Mr. Grimwig was sure to combat it with all sorts of reasons why it shouldn't be so, and why Oliver should be sent back to the workhouse posthaste. All of this had been expressed by Mr. Grimwig for years.

"The work would be too hard for the boy," said Mr. Grimwig. And just to prove he wasn't saying this out of sympathy or concern, he added, "He's never done a day's worth of work in his life, but spends it reading and walking and begging for money to go to the theater. He wouldn't last a day in a shop."

"Hard work would do the boy some good, I should think," said Mr. Beauchamp, nodding and waving his hand at the girl with the tray of sherry to come closer. "I've never seen a boy, regardless of his circumstance, who didn't benefit from a bit of hard work."

"Be a good man, Mr. Grimwig, and give Mr. McCready a chance to know about the boy at least." Parson Greaves nodded. "It wouldn't hurt, and the boy's got to make his way in this world sometime. Mr. Brownlow would have approved of McCready, at any rate."

"He's just there," said Mr. Beauchamp. "Over by the cakes. Blessedly good cakes, by the way. Why don't I just go and fetch him, and then we can be going on with our good deed?"

There was nothing Mr. Grimwig could do, not even make taciturn remarks about upstart young men and the inelegance of being in trade. That Uncle Brownlow had friends not only in banking and in the church but also in trade never seemed to matter. The fact that Oliver might want to go into trade was enough to make Mr. Grimwig dislike anyone who put on an apron and waited behind a counter.

Mr. Beauchamp didn't even put down his cake plate or cup of

tea, but strode boldly over to where a group of men stood near the arched doorway. As he chatted with one of them, that man looked over at Oliver. Then he nodded and came with Mr. Beauchamp. The new member of their party was tall and had a clean, tidy air about him in spite of his shaggy sideburns.

"Gentlemen," said Mr. Beauchamp, "may I introduce my friend, Mr. McCready, haberdasher extraordinaire."

Mr. McCready nodded his head in greeting. As he did not know Mr. Grimwig, it might be that he did not know the story about Oliver's illegitimacy. On the other hand, as Oliver had learned from Mrs. Bedwin, there was nothing people loved to do more than gossip.

"Yes, I do own a shop. A haberdashery." As Mr. McCready spoke, he had a special little smile that seemed to announce his feeling of both contentment and superiority, as if there were no greater felicity in the world than to own a shop and wear an apron and stand behind a counter all day.

"There's nothing more pleasant than a well-run haberdashery," said Mr. Beauchamp, chewing his cake with relish as if, when he left Mr. Grimwig's, there would be no more cake to be found.

"I like to think so," said Mr. McCready. "I like to think of my little shop as a pleasant respite from the hustle of the street where one can browse for essentials as well as fripperies." He nodded at this statement, seeming well and truly satisfied with his shop and his life. "I've recently added draperies and cloth to my stock, which has widened my clientele."

"That can only be good for business," said Mr. Beauchamp. He patted his waistcoat as he brushed some small crumbs away. "When you widen your scope, you widen your net, and the cash rolls in."

"Indeed," said Mr. McCready with a glint in his eye. "I am truly blessed in this. My shop might not be a palace lined with marble and gold foil, but it is clean and respectable enough for the Queen herself, and I would not be ashamed to have Her Majesty alight on the pavement before my doors."

"Do you still take apprentices, as we were talking of only last week?" asked Parson Greaves, with an abruptness that took Oliver aback.

"Indeed, I do," said Mr. McCready. "I take in apprentices, boys as young as twelve years and as old as fifteen."

"Young Twist is seventeen," said Parson Greaves. "Barely too old, though in spite of that, perhaps just right for a shop such as yours. Would you be up for the work, Oliver?"

Oliver tried to think of something to say in reply to this, something that wouldn't reflect anything scathing that he thought about a shop that didn't sell books. He also felt some shock at the rushed and pragmatic direction of the conversation.

"You waste your breath talking of work, gentlemen," said Mr. Grimwig. "Because here before you is a head that is addled with novels and books, and a body that expresses the laziness of a young man upon whom every indulgence has been lavished."

This was true, this was so very true; there was no way Oliver could make Mr. Grimwig revoke it because since the day Uncle Brownlow took him in, Oliver'd had every care in the world lavished upon him. There had been a parade of attendance in the form of private tutors, as many books as he could read, and cake and puddings for his sweet tooth that Mrs. Bedwin had ever despaired of but had never attempted to curtail.

But while it was true he'd been indulged, it had never been true that he'd not appreciated it. After the first nine years of his existence at Mrs. Mann's baby farm, which was later echoed in the dark room at Hardingstone Workhouse—a dank place with no windows and no door—coming into the light under Uncle Brownlow's kind care had created a contrast of which he never needed reminding.

He knew what it was like to be treated with cruelty and to be disregarded, as if he weren't a human being at all, but merely a creature barely deserving of being fed and clothed. When comparing his memory of the workhouse to the image of Mrs. Bedwin tip-toeing into his room in the morning to open his curtains and bring him a cup of tea, sweet with cream and sugar, well, the contrast was firmly drawn.

Not that he could talk about any of this to the assembled company, for he'd wager that none of them had suffered a day's deprivation in their collected lives. But he could defend himself from the charge of laziness; Uncle Brownlow had always encouraged an honest response, saying it was a mark of a gentleman to speak his mind.

"I intend to work," said Oliver into the small silence that had fallen at Mr. Grimwig's remark. "But I intend to work toward owning a bookshop when I gain my inheritance at twenty-one."

"It's only three thousand pounds," Mr. Grimwig said to everyone, in spite of the comment about money being in very bad taste in such a setting. To this bald pronouncement, Mr. Grimwig followed up with a tart and completely unnecessary explanation, "To be kept by me until he's twenty-one, if he doesn't end up a criminal first."

"I beg your pardon?" asked Mr. McCready, which was indicative of the fact that he was the only one of the assembled company unaware of the stipulation of Oliver's inheritance. His thick, dark eyebrows flew up into his forehead, perhaps at the crass mention of money as well as the amount, for three thousand pounds was indeed a fortune for an illegitimate parish boy.

"There was some sort of arrangement in the will of the blighted boy's father," said Mr. Grimwig, telling the story that, indeed, was not his to tell, but that he told to anyone who would listen. "If Oliver Twist can abstain from a life of crime, if his record is clean and unbesmirched by the time he reaches twenty-one years of age, then he shall inherit. But if there is one single blot, then he inherits nothing. And, gentlemen," said Mr. Grimwig as his chest puffed up, "I would lay claim to the fact that the latter is more likely than the former."

"It's an odd arrangement that was dreamt up during a death

fever, I dare say," said Parson Greaves, as though attempting to brush over Mr. Grimwig's unkind remarks.

Mr. Grimwig shrugged, as if it were of no consequence to him. "Death fever or no, the arrangement is in the will, duly witnessed and signed. A half portion of the original amount of the six thousand pounds was given to Oliver's half brother some years ago, but that gentleman, a Mr. Edward Leeford, went to America directly after, and no one knows what happened to him."

"But I know." Oliver swallowed and made himself say it, although even the memory of Monks and his peering, skulking ways was enough to give him nightmares. "He went to America and squandered the money. Uncle Brownlow said that he died in prison, a pauper."

"Which is how you'll end up, Oliver Twist, if you can't refrain from speaking until you are spoken to."

Mr. Grimwig's voice was loud enough to carry over the reception in general. A low silence fell for a moment before polite voices took up various conversations once more, and Mr. Grimwig's face had a chance to settle back from a sudden puce color into its normal, hearty red.

"Oh, I doubt he'll come to that," said Parson Greaves. "He's got the face of an angel, as it is, and a voice like one as well."

"Yes," agreed Mr. Beauchamp. "No one with a face like that could ever come to crime."

The gentlemen looked at Oliver, frankly appraising him, and Mr. Grimwig did as well, making Oliver want to squirm. Their statements were of the kind that Oliver had heard often, ever since he'd come out of the Hardingstone Workhouse, but that never made it any easier to hear. People everywhere—in church, in the shops, or on the street—stared at him raptly, as though he were something that they felt they wanted. He couldn't help the way he looked and, besides, no one knew better than he what evil beauty could hide.

"Work is what keeps people out of the workhouse," said Mr.

McCready. "Even if that abode casts a long shadow over their lives."

Of course, it might be that Mr. McCready knew, at the very least, that Oliver came from a parish workhouse, but he tried not to show his surprise at this statement. Oliver had never expressed his fear of one day going back to the workhouse, because he'd never wanted anyone to know. A true gentleman never worried about going hungry or about being admitted to a workhouse, his body stripped of its own clothes, to be given the grim, threadbare workhouse uniform.

"I do have work, young Oliver," said Mr. McCready. He held his cup and saucer in one hand but had not drunk from it, not the whole time that he'd been standing there. He'd not taken any cake either, though from the breadth of his shoulders it did not seem that he abstained from eating sweets on general principle. "I could use another apprentice in my shop, someone to work in the warehouse, count the stock, make deliveries—"

"Oliver has said that he only wants to work in a bookshop," Mr. Grimwig said, interrupting. The statement didn't surprise Oliver overly much; the protest was merely for form's sake and to be cruel. "He's made that quite clear, though what's to actually be done with him except send him to the mines is beyond me."

Parson Greaves almost choked on his tea. Both he and Mr. Beauchamp tipped their chins low and chortled at the nonsense that someone as beautiful as Oliver would ever be sent to the mines. But they couldn't laugh outright; that would be rude.

"As I was saying," said Mr. McCready, as if Mr. Grimwig had not spoken. This gave Oliver a little shock because no one had ever ignored Mr. Grimwig. "I could use another boy. And, if you'll pardon me, Oliver Twist, with a face such as yours, you could make plenty in tips doing deliveries to kind ladies who don't want to brave the busy streets and who are full of gratitude for the receipt of their laces and ribbons."

Mr. McCready turned his face to Oliver as he made his offer. His eyes were serious and steady.

Oliver felt his whole world come to a complete stop. His ears rang, and, in his mind's eye, he saw his future shop, situated at the end of a tidy cobbled lane and made of red brick, with paned windows on either side of a large wooden door that had a polished brass handle.

The shop would be clean and would smell of paper, and there would be a small iron stove in one corner to keep the books dry, with chairs for patrons to sit on while they thumbed through their chosen volumes. And over the shop would be Oliver's rooms, with large windows to let the sun stream in when it was shining, and a snug little chair in which to sit and watch the water sheet down the glass when it rained.

He did so want to own a bookshop and had plenty of ideas about what books he would procure for it, but he had only the vaguest idea as to how to establish the business itself. If he worked for Mr. McCready, he would be better able to acquire his heart's dream.

"I've an eye for a young man with gumption who wants to make his own way in the world," said Mr. McCready. He beckoned to one of the servants to take his teacup away from him. Then he reached into his inner breast pocket and pulled out a long wallet. From this, he took out a card, which, in deference, he handed to Mr. Grimwig. "Oliver and yourself might come by the solicitor, Mr. Bond on Oxford Street, if you are in agreement. Then we could sign the papers, and Oliver would work for me and be a burden to nobody."

It was then Oliver realized that, for the whole conversation to have come so smoothly to this point, it must have been orchestrated by Parson Greaves and Mr. Beauchamp. As for Mr. McCready, he also seemed very aware of Oliver's predicament. Oliver looked at the three men, and their eyes were kind as they nodded at him. He felt a flood of gratitude and nodded in return.

"I know it is very soon," said Mr. McCready, as he watched Mr. Grimwig flicking the edges of the card with his fingers. "So soon after laying your beloved benefactor and friend in the ground only this morning."

"God rest his soul," said Parson Greaves.

"He was a good man," said Mr. Beauchamp. "And as constant a customer as anybody could hope to have."

"We should wait some days, out of respect," said Mr. Grimwig. He slipped the card into his breast pocket, mussing up the carefully arranged white handkerchief there.

Oliver considered that if Mr. Grimwig lost the card, either accidentally or on purpose, Oliver had only to contact one of the gentlemen gathered around him and ask them, or walk along the pavement of Oxford Street and inquire for the office of Mr. Bond.

"But in these modern times," said Parson Greaves smoothly, "we don't have the leisure to observe traditional mourning periods of weeks or months. You must make your way in the world, Oliver Twist, and good, honest work is sometimes the best panacea for a saddened heart."

"Monday, then," said Mr. McCready. "Would you be willing to meet me at the solicitor's in the afternoon, say, at four o'clock?"

"We could, perhaps," said Mr. Grimwig. "If the weather doesn't turn sour. I'm not desirous of making haste in a sleigh down London's streets for an appointment with a shopkeeper."

The comment was rude, as was to be expected from Mr. Grimwig, regardless of the present company. Mr. Beauchamp and Parson Greaves had shared expressions of wishing the conversation could continue apace, as though the words had not been said at all, and as for Mr. McCready, he frowned, his dark brows a bit thunderous.

It did Oliver's heart good to know that this new acquaintance did not approve of Mr. Grimwig. Besides, that the recent weather had been icy and cold was true, with storms sweeping through the snow-packed streets almost every afternoon. At the same time, Oliver didn't think that Mr. Grimwig would actually let a little bit of bone-freezing, traffic-snarling weather keep him from getting Oliver off his hands and out of his sight at long last.

Mr. McCready gave Oliver a kindly nod, as if to say that all would be well. Oliver wondered when he would really begin to believe that was true.

"Monday at four o'clock it shall be, then."

"Yes, thank you, Mr. McCready," said Oliver, being his most polite. He wanted to be gone from the townhouse with every breath in his body, even if it meant working in a shop that sold no books.

Mr. McCready nodded again, a little smile on his face, and his eyes were bright. He was obviously a man who liked making plans and enjoyed seeing them come to fruition. "I'll expect to see you then. Your guardian, Mr. Brownlow, would have been pleased, I think."

"An apprenticeship at his late age should be rather difficult to arrange, I'd say," said Mr. Grimwig.

"I'm only just seventeen," said Oliver, before Mr. Grimwig could respond with a nasty observation about the uselessness of youth. "Turned this January past."

"A rather cold month to be born," said Parson Greaves.

"His mother had fallen on hard times, you see," said Mr. Grimwig almost conversationally, as if he'd been telling this story all along. "She suffered the misfortune of giving birth to an illegitimate child in a parish workhouse."

Oliver could see by the expressions on all three of the men's faces that they were somewhat taken aback by the baldness of this statement, as if they'd not heard this particular tidbit before. As if they'd not heard it a *hundred* times before. Most days it wasn't even noon before Mr. Grimwig had reminded anyone in close company of that very fact. Oliver curled his hands into fists to keep his pounding heart from galloping away from him, but he opened his mouth anyway to try and change the subject.

But just before he was about to speak, one of the men beat him to it.

"From whence came your cake, Parson Greaves?" asked Mr. Beauchamp. "I don't see the girl with the tray."

"She's right over there," said Parson Greaves, waving his fork over his plate, which was picked quite clean. "Raise your hand, she'll see you. Be sure to have her bring you one of the raspberry tarts; they're delightful."

Oliver waited with what he assumed was a polite mien while the servant came over with the tray and busied herself by serving the men various slices of pastry and necessary cups of tea.

Mr. Grimwig did not accept anything, not tarts or cake nor even more tea. Instead, he looked at Oliver out of the corner of his eyes, a curl to his mouth, as if daring Oliver to defend himself and his long-dead mother.

Oliver knew that if he said even one word on his own behalf, let alone that of his mother, he might actually start yelling, his temper overcoming him to the point where propriety was well lost and his reputation ruined. And all the while, Mr. Grimwig would smile, as if satisfied that his point regarding Oliver's low birth had been proven right.

Oliver turned away. He didn't want to hear Mr. Grimwig say any more cruel things to these men who were trying to help him. He didn't want to see the sympathy on their faces or witness their attempts to smooth things over. So instead of remaining, as would be most polite to do, he allowed himself a small nod to nobody and slipped out of the circle of wool-clad shoulders, intending to make his escape while he could.

## ❧ 3 ❧

# WHEREIN OLIVER ONCE AGAIN
# ENCOUNTERS A STRANGE SORT
# OF YOUNG GENTLEMAN

O liver walked with hurrying steps to the servants' door at the back of the townhouse and grabbed his great-coat from the rack.

"You shouldn't go out, young master," said the housekeeper from behind him, her heavy skirts swishing over the sound of her footsteps clacking on the tile. "It's not fitting to be out so soon after a funeral."

Oliver shrugged on the greatcoat and buttoned it, and tied his red wool scarf around his neck as he pretended not to hear her. When he pulled on his thickest leather gloves, he couldn't bend his fingers enough to pick up his cap, but she kindly gave it to him just the same.

"Thank you," said Oliver. He couldn't remember her name, but that wasn't exactly his fault. Mr. Grimwig had hired all new staff the moment he was able, and since then, the staff, never up to his expectations, came and went before becoming known to Oliver.

"I won't be out long," he said, as she opened the back door for him.

Snow swirled across the brick steps that led down to the cobblestone yard that led to the alley, but the drift was thin, as if the snow intended to give up quite soon. The sky above, boiling with low clouds, belied that fact.

"Not long," he said to her.

His heart expanded with a lurch inside of him, seeming thick in his throat as he blinked hard and did not let himself look at her. He could *not* look at her, or his hard-won semblance of calm and control would become undone. Instead, to be polite, he tipped his cap and went down the steps, hurrying, not letting himself stumble or slow, trying to leave before Mr. Grimwig might chance to look about him and notice that Oliver had slipped away.

OLIVER WALKED ALONG THE PAVEMENT, HIS CHIN DUCKED into his red scarf, the snow almost up to his ankles, until his heart settled in his breast and his rage dulled to a low ache in the shivery air. The row of white townhouses, all neat and tidy, looked cream-colored against the smudged sky, their green-painted ironworks hidden by layers of snow.

The world was white all around, a thin swirl about his head and dark flakes coming down from the smoking chimneys, black against the newly laid white. There was, at this hour in the afternoon, yet a gleam of sunlight slanting over the chimney pots, silver through the clouds.

The street was not very busy, as was typical during the late afternoon hours, especially when a deep cold was coming on. All the deliveries had been made, tomorrow's milk and eggs ordered, and toast and tea were being prepared in houses all up and down the tidy street.

People were inside, as they should be, but Oliver needed to be outside. The townhouse was too full of memories of good things, many of which he'd taken for granted, in a way. Not that he was ever less than mindful of always having a full stomach. Or that his boots were sturdy and without holes, that his stockings were woolen and thick against the cold. And, best of all, he always had books aplenty to read and considerable amounts of time to read them.

It had been Uncle Brownlow that Oliver had been careless about, and the thought of this felt sharp in his chest, as it had been since the day Uncle Brownlow had passed away. Uncle Brownlow had always been old, but uncles lived forever, everyone knew that. Or at least the ones in books did; uncles lived to see their young charges settled in life, happy, perhaps even married. Or if uncles did die unexpectedly, it was under mysterious circumstances, which would, eventually, lead to a surprise happy ending where the young charge inherited a great deal of money.

Yes, part of that was true; Oliver *had* inherited money. And more, Oliver had gained an uncle in Mr. Brownlow, relatives in Aunt Rose and Uncle Harry, along with two fine nephews, and a circle of acquaintances spreading out from that. But now, close to hand, all he had was Mr. Grimwig, who in no way was going to become the kindly replacement uncle whose sole purpose in life was to see Oliver settled and comfortable. Which made the conversation at the funeral reception even more remarkable. Much like what happened in books, he'd met with three men who were willing to help him, willing to see him happy.

When Oliver got to the corner of Old Church Street, he turned in the direction away from the church and the dark grey workhouse, not wanting to be faced with the reminder of the funeral that morning nor the dark, towering walls that represented his past.

He could go into Elm Street Park, where the path was likely to be shoveled and trampled. Though now the dark treetops were humped in soft white, in springtime the path was kept private by boughs of willows and thickets and smelled of greenery and flowers.

Oliver determined he would think of that, instead of the snow that now bowed branches and lumped over shrubbery. He thought maybe that the snow would forever remind him of Uncle Brownlow, catching a chill, growing weaker, the fever taking him, and then this emptiness. Surely spring would come. Surely the memories would fade into something more pleasant than the ache in his heart.

Oliver walked along the street till he got to the path that wended its way through the park. He faced the wind as he went; it was prudent to do this, for then he would be able to walk home with the wind at his back and his face turned away from the cold as he retreated from his memories. But for now, he walked face in the cold, shoulders back, braced against what might come.

The trail beneath the snow was a little slippery, but there was enough traction from stones and branches and roots of trees to help keep him upright. A gust of snow caught an exposed part of his neck, and his cheeks were burning with cold.

A group of men with shovels over their shoulders came walking toward him on the path. Their boots were thick and their clothes were thick, but they were bare-headed, their faces gleaming with sweat from their efforts to clear snow. As they walked, the heads of their shovels knocked snow from the upper branches, and they seemed neither to notice nor care upon whom the snow fell. Oliver hesitated on the path, and then, at the last moment, jumped out of their way, to the edge of the path, shivering as a face full of snow caught him anyway.

Sputtering, he wiped his face with his gloves. He should get back to the funeral reception anyhow, before he was missed. Even though there was really no one to miss him now, and the reception was mostly full of conversation of the idle type he'd never much cared for, there were expectations of propriety and guests waiting.

He felt a hand on his arm and jerked backward.

"Leave me be," he said, low, almost muttering. "I've got it, I say."

"Leave you be, Nolly?" said a voice, using the pet name that no one had called him in years. "That's all anyone's ever done, is leave you be."

The voice was close, and Oliver could smell small beer and unwashed skin and something familiar that made him freeze. He did not know that voice, and yet he did. He shrank inside his greatcoat, but the hand jerked him again and pushed him against a tree, where the snow rattled down and obscured his vision again even as he opened his eyes.

When he could see through the curtain of snow, there, to accompany a voice from long ago, was a face from memory, five years on. The face was thin, hollow-cheeked, the skin sallow, as though fading from being sunburnt, with snapping, bright green eyes, that rough face grown into itself. It was, impossibly so, the face of the Artful Dodger, also known to his more intimate acquaintances as Jack Dawkins, back from the grave, back, back from wherever he'd been. And he'd found Oliver.

"Oh," said Oliver. "*Oh.*" A prickly feeling rose along the back of his neck and along his scalp, and he was cold all over. He felt as though something had punched him in the gut, a deep blow that sent his whole body reverberating with shock waves that made him reel, unsteady, on his feet.

In spite of this, all of a sudden part of him flickered with the memories of Jack from so long ago. Jack, taking Oliver by the hand on a crowded High Street in Barnet; Jack acquiring ham and bread, and feeding Oliver with it till Oliver's stomach had been as full as it had ever been, more full than he could ever remember. And then how Jack had pulled him through the streets of Barnet and Islington, to the thickness of London, darting across posh, wide boulevards, and trotting down rackety-packety back lanes full of sewage and open doorways with dark figures looming inside.

There was, as well, the memory of Jack's touch in Fagin's den. Jack's hands pulling him back, Jack putting his body slightly in front of Oliver's when Fagin ranted, waving his iron fork about. Jack, with his hands in Oliver's hair, or patting his cheek, stroking his arm. Jack had been a constant part of that time, his hands leaving a sensory memento of those days so long ago. The echoes of which Oliver realized he were now stirring inside of him, and which he did not quite know what to do with.

And then, sometime along when Oliver had been snatched off the streets by Nancy and Bill Sikes, Jack had disappeared, never to be seen again. No one had ever told him what had happened to Jack, and Oliver had never known whom to ask. And yet here Jack was, cutting a bright figure in the snow, dapper in a new greatcoat that was no doubt, *no doubt*, stolen from some fine establishment, where the staff were, even yet, quite possibly peering through the racks and crates and boxes, trying to figure out where the coat had gone. They'd probably never even seen Jack, neither coming nor going.

Oliver thought to say a word, and he opened his mouth to say it, but his confusion over whether it should be of welcome or recrimination stopped him. Jack was not his friend; that finely drawn illusion had been shattered some time after Jack had dragged him into a den of thieves. Oliver had been taught how to pick pockets and how to break into homes.

And yet. Jack had been the first person to show him any real kindness. In the midst of Oliver's exhaustion after his walk from Hardingstone and his confusion as to what to do next, Jack had taken Oliver under his wing, fed him, had given him a smile and a pat on the head, and Oliver had been so grateful, so *unbeliev-ably* grateful. Yet, it was hard to separate what had happened on the High Street at Barnet from what had come later. Jack Dawkins had found the life of a thief a grand one; in his mind, it was something to be grateful for. So he had not meant—

But now, Jack's eyes were narrow, and his thin face was shadowed and grimy from cold and exposure. With a snap, he shoved Oliver against the tree, sending snow to sift inside the red scarf folded about his neck.

"You're goin' to tell me what I want to know," Jack said. His teeth were gritted together, and the accommodating smile, which had flitted among Oliver's memories through the past five years, was nowhere to be seen.

Lurching forward, Oliver tried to push past, but Jack caught him, the breadth of his shoulders creating a barrier. The group of men who'd been shoveling snow was too far gone, and there was no one else near the little copse in the park, no one to help. When he'd gotten snatched by Bill and Nancy, he'd shouted, and although there'd been plenty to hear, no one had believed him. This time, there was no one even to hear.

"Let me go, Jack," said Oliver. His teeth were chattering. He wanted to tell himself it was from the cold, only his knees felt as though they'd lost bone and were ready to give way beneath him at any moment. "I won't tell anyone you're here, I won't, promise."

"Tell anyone what, then?" asked Jack. He pushed Oliver hard against the trunk of the tree with cold, gloveless hands, his smile showing the tips of his teeth. "I'm here on orders of the Queen an' all; got papers an' everythin'. Been hextricated an' that. Five years, served me time."

"Extricated from where?" Oliver had no idea what Jack was talking about, and yet it seemed that Jack assumed he did. He didn't correct Jack that the word *hextricated* was pronounced *extricated*; it wouldn't help, and Jack would hardly appreciate the difference, anyway.

"Got shipped back, by orders of the Queen. Been deported to Australia, to the colonies, haven't I, but now I'm back. On good behavior, no less." Jack smirked, still pressing Oliver against the tree.

"They don't let you come back; they send you there and you *never* come back," said Oliver, his jaw tight. He couldn't believe that Jack had actually been deported, let alone returned.

"And yet here I am," said Jack, smiling fully now, showing more teeth, his green eyes flashing.

Oliver's rage during the funeral reception, which had begun to turn into grief, sprang anew within him. His heart raced, as it had so many times in the past, pushing against his breastbone in a painful, sharp way, as though battering its way through his chest. But Jack did not notice or care as he held Oliver's shoulders. And even though it seemed Jack did this as if by afterthought, no matter how hard Oliver twisted and pushed, he couldn't move.

"I come to London three days ago an' go straight to the bottom of Saffron Hill. The Three Cripples was there, but no Fagin, no gang," said Jack. The words came in a blast from Jack's chapped lips. "I asked; no one knows the story. I go to the other hideouts, the perches, the dens, an' then ask around some more. I hang about the Three Cripples till they almost throw me to the peelers. But no one's seen anythin' of Fagin's gang, an' no one will tell me exactly what happened, why they're all dead an' gone. An' no one'd ever heard of me neither. It was as if I t'weren't never there."

The words and the grip took Oliver back in an instant, as if the intervening years had never been. As if the last door he'd stepped through had not been the cream-trimmed one at the townhouse on Old Church Street, but the one to the room in Fagin's backup den, where Oliver had been kept forever. Kept in semi-darkness and utter silence and fed a meager diet and given books about criminals to read until he'd all but broken.

"Let me go, let me *go*," said Oliver. He could hardly breathe to get enough air in his lungs, and the words came out thin.

Jack laughed a little under his breath and seemed only amused by this rather than moved, though he stepped back and dropped his hands from Oliver's shoulders, as though to let him pass. Oliver took a single step, and then, in a blur, he was on the ground, shoulders and back pushed into the snow, almost smothering from the weight of Jack on top of him. Jack held Oliver's face between two hands.

"You tell me," said Jack, low, snarling, his breath warm, shocking, on Oliver's face. "You *tell* me where they are."

Oliver could hardly move. Dizzy from lack of air, he could

only blink the snow from his eyes and stare at Jack. When he tried to inhale, his breath throttled in his throat, and Jack still didn't seem to care.

"Who?" Oliver managed. "Who?" He couldn't imagine who Jack was looking for after all these years.

"Them! Everyone! Like I told you! I'm lookin' for 'em." Jack slammed Oliver's head deeper into the snow until the white walls cupping around his ears threatened to collapse in on him and smother him. "Charley, Nancy, even Bill Sikes. And where's Fagin? *Fagin!*"

Oliver's eyes fluttered half-closed. He didn't want to be the one to tell Jack, Jack who had come so recently back to England and didn't know. The newspapers depicting the events were five years old, and even if Jack could find them, Jack's reading skills had never been a known thing. But to *tell* him? To be the one? Jack would surely kill him then.

Oliver shook his head and clamped his mouth shut, and was shocked to feel Jack's fist slamming into his face. He inhaled snow up his nose and coughed and thrashed as Jack held him down. His struggles only shifted Jack's body till Jack's legs were between his own, warm and heavy, shoving, part of Jack's body pressing like an iron brand against the inside of his thigh.

"Tell me," said Jack, thrusting forward. "Tell me or I'll bury you in snow."

It would be foolish to doubt this. Oliver felt the warmth on his face and was sure his nose was bleeding as his jaw throbbed. The press of Jack's chest on his was pushing him further into the snow, and whether Jack buried him or used more of his fists, it didn't matter. Oliver was already marked up, and he was to see Mr. McCready the next week—

Oliver pushed up, growling, and for a second, this seemed to surprise Jack, who pulled back, only to slam down again as he punched Oliver right on the mouth, sending hot blood from his mouth to sear on the snow. Gasping, Oliver sank back, trying to shift his legs so that Jack's weight didn't press so *close* against him.

Jack brought his face very near Oliver's. He wasn't looking at Oliver directly; it was as if he didn't care what Oliver looked like. He breathed through his nose, and when he spoke, his lips almost brushed against Oliver's.

"You'll tell me," he said. His breath skittered across Oliver's skin. "Or I'll bury you."

"Jack," said Oliver, unable to breathe.

"I'll *make* you," said Jack. He drew back his fist.

"No, wait," said Oliver. He turned his face away. "I'll tell you."

It would be useless to try to explain to Jack why Oliver mustn't look like he'd been getting into street fights. Why it was so important that he get away from Mr. Grimwig and start his new life, start working toward that bookshop he'd always wanted. He couldn't tell Jack any of that because Jack was likely to use that knowledge somehow, to control Oliver and make him turn back into one of Fagin's boys. To make him sink to the level of the street, to the throng and pall of those who barely had enough to eat, and where there would certainly be no quiet corner in which to read.

Too much was at stake. He'd tell Jack what he needed to know, and then Jack would leave him in peace.

Jack moved. Half his weight was off Oliver now, and Oliver felt the relief in his chest, gasping with it, even though Jack's legs were still tangled with his, sending some humming thing moving through his stomach. But more, he shivered with the touch of Jack's skin, warm against the coldness the snow had left behind, the tiny roughness at the ends of his fingertips against Oliver's jaw, the heat and pulse beneath Jack's skin.

"You goin' t'start talkin'?" asked Jack. "Or do I get to shove my fist down your throat?"

"It's difficult to begin," said Oliver. On top of shaking with cold, he could hardly believe that he was having this conversation, which threw him back in time, back to when he'd been a child of the streets, a poor orphan that nobody wanted and could never love. Oh, Fagin had once had use for him and his pretty face, that was certain, but it was for his own gain and never for Oliver's.

"Try."

"You have to promise—"

"Promise what?"

"I wasn't there, Jack," said Oliver. "I wasn't there for any of this, you have to understand it, you *have* to—"

Jack tightened his fist; Oliver shied back and put his hands up to his face, but Jack's hand upon him was firm. Snow flew up around Oliver's arms like white lace, beautiful but cutting and cold.

"I can't tell you more about where they've gone," Oliver said, thinking to take the gentle road, something comforting and soothing, as might be said, even regarding the likes of Fagin and his gang. "Unless it is to the hereafter, and God speed to them."

"What the fuckall does that mean?" Jack spat this, as if his temper had been frayed by hours of attempting to lure the truth out of him rather than only two moments in the drifts of snow.

"Something happened to Fagin's gang," said Oliver. His lips felt numb. "I don't know exactly, but that's what Uncle Brownlow told me. It was in the newspapers, but that was five years ago, and they never let me see them. They said it would be too much for me, after—well, after everything."

With a shove, Jack pressed close, his hand clenched around Oliver's jaw. "I know you know more, an' you better tell me quick, or—"

"Wait!" Oliver took a breath. Cold air whistled down his neck where the red scarf gaped. "It all happened so fast, you realize. Once Nancy was killed, the hunt was on, and the courts, they took it personally, having let Fagin's gang go on so long. So they hanged him. They hanged all of them, as far as I know."

"Where?"

"Where *what?*"

33

"Where did they *hang* him?"

Then it became clear. Where a criminal was hanged was markedly important; Oliver remembered this from the books on criminals that Fagin had made him read. This, then, was the crux of it for Jack.

"Fagin was hanged at Newgate," said Oliver, as plainly as he could. "I went to see him, to pray—"

Jack slammed Oliver in the chest with the flat of his hand, then pulled him close again, breathing right into Oliver's face. Cold snow slithered down his neck; Jack's hot breath simmered against his cheek. A low, cold wind whistled around them both, the dark branches stirring overhead, sifting down snow as delicate as though from angels' wings.

"Prayers? For Fagin? From *you?*" Jack looked white, his eyes enormous dark spots, the breath winged out of him, as though he'd been struck in the gut.

"I stayed with him to give him some comfort," said Oliver as quickly as he could. Only it had been so long ago, and Oliver had buried much of it, and couldn't dig up enough of it fast enough. But he had to try. Something, somehow—

"It was a horrible place. There were two guards outside of Fagin's cell—"

"Of course there would be two, for someone as dangerous and canny as ol' Fagin," said Jack, arching his neck proudly. "Go on."

Now Oliver understood, and he stopped thinking about what he could recall and instead began to imagine what, exactly, it was that Jack wanted to hear. Jack wanted the romantic story of it and not Christian platitudes, that was plain enough.

"It was one of the most secure cells, guarded by the warden, an important cell," Oliver continued. He focused on Jack as this news, only slightly false, fell into the cold, raw air.

"Because he was an important prisoner, of course." Jack nodded, some color coming back to his cheeks. "Then what?"

Oliver considered the reality of what had actually happened

that day. Fagin had gone mad with terror, had crouched on his pallet, shivering and shaking and spouting nonsense. He'd continually muttered about a man who *should* have his throat slit, someone who had betrayed them all. Someone who had peached.

This last was the worst possible sin for anyone of Fagin's ilk, so Oliver could well imagine that the person in question should have his throat slit. At least according to Fagin. And, probably, according to Jack, who was waiting for more of the story. Oliver swallowed, settled his chin, and determined to make the best of it.

"He didn't want my prayers," said Oliver, the lies, like the words in a story, coming more easily to him now. "The major of the guards had questioned him for some time, Fagin told me, wanting to know details and names, but even on promise of a lighter sentence, Fagin never gave anyone up. He waited, upright and strong, for his fate."

At least part of the story was true. Fagin had been too busy trying to pretend that Oliver was going to escort him out of Newgate, as innocent as you please, to even come close to naming names. Except there had been that one name, new and unknown to Oliver at the time, and which now remained firmly out of reach. It didn't matter, anyway. At that point, the guards hadn't cared who Fagin had been able to mention, so in effect, he'd peached on no one.

"Of course not," said Jack. "I always knew he'd go like that."

Jack's eyes were blind to Oliver now, as though he was miles away, back where he'd come from, back in some moment of his own past. He made a small gesture with his hand toward Oliver, as if asking for something.

"What is it?" said Oliver.

Jack focused on him then, but didn't say anything.

"That's all I know." Oliver said this as quickly as he could. "Something happened, I don't know what, but Bill killed Nancy. A mob chased him through the streets and he was shot. Along the way, as he ran, he must have led constables to the various hideouts, and they were able to track their way to Fagin, and—"

Jack pulled his hand away, and he sat back on his heels, the edges of his coat digging dark trenches in the soft snow that sparkled whiteness all around. He pulled Oliver to sitting but kept him close by, hip deep in snow, and banged his fist gently on his own bent knee.

"Hanged." Jack's voice quivered, and it seemed as though he were trembling.

Teeth chattering, Oliver looked up at Jack and tried to shift to a more comfortable position in the snow, but Jack gave him a shove and refused to let him move.

"Stop," said Jack. His face was the color of iced paper. "Fagin was *hanged* because of you. You an' your snivelin' face an' your stupid, pious—"

Oliver felt the rush of his temper, like flames shooting out of his belly. He rolled to his side and shifted to his feet, ready to be away from Jack and his fists, poised, ready to run. The snow flew about him, and his red scarf fluttered loose about his neck.

"I wasn't there for any of it!" He almost screamed this. He had been there for part of it, but if Jack was going to keep at him like this, then maybe Jack *did* deserve to know that his precious mentor, his leader, went so mad in the head that he thought Oliver was there to take him away from that horrible place. Fagin had kept babbling about someone who had sent them all to the gallows, leaving Oliver unable to make sense of any of it. "I was in the country, I was at church, I was studying my new textbooks; I simply wasn't *there*."

Jack bent low and scooped up some snow with his bare palm and placed it on Oliver's jaw. Without thought, Oliver knocked his hand away, making the snow, already dappled with blood from Oliver's nose, fly and drift down anew.

"Stay away from me," said Oliver, low, his voice rough from the distaste of having his past, *this* past, barrel its way into his life just when he was taking a new direction and starting over again. He felt rough, as well, from his shock at the unexpected but not unfamiliar touch of Jack's hand, the gentle kindness, the casual intimacy of the gesture. "You stay away from me or I'll call the constable and explain to him exactly who you are and what you were arrested for." Oliver could almost taste his disdain for Jack. "And this time? They'll carry you off for good."

Something flickered across Jack's face, and there was a twitch along the edge of his mouth. Oliver knew he merely imagined he saw the hurt there because Jack had been on the streets most of his life; no hard words could ever hurt him. If Jack was wounded, it was because Oliver had threatened to break the code, the one that dictated that none of Fagin's boys ever peached.

Jack straightened up and took a step back, stumbling against the roots buried beneath the white lumps of snow.

"As you wish, Nolly," he said, smirking. "I'll leave you be, but you know, Fagin's boys got to stick together, help each other out. Find good jobs to get to the glittery stuff an' that."

Jack had always been happier in a group, and if he couldn't find his gang, he'd be all alone. But then, it wouldn't be too long till Jack had another gang, would it. Though that was none of Oliver's concern, and bad business besides.

"I'm not one of Fagin's boys," said Oliver. "And I've got nothing for you. *Nothing*. Stay away from me, or I *will* call the law."

"You won't do that, Nolly," said Jack, not at all worried, it seemed.

"Good-bye, Jack," said Oliver.

He picked up his red scarf that had fallen in the snow and started to push past Jack, stepping back on the path, shaking snow from his shoulders as he went. He could sense Jack standing there, watching him, but he didn't turn back to meet his gaze. Those old days were gone, and Oliver wanted nothing to do with them.

"Hang on, then," said Jack, in that voice he had used in the past to distract a pedestrian and redirect their attention while snatching a handkerchief or a wallet or a pocket watch or what-ever he felt was on offer that day. "I'll be takin' that."

With a deft hand, he snaked the scarf from Oliver's hand, where it ran against his dirty, calloused palm like a ribbon of blood.

"Give that back!"

Jack shook his head and wrapped the scarf around his own neck, tucking it inside his coat, in spite of the clumps of white snow that clung to it. It had to be cold and icy-wet, but he didn't even shiver.

Oliver leaped toward him; Jack nimbly jumped backward and laughed.

"I'll be keepin' this for a while as you look like you can easily afford another'n," said Jack. "Say it's a present from one mate to another—yes, let's call it that. Your welcome-home gift to me."

"It's not a gift and you're not welcome!" Oliver tried grabbing the scarf, but Jack was too far away, and Oliver's knees were still shaking. "And you're *not* my mate!"

Something smoked dark and hot in Jack's eyes, but Oliver refused to feel badly for it. How was he going to explain the loss of his scarf? And with the bells tolling the hour, the very late hour, how on earth was he going to explain his absence to Mr. Grimwig and the rest of the people at the funeral reception?

But Jack had turned his back and was walking up the path, churning up the snow as he went, his shoulders brushing the snow-covered trees, sending a cascade of it to fall around him till finally he was obscured by a misty curtain.

Oliver watched him then turned to spit in the snow, leaving blood-red dapples across the white.

## ❧ 4 ❧

## UPON HIS RETURN FROM A
## SOJOURN IN THE STREETS

When he arrived at the townhouse, Oliver was still shaking, but he managed to slip up the narrow brick stairs from the back courtyard and hang up his greatcoat and cap in the servants' hall, flipping the snow from his gloves. Snowmelt dripped from his hair down the back of his neck, and he wiped it away with his bare hand.

He turned to look up the hallway. The back entryway was empty, though he could hear the cook and the girl in the kitchen below. With his heart in his throat, water drying on his cheeks, blood drying on his upper lip, he tugged on the hem of his jacket, and straightened his lapels. By the time he'd gotten himself settled and walked up the passageway to the front foyer, he realized the house was quite empty, and the funeral reception was long over.

He rubbed his arm through the cotton of his sleeve, though feeling the length of the scar didn't seem to help as he got closer to the sound of things being moved about. Two servants were in the parlor to the left of the front door, gathering up cups and plates from the tables, dusting around the black wreath in the corner, and tidying the black cloths draped over the looking glasses and the clocks. They hadn't got to the study on the other side of the hall, which meant that the reception was over. *Just* over, but he was too late to avoid the recrimination he'd so rightly earned.

He heard a step behind him, and he turned around. Mr. Grimwig stood there, unsmiling; it was always the same, whether or not Oliver was considered to be a disgrace. Mr. Grimwig had a glass of sherry in his hand, which, under the circumstance, could go unremarked. But in his other hand, he held an envelope, which he did not quite hold out to Oliver.

"Where have you been? All of your guests have left, you know, each one of them asking to take their leave of you, and you nowhere to be found." Mr. Grimwig barely took a breath, and the diatribe continued. "And what are you doing, coming in like a street urchin, with blood dripping on your shirt, tracking snow and mud on the carpets? Oliver, what have you been up to?"

Oliver shuddered in a breath, fighting against the memories of Jack that swirled in his mind. It wouldn't do to explain what had actually happened, and it wasn't to protect Jack, so newly returned from being deported; Mr. Grimwig would hardly care about that, anyway. It didn't have to be Jack that Oliver had been with—any lowlife or commoner would do; it was Oliver's actions that would be seen to be the fault.

"I was attacked in the street," he said, shrugging. "Someone stole my scarf."

"Probably because you were waving it about as though it were a banner," said Mr. Grimwig.

He finished off the sherry and left the glass on the table, not seeming to care that it might mar the wood, leaving a white ring that would never come out. Then he lifted the envelope in his hand a little closer to Oliver and shook it.

"You received a letter today. From someone in Hardingstone." He peered at the return address. "It's from a Mr. Sowerberry. Do you know this person?"

The question jerked Oliver to attention. Sowerberry? The

40

name was from so far in his past it surfaced to the top of his memory like dislodged moss from a stagnant pond. He knew the name; the branding of it on his soul had been quick and nasty.

He had not allowed himself to think about the undertaker's shop since many seasons ago. But the sensation of the dark, damp cellar still lingered, and with it the puffy, cool feel of the casket lining beneath his hands. The weight of the shutters and the feel of Noah's clammy hand slamming into the back of his head.

Mr. Sowerberry had never stopped the blows, and Mrs. Sowerberry had obviously felt Oliver was a badness she had to control. He'd often felt her switch and her intolerant looks, both of which brought him to heel faster than he liked to remember.

And everything had smelled bad—some dusky, unwashed, lingering scent that came from the bodies that the undertaker watched over, though sometimes it had been Oliver's job to ensure that the body was too far gone by the time it was buried to keep body snatchers from making off with it. Even Oliver's own bedding had smelled of it—that same sweet, oily smell—and years later, from time to time, he would recognize it when passing a butcher's alley.

"Yes, I know them, sir," was all he said now. "I worked for them after I left the workhouse. I was apprenticed at an undertaker's."

Anything would have been better than the workhouse, but the undertaker's shop had been almost as bad. Sometimes, such as now, it felt that it would never get better and he would never reach the blue sky above.

"You worked for them? Brownlow never told me this. You have experience at an undertaker's?"

"I was nine at the time," said Oliver, the words of explanation slipping out before he could stop them. "But I ran away."

"You ran away? From such a good living as that?"

It was clear that Mr. Grimwig was not only astounded to find out something he'd not previously known, but was also surprised that Oliver was not desirous of becoming an undertaker himself one day. Uncle Brownlow had understood that for a sensitive boy such as Oliver, the darkness of the cellar and the black paint of the coffins had been nothing less than terrifying. The loss of a good living was all that concerned Mr. Grimwig, of course.

"Oliver? I asked you a question, and I would like an answer."

Oliver nodded as if he'd just been thinking. "I ran away, it's true. But they were cruel there and were going to send me back to the workhouse."

"Young men's struggles are often overstated," said Mr. Grimwig. The candlelight glistened on the moistness of his lower lip, and there was an unpleasant, sullen droop to his eyes. "You ought not to have done that. I wonder if Brownlow knew of your propensity to avoid those duties which were properly assigned to you."

Oliver thought of the way he'd come to the funeral parlor, from the dark room at the workhouse and all those beatings, and of the living he'd barely escaped before that, being a climbing boy for a chimney sweep. In Mr. Grimwig's mind, no doubt, those who worked for chimney sweeps or who were apprenticed in funeral parlors deserved their low, difficult status and should remain there till the angels determined they should be called home again.

Fearing he might start shouting at Mr. Grimwig to keep his ill-spoken remarks to himself, Oliver breathed hard and almost choked on the stink of old, withered flowers in the room. The memory of Uncle Brownlow, and how disappointed he would be in such a display of temper, was all that held him back. He clamped his mouth shut and looked at Mr. Grimwig.

Mr. Grimwig, without asking, opened the folded sheets, tearing open the seal as if the letter were his, and began scanning the contents. He squinted a bit as he read, his mouth moving. The letter must have been short, for he soon lifted his head and raised an appraising eyebrow.

"They send their condolences," said Mr. Grimwig. "As they

should, as is proper, of course. Probably only scouting for business, I suspect, knowing that if there is one death in the family, there is likely to be another. Although this family was shamed by your early departure and your lack of a proper good-bye to our guests."

"I know it was rude," said Oliver, his lips curling in an effort not to scream the words. He regretted not being able to properly thank Parson Greaves and Mr. Beauchamp, to shake Mr. McCready's hand and bid him good-bye until their meeting at the solicitor's office. "You don't have to tell me."

"What I shouldn't have to tell you," said Mr. Grimwig, his eyes snapping, "is how to be respectful when you speak to your betters."

"I would be," said Oliver. A low fire sparked in his breast. "If there were any of my betters here to speak to."

Mr. Grimwig turned white, and in another moment there would be shouting. But that didn't matter. If all went well at the solicitor's on Monday, Oliver would soon be out of Mr. Grimwig's circle of influence, gone for good and all. Oliver would remain in Mr. Grimwig's memory as only a story to tell on a rainy night, with mockery and grievances aired, and no reason to stop, not even out of respect for the dead.

What mattered now was the letter. Oliver reached out and snatched it away from Mr. Grimwig. Without looking back to mark Mr. Grimwig's startled expression, Oliver turned and hurried up the stairs, knowing that his boots were leaving a muddy tread on the darkly colored swirls of the runner. He should take them off and carry them and not make the maid work at cleaning both the stairs *and* the boots. But to do that would mean pausing and sitting on the steps while Mr. Grimwig watched him, and that he could not bear.

He heard Mr. Grimwig walking away from the bottom of the steps, muttering under his breath, shuffling with his cane, but Oliver did not stop till he'd reached his door on the top floor and opened it. He stepped inside and closed the door behind him, letting the sober dimness and the smell of the single beeswax candle the maid had lit, quiet him. Then, with the edges of his fingers pressing open the folds of paper, he stepped close to the candle and read as quickly as he could.

The elegant script was a reflection of Mr. Sowerberry's occupation; undertakers had beautiful handwriting, as if to offset the sadness and grief of their business. Beneath that, the letter was simple, containing *solemn condolences, respectful regrets*, but nothing personal, nothing for or about Oliver specifically. Mr. Grimwig was right; the letter contained only an attention to the undertaker's business and could have been sent to anybody.

At the uncomforting nature of the letter, a raft of bleakness now swamped him. The loss of Uncle Brownlow was a sheer weight hanging overhead that had been waiting for just this moment to rush into the blank spaces of his heart, and he flinched against it.

He walked over to the fire that was burning in the shiny black grate and tossed the letter into the flames. He watched till it crisped in the heat, burning down to black curls. Then he sat in his chair by the hearth to soak up the warmth.

The chair was a former occupant of the study downstairs, but the old-fashioned silk pattern was worn and had been considered too old for use there, and so had been given to him. Oliver had barely been able to stop himself from bragging that the chair, though shabby, was well made and so fantastically comfortable that he'd often fallen asleep in it. But he'd not wanted Mr. Grimwig to suggest that it was too fine a chair for such a boy, so he'd kept his mouth shut and, later, in private, had profusely thanked Uncle Brownlow for the gift.

He undid the laces on his boots and got up to scuff in stockinged feet to place them outside the door. Once he'd closed the door and latched it, he let his shoulders sag. Now he was alone with his thoughts and the complete absence of any prayers, and the comfort and solace they were said to bring. He'd tried very hard, praying at the church and at the graveside, and once when the local parson had come to tea the day after Uncle Brownlow had passed away. None of it had done any good, and the echoes of those efforts were of even less use still.

All that remained was the emptiness left by the absence of Uncle Brownlow, and the lack of anything to do about it. A great, enormous, monstrous lack that rolled into a blankness that filled his chest, tinged only with the weak gratitude that he'd no longer have to watch Uncle Brownlow struggling for each breath as he attempted to light his eyes on Oliver to let him know everything was going to be all right.

It was not all right; Uncle Brownlow had suffered, not wanting anyone to know how ill he was. When Oliver had found out, he'd watched his guardian waste away amidst the stone-white bedsheets, the medicine of the bewigged apothecary, the ministrations of the housekeeper, and the prayers of the parson, none of which had done any good at all.

Oliver had held Uncle Brownlow's hand for hours each day. And then once, Oliver had gone down to the kitchen to get away from the sickroom, just for a moment. When he returned, Uncle Brownlow had breathed no more. The room had quickly been spread with herbs to cover up the miasma of the fever and then closed immediately till the undertaker could come.

Horrified, Oliver had struggled with the butler as he'd locked the door, and when unseen hands had pulled him back, he'd raced down the stairs and flung open the front door, gasping in cold breaths as the snow came down thick as cream, filling his mouth and his eyes and slatting against his chest.

Someone had pulled him back. He flushed to think it had been Mr. Grimwig, who struggled even to climb the stairs. But it *had* been Mr. Grimwig. Though for once, the only time, he'd not scolded or berated Oliver in any way, even though he'd been standing with the front door fully open in his stockinged feet, letting in not only the snow and the cold but the stares of vendors and servants and everyone passing on the street.

Their street was busy, and everyone and anyone had seen

Oliver with his mad hair and open mouth and shirt unbuttoned to the waist. They'd stared and then turned away, and he, according to what Mr. Grimwig said later and quite stoutly, he, Oliver, had been the talk, all right. From coffee shop to tobacconist, from basket maker to bonnet maker, simply the *talk*.

Not that it mattered. In a short while, peace and God willing, Oliver would be gone from the house where all that had kept him from Mr. Grimwig's derision had been Uncle Brownlow's mild disapproval. At least Uncle Brownlow had had a constant companion in Mr. Grimwig, who now didn't want Oliver there. Oliver didn't want to be there, either. Which didn't help, the anger didn't help, and trying to use it was like trying to hold up a thin piece of shaved wood to block a flood.

He sank onto the bed and struggled to tear off his cravat, which, as he tugged, snapped in his hands. It was rented funeral garb, so it didn't matter. In little more than a week, he'd take up the costume of his new position. Regardless, Mr. Grimwig was sure to vent his displeasure at the thought of not getting that deposit back. But as Oliver held the bits of the cravat in his hands, he realized his hand was shaking.

It was as plain as the black cloth across his palm: Uncle Brownlow was the last person in the world who'd cared about him. Oh, yes, Aunt Rose and Uncle Harry always welcomed him upon his arrival to their home, but Oliver was now only a visitor to them, not a member of the family. Mrs. Bedwin was two years gone, and other than that? He had no one. Everyone died.

He braced his stockinged feet against the hard iron bedrails and covered his face with his hands. But it was no use, the pain across the soles of his feet didn't even make it up his legs, and however hard he held his jaw, it trembled, and as he shivered all over, it took him, a swamp of blackness that slammed into him hard like a blow to the face. It was like being shoved into a dark room where the only moment of daylight was when someone came in with the lash to beat him, making him bend to the realization that it would always be dark like this. That he was alone. That he couldn't be loved.

His face was hot with tears, but he was shivering all over. He tried stiffening his whole body to stop crying. But he couldn't by force, so he let the sadness come, soaking his hands and his shirt bosom as he tried to wipe his face with it. The rough feelings inside of him faded in an odd way, growing in his chest and then sinking back, till at last he was left shivering on the bed.

His feet hurt, his face was tired, and his chest ached as he stumbled to the chair with its pale green and gold-shot silk. Sinking into it, he curled himself into a ball, tucking his feet up under him. It was how a young child might sit, not a young man about to embark upon the world, but he didn't care. There was no one to see, and this way the fire in the grate could reach all of him now.

The fire was small, as befitted the grate of an attic room, but it sparkled and flicked its shadows brightly about the room. As his tears dried, he rested his head against one wing of the chair and wondered if perhaps he should go down for something to eat, or if one of the servants might bring him a tray.

Though, as to the latter, Mr. Grimwig might take it upon himself to make Oliver come down, instead of being waited upon like a young prince. *That young prince*, Oliver had heard Mr. Grimwig say more than once. *Prince of the May Dance, he thinks he is, and the world should be better served by making him scrub floors!* Not that this made any sense. It never did, but perhaps after years of derisive remarks, Mr. Grimwig was simply running out of fodder. Not that that had ever stopped him.

This almost made Oliver laugh out loud, feeling an odd relief that he could. As he stroked a hand across his belly, it grumbled down deep, bringing a real and insistent hunger to the surface. Something flickered in his mind then, the idea of being warm and hungry at the same time. He considered the odd juxtaposition of the two. When had that happened? Oh, yes, in the bad old days.

47

But why was he thinking of it now? Oh, yes. *Jack*. Jack with his whole body next to Oliver's, pushing him down into the snow, their legs tangled together. There had been, between them, between their bodies, a rough, emboldened familiarity, as if the distance caused by the last five years had never been.

Oliver shook this off and thought about the old days when Fagin's boys had lined the floor around the fire. Even if there had been nothing to eat, at least they'd all been warm, they'd all been hungry together. And in the morning, mysteriously, there had been sausages and bread and gin, and sometimes even sugar, when Fagin would take the time to heat the gin.

It had almost seemed to make the night of an empty stomach worth it. Especially when the boys would sit in front of the fire, their bare feet stretched out to it, shoulder to shoulder, warm together against the morning chill. It hadn't mattered then, or even later, that he'd been amongst thieves, because there had been those moments of connection, of belonging.

He could almost understand why Jack looked as though he'd been truly grieved to hear of Fagin's death, of the gang disbanded, of all he'd ever known gone. With moments like those, of being circled around the fire, in company, and the company pleasant if not good, especially with draughts of sugared gin, who would not miss it? Especially when the experience of that had been the best one he had ever known?

Oliver stood up and tried to think more clearly. He needed to wash his face and hands and change his shirt and go down to see if the cook would let him eat in the kitchen. The previous cook had sometimes let him.

Mr. Grimwig was probably locked in his own room now, as the evening came on. With nothing to plan or rent or arrange, he would be at as much of a loss as Oliver was, perhaps moreso. Uncle Brownlow and Mr. Grimwig had been good friends for many years. Not that that made Oliver feel any more sorry for Mr. Grimwig, no. But was it better to think upon that than to think of Jack, standing in the cascade of snow, in a stolen coat, with Oliver's red scarf wrapped around his neck as he laughed?

Instead of dwelling on Jack, as part of him wanted to do, he went to the washstand under the eave in the corner of the room and touched his fingers to the surface of the water in the pitcher. The water was still warm. This meant that one of the housemaids had taken it upon herself to bring him hot water when she'd lit the fire and the candle, in spite of anything Mr. Grimwig might say. The water that had cooled as he'd wandered the streets, and met up with—*Jack.*

Oliver heard a knock on the door. When he went to open it, the kitchen maid stood there. He still didn't know her name, but she carried a tray with a pot of tea, a pile of sliced sandwiches, and a pudding with a small pitcher of custard that was warm enough to steam in the hallway.

She looked at him, as though she didn't notice the blood on his shirtfront or the smears of blood on his chin, his rumpled hair, or any evidence of his unsettled state.

"Here you are, sir," she said. "I thought you might need this after today."

She held the tray out, and Oliver took it. Mr. Grimwig might have called her bold to take it upon herself to talk so plainly, but Oliver knew it was kindness, pure kindness, on her part.

"Thank you," he said, almost choking on the words.

"You're welcome," she said. "Things will look better in the morning, I'm sure." She bobbed a small curtsey

After a moment's pause, as she turned to make her way down the stairs, Oliver shut the door with his foot. He walked over to the fireplace and set the tray on the rug in front of it. Sitting cross-legged near the tray, he faced the fire, nodding as the warmth from the hearth radiated out at him.

Yes, he would eat like this, though he shouldn't; young men didn't. But Mrs. Bedwin would have said that a young man sometimes needed to eat like this, as close to the fire as he might. The memory of her kind regard was all the approval Oliver wanted at the moment.

He poured himself some tea from the teapot and brought the thin china cup to his lips. He could smell the sweetness of the tea and see the ripples of fat from the cream, the shadow of the edge of the cup across the brown surface. He took a sip, letting the warmth run through him, and thought of another fire, with a semicircle of barefooted boys around it as they warmed their feet and sipped sugared gin.

Of course, he didn't care where Jack was tonight, whether he had a roof to sleep under, but he couldn't help memories of other fires crowding around him, could he? No. So he drank his tea with one hand and idly poured the custard over the pudding with the other, watching the steam fade as the custard cooled, and let the memories come. They were all he had.

## OF SILENCE AND TIME,
## WHEREIN OLIVER IMBIBES IN A
## LOW TAVERN

The days until Oliver and Mr. Grimwig would sign the papers at the solicitor's passed slowly.

Each morning, Oliver woke up, thinking of the bookshop he would one day own. He washed at the washstand, got dressed, ate breakfast, thinking of the rooms above it where he would one day reside. After which, there was nothing much to do except sit in his green- and yellow-striped armchair and read. It was either that or take tea with Mr. Grimwig in the front parlor with the green wallpaper that he'd helped Mrs. Bedwin pick out some years ago.

Taking tea with Mr. Grimwig felt somehow required and was perhaps expected, even if he and Mr. Grimwig said no more than *pass the cream* or *are we out of cake*? The atmosphere, with or without those polite and short exchanges, was always severe and tense. And, in such stilted circumstances, the tea was not enjoyable, and the cake never satisfied.

Other than taking miserable teas with Mr. Grimwig, Oliver dawdled over which books to pack, wondering how much of a scolding he'd receive if Mr. Grimwig discovered he had the temerity to think he'd have time to read. Or whether Mr. McCready would be of a like mind to Mr. Grimwig and confiscate Oliver's books. Oliver couldn't bear to leave any of them behind, so what was he to do? So he ended up packing all of them, even his books from childhood, among them the well-worn *Lessons for Children,* and a tea- and jam-stained copy of *The History of Sandford and Merton.*

Once or twice, when he went on an errand to save the house-maid from having to go out in the frosty cold, he kept an eye out for Jack. Jack should not have talked to him, had been out of bounds to talk to him, and Oliver, for his part, had been remiss in allowing the conversation to continue as long as it had. The second Jack had been rough with him, Oliver should have called for the constable, and never mind the trouble and scandal that would have caused back at the townhouse.

But he'd not seen Jack, and none of the servants shared any talk about a stranger skulking about, so perhaps Jack had gone away, out of London, and Oliver would see no more of him. Certainly, once Oliver had moved to Mr. McCready's, not only would Jack not be able to follow him there, Oliver would be far too busy to partake in anything so unsavory as rude conversations with Jack Dawkins. Which was probably for the best, as he didn't need to get himself into trouble at his new place of work.

And Oliver wanted to go to work; he didn't think he'd ever wanted anything so much. Well, yes, there had been that pony that he'd never gotten, but in the City there would have been no place to keep it, and at Aunt Rose and Uncle Harry's, he'd run in the fields barefoot, the back of his neck and arms growing brown as he'd tagged with the local country boys and splashed in the creek, chased after crows, made grass whistles.

Now, of course, he was a young man and didn't have time to play. He felt eager to start anew, in a new place, doing something useful, earning money. Uncle Brownlow had taught him the value of money, and the value of well-made goods and how to treat them. He'd learned to be careful of his shoes, handing them over to be cleaned and polished on a regular basis, walking around puddles instead of through them, and never letting his boots dry without stuffing them with rags first.

On another day in that slow time, on a wet and chilly day when the snow had melted into a muddy sludge, Oliver put on his grey jacket and trousers and went down to the back landing to get his greatcoat and find a scarf to keep out the damp. On a peg on the wall next to the coat rack, there happened to be an old, rather taggle-ended grey scarf that looked as though it had no prior claim upon it, and so Oliver wrapped that around his neck. With his gloves in hand, and a few shillings in his change purse, which he put in his trouser pocket, he walked boldly out the front door. He was determined to get a breath of air, even though the wind was brisk, making the low clouds cut through the tops of church steeples, and the foggy, moist air slice through the winter-dark trees.

His feet, naturally enough, took him to the closest bookshop, which was on King's Road. The wind was in his face the whole way, so strong there were few ladies about, only a shawl-wrapped maid on an errand, and a few well-dressed gentlemen who held onto their top hats with gloved hands. Oliver put on his gloves as he walked and held onto his cap with one hand, hurrying along the pavement as passing carriages tossed up a great deal of muddy, half-melted snow.

Hillyard's Books, just a few steps along King's Road, was almost too grand for Oliver. It was on a main thoroughfare, and therefore was of the type to be staffed by white-aproned clerks with a rather superior air. But he was fond of the shop and went there often, as he did now, when he needed, so desperately needed, to breathe the dry, clean air of a bookshop and quiet his mind as he looked at the decorated spines, to become lost in the idea of the books and the stories they told.

He took off his cap and gloves as he entered, moving the door slowly to keep from clanging the entry bell too loudly. Politely, he dismissed the first clerk to approach him, asking if he needed any assistance. This was always annoying, but in any well-bred shop, it was inevitable.

Oliver had long ago decided that in his bookshop, neither he nor any clerk would interrupt a potential customer's musings. He would greet the customers when they entered his shop, and he would tell them to return to the counter if they had any questions. That way, they would be left alone to dream and ponder as they needed, and never feel irritated as Oliver did now. Obviously, he could read the titles and the placards on the shelves; he didn't need any assistance. He needed to be left alone.

It was natural for him to seek out the newer books near the front door; he had been so often in this particular bookshop he knew its regular contents. The collection of books on the deal table, however, seemed made up of recent rental-returns or books exchanged for new. But as Oliver came closer, he saw that there was a slightly used copy of *The Arabian Nights*. He'd asked for it for his birthday, but Uncle Brownlow had said that it was far too—what was the word he'd used? Far too—*provocative*, especially for a young man such as himself.

But now there was no one to restrain him, so Oliver picked up the book, and instantly there was a clerk at his side.

"Will the young man be taking this book today?"

"Yes, please," said Oliver.

He handed over the book, feeling reluctant to do so when he'd only just found it. But that was the way of this particular shop, the graceful attention, the careful ringing up, and the solicitous handing over of change.

By the time the clerk handed him the book, wrapped in white paper with the edges carefully folded in, Oliver had already put away his change purse and knew he could have been well into the first chapter. But there it was. Hopefully, near the haberdashery, there might be a less formal and far less grand bookshop for him to frequent.

"Good day to you, sir," said the clerk as Oliver tucked his new purchase under his arm.

"Thank you," said Oliver, as it was only good manners to do so, though he suspected it wouldn't matter what he'd said, as this was probably the last time he'd be at Hillyard's Books.

He left the shop with the bell clanging in his ears and, struggling, kept the book tucked beneath his arm while he put on his cap and gloves. The grey scarf was scratchy and, at most, kept out some of the damp even while it let in the cutting wind. But there was nothing to be done about it but walk back to the townhouse as quickly as possible. No one would have missed him upon his return, of course, but he was cold, and the thought of reading a new book by a warm fire was a good one.

Hurrying along, he avoided puddles when he could, keeping his head down, tucking his chin in the coarse scarf, glancing only slightly at passersby to keep from bumping into them. Black top hats glistened with wet, though a few gentlemen carried black umbrellas, which were stylish but seemed to have the tendency to fold inside out when held the wrong way.

Ignoring that, Oliver concentrated on getting back without tracking too much mud and street dirt on his boots, and planned to go in the back way, in case he'd not been able to manage it.

The servants' entrance to the townhouse was already open when he arrived, and was bustling as the cook and the maid accepted a delivery of meat and eggs and whatnot from a damp-coated delivery boy. Supper wasn't for a while yet, so Oliver skirted past them to hang up his greatcoat and cap, laid his gloves on the rack without a word, and resettled his book under his arm as he walked up the passage to the stairs. It was when he was by the front door and turning to go up the stairs that he caught his reflection in the gilt-edged hall mirror.

Dressed in grey, as he was, with the wall behind him a soft, almost-matching color, he felt as though he was seeing an image of someone who was about to melt away. It wasn't merely that the ghost-like properties of his clothes blended in with the wall. More, it was the expression on his face, white and still. And his eyes, in which, were he not himself, he would not have been able to discover a single emotion or uncover any attribute of the type of person he was.

Except, yes, there it was, that flicker that announced that the world was let in and the raw, unhampered feeling of missing Uncle Brownlow came in a rush, all the way from that dark, tender spot inside, flooding him with its misery. Turning away and hurrying up the stairs, he wiped the tears on his cheeks with his cold fingers and told himself he was pathetic to be acting this way. To be thinking that he shouldn't have bought this particular book because Uncle Brownlow wouldn't approve, but at the same time, being unable to forget that Uncle Brownlow was no longer around to approve or disapprove of anything Oliver did or intended to do.

By the time he reached the door to his room, he was miserable and crying as hard as a small child, and very grateful indeed that he had encountered no one on the way up the stairs. As he closed the door behind him and leaned against it, the spate ended, leaving him exhausted. He wiped his face again and looked around the room, as weary as if he'd walked a dozen miles instead of only a handful of city blocks.

Once again, the maid had come—some maid, one of the maids, he would never know which one—and scrubbed the grate and lit a small, bright fire, and even opened the curtains a little to let in whatever daylight might be allowed by the weather. There was a tray on the table next to the green easy chair, upon which had been placed a teapot covered with a tea cozy, a white china sugar basin, a jug of cream, and a plate of iced biscuits.

He was about to collapse under the weight of this kindness, in spite of himself, but he tightened his mouth and managed to stop it. He should be grateful that now he had no need to go back downstairs until suppertime. He could have his tea and read his book by the fire, and when the biscuits were gone, he could lie on top of the quilted counterpane and lean against the pillows and read until he could fall asleep. That was the best option, the easiest option, for in sleep, there were no dreams, no memories, nor any grief. At least for now.

~

By noon on the day of the appointment with the solicitor, Oliver could stand no more of the solitary silence and wanted fresh air. He'd been hiding in his room since the funeral, even though Mr. Grimwig had also followed solitary pursuits, and would not be chance met in any room or passageway.

Oliver had come upon him only once. Mr. Grimwig had been sitting, just sitting at the chess table in the parlor, just sitting there, the pieces half-moved, as if waiting for the next turn, which would never come.

When Oliver came downstairs now, Mr. Grimwig was again staring at the chess set. Therefore, he wouldn't see Oliver making his way into the street, regardless of which door he used.

Oliver put on his greatcoat and cap and the old grey scarf and left the townhouse boldly by the front door. He walked amidst the bustle of traffic and the clang of iron wheels against stone as carriages and carts moved briskly along, threading himself among the people on the pavement, the hawkers, and the beggars. He headed east in the icy air, fragrant with street muck, and then toward the river, where he soon found himself at Westminster Bridge.

Oliver leaned against the cold stones of the edge of the bridge, and almost directly below him there was a low skiff with a lone boatman struggling along the sliced ice at the edge of the Thames. It was low tide along the banks of the river, and snow had fallen during the previous night, thickening the ribbon of shore water, making it an almost impossible task to bank the skiff.

Oliver could see that the boatman was trying to get around paying the fee at the dock and was getting stuck in the mud. But it was too late, as the local muscle that collected the rent was already coming for the boatman, and Oliver turned before he could see the tussle in the frozen mud, instead turning his face up to the sky, looking for blue but catching only frosty, sharded clouds.

The City traffic hustled by him on the bridge, people hurrying to or from errands or to home, a pair of dray horses pulling a thick-wheeled cart across the stone. Thunder rumbled across the ice on the water that was hardening as the sunlight waned thin. The smell of the river grew dank as a sharp breeze buffeted across the ice and up over the bridge. Oliver clenched his fists around the railing, realizing that he'd left his gloves behind, though that was probably for the best; the fine leather gloves that he'd gotten on his birthday last year would have been ruined in short order by the roughness of the metal rail.

Oliver stood alone, feeling lost as he traced the patterns of smudged footprints of the mudlarks across the ice. He knew death would come to them all someday, but it seemed unfair that Uncle Brownlow would be taken so soon, just as, through the years, all the others in Oliver's life had been taken. Until anyone who he'd ever cared about, who'd ever cared about him at all, had gone, leaving him in the company of the ill-tempered Mr. Grimwig who, at this moment, was waiting upon Oliver's return to go to the solicitor.

Well, Oliver couldn't blame Uncle Brownlow for leaving him with Mr. Grimwig. It was not Uncle Brownlow's fault that Mr. Grimwig had never found Oliver to be a particularly pleasing boy.

In spite of his thick coat, he was cold, shivering as the dank, earthy breeze from the river blew up toward his face and circled around his neck, which felt bare in spite of the grey scarf. Mr. Grimwig had not offered Oliver any money to replace the scarf that Jack had stolen from him, though it might be that Mr. Grimwig assumed Mr. McCready would cover the cost of a new scarf. Oliver had some coins left in his change purse, but it was not enough to purchase a scarf.

As he turned away from the wind, he saw the sign for the Green Dragon at the south end of the bridge. The tavern was fairly close to the river, enough to give it a slightly dubious reputation. But the street alongside the tavern seemed well-trafficked; there was a coffee busker, a small, narrow horse-drawn wagon hauling coal, and a man and a woman with a donkey and cart, all shivering in the wind as they hurried about their business. It was enough to make the establishment more salubrious than it otherwise might have been, so Oliver opened the door and went in.

The low ceiling was dark with smoke and oily with years of sweat and dirt rising from a type of custom that couldn't care less about the grime and would have been turned away at the door of any establishment Oliver usually frequented. But the tavern was warm, with a smoking open fire at one end, and a large kettle with a fire underneath it at the other. There was a stew being cooked in it, with ingredients no doubt known only to the pot and perhaps the long metal spoon that stirred it. Oliver thought he smelled chestnuts, bursting with sweetness and about to explode their skins, but he couldn't see anything being being roasted.

There were a few rows of dark wooden tables and scattered chairs, placed either close to the windows for the light or near the fire for warmth. Though the majority of the patrons were quiet, concentrating on their drinks, there was some rowdiness going on at the bar. But in this part of London, by the river, where the streets were narrow as though shrunken by time, and the smell of the Thames seeped through every fiber of wood and stone, well, nobody would turn away anybody with a penny to spend.

Oliver kicked at clumps of rubbish under his boots and ordered a tot of gin at the counter before he could think about how indecent it was to have a drink like this in the middle of the afternoon. But the gin was delivered faster than he could remonstrate with himself, and he watched his pennies being swept up with a grime-streaked hand without attempting to stop the exchange.

No words were said, no *thank you for your custom, young master*, which Oliver found he missed more than he imagined he might. But then, he'd long ago realized that getting used to something meant that it was much more difficult to attempt to go without it.

He sipped at the gin and thought that it sat nicely in his stomach, sending out pumps of warmth and relaxation. And, as long as he kept drinking it slowly, the gin would keep him in a nice steady state of not feeling very much for the next hour or so. Another sip from the glass warmed him, but only barely. It was, he realized, watered-down gin, not very potent, and it left a slimy coating in his mouth, giving indication of having been served from a not very clean bottle. He sank his nose in the glass to smell the gin and absorb the fumes that way, to warm himself.

If it were true that time flew on wings toward only horrible destinations, the reverse was also true: it dragged itself on broken legs toward a good one. Oliver knew that his good destination was waiting for him simply because he felt it would never come. It seemed out of reach, like a blue sky, and him in a place of limbo, never moving forward, never arriving.

With the customers crowding around the fire and blocking the heat, it was getting a little cold where he was at the end of the bar. He ordered another gin.

Uncle Brownlow would not have approved, not of the second gin, let alone the first, nor of Oliver's sense of relaxing in such a place as this, yet his shoulders came down and he sucked back a large mouthful of gin. In spite of the press of late afternoon bodies, the scent and salt of laborers, the frozen snow melting onto the floor near the door, and the drifts of damp dust and spilt beer, he felt somehow at home. Even though he shouldn't.

Uncle Brownlow never liked hearing the story of little Oliver's early life and had listened only once or twice before he'd declared he'd had enough. He didn't even want to hear the part about how Fagin, upon seeing the many holes in Oliver's old stockings, had stolen him a new pair. Nor had Uncle Brownlow wanted to hear how Fagin had, with his own hands, stuffed straw around the windows to keep his boys warm. None of that mattered, only that Fagin was a fence, a flash man living at the bottom of a very hard world. That he was a thief and a Jew seemed to matter less than that he'd stolen Oliver away.

Uncle Brownlow's disinclination to listen didn't make what had happened not so, however. Oliver knew that. And he suspected that Uncle Brownlow did, as well. But nobody else had specifically asked to hear of his adventures, so he'd stopped telling them. Soon, it was as if they'd never happened, except in Oliver's own mind. And in Mr. Grimwig's memory, of course.

For some reason, Mr. Grimwig was always able to work the torrid details of Oliver's story into any conversation, especially to those persons with whom Oliver was making his first acquaintance. Mr. Grimwig always saw to it that everyone he met knew exactly the low places that Oliver was familiar with. Such as this tavern. Mr. Grimwig would indeed be satisfied to know that all his opinions about Oliver might be more true than he suspected. Not that Oliver would ever tell him.

He took another slug of gin and considered the glass in his hand, smeared with grease and not very clean. He realized quite clearly that Uncle Brownlow would be shocked to see him drinking out of such a vessel, and that opinion, so dearly missed, was making him feel very badly about being where he was, and on such a day.

"You'll be wantin' better than that, you will, my flash companion."

Oliver heard the jaunty voice from over his shoulder, and it came at him as if pressed through some kind of chamber, sealed at one end so that it echoed back at him without ever having been spoken. The hair on his neck began a creeping dance, rather as if it were trying to slide beneath the collar of his woolen greatcoat. The skin across his shoulders soon joined it, and he turned his head, wondering if there would be something to scare him, or if he would only find the sightless eyes of a beggar wanting a sip of the gin that had suddenly turned to ash water in his mouth.

He was badly drunk, drunk enough to be dreaming, but there Jack Dawkins stood with his heavy brow and that wide mouth, smiling far too broadly. On his head he wore a ragged, once-shiny top hat. Stolen, no doubt, as had been the coat, for such articles would not have been purchased, not by someone who possessed such talented hands, which were now jammed into pockets, ruining the elegant lines of the coat.

Jack was of a height with Oliver, though not quite as broad or well-fed as the gentleman for whom the coat had been designed. But yes, he wore Oliver's red scarf around his neck, boldly tied, of course. Only Jack Dawkins could wear a scarf in that manner and call it fashion.

Still Oliver could not speak, could not greet Jack and call him by name, for to do so was to bring back the past to the now. Particularly to the now where he'd been caught with his second gin in his hand. In a tavern near the river, in a rough part of town. He saw Jack's eyes take in the ugly grey scarf that Oliver wore.

"Have you been following me?" Oliver asked. His mind froze at this; if Jack could find him on a snowy, ice-crusted day in London, then Jack could find him anywhere.

"Why are you always so surprised to see me, eh, Nolly?" Jack smiled the smile that Oliver knew so well.

"Anyway, you're the only person I know in London," continued Jack with a shrug. "Besides, that muck'll give you belly rot," he added, nodding at the glass in Oliver's hand.

Jack didn't truly care, of course. Oliver could sink into drunken madness at that very moment, and Jack would only be concerned with what he wanted, with what was good for Jack. Jack Dawkins. The Artful Dodger. Mr. Artful, if you please.

Oliver opened his mouth to speak, and someone bumped

into him. Oliver jerked his hand, and the gin spilled all over his trousers. The gin oozed down his leg and reeked through the air, and all the while those green eyes, sparkling beneath the brim of that hat, watched him.

"I've got an interview with a solicitor today," said Oliver, his mouth thick over the words. "And no time, not any, to spend in idle talk with a pickpocket." His hand shook, and he spilled more of his gin on the floor so that there was only a draught or two left in the glass.

"How much have you had, anyway?" Jack sat on the stool next to him, and Oliver shifted back.

There was something sinewy about the way Jack moved. And, as Oliver looked at that coarse skin and the fringe of dark hair coming down the hard jawline, he thought about the five years since Jack had been deported. It was from that faraway place that Jack had returned, looking more a young man than the boy Oliver remembered. Regardless of when and how, Jack's one major task of consequence, to wit, was to pester his old pal.

Oliver really couldn't understand why Jack had sought him out yet again. Oliver had told Jack everything he knew about Fagin's gang, or at least what he could say. That everyone from Fagin's gang, from the smallest lad to the man himself, had been scattered to the winds. He shoved away the memory of Fagin's last night in Newgate and thought of Nancy's death. Though with no details forthcoming, he could only imagine her blood running across the cobblestones till the street ran red like those at Smithfield Market. And of Sikes's body, shot, hanged, dead, something like that—

"Some air," said Jack.

He took Oliver by the arm, as though they'd been in the midst of discussing it and Jack had just decided. He got up and pulled Oliver to his feet and made him walk outside.

The air on the street was painfully cold, now that he'd been breathing in the warm funk of the tavern, and fresh, in spite of the smack of the scent of the river in his face. His blood was racing through him, courtesy of the gin. The heat of his skin became flecked with frost as it cooled, and he wondered why he'd not worn a different scarf, such as his red one, and then remembered that Jack had stolen it, was wearing it even now, the soft red wool swirling around his ex-convict neck.

Oliver shook his head and let himself be dragged, which was a sad mistake because if Jack meant to haul him somewhere quiet and dark and hold him there till Oliver gave up whatever Jack wanted, well, it would be a short wait. Jack was all bundled up, prepared for the weather, and Oliver was not.

But once Jack got him into the street, he stopped and released Oliver. They were still close to the overhang of the sign for the Green Dragon, where people passed in and out of the door. And the snow, as it blew off the roof, slanted toward them; splats of snow landed on Oliver's neck.

Jack patted the front of Oliver's greatcoat. And, as Jack leaned toward him, Oliver found he was too close to the swath of dark hair that spilled across Jack's forehead in greasy strands from beneath the ragged edges of that hat. The warm, steady touch of Jack's hands overwhelmed him. Oliver tried shoving backward, but Jack gripped the edge of his lapel. His own glove-less hands tried for purchase on Jack's thicker coat, but it was useless. He was about to fall on his backside in the snow. Right there in the street.

"Let go of me," said Oliver, flushed, feeling that his words came out indistinct, to be regarded by nobody.

He tightened his whole body to pull away, but Jack pulled him close, close enough to almost touch Oliver's face with his own. Close enough that Oliver could smell the smoke and sweat on him, see the wreath of grit on his neck.

"There's no sense in that, Nolly," said Jack, tugging on Oliver's greatcoat to keep him still. "Seein' as I've got you."

For a moment, the hardness of that voice erased almost every bit of boyishness Jack possessed. Almost. The street thug was there too, in the husk of air as it pushed out of his lungs. Oliver watched the frost of breath from Jack's lips and felt himself shake his head, as if he were saying no to one of Jack's suggestions.

Jack laughed and pulled back, twitching his head to resettle his hat, and Oliver sank back against the wall, his boots slipping in the snow, melted ice from the sign dripping down his neck. Jack grabbed his arm again and pulled Oliver up the street to where it narrowed to a mere lane.

"Let go, I say," said Oliver, trying for force, teeth grit, but not wanting to make a scene, not wanting word to get back to Mr. Grimwig for any reason at all. "Let go!"

He threw a punch, wide with his bare fist, hitting Jack in the arm. It was ineffectual, but it did stop Jack. Jack bunched up his shoulders, as though he were going to strike back, but then he lowered them. When he reached out his hand, it was to push the moist hair from across Oliver's forehead and to gently pat Oliver's cheek.

Oliver staggered, as though he had been struck, clutching onto Jack's wool-clad arm, dazed and staring, feeling as though he should understand what was happening, could understand it if his head wasn't ringing. When Oliver tried to pull away again, Jack gave Oliver's arm a rough shake. Then he walked a few paces, pulling Oliver with him.

"I'm hurt that you would think I meant you ill," said Jack. "*Wounded*, even."

Oliver rubbed his coat sleeves with his bare hands and tried to be more worried about his soaked trouser leg and the tiresome explanation he'd have to make when he got back to the townhouse. Better to worry about that rather than how close Jack was, and how the curve of his mouth and the smell of his skin, warm in the cold, took Oliver right back to a place he'd never thought to return, and from which he'd come so far.

"Here, what money you got? Any change? Be a good boy and hand it over now.."

Blinking, Oliver thought of the small change purse in his

pocket from whence he'd brought forth enough for two measures of gin. He'd been a good boy for so long, but with the right sort of people, he might be a bad one. But Jack's expression said, in dark familiar lines, that the kind of boy Jack wanted him to be was an obedient one. One that would hand it over, and that right quick.

How much money did he have left, and what did Jack want it for? Maybe Jack wanted lodgings and someone to recommend him; Oliver couldn't think straight enough to figure it out. And all the while, Jack's eyes were watching him. As Oliver jerked his hand near his pocket to protect it, Jack reached out and grabbed him by the wrist.

"Pull it out, or I pulls it out for you."

Something warm and dusky was in Jack's voice; Oliver believed he meant to do what he said, though Oliver couldn't imagine anyone doing what Jack was suggesting. To put his hand in another man's *pocket*—

"Just hand it over, Nolly," said Jack, shaking his head, the velvety tones of his voice slipping away to the street-bright ones. "We're goin' t'get somethin' to sober you up. Here."

Jack made a wide gesture with his hand, and Oliver made himself focus. They were directly near a coffee busker, a cart on wheels with its slanted canvas roof clean of snow, the wheels painted a bright blue. The cart had a little hob over which hung a silver pot with a short, curved spout.

Jack nodded at the man, who tilted the pot and poured out a large dose of coffee into a dented metal cup. Into this, he tipped some brown sugar and handed it to Jack.

"Bread as well, then?" asked the busker.

"With butter," said Jack. "Is it salted?"

He gestured to Oliver to pull out his money, and this Oliver did, feeling half-stupid and far short of being half-sober. Jack took the change purse, and, without asking, pawed through it for a handful of pennies, which he handed to the busker. Then he held out the tumbler.

"Extra sugar in that, if you please," Jack said, pocketing Oliver's change purse so quickly that Oliver blinked. "My mate here likes it that way."

When the busker handed over the slices of buttered bread and the large tumbler of hot coffee, Jack handed the tumbler to Oliver.

"Here, get some of that into you." Jack even tipped the container toward Oliver's mouth to encourage Oliver to drink.

Oliver took the tumbler in both hands and put it to his lips. The metal was hot, but in the cold air, quickly cooled as steam rose from the surface of the coffee in mad swirls, dissipating somewhere near his forehead. It was occurring to him, through the fog the gin had created, that Jack meant to help him rather than to hinder.

He took a small sip of the hot coffee. It warmed him through as he watched Jack take a bite of the bread and butter, his lips smacking around the bite, as if it were the best he'd ever eaten. It might have been, for all that. Oliver found himself strangely disquieted by the fact that he didn't mind that Jack had spent his money, though he did want that change purse back. Uncle Brownlow had given it to him at Christmas, and the clasp was guaranteed for life.

"There's no cream in it," he said. "But it's what you need."

Jack took the coffee from Oliver and took a large swig. Then he handed the coffee back as he ate the rest of the bread and butter, rather as if he were starving, which Oliver imagined he might be. After all, what did an ex-convict, recently *hextricated*, do for a living? Never mind. He had no intention of asking.

"Our own dear Nolly," said Jack, after taking another swig of coffee and handing it back to Oliver. He tapped the cup, as if to encourage Oliver to drink still more. Which he did, taking a large swallow that was not quite hot enough to burn his tongue.

"Sweet Nolly," Jack said now, still watching him. "Suckin' back a glass of gin from a dirty glass, no less, with his elbows on the counter, for all the world like a down-and-out sailor."

Frowning, Oliver handed Jack the coffee, only now realizing that they'd been sharing the same container. But then, what of that? In the bad old days, there'd been fewer mugs and tumblers than there had been boys. Fagin's lads shared what they had, from cups of coffee to slices of bread. Rough pillows and worn blankets. The circle of bare feet around an open fire in a raggedy hearth.

He watched Jack licking his fingers and tucking them around the metal tumbler to warm them. There were new scars along the backs of his fingers, and the bones on his hands and wrists seemed too near the surface. It made Oliver want to ask what Jack had been doing while he'd been away.

Jack tipped his head back, his throat working as he swallowed the rest of the coffee. Then he gave the metal cup back to the coffee busker. He patted his stomach, seeming content as he gave Oliver a quirky half smile.

"Filled now," he said. "And you're more sober."

"Yes," said Oliver.

His body was beginning to feel the steadying effects of the gin being chased away by the hot coffee. And by Jack's presence, which was, in truth, as good as a slap in the face. It reminded him that if he didn't sign those papers, he wouldn't be able to work for Mr. McCready. And then he would end up like Jack, a vagrant in the street, with nowhere to go and nothing to do. Well, nothing *respectable* to do.

"I have to go," said Oliver quite bluntly.

Watching Oliver with an intent expression, Jack reached into his pocket and jostled Oliver's change purse in his hand, up and down, as though he were tossing a child's ball. He didn't offer the change purse back to Oliver, and Oliver didn't dare try to grab it, for Jack would just laugh and pull away, as if the whole of it were some game. That change purse was as long gone, as gone as if Oliver had thrown it into the Thames with his own hands.

"I can catch up with you later," said Jack. "I'll come tomorrow."

"But you won't," said Oliver, saying this before he realized he should just let the comment remain where it was without an explanation. He stepped back from Jack, his boots slipping a bit in the wet snow that had gathered around his feet. Though he was an orphan still, he was no longer a small boy to be detained by a street thug, and he had somewhere to be. "I'll be moving on. I've got an interview this afternoon, and then I'll be in a different part of London."

"Well," said Jack, tugging at his lapels and tipping his head back to look at Oliver down his nose. "That ain't no matter to me; for I'll find you, just the same."

Of course, Jack would. He had before; there was nothing to stop him from doing it again, not when the whole of London belonged to him. Then Jack turned and walked up the slanted street without a backward glance, and, in a moment, he'd disappeared around a corner as if he'd never really been there.

Oliver straightened the lapels of his greatcoat and tried to brush the snow from his trousers. He should not have gone for a drink. More, he should not have gone with Jack anywhere, despite the fact that Jack had rescued him from a bottle of gin. But it was too late to think about that. He looked as though he'd rolled in a snowbank, and not a very clean one at that. He picked up his pace to get back to the townhouse in time.

There was a low sound as the local church began to bong out the hour, and Oliver realized with a shock that it was three o'clock. The wind whisked up behind him, chilling him where his clothes were damp and finding its way through the seams of his collar.

Oliver turned and started pushing past people to get to the center of the bridge, and when he got there, he plowed along, fists in his pockets, cap tilted low over his forehead, wishing the grey scarf were better suited to the wet weather.

When he was almost to the end of the bridge, he heard the bells from St. Margaret's Church. And as they faded away, and as the cold air started blowing snow in a thick cloud around the portals on the north end of the bridge, he knew there was nothing for it but to hurry. He walked faster, and trod on toes, and slipped in the mud and refuse on the bridge, and felt his breath coming sharply in his throat as he hurried, uselessly hurried.

He'd wandered the streets for a good long while before stepping into the tavern, and now Jack had delayed him even longer. There was no way he'd be able to stay in Mr. Grimwig's good graces now, if there ever was a chance, which there never had been. But he had to get back home; the meeting with the solicitor was a pressing matter.

As he headed west toward the nicer part of town, the gas lamps were being lit against the fog and the smoke and the setting sun. The streets were being swept as darkness came. The pavements became rushed with people and the streets filled with carriages and horses, the rooflines only a smudged, dark cut against the growing darkness.

His head pounded as the gin faded away, and the streets became colder, and he realized his boots were soaked through. His feet ached with dampness, and there was a large, greasy blotch on his trousers that also managed to smell like freshly spilled gin. He took his hands out of his pockets to blow on them, then, thrusting his hands back in his pockets, he tipped his chin down and hurried up the street and down the lane and across the park, when it started to snow again.

## ❧ 6 ❧

## AT THE SOLICITOR'S

He was damp through by the time he skirted the front door and took the short flight of iron stairs that led down to the kitchen area. The smell of hot food and grease hit him even before he'd opened the door, though the kitchen was empty when he did. He heard the sounds from the floor above, the sound of footsteps and skirts against wood and boots on the carpet and the short bark of an order.

Oliver didn't know if he could make it up to his room or even past the parlor, where, no doubt, Mr. Grimwig was waiting. Oliver looked at the open door that led to the servants' staircase. One of the maids came down in her plain dark dress that reached the floor, her white apron crisp against the black wool

"Mr. Grimwig has been looking for you," said the maid. "He knows you left the house," said the girl, passing him as she went into the kitchen.

Oliver nodded. It was obvious from her expression what had happened. And it wasn't that Mr. Grimwig had yelled or scolded the maid or threatened to sack her for not stopping Oliver from leaving. If anything, Mr. Grimwig had taken out his watch and looked at it, a sure sign of his agitation. He probably thought he was justified in everything he'd ever thought about Oliver. The

71

years had not erased his initial opinion, and no passage of time would do anything more.

"I'll go up," Oliver said. "I'll change directly."

The maid tried smiling, but it wasn't working, and so he slipped past her to tread up the stairs to the polished passageway, and then down the hallway to the front door. He pushed through to the parlor. Better to have it over with, better to face up to Mr. Grimwig's disapproval.

Mr. Grimwig stood by the front table in the parlor, cane in one hand, his opened watch in the other. The fob and chain against his black waistcoat glittered in the light of a newly built fire in the fireplace.

"Well, young Oliver," said Mr. Grimwig. He was trying to smile politely, but there was nobody but Oliver and Mr. Grimwig standing there, and no need for it, so the smile turned into a grimace. "Are you ready?"

Oliver stared hard at the looking glass, covered still with black crepe, and at the green silk wallpaper that shimmered in the candlelight from the sconces over the fireplace. The drapes were green too, though they looked black in this light.

He chewed the inside of his lip and tried not to think of the gin house he had so recently been in. Tried not to think of Jack, green-eyed and canny, patting Oliver, stroking his forehead with complete equanimity, as if all of this were under his discretion, solely his, and not Oliver's.

"You don't look well," said Mr. Grimwig, entirely without sympathy.

Oliver wasn't going to argue about that. The gin was making him sick; it had been very bad gin, it seemed, not even worth the pennies he'd paid for it.

"You should freshen up now, Oliver." This was delivered in more caring tones that sounded entirely false to Oliver. Mr. Grimwig controlled all now, and it was plain to see he had the confidence of it. "We leave for the solicitor's within the moment."

"Yes," said Oliver. His knees were knocking, and there was a sudden slick feeling in his throat. He would walk smoothly out of the parlor and head to the back stairs. There was a dustbin there, an empty one that had, of late, held old rags. He could use that to throw up in. Or maybe he would tear open the door to the back garden and use the hollow beneath the winter-bare rose bushes. It all depended on which servant was nearby and how fast he could get past them.

"And Oliver?"

"Yes?"

"You will make sure to change altogether; I can smell the gin from here."

Looking down at himself, Oliver saw again the greasy patch on his trouser leg. He reeked of the gin house, of the street, of coffee, of Jack.

"I'll go directly and get cleaned up."

"See that you do."

Mr. Grimwig put his pocket watch away and wiggled his cane. Tucking one hand behind his back, he pushed out his stout stomach that glistened beneath its sheath of black silk. A threat lingered in his voice, unspoken, and Oliver knew that Mr. Grimwig's intolerance for Oliver's lack of temperance, long buried, would remain buried no longer.

Oliver found he wanted another drink of gin very badly. But he'd already done his drinking, and the tears that boiled behind his eyes refused to come to the surface. As a small boy, crying had come at the flicker of an eyelash. Not that it stayed anyone's hand or made the angels come to carry him into the arms of his dead mother. Tears had been like rain to him just the same, affecting no one and making him feel as though he'd been pressed between millstones. Wrung out like a bottle rag.

Now he felt that way, even without the tears. He wanted nothing more than to scream and pound the walls and make Mr. Grimwig's placid, self-satisfied expression explode into shock.

His hands pressed against his thighs like hot brands, and the candle flames over the mantelpiece shimmered.

Oliver turned and went along the hallway as fast as he could, knowing he was tracking mud, unable to stop. He went all the way to the bin near the back stairs. It was gone.

Sweating, he realized he had about two seconds before he spoiled what remained of his good clothes or the woolen runner on the floor. He dashed to the back door, threw himself into the mist and snow among the bare rose bushes, and vomited into the frozen mud with a splash. Fresh gin would taste very good right now, or another cup of coffee. Even some cold water would help.

WHEN HE'D WASHED AND CHANGED HIS SHIRT AND TROUSERS, Oliver went back downstairs, his head feeling somewhat clearer now that his stomach was empty of gin. Under Mr. Grimwig's glower, Oliver put on his coat, leaving behind the grey scarf that was far too scratchy. With his cap in his hand, he turned to Mr. Grimwig. The parlor maid held the front door open, and snow swirled in, bits of speckled ice that landed on the black-and-white squares on the landing and winked out of existence in the warmth.

Of course, if Oliver acquired the position with Mr. McCready, then he would, most likely, go to live in residence, over the shop, perhaps, or maybe in lodgings. Either would be hard, mostly in the leaving of the place where he'd shared so many good memories with Uncle Brownlow. But staying would be hard as well; living with Mr. Grimwig, alone, with no one to stand between them, was liable to make one or both of them come to blows.

"In the cab, boy, we can't be at this all day. I've an appointment, and I shan't let you keep me from making a timely appearance."

Oliver nodded and slipped past Mr. Grimwig's scowling face

and the cane held in one gripped fist. Oliver slipped on the pavement and scurried into the cab: a one-horse hansom that would move fast and get them there without too much delay. But it would also mean sitting quite close to Mr. Grimwig beneath the woolen blanket the coach had supplied. As Mr. Grimwig lumbered to sit beside him, Oliver realized that at least it would be too cold to talk, although Mr. Grimwig managed it just the same.

The driver flicked his whip and as the cab lurched off down the street, Mr Grimwig said, "Trust you to pick the most miserable day on record for a fool's errand."

Oliver kept his mouth shut and didn't remind Mr. Grimwig that he'd said the same thing the day they'd buried Uncle Brownlow.

Heading toward the center of London, the cab trotted through the streets, which were thick with traffic in spite of the weather. It was cold, but the snow coming down covered the black soot on the pavement and the piles of horse manure and the lump at the end of the street that he knew to be a dead dog. Everything at the roofline, however, was white and soft, the slate roofs fur-edged, the church steeples laced with scrolls of snow.

In spite of the weather, the cab passed a group of quality folk on the pavement, the ladies in fur-trimmed bonnets, and the gentlemen in fine, thick coats. Maybe they were a skating party, or perhaps they planned a trek through one of the parks. They looked merry and warm and probably had hot drinks waiting for them upon their return home. Oliver watched them until the cab had passed them, and then focused on the front of the interior of the cab.

"We'll be there shortly," said Mr. Grimwig. "Be sure and mind your manners."

"I will," said Oliver. "I always do." He grit his teeth to keep anything harsh from coming out; the last thing he needed was to alight from the cab with his clothes rumpled from an elbow-to-elbow pushing match with Mr. Grimwig.

"That remains to be seen," said Grimwig. Then he thumped the roof of the cab. "Driver, can you hurry? I've some better place to be."

With a flick of the whip, the cab lurched forward, and Oliver gripped his thighs with his hands. If he grabbed the wooden rail, Grimwig was sure to mention to one and all what a silly, nervous boy Oliver was. But if he tumbled to the floor, that would be worse. The best he could do was brace his feet on the floor of the cab, press himself into the corner of the padded leather seat, and try to stay upright and balanced.

As the cab followed the curve along Oxford Street, with St. Paul's grey outline looming over the chimney pots, the wind changed direction and came in through the canvas-framed windows. It hit the side of Oliver's neck and, for a moment, he felt as if he ought not to have agreed to this wild choice, to leave the comfort, relative though it might be, of Mr. Grimwig and his late Uncle Brownlow's abode. There, it was warm and safe and dry, and there was food, and even though the present company was none too good, it was known and familiar.

Oliver had to bite his lip to keep from saying it aloud: *Take me home.* Except he hadn't any. So instead, he stared fixedly out of the window, watching the street go by, determined to keep his mouth shut for the duration of the trip.

"You'll find this a good establishment, I'll wager," said Mr. Grimwig from beside him.

He leaned forward on his cane, as if to catch sight of what had his charge so riveted. He did not add, to Oliver's relief, that if it were otherwise, he'd eat his head. He'd not said that phrase, not at all, in the days since Uncle Brownlow's passing, as if, after all, the point in saying it had passed as well. Oliver had never known whether Uncle Brownlow was laughing to himself or laughing at Mr. Grimwig. He would never know now and didn't really want to. Oliver was heartily sick of the phrase, anyway.

"Did you hear me, Oliver?"

"Yes," said Oliver, hearing the flatness of his own voice.

"I hear it from Parson Greaves that Mr. McCready only takes in a very few boys. You're privileged to be considered for a position without waiting."

Oliver already knew this. It had been said to him for days since the reception.

"This is a rather suitable area for a solicitor," said Mr. Grimwig.

He had turned the other way now, and Oliver flicked his eyes across the space of the carriage and looked to where Mr. Grimwig was looking. Though he couldn't see the whole of each building, they appeared to be as shops and offices ought to appear.

It was a good street. The cab had passed through one or two insalubrious areas, but now the pedestrians once again looked hale and hearty, bundled to the cold. They're out in the sharp weather because they wanted to be, because they had a new cloak to show off and boots that could bear the dampness of snow and ice. And they had servants standing by later to clean and brush and press and dry.

"Don't you agree, Oliver?"

"Yes," said Oliver, but that was all he could manage without bursting out shouting.

When he turned twenty-one, the three thousand pounds left to him by his never-met father would be his. He'd do what he had to at Mr. McCready's because he wanted to buy a bookshop with that money, and he wanted to be ready when that day came. Which was, at present, an eternity of four years away.

The cab pulled up to the curb, the wheels jumping in the stone gutter for a jarring second before coming to a halt. The squeak of leather harness and click of metal-clad hooves echoed in Oliver's ears, and then it was still.

Mr. Grimwig was already lumbering out of the cab, handing

up money with a tight fist and gesturing with his cane for Oliver to alight also, to hurry and be quick about it.

"Come back at a quarter to the hour," said Mr. Grimwig to the cab driver. "If you are late, I will simply hail another cab. But I'd just as soon ride in this one, for I already know that it is clean."

The cab driver tipped his hat and flicked his whip to get the horse going in a quick trot down the busy street. Oliver couldn't have assured Mr. Grimwig that the cab would be back because unless one gave them money first, cab drivers of Oliver's experience did as they pleased. Not that this was anything that Oliver needed, or wanted, to concern himself about.

"They are expecting us, Oliver," said Mr. Grimwig. "Even if we are late, which is your fault."

A gentleman in a dark black waistcoat and jacket, his white shirt gleaming against the wool, came out on the front step to greet them.

"Mr. Grimwig," he said. "I'm Mr. Bond. It's a pleasure to meet you. Let me shake your hand, and that of young Twist. Then come away into the shop, where it is much warmer than it is on the street."

Mr. Grimwig shook the offered hand and then tipped his head in Oliver's direction.

"I brought him," Mr. Grimwig said. "Though he's still not sobered up from his sojourn to a tavern today. The street never leaves the boy, who, I fear, has a taste for the gin."

"Surely you must be joking," said Mr. Bond, his voice thin in the cold air.

"I never joke about intemperance," said Mr. Grimwig. "It will be the ruin of our civilization, or I'll eat my head."

Oliver was not actually surprised but merely startled that in such company Mr. Grimwig had been so bold about Oliver's current state and, not only that, had voiced such a sly rejoinder at how horrible Oliver's past was. But after today, Oliver would be leaving all of that behind him. Mr. Bond took Oliver's hand

and shook it, just the same, and Oliver returned the gesture, with his nervousness zipping through him.

"I had a glass with a friend in remembrance of my Uncle Brownlow, and the time got away from us, that's all." Oliver said this while looking only at Mr. Bond.

"A *friend?*" roared Mr. Grimwig. "You have no friends, save that low family of yours in Chertsey."

Oliver could only glare at Mr. Grimwig. If he leapt to Aunt Rose and Uncle Harry's defense, both he and Mr. Grimwig would come to blows, right there on the pavement.

"In remembrance," said Mr. Bond, rushing into the boiling silence. "Which is always a good thing, and time does not matter upon those occasions. But perhaps you should both come in out of the cold and the weather. I have an office where we can conduct our business, and Mr. McCready is already arrived."

Oliver took a deep breath and followed as Mr. Bond and Mr. Grimwig went up the short flight of freshly cleaned stone steps. He stood back a little and let the two men pull ahead, and then stepped over the threshold and absorbed the warmth of the building, which seemed to reflect the promise of a new life to come.

As they entered Mr. Bond's wood-paneled office, Mr. Grimwig greeted Mr. McCready, who stood up. After everyone shook hands, they sat down in the leather-backed chairs opposite the solicitor, who sat behind a desk stacked very high with papers. Oliver could feel the stiff cushions beneath his thighs, see the clock with its severe face ticking out the time, and thought for a moment that he'd made a grave mistake.

"Your uncle was the most Christian of men," said Mr. Bond as he opened the meeting with some kind words. "And I know that this move to employment would have been what Mr. Brownlow would have wanted."

"I agree, this is the best course of action to take," Mr. Grimwig said, directing his words at Oliver, turning the kind words into severe ones. "With your past record and your questionable birth—all of these things I've taken into consideration before allowing you to take this apprenticeship."

A silence fell because there was nothing Oliver could say that wouldn't set Mr. Grimwig off, and it wouldn't be seemly to bring their shared animosity out into the open in an important solicitor's office on Oxford Street.

For his part, Mr. Bond merely regarded Mr. Grimwig from above his half spectacles.

"Oliver Twist is going to be making his own way now, and would be self-guided," said Mr. Bond. "And I have every faith that Oliver will do well and make us all proud."

Nodding at the solicitor, as though thanking him for his intervention, Mr. McCready leaned back, steepling his hands while he rested his elbows on the arms of his chair.

"You now know most of what I am about here," Mr. McCready said. "You know how I train and what I train in. I take in boys at a young age and keep them until they are twenty-one. At which point, they are fit to work their way up in any shop in London. In the world, I daresay, though none of my boys has yet tried it." A smile pulled at the hard muscles of his face.

"Do you have any questions, Mr. Grimwig? Or you, Oliver?" asked Mr. McCready.

Oliver shook his head and was about to politely say no when Mr. Grimwig interrupted him.

"I understand that you give the boys a pay packet each week," said Mr. Grimwig, thumping his cane.

"Indeed. I believe boys need the wherewithal to test their boundaries and independence. Boys work harder for it and spend more wisely knowing how it is earned." Here Mr. McCready paused, then he said, "I give them a shilling a week."

"An entire shilling? *Every* week?" Mr. Grimwig thumped his cane louder this time.

His voice had risen so high that Oliver considered it very possible that the next utterance out of him would be a proclamation that if any apprentice boy deserved that much, he'd eat his head. But his astonishment seemed to please Mr. McCready, who dropped his hands and laughed out loud.

"Unless, of course, the shop is doing so poorly that I cannot manage it, as sometimes happens during the slow season. But then the boys learn that their fortunes are tied in with how the market is going. Again, another lesson to be learned."

"*Every* week?"

"And then I give them a penny for the plate on Sunday. Attendance is, of course, required."

"*Every week?*"

"In addition, I supply all their clothes and smalls. Wear and tear is accounted for unless a boy damages some article by carelessness. Then the money comes out of his pocket, which teaches him responsibility."

Mr. Grimwig opened his mouth again, and Oliver thought surely he was going to repeat his statement, but this time he only shook his head and looked at Oliver. Oliver felt it was up to him, then, to say something. To make a decision.

For a moment, he looked at the office lined with shelves, crowded with papers and books, the whole of which was made warm by the fire and bright by two lamps. He heard, through the open doorway, the industry of the several office boys as they went to and fro.

"So then, Oliver," said Mr. McCready, whose dark eyes were steady. "Will you make something of yourself?"

"Yes, sir," Oliver said, not hesitating. "I would like to very much, if I may."

"It is acceptable," said Mr. Grimwig suddenly, as if the final decision rested with him. This surprised no one, least of all Oliver. "It will be a good thing for the boy to make his own way, and have a purpose in life other than sticking his nose in a book. Why his eyesight hasn't failed him with all that reading is beyond me."

This final comment was ignored by both Mr. Bond and Mr. McCready. Then, with a nod from behind the stacks of books and papers on his desk, Mr. Bond began to review the paperwork ever so slowly.

Time stretched out till at last he pulled out a pen and signed. Then he made Oliver and Mr. Grimwig sign and handed the papers to Mr. McCready to examine.

Oliver could see that Mr. McCready's signature was already in place. That he'd done this before they'd arrived meant that Mr. McCready truly wanted Oliver in his shop. Someone handed him a penwiper, and Oliver wiped his fingers with it, knowing that his most immediate future was sealed. It felt good.

Mr. McCready stood up and straightened the edges of his frock coat.

"Shall we have young Oliver start as soon as may be, Mr. Grimwig? Perhaps on Monday? I'll send him his uniform to be fitted, but I'm afraid I must leave you and get back to my shop, for, as you know, the wheels of commerce never stop."

They shook hands on it, and Oliver felt the firm grip of Mr. McCready's fingers.

"I look forward to it, sir," said Oliver. "And I thank you for the opportunity."

He didn't know if that last part was important enough to add, truly, but he meant it. Perhaps it had been to show Mr. McCready that he understood the connections between gentlemen; he wasn't sure. He knew, though, that he wanted to please Mr. McCready. As he had pleased Uncle Brownlow and his Aunt Rose and Uncle Harry. And Mrs. Bedwin.

"Till then, sir," said Oliver.

Mr. McCready hastened out, and after bidding farewell to Mr. Bond, Oliver and Mr. Grimwig left the office through the front door, making their way amidst the crowd of dark-garbed workers, and slowly, for Mr. Grimwig's limp. Monday, and all the days that followed it, could not come fast enough for Oliver.

# 7

# ARRIVES LATE, WHICH IS NOT CONSIDERED AN AUSPICIOUS BEGINNING

"Inf not for the commodious amounts of personal effects that you insist on carting about, you would have been able to walk to this new position," said Mr. Grimwig.

It was snowing again, and one of the servants had ordered a cab without, exactly, asking Mr. Grimwig's permission, but there was a delay while they waited for the transport. All of which had made Mr. Grimwig quite cross.

In spite of Mr. Grimwig's rantings, Oliver wasn't taking much with him. Just mementos of his time with Uncle Brownlow: a lace-drawn card from the chapel where Aunt Rose and Uncle Harry had been married, the small picture of his mother, wrapped in a soft cloth, and of course, there was his collection of second-hand books, purchased from Mr. Beauchamp's store, where Oliver and Uncle Brownlow had, so to speak, met. Tucked at the very bottom of his case, hidden beneath his nightshirt, was his copy of *The Arabian Nights* that he'd bought at Hillyard's Books. It wasn't very much that he was taking with him, surely nothing to express how happy he had been living there.

Oliver was ready, even though he was running late.

He was dressed in his new uniform, which had been sent to him the day after the papers had been signed. One of the maids had him come down to the kitchen so she could take the trousers in and let the jacket out, as needed. The whole of the uniform was made of a sensible warm, brown wool, from his cap to his trousers. Even his waistcoat was brown, as well as his boots.

Only his scarf was a different color, a deep, brilliant green; his white- and green-striped shirt was hidden beneath the layers. The scarf would make him stand out, he supposed, when he went on errands or was anywhere in the City; it would mark him as one of Mr. McCready's boys. And that was all right, wasn't it? A thing to be proud of.

His fingers were numb around the handle of his case, and a small collection of the staff of the house stood silently in the hall as the cab arrived in front of the townhouse with clops of shod hooves and the clank of iron wheels over icy cobbles. Mr. Grimwig handed Oliver an envelope that contained his papers and the address of the shop for the cab.

"You're to go to Mr. McCready's directly," said Mr. Grimwig. "You're not to make any stops along the way. No loitering and no stopping at any bookshops. The faster you get yourself settled there, the more content you'll be."

And this said as if Oliver had expressed any intention of not going, of not being willing to go. Mr. Grimwig was turning it all around, as usual, to make the positive aspect of the whole arrangement his own, thus leaving Oliver to play the part of the reluctant miscreant.

"Yes," he said, his heart thudding.

Mr. Grimwig nodded at the envelope in Oliver's hand. "That's to pay for the cab, and any small thing you might need before getting your first pay packet."

To send Oliver off with money was for Mr. Grimwig's own benefit, and to entertain anyone who might hear about it.

"You'll find exactly five pounds in there," said Mr. Grimwig, a smirk dancing across his eyes. "Exactly the amount you typically like to find yourself holding when you go out and about."

It was a slap, a rude, cruel slap. It had been five years since The Incident, and everyone, even the servants, knew the story, knew the truth of it, that Oliver had been *taken*—

That errand, which sent Oliver out into the dangerous streets of the City, had been Mr. Grimwig's idea. It was he who had suggested that Oliver take the books back to the shop for Uncle Brownlow, and a wager had been placed the moment Oliver had left the townhouse. And, as Mrs. Bedwin had told him later, Mr. Grimwig had been most insistent that Uncle Brownlow was about to be taken for all he had.

*The boy has a new suit of clothes on his back; a set of valuable books under his arm; and a five-pound note in his pocket. He'll join his old friends, the thieves, and laugh at you. If ever that boy returns to this house, sir, I'll eat my head.*

While Oliver had not come back, it was because he'd been taken in the street, and he'd not laughed about it, not then, not ever. But it didn't matter now. Any protestations from Oliver, and especially in the absence of taking the time to explain the whole story, would be a waste of time. He was eager to be on his way, besides, so he merely nodded his head and tucked the envelope in his pocket.

"Yes, thank you."

Mr. Grimwig patted Oliver on the head, which he tended to do when he wanted to show how amiable he was. The cap on Oliver's head padded what was almost a blow, and he ducked his head to stave off any more.

One of the servants opened the door, and the warmth of tea and toast and the morning fires whisked past him across the polished black-and-white floor and pulled him out into the day. Into the snowy cold of the March morning that, like most March mornings, was cold enough to make him believe that spring would never come. That winter had won, at last, and that the snow-laced branches would always look that way. That it would always snow, the steps perpetually coated with some ice that had not been properly scrubbed off. That, as he stepped out and went down the steps to the carriage, he was the coldest he'd ever been. And colder than he'd ever been at Fagin's den, though that was a memory best left alone.

Oliver turned back to look at the open door, at the faces that did not look sorry. At Mr. Grimwig's satisfied expression, framed by slowly drifting morning snow. Not obscuring it, but taking it into his memory. Had Uncle Brownlow not died, the picture before him would never have been.

"I will be getting reports on you, young Oliver," said Mr. Grimwig, which was obviously his best attempt at a tearful farewell. "I expect they will be good reports, or we will have to move you, after all. Perhaps a factory up north might better suit you? Or the mines?"

Oliver shook his head. Not either of those, not if he could help it.

The cab took Oliver through the cold morning streets of London, around St. James's Park, past the formal buildings along Whitehall, and as briskly as it could through the busy traffic at Charing Cross. At Haymarket, where the fronts of the shops and offices clustered in more closely, the cab had to slow down, enough so that as it headed up Windmill Street, Oliver could observe the type of neighborhood it was. It was not posh, such as the Strand, but it displayed tidy front steps and enough ladies to indicate the health of it.

Then, when the cab turned right on the even more narrow Broad Street, Oliver got an all-too-thorough look at the local workhouse. It was located just along Poland Street, the firm grey brick rising in a wall around it and the even darker brick of the building itself. Oliver had a brief glimpse of the sign that indicated it was St. James's Workhouse, but that was enough to see. Oliver looked the other way and concentrated instead on the rocking pace of the cab as it went as briskly as the narrowing lane would allow it.

Then with a lurch, the cab came to a stop in front of a building with a glossy, green-painted sign with gold letters that said: *McCready's Haberdashery*.

Oliver lingered in the doorway of the cab that he had opened himself. He did not expect any assistance, didn't want any. For one moment, he wanted to be invisible. And it was not that he imagined his life here would be so bad, only that it was, for the moment, so very different. If Uncle Brownlow had been with him, he would have been very willing to explain to him what he was seeing, but Oliver felt he might be able to see it on his own, concentrating on the details while waiting until two country gentlemen dressed in thick smocks passed by on the pavement.

Street traffic, made up of, as Oliver could see, the sturdy, industrious, and upwardly climbing type, kept the area relatively clean and safe. But while the neighborhood was nice, the location of the shop was too near the back streets. However, the haberdashery itself was saved from being too insalubrious by the fact that it was near St. James's Church, and only one street off a main omnibus line, which made it somewhat more genteel, being near to Oxford Street, and only one or two blocks from Soho Square.

The brown-brick building was near the middle of the street. It attached on one side to another building, and had a tall set of doors on the other corner, and an alleyway alongside of it, leading to a dark court.

When Oliver alighted from the cab, he pulled out the envelope Mr. Grimwig had given him and paid and tipped the driver out of the five-pound note. The driver grumbled and dug into his pockets for enough change. It took him a moment, but when he gave Oliver four pounds and ten shillings, he was shocked at how much the trip had cost, and resolved to keep closer track of his money and walk when he could. The driver handed Oliver's case to him and then flicked the reins to trot off to circle around and return to the main thoroughfare.

Puffs of steam rose from the bodies of the horses pulling other cabs and from the dung steaming in the street. Over the roofline, he could see the grey hulk of the workhouse, and ignoring his dismay at seeing it so close to where he would be working and living, he resolved that when he set out on any errands, he would give it a wide berth.

To distract himself further, he looked up at the shop in the bright, cold air, then looked along the street. The haberdashery was in the middle of a lane, with an alley on one side, a lane was filled with shops, all painted in bright, rich colors, with huge windows and drapes of cloth in them. Or bonnets. Or shoes. Or baskets. Whatever was for sale. From down the street, Oliver could smell bread baking, or perhaps it was beer being brewed in a shop nearby.

The haberdashery itself had narrow double doors at one corner, with three stone steps that led up to them. Though each step that led to the doors sagged in the middle from years of foot traffic, they were free of snow and dust, a creamy white from many scrubbings. The double doors were a dark clover green, painted glossy and new with generous strokes, and had bright brass handles and fittings.

The tall windows of the shop, draped with cloth and hung with articles to buy, were shining clean. The brass handles sparkled. Overall, it seemed the sort of shop that Uncle Brownlow would not only have approved of, but would have frequented, and it was of the class that he would have been proud to say that he did.

A lad came out of the shop. He was a short, ginger-haired boy and was wearing a white apron, and under that, the same thick brown trousers and striped green-and-white shirt that Oliver wore.

The lad carried a bucket and shovel and, in perfect silence, stepped into the street and shoveled the manure into the bucket.

Then he whisked the remainder with a broom, sending it into the center of the cobbled street, and hurried with his gear into the alley at the side of the shop. Of course, he would come out with an empty bucket, but it would be a foolish shopkeeper who allowed his lads to come back through his store with a full or fouled one.

Oliver hesitated at the bottom of the steps and waited, thinking that he was lucky his feet weren't going numb, as it felt as though it had grown much colder since he'd gotten out of the cab. Better these mundane thoughts than to concentrate on the wild beating of his heart.

It was so ordinary, what he was doing, so very, very ordinary, a young man walking into his first apprenticeship. But it felt as though he was about to walk over an immense chasm from his bleak situation at Mr. Grimwig's, where his rotten, dark past was never allowed to stray far behind him. From that into a clean, bright place with kind, upstanding, and hardworking people, who, while they might know the story, would not, perhaps, be inclined to bring it up every other half hour.

He heard footsteps from within and straightened, bringing up his chin to look the approaching person in the eye, as he ought, and felt the churn of his stomach. How many doors had he gone through in his lifetime, never knowing what was on the other side, who would be there, and whether they would be kind. Would this be the last door? Or would it be just the next door in a very long line?

This pair of doors had long narrow window on each side and a transom above. The doors opened and out stepped Mr. McCready, his broad shoulders cutting the air around him. As he looked at Oliver, he was, naturally, standing on the top step and looking down his nose. For a moment, he reviewed Oliver, a haughty downward curve to his mouth, an assaying expression in his eyes.

"You're late, Oliver," Mr. McCready said, his mouth thinning.

"It was the traffic, sir," said Oliver. "It took a good quarter of an hour longer than we—that is, Mr. Grimwig, indicated—"

"That's enough, Oliver. But in future, you will not be late. It's not suitable and sends the wrong message to our customers."

Mr. McCready was truly irritated, that was easy to see, from the cold morning, perhaps, and most assuredly from Oliver's lateness. Snow whistled around Oliver's feet as he waited for his orders. Perhaps Mr. McCready would turn him away for this one small slight, though where Oliver would go, he hadn't the faintest idea.

Some small part of him thought about Jack and where Jack was and whether he'd take Oliver in, though the very thought of that was foolish. The last thing Oliver needed at this point in his life was to throw in his lot with a pickpocket.

Then Mr. McCready nodded, holding the door open with one strong hand.

"Come in, then, Oliver," said Mr. McCready, as if he felt his point about lateness was both made and taken. "And you will begin to learn."

Oliver took off his cap and stuffed it into his pocket as he followed Mr. McCready into the shop, his large case banging against his knees. It was early, so there were no customers. Mr. McCready walked up to the edge of the main counter, long and glossy, and tapped it.

"This is the center of the shop, Oliver, the heart," he said, his loud, clear voice finding its way into every cranny of Oliver's brain. "If you have any question as to what you are about, you come here and ask. But stand at the edges while you wait; I will not have lollygagging in the center of my shop, as it presents a very untidy image to the customers."

The shop was set up as many a haberdashery was, with shelves all around the walls, in front of which waited a rolling ladder. There was a series of display cases framed with dark, polished wood and with glass tops and brass frames. There were scissors on strings and several small bales of twine and rolls of brown paper, both on brass pikes. Little drawers were set into shelves along the walls, with labels written in fine cursive script that read *Buttons* or *Pins* or *Hooks*. Open shelves held starched collars or stacks of suspenders.

Oliver felt overwhelmed as he looked at the array, especially as he realized that the location of each was something he was going to have to learn. Not just admire and select from, but actually know. And the floor. It was polished to gleaming, with not a fleck of dust to be seen anywhere. A great deal of work obviously went into keeping the shop as nice as it was. It suddenly occurred to him the amount of work that it was, that the boys who worked for Mr. McCready attended to. That *he* would be attending to.

The shop boy who had scraped the horse leavings from the street was now waiting on a lady customer who had just come in. The boy barely paused in his attendance to the lady to note the presence of anyone else. He didn't appear an unfriendly boy; it could be that he was merely busy. Oliver nodded at him just the same.

"The most important thing is that the boys in my shop are known for their politeness," Mr. McCready said. "We open the front doors for customers, whether they are coming or going. We thank them for their custom, if they have purchased anything, no matter how small or insignificant, and hand them their carefully counted-out change."

"Yes, sir," said Oliver. The shop, he was beginning to see, was more like Hillyard's Books than he was comfortable with, but perhaps if he were one of the lads with a superior air and a clean white apron, he might feel differently about that.

"Well, now that you've seen the shop, we shall go see the quarters upstairs."

Oliver nodded and followed when Mr. McCready led the way up the stairs, almost bouncing on his toes on each riser as they went up the two flights of stairs. Oliver had to trot to keep up with him, trying not to smack his heavy case against each step.

By the time they reached the top landing, Oliver was almost out of breath and marveled at his new master's stamina.

The landing was small and made up of a short passageway, with two doors on the left and one on the right. There was a small window at the far end that let in a vague gleam of morning light that lit up the white-painted walls. As with the downstairs, the wooden floor was clean, and the window was fairly free of streaks; most of the dirt was on the outside, but then the outsides of windows were always hard to keep clean in winter.

Mr. McCready smiled and opened the nearest left-hand door, which showed a small sitting room with dark, striped wallpaper, and a pair of older but still plush armchairs in front of a fireplace, which was dark without a fire in it.

"This is my private sitting room, Oliver, and beyond it, my bedchamber. I sometimes take my meals alone here, but mostly I take them in the kitchen with the boys. No boy is allowed in here without my permission, and indeed, without my presence, which, I'm sure, only makes sense."

"Yes, sir," Oliver said, nodding. "I see."

"I'm not at liberty to show you, but those are Mrs. Pierson's rooms." Mr. McCready waved at the other door on the left but didn't open it. "She's the housekeeper and cook. We have a girl come in most days to help, and she lives elsewhere."

Mr. McCready moved past Oliver to open the door on the other side of the small passageway. His body seemed large for a moment as he shifted to open the door, and so Oliver had to step back. Mr. McCready motioned with a wave of his hand for Oliver to precede him.

Feeling that Mr. McCready was just at his heels, Oliver walked into the room. There were three iron beds, all tidily made up in the middle of the day. The single window at the far end of the steeply gabled room let in only enough light to douse the beds and the floor with gloomy flickers of shadow and light.

Mr. McCready came next to him and pointed to the bed nearest the window and farthest from the door.

"You're the newest apprentice, so it is tradition that you shall sleep closest to the window."

Oliver looked at the bed and walked over to it. He put the heavy case down next to it with a sigh.

"You can unpack later; you may have the pegs on the wall and the chest at the foot of your bed for your own personal use," said Mr. McCready. "Now, take a look at the room here, and tell me what you see."

Feeling a little numb, Oliver did as he was told and turned around. Now that he was facing the room with the window behind him, he could see a little better.

There were three beds lined up like coffins under the eaves, the head of each iron bedstead coming just to where the slanted ceiling met with the wall. Beside each bed was a chair with a candle in a small stand. On the wall was a series of pegs; the set nearest Oliver was empty, and from the other two sets hung white nightshirts, and perhaps an extra shirt and a pair of trousers. At the foot of each bed was a small wooden chest.

The other side of the room had a single washstand with a pitcher stored neatly in the bowl. Next to the washstand was a low, battered couch. All in all, it seemed rather severe a place after his snug little room at Uncle Brownlow's.

"Well, Oliver, what do you see?"

Pausing a moment, Oliver said, "I see three beds, sir, and three chests. I see—"

"You see order, Oliver. Each boy has what he needs. Each boy takes care of what he is given. Do you see any dirt on the floor?"

Oliver looked, wishing he knew whether or not this was the customary way of things, or whether this was a trick question of some sort.

"No, sir, I don't."

"Do you think the boys clean the floors here?"

"No, sir."

Mr. McCready gestured to Oliver to come to him, and

clapped a hand on his shoulder again, and Oliver wondered if he'd have bruises there in the morning.

"They do indeed, but not up here. In the mornings, after breakfast and before the shop opens at nine o'clock, the boys take down the shutters, wash windows, weather permitting, check the count in the change box. They make sure the girl has cleaned the grates and lit the fires properly in the stove in the main room, my office, and the warehouse. At night, the boys dust and polish the shelves, replenish stock and sweep and mop the floor. But up here, the girl comes in and does the cleaning. That way, boys know what it is like to both clean floors and have floors cleaned for them. Do you understand what this means?"

Oliver turned around and struggled with an answer. He could recall Uncle Brownlow talking about something like this. It had been just this Christmas past when they'd discussed what they could do for the poor, and how they could best show the housekeeper and the other servants how much they appreciated them. Mr. Grimwig had thought the whole thing a waste of time, but Uncle Brownlow had enjoyed giving out gifts very much.

"It has to do with...it has to do with knowing your place in the world, doesn't it, sir? Only kings and queens never clean their own floors, only the poorest never have their floors cleaned for them."

"Very good," said Mr. McCready, nodding. "You've had good teachers. It is imperative that someone who serves knows what it is like to be waited upon. It is in this way that we can give customers what they want because we know what it might be that we would want. Never forget that."

Mr. McCready turned to go. He opened the door to the hallway and motioned that Oliver should follow him.

"We'll catch up with Tate in the warehouse. He's a good lad, and useful too, for all he's not very easy with customers."

Mr. McCready trotted down the stairs, and Oliver followed, his legs already feeling like stumps. How long would it take him to get used to moving so fast?

# 8

## OLIVER JOINS WITH A NEW
## COMPANY AT MCCREADY'S
## HABERDASHERY

At the bottom of the step on the main floor, a short passageway led from the shop to a back hall. It was there that Mr. McCready took them, his dark, oiled head set at a confident angle as Oliver followed him.

"The warehouse is this way," said Mr. McCready, opening the door at the end of the passageway. He smiled as Oliver caught up to him, stepping over the slight hump that the floor took as it led through the passage.

As Oliver followed through the doorway, he found himself on an elevated landing of rough wooden boards that had a set of stairs leading directly down into the open area of the warehouse. The unplastered ceiling above was quite high, and there were long, horizontal windows on tops of the long walls, also very high up, which let in the soft winter light.

Between the unpainted brick walls, the room was full of shelves filled with boxes and slatted crates he presumed held more goods for sale, and bundles that looked as though they were waiting to be unpacked. Near the large doors at the far end was a small cast iron stove, glowing with heat. There were small irons on the top, heating, and along the wall was a deal table with a cloth on it and a pile of ribbons waiting nearby. A tall, dark-haired boy stood next to the table, arranging the ribbons into long, colored strips.

"All nice and tidy then, eh, Oliver?" asked Mr. McCready as he looked at Oliver. "Each boy has a task assigned to him until he is called or directed to another."

Oliver nodded.

"Then, of course," Mr. McCready went on, "each boy is taught how to do each task and is allowed time to perfect the doing of it. Boys must be given time to learn."

Mr. McCready turned to the floor and gave a quick shout. "Tate! Tate Maxwell."

The boy at the table lowered a trail of ribbon and raised his head. "Yes, sir?" he asked, his voice loud enough to carry.

"Come here a moment, would you? I've someone for you to meet."

Tate laid the ribbons down, checked the irons on the stove to make sure everything was to rights, and hurried over to them. His passage up the wooden steps was so quick that his hands barely touched the rough, unpainted railing.

"Yes, sir?" Tate asked.

Though taller, he was some years younger than Oliver, with wide brown eyes and a smear of high color on each cheek of his thin face. He had on a cream-colored apron tied around his middle that came just past his knees. Beneath his brown uniform that matched Oliver's, Tate wore a white shirt striped with green, as Oliver did, and it was a green that Oliver suddenly realized matched the painted doors out front. And even though Tate's shirtsleeves were folded up, there wasn't a rip or darn or any sign of wear in the cloth. His boots were sensible and brown.

"This, Tate Maxwell, is Oliver Twist, who is going to be an apprentice with us. Oliver, this is Tate."

"Pleased to meet you," said Tate, looking at them with eyes that darted over their faces. He offered his hand to Oliver. Oliver shook it, feeling the faint calluses on Tate's palm.

"And how do you like your work here, eh, Tate?" asked Mr. McCready.

"I like it just fine, sir," said Tate. His voice came out quick and slightly breathless, as if he feared he wouldn't be given enough time to say what he needed to say.

"And you're not just saying that because I'm standing here, Tate?" Mr. McCready winked at Oliver. "Now, be honest."

"God's truth, I've learned ever so much here."

"Ah," said Mr. McCready. "What have we talked about using the Lord's name in such a way?"

"Sorry, sir, it slipped. I won't forget again." Tate blinked several times, as if startled by being remonstrated, but he didn't seem to be taking it badly, and in a moment, shrugged his shoulders as if through with it.

"Off with you, then," said Mr. McCready, as if he, too, was done with the issue. "How long till you are finished with that shipment of ribbons?"

"Another hour," said Tate. Tate waited for Mr. McCready's silent nod and then hurtled himself down the steps as if there was nothing more he wanted than to return to his task.

"You see the ribbons, Oliver" said Mr. McCready. "And over there, beeswax candles. Isn't that a bit old-fashioned to be selling those, you might ask? And at such an expense when paraffin ones are so ready and cheap to buy? So much cleaner to burn?"

Oliver didn't know what, exactly, to say to this, but he stopped himself from shrugging. "Old-fashioned?" he asked.

"Indeed," said Mr. McCready, leaning for a moment on the balustrade, surveying Tate working below. "Old-fashioned it is, and charming, too. There's nothing like the smell of a beeswax candle, and so many who remember it prefer it, even. The chandlers mostly make paraffin candles these days, but I'm offering something special. You see?"

Oliver nodded, as if the demands of the consumer and the theories behind offering them one thing instead of another were a subject he knew all about.

With a satisfied nod, Mr. McCready patted Oliver on the shoulder.

"Go down to the kitchen, and I'll be there in a moment to introduce you to Mrs. Pierson."

Oliver followed Mr. McCready back into the shop, where Mr. McCready went over to a customer and gave a little bow. So Oliver went by himself down the flight of stairs that led to the kitchen. They were steep and unpainted, and as Oliver paused on the small landing where the stairs turned halfway down, he could hear the sound of crockery and felt the warmth of a fire. A second later, he smelled butter and roasting meat.

At the bottom of the stairs, the kitchen had a flagstone floor, well swept and even. A corridor led from the kitchen to back rooms that looked like they held a laundry area and a boiler. The main room held a table that would not have looked out of place in a farmhouse, but it had been wiped down so many times it was glossy in the light coming from the windows that looked out on the kitchen area.

At the far side of the room was a brick-lined fireplace. There was no fire in it, but it was swept clean. Through a little alcove, Oliver saw an iron stove, glowing with heat.

A woman stood in front of the stove. In a moment, she turned, her large skirts sweeping the floor, her white apron going from neck to hem and almost free of stains. She had her dark hair done up, as ladies did, eased over her ears in front of the laces of her cap. Her skin was fair, though flushed with heat from the stove, and her eyes snapped like dark, shiny buttons.

"Yes, young man?" she asked, as if he'd inquired after permission to ask her a question. "What might I do for you, or shall I find you are in my kitchen quite by mistake?"

"I'm—I'm Oliver Twist," he said, worrying his hands together. She reminded him of Mrs. Sowerberry in the way she was so dark, her eyes so severe. He swallowed. "Mr. McCready said, that is, he told me to come down, I'm to—"

"Oh, I see," she said. It had the sound of a box shutting.

"You're the new boy. Have you come to inspect my kitchen, then?"

She spoke as if, although he might have the temerity to try, he would not be able to find fault with her kitchen. And even if he had, she'd thrust him out on the pavement so quickly that his presence would be a lost memory. He hated the thought that he'd made her dislike him so soon in their acquaintance; his mind scrambled for a way to set things to rights.

"No, ma'am, no indeed." He bobbed his head just a fraction. "I can see how clean it is, and I know that Mrs. Bedwin would have felt right at home here." His face, unbidden, tightened because he could see, directly and without hesitation, Mrs. Bedwin sitting there at the glossy table with her fussy white lace cap, and her hands, wrinkled and calm, holding a cup of tea, with a napkin in her lap.

"Mrs. Bedwin?" asked Mrs. Pierson, peering at him more closely now.

"My old nurse," said Oliver. "Gone these two years past." His throat tightened, and he had to look away.

From behind him came the quick trot of someone moving down the stairs apace. Oliver turned, quite grateful for the interruption of his sad thoughts, to see Mr. McCready, who was not even out of breath as his boots hit the flagstone floor.

"We've come not to inspect your kitchen, Mrs. Pierson, but to allow Oliver to salivate at the thought of eating your good cooking."

The corners of Mrs. Pierson's mouth turned down, as if she were, at that very moment, deciding whether to accept his compliment or reject it as insincere.

"Very well," she said, smoothing her apron with both hands in long, broad strokes. "Have him come take a taste of my bread, freshly risen and baked today. And if he promises not to sneeze on it, he may have a quick peek at the chicken stew I am making for supper. Then there's the tea I've got to be getting on."

With a flip of her hand, she bid him to come forward.

Looking at Mr. McCready for confirmation, Oliver stepped up to the stove on which sat a large covered pot. Mrs. Pierson took a cloth from her apron waist and lifted the lid. Warm odors of onion and salt rose from the golden broth. Just as quickly, Mrs. Pierson replaced the lid. Then she turned to the sideboard and handed Oliver a piece of bread. As he took it, he saw it was already spread with butter, and that there was an entire plate of buttered bread sitting on the sideboard, covered gently with a thin cloth.

With his mouth already salivating, Oliver brought the slice to his mouth and bit into it. He knew it was rude not to tear the slice in half before he ate it, and he knew that he'd taken off a rather big bite, showing his teeth as he chewed, but he couldn't stop himself. But then, he'd never been able to eat slowly, even after all these years.

"Boys are always hungry," she said, watching him. Though, as she handed him another slice as soon as he'd finished the first one, it seemed the idea of his hunger recommended that he be fed rather than the other way around. Her eyes regarded him as he chewed and swallowed.

"It's very good," he said, when his mouth was empty. The last time he'd tasted butter that creamy was last summer when they'd gone to Chertsey to visit Uncle Harry and Aunt Rose.

"Only the finest for Mr. McCready's boys," she said, her mouth curving, pleased.

"Mrs. Pierson, this is Oliver Twist. Oliver, this is Mrs. Pierson, who is my cook, and a fine one too, and my housekeeper, as well. We have a girl, as I've told you, but she is out at the moment, I presume, Mrs. Pierson?"

"Yes, indeed, to do the shopping, though whether she'll be back in time to help with the cooking and washing up is another matter."

Mr. McCready *tutted* under his breath; it seemed an old disagreement between them that had yet to see any resolution.

"Well, Oliver," he said. "What do you think? The boys who

work for me work hard, but they are well fed three times a day. Along with the training I give them, well, it's more than that you'd be hard pressed to get elsewhere."

"Yes, sir," said Oliver, unsure as to what sort of reply he might make in the face of such satisfaction on Mr. McCready's part. The ginger-haired boy with the white apron that he'd seen in the shop, and the one he'd spoken to, Tate, had seemed well enough, with faces brighter than most of those he'd seen in other shops he'd been to.

With a smile, Mr. McCready turned to the stairs, calling after him as he went up. "Come along, then, Oliver, don't dawdle. I'll show you the office and then you will have seen all there is to see before we put you to work."

Oliver followed Mr. McCready up the narrow stairs, trotting to keep up, his face cooling as he left the warmth of the kitchen for the more chilly air of the shop. There were no customers at the moment, though the ginger-haired boy he'd seen before was standing at a glass-topped table near the door, folding long strips of cloth and stacking handkerchiefs, his eyes intent on his work.

Mr. McCready walked up to the boy and Oliver followed. The boy stood up straight and stopped his work, but he looked at Mr. McCready directly, without the sullen expression of many shop boys toward their masters and, in fact, without the least bit of fear.

"All right then, my lad. This is Oliver Twist, who has signed on as a new apprentice. Oliver, this is Henry Poulton."

As Mr. McCready pointed to him with all apparent fondness, Henry dipped his head and Oliver did likewise. Henry Poulton was slight and compact, with fair ginger hair. For all the cravat on his neck was slipping to one side, he seemed tidy, and looked at Oliver with grave, brown eyes.

"Henry is my senior boy," said Mr. McCready, slapping Henry generously on the shoulder. "He's almost too smart for his britches, but I don't know as how I'd manage without him. When you're ready, he'll teach you everything about the front shop duties. Tate will teach you the back shop duties and will move up to help Henry. That'll leave me a free hand to work on expanding my stock." Mr. McCready seemed to sigh then, as if Oliver's arrival was a relief he didn't know he'd been waiting for.

"Am I not to work in the front shop directly, Mr. McCready?" asked Oliver, realizing too late that perhaps he should have asked permission to speak before he spoke. Or that his question was altogether too bold for the new boy.

"No, indeed, Oliver," said Mr. McCready. "But it is not any slight against you or any apprentice, new or old. I have a system, you see. I've had many boys work their way through it, and all of them have started in the back shop, learning the business from the ground up. Then, when they are ready, the boy comes to the front shop and learns to interact with customers and learns that end of the trade."

"Don't worry, Oliver," said Henry, with a slightly musical up-and-down rhythm to his voice. "It won't take you long till you're working in the front shop."

"That's right enough, Henry," said Mr. McCready, again smiling fondly at Henry. "He's been here long enough to know how things work. Why, if I took off on holiday tomorrow, he'd be able to run the place without me for a fortnight."

Henry nodded and seemed unabashed at the compliment.

"Boys are trained by me in all aspects of running a business such as this. For example, you'll not only know how to receive stock, but how to keep track of it and order more. My boys do everything from the most common tasks to waiting on the ladies and gentlemen of quality who come through those doors. Eventually, each boy performs some of every duty, every task."

"I see, sir," said Oliver.

The numbness he'd been feeling all morning, and indeed since Uncle Brownlow's funeral, began to fade away a little. This was a good place, he could see that. It was a fine shop, with well-trained, well-treated boys who could eventually make their way in the world when they left the confines of Mr. McCready's establishment. Though it was not exactly as he expected, surely it was a good start for the bookshop he wanted to own one day?

"Besides, young Oliver," said Mr. McCready. He looked at Oliver appraisingly in a way he'd not done, not even at the funeral. "With that face and your knowledge of the streets, I think I'd do best to put you on deliveries almost right away. You'd bring in extra custom, and, as you know, my lads keep their tips."

Oliver flushed and opened his mouth to protest. Yes, he'd been told he had the face of an angel so many times, but he'd never really been asked to use it to make money. Nor did he know the streets as well as one might think, or have much experience talking with ladies, given his background. Yes, he'd assisted Bill Sikes with breaking into the Maylie house, but that didn't make him a criminal! And it certainly didn't make him the type of lad who—

He felt hot and flushed, and his collar felt tight as his chest swelled with indignation, but a customer came in, and Henry turned away to attend to the gentleman.

At the same time, Mr. McCready waved Oliver to his office and Oliver followed, swallowing his spark of anger. It really wouldn't do to say what he felt, not when this was the best offer going. An added benefit was now that he'd moved across town, Jack would be hard pressed to find him, at least not easily. As well, being a part of a respectable shop such as this might be what would keep Jack away, and help to rid Oliver of some of the tarnish he was apparently still carrying around. Furthermore, perhaps most important of all, he would be busy, too busy to spend any more time grieving over Uncle Brownlow, which tended to tear him down to his very bones, making it almost impossible to get through a day, let alone a single moment.

When he got to the door of the office, he saw it had a desk against one wall so that Mr. McCready could sit at it and see anyone passing through the small corridor. One wall was lined with shelves and a series of cubbyholes that were labeled with slips of paper that said things such as *Incoming, Ordered, Special Order, Arrived, Outgoing.* Toward the middle of the room was a small fireplace with a comfortable chair and hassock, presumably for when Mr. McCready felt he needed a break from the hectic swirl of his shop.

"This is my office, Oliver. If you need anything, and I am here, simply knock at the door, whether it is open or closed."

"Yes, sir," said Oliver. "Thank you."

"Then we'll begin," said Mr. McCready, as he stepped out into the small hallway.

"Henry, come here." Mr. McCready gestured to Henry, who was just finishing with his customer. With the aplomb of confidence, Henry smoothed his apron and came over to them.

"I'm handing him over to you now, Henry. Show him the outside tasks and then give him to Tate, who will show him the warehouse duties. Can you manage that before Mrs. Pierson calls us for dinner at noon?"

Henry nodded, sage and sure in his knowledge and his position in the shop.

As Mr. McCready moved behind the counter to wait on a lady customer who had just come in, Henry turned to Oliver.

"I've been at the shop for two years," Henry said, even though Oliver had not asked him anything. "In a few more, I aim to be the best shopkeeper in the City."

Henry was shorter than Oliver and was younger in years, yet his voice had such conviction that Oliver didn't doubt him.

Henry led Oliver down the back hallway, away from Mr. McCready tending to customers, past Mr. McCready's private office, and down the back steps into the warehouse. Tate was sitting on a high stool next to the deal table against the wall, having left the ribbons in a heap. Now he was sorting through a box of what looked like buttons, carefully writing down amounts on a slate. His mouth moved as he counted, isolated and alone in the chilly warehouse, but seeming content, for all that.

In the snowy morning, the large wooden doors to the courtyard were shut, so the warehouse would have been dark, save for the light from the high windows. Henry took Oliver around the wooden stairs to the cupboard against the wall where the supplies were kept. He drew out the bucket and brooms, the cleaning cloths and the polishing stones for the stone steps that led up to the shop's front door.

"Here's an apron for you. It's a little worn, but it's for outside work. When we make deliveries, which I imagine Mr. McCready will have you doing mostly, we take them off, of course. Use a clean one if you are working in the shop at all, either in the warehouse or out front." Henry pointed to two large hooks that stuck out of the wall.

"Clean aprons are on the left, of which you get two a week. When they are too filthy to be worn, you hang them on this peg; Mrs. Pierson sends most of the laundry out once a week on Monday, and the rest the girl does. Do not put any soiled laundry in the basket or the mice will get at them." Henry gestured to an oval wicker basket on the floor, which was empty except for a few scraps of metal, perhaps being kept for the dustman. "For now, leave your coat and jacket on that peg. And your cap."

"Of course," said Oliver, slipping his greatcoat and brown jacket off. He pulled his cap out of his pocket and stuck it on a hook. Then he ducked his head to pull the yoke of the apron over it. He kept his scarf on, but even so, he was chilled without his jacket and coat. Henry, on the other hand, seemed unconcerned that his lips were already blue, so Oliver shrugged it off.

"I see you got your scarf. We all heard some street thug stole your other one."

Henry was almost smirking as he said this, but it was the fact that the story of it had gotten so far, so fast, that startled Oliver the most. Trust Mr. Grimwig to take one last stab at what was left of Oliver's reputation. It was in tatters already, added to by his being late on his first day. Would it have troubled Mr. Grimwig overly much to keep his mouth closed for once?

There was nothing to be done about it now, so when Henry

picked up the bucket and the bag of stones and cloths, Oliver picked up the broom and followed Henry through the small door that was set inside the big door, out of the warehouse and into a small courtyard. The brick walls around the yard were capped with stone and shimmered with ice and snow. The yard was cobbled and had a tall, green-painted wooden gate with an iron latch.

"Never take this gear through the shop," said Henry over his shoulder as he led Oliver into the alley. "Mr. McCready won't like it. All gear, all deliveries, come through the back door."

"Yes," said Oliver. It made sense, of course, but knowledge that there were tight rules with unspoken but dire consequences made him feel fatigued before he'd even begun.

They made their way down the ice-bound, cobbled alley that ran alongside the building to the pavement in front of the shop. Once there, Henry laid his bucket and broom down and placed the sack with the cleaning stones on the wooden ledge that the empty flowerbeds made.

"It'll be your job to keep this area clean and tidy," said Henry, scanning the pavement in front of the shop that was bare except for a dusting of snow. That there were piles of snow elsewhere, in the gutter, in the center of the street, on other pavements in front of other shops, hampering passersby, did not seem to concern him.

"Every day, you will need to give the pavement a sweep and a cleaning, or shovel snow and cast it with sand. Depending on the weather, you will scrub the steps each morning and whiten the stone. Not today, though, as the washing soda and water would only freeze."

This seemed obvious, and Oliver had seen this logic being applied at many shops over the years. The clean shops, the ones with swept pavements and scrubbed steps, attracted the better type of customer. He could see that there were long, narrow iron bars nailed above the windows that could, at various times, be hung with banners and colors draped over the glass to give the shop a festive air. Surely Uncle Brownlow would have thought it a good shop.

To stave off pangs of loneliness, of home, Oliver turned his attention back to Henry, who was still talking and instructing.

"In warm weather, you'll wash the windows daily. In cold, you'll carefully scrape the ice and dirt off." Henry pulled out two slats made of iron, each with a razor-sharp edge. "Don't break the glass when you do it. We'll start with that."

He handed Oliver one of the slats and demonstrated a curved-wrist movement that tucked beneath the edge of the ice and popped it off to clatter to the pavement. Together he and Oliver scraped at the ice, leaning over empty flowerbeds, moving the slats over the bottom and edges of the window where the melted snow and water had hardened into ice the night before.

Oliver tried to keep up with Henry, who was fast and efficient, wiping the ice off the slat with his apron and working with a little hum under his breath. Always moving, always pointing out spots Oliver had missed. Within a short period of time, Oliver was warm, and he realized why he didn't need his jacket. But his hands were numb, stiff as pieces of chalk, and his ears felt as though they were tipped with frost.

When they were finished with the windows, they wiped the pieces of iron down for the final time and slipped them in the sack. Then Henry took the broom and showed Oliver how to sweep the ice and any other debris into the gutter, what the most efficient strokes were.

"We'll come out after the dinner break to check," said Henry, "but there's not much that can be done in such cold weather."

But a little more they did, picking up the odd stray piece of paper, staying out in the cold, snappy air for a good ten minutes or more. They even assisted a lady from her sturdy black barouche when it stopped in front of the shop.

Henry held out his hand to her in an almost obvious way, with his other arm tucked behind his back, as though showing Oliver how it was to be done, as if suspecting that Oliver had never helped a lady from her carriage before. Which, truth be told, he hadn't. Henry was so quick that he even beat the footman to this task, though Oliver wondered at the entire exchange, as the lady only nodded at them and walked up the street to a different shop.

Before Oliver could point out the wasted effort, Henry smiled at him. It was a genuine smile this time, giving Oliver the decided opinion that Henry enjoyed working at the shop, liked doing what he was doing.

"She won't soon be forgetting us, that's what Mr. McCready says."

What Mr. McCready knew about keeping a good shop, Henry was, apparently, willing to learn and take to heart.

They were picking up the broom and tools when from the alley came Tate, his dark hair flying around his white face as he ran, slipping on the icy cobbles in his haste.

"Henry!" he said. "Mr. McCready wants you for a delivery. Bring the new boy; you're to show him how it's done."

"You'll be taking over for me in no time on those deliveries, I expect," said Henry.

Oliver followed Henry through the alley and into the court-yard and tried to remind himself that being a merchant was more like being a bookseller than anything else he could be doing, and being a bookseller was what he wanted to do. Although, at this moment, chilled through as the sweat from the cleaning dried on his brow and the back of his neck, what he really wanted to do was find a soft couch somewhere and curl up on it till Uncle Brownlow came home. But it was too late for that, too late for couches and cups of tea and soft chats until the girl came to call them for supper. That life was forever behind him now.

Henry showed Oliver how to put the supplies away in the cupboard at the bottom of the stairs, and they both hung up their aprons on the pegs in the wall. Pulling on their coats, caps, and Henry his scarf, they met Mr. McCready coming toward them in the hallway.

"You took your time," he said, almost snapping. He held out a parcel wrapped in brown paper and string. "These are the silver buckles Mrs. Acton has ordered; you need to take them to her quickly. Do you remember the address?"

"Yes, sir," said Henry, who had finished buttoning his jacket and took the package with two hands.

"Take Oliver with you. And don't take the omnibus, as I've no pennies to spare you. Then come back and hand him over to Tate."

In the narrow passageway, with no pennies to be spared, Oliver felt the sudden rush of urgency and matched Henry's movements and speed as he grabbed his scarf.

"Here, Oliver, you should be tidy when you are in the streets representing the shop."

As Oliver turned, Mr. McCready tugged on his neck, tying his scarf so that it was warm and plush around his neck and draped just like the scarf Henry had on. Mr. McCready didn't mention the stolen scarf or the street thug that Oliver reported had taken it off him, but the memory of the incident might be there in his eyes, hidden away behind the sudden display of kindness, along with his barely checked temper at the need for haste.

Oliver tugged on the scarf to loosen it a bit, then followed Henry and the packages and bundles out the front door and into the street. He took a deep breath as he kept up with Henry's quick pace.

Being out in London, swerving in and among the warmly dressed people on the street, hearing the busy clatter as the carriages and wagons tried to outpace each other, was exciting. As to being out on his own with another boy, without Uncle Brownlow, it was like breathing new air. Not to mention that he'd have someone with him if they chanced to cross Jack's path. Then Jack wouldn't be able to say anything more than hello or good-bye.

Even so, as Oliver walked at Henry's side, he cast an eye about him, looking for the shape of the figure that his brain would never lose the memory of. And, in spite of himself, listening for an echo of the long-ago, high dog whistle and the snap of a command barked out to all that instantly cowered and shrank from it. But Mr. McCready was no Sikes, Oliver was sure, and no Fagin either. Though why Oliver was making this comparison, here on this snowy street, he had no idea.

Henry tugged at his sleeve. "Come on, new boy. We aren't to dawdle, you know."

Henry didn't say this with any meanness or with any implied threat to report him back to Mr. McCready. He just meant for Oliver to hurry so that they could both perform this task to Mr. McCready's satisfaction. Henry was looking out for Oliver, which was quite different from the last time Oliver had worked with another boy. Back at Sowerberry's, Noah Claypole would have tripped him as soon as he looked at him.

## ❧ 9 ❧

# IN WHICH OLIVER MAKES HIS
# FIRST DELIVERY

O liver was glad that, as they headed toward Oxford Street, Henry led them along Wardour Street in the opposite direction from St. James's Workhouse, with its hard angles and dark, rising brick walls. Henry even had them avoiding the crossing sweepers by hurrying quickly behind a carriage as they headed out to the main thoroughfare.

The entire way, Oliver kept his eyes on Henry and pretended he didn't see the beggars at the corner—two men, one with a hideously scarred face, the other with only one leg. He had no money in his pockets, and if Henry had any to spare, he was moving too quickly to be parted with it. Oliver wanted someone to come and shoo the beggars away, but Henry walked fast and Oliver trailed close behind him; the beggars never had a chance.

Mrs. Acton's residence was a good way uptown, and they had to hustle up Grey's Inn Lane till they got to the corner of Doughty Street. When Henry allowed them a breather on the pavement, Oliver looked at the residence that was his first delivery on his first day of his apprenticeship. It was a cream-colored brick townhouse, tall and narrow, in the middle of a tidy block of townhouses just like it. Along the roofs of the townhouses was a neat, narrow row of chimney pots, all pouring out fine, almost identical black trails of smoke.

The carriages and barouches that passed on the street had no less than two horses each; the drivers were brisk with their whips, and the wheels made only the faintest of clatter on the cobblestones as each passed by. No milkmaid tarried anywhere, no sandwich men, no street sweepers holding out grubby hands, waiting to be tossed a penny for their labors.

There were no geese or cows being driven through the neighborhood on their way to Smithfield, and there certainly weren't any remains to mark any animals having passed this way in many a day. The entire street, and several blocks in either direction, bespoke a place inhabited by a higher quality of people who expected the best and were able to pay for it.

The front steps of Mrs. Acton's townhouse were clean and well scraped, but Henry took Oliver down the slanted iron stairs that led to the kitchen area.

"You make deliveries at whichever door they say, whatever they say, right?" Henry asked as he knocked on the white-painted wooden door, and peered through the small square of bullseye glass.

Oliver nodded.

"If you don't know, use the side door, or one like this, till they tell you different."

The door opened, and a lady's maid stood at the threshold in a striped dress and clean white apron. She looked severe until she saw who it was and then she had a smile, for Henry, at least.

"Who's that, then?" she asked, looking at Oliver as she held out her hand for the package.

"That's the new boy," said Henry. "He's Oliver Twist, and he'll be making deliveries from now on, I reckon."

She stared at Oliver, almost out of the corner of her eyes, as if she were trying very hard not to stare. "Mrs. Acton doesn't want mud tracked about, so scrape your feet next time, you."

Oliver looked down at his boots, which had tracked only the

faintest of dirt on the clean stone. "Sorry, miss," he said anyway, just to stay within her good graces.

"Ah, we'll forgive you, with a face such as yours." She reached into her pocket and handed Henry a penny. Then she held one out to Oliver. "Go on, take it. It's only a penny, but they add up."

Henry jostled him with an elbow, so Oliver took the large copper coin, still warm from her skin, and put it in the pocket of his trousers. He would find a box to keep his tips in, and he would never spend any of it. All of it would be to purchase his bookshop one day. He wouldn't even spend it on books, let alone gin. And, perhaps, though he had no idea how, he'd be able to get his change purse back from Jack.

"Tell Mr. McCready she wants a dozen of those beeswax candles next time you come this way. She needs them for her prayers."

"That's fine, missus," said Henry. "I'll tell him."

He tugged at Oliver's sleeve and led them up the stairs and onto the pavement. From an upper-story window, Oliver saw the curtains twitch as a woman in a white morning cap and robe looked down at him from her higher perch.

"And that's it?" asked Oliver, looking away from the woman. From the way Mr. McCready had talked about it, he'd expected the transaction to be somewhat more complicated. "She didn't pay us."

"She's on account," said Henry, shoving his hands in his pockets to keep them warm. "Some are, and some aren't, and it's up to you to remember which."

Oliver nodded again. That's how it was complicated; it sounded as though nothing were written down. Or perhaps Mr. McCready had it written down, and his apprentices were simply expected to remember everything.

His head was aching from the cold and the activity and the overwhelming sense that he was never going to catch on, never be as adept as Henry. For surely Henry was the high-water mark at the haberdashery; Tate was the youngest and—Oliver ground his teeth and made himself stop. He wasn't, didn't want to be, in competition with his fellow apprentices. He wanted to learn what he needed to learn, and then he wanted his own bookshop. And that was it, full stop.

"That was Mrs. Acton's, at any rate," said Henry. "She's a very particular customer of ours."

Henry trotted ahead as the snow started coming down in little whispers. "Come along, Oliver. We must get back as there's plenty to do at the shop, as Mr. McCready likes to say."

Oliver hurried and was able to keep up, but he wondered how long it would be before he felt as tireless as Henry seemed.

THE WAREHOUSE WINDOWS, FOGGED FROM LAYERS OF moisture and dirt from the alley, seemed dark. The little doorway was opened to let the light in somewhat, but the cold air came in as well, and battled with the heat of the potbellied stove.

Standing near the stove, Oliver numbly witnessed the short, heated discussion between Henry and Tate over opening the big doors. Henry insisted the day's delivery from their supplier was to come soon, and Tate insisted it wasn't till after dinner, in the afternoon. But Henry won out, and now he marched to the double doors and flung them open.

The sky looked as though it was going to shrug down more snow, and, standing only paces away from the open door, Oliver knew he'd be chilled through quite soon. He watched Henry's retreating back as he marched up the steps to the shop. Tate tiptoed over and closed the big doors most of the way.

"They're still open," said Tate, in a whisper. "But there's no sense catching our deaths simply because he thinks he owns the place."

Oliver didn't let himself smile, but it was nice to be included in Tate's small act of rebellion. Tate didn't know him from Adam;

how was he to know that Oliver wouldn't side with Henry? But Oliver wouldn't. He wouldn't side with anyone; he would be on his own side.

Tate shifted the next box of stuffs on the deal table to be unpacked and sorted. When he opened the box, Oliver saw it was yet another box of spooled silk ribbons. Only the ribbon had become unspooled and had traveled in a mangled, twisted mass, causing creases in the silk and winding all the colors around each other.

"Don't cut them apart," said Tate. "No matter how much you are tempted. Here, we spread this old cloth on the table—"

He shook out a faded muslin sheet from a hemp bag beneath the table, spreading it on the table. Then he upturned the box and let the ribbons tumble out. With deft hands, he began to untwist the ribbons; there had to be yards and yards of the colored silk: pale yellow, bright pink, green, blue, purple—

"How long will this take?" Oliver managed at last.

"Oh, we'll get a good start before dinner. Mr. McCready would rather we take the time here than to make a lady wait for her ribbons. He calls them impulse buys, bright things such as this. A lady cannot resist when she sees them, and often doesn't. And just wait till you see the buttons."

Tate smiled and nodded, as if this was very exciting. Oliver supposed that if one was stuck in a warehouse all day, shiny buttons coming out, all a-tumble, might be the very thing to brighten up your day. He hoped the time would never come when a bright button would be all that was needed to make him smile.

"We'll heat up the stove," said Tate. "And iron them, probably this afternoon. But for now, we twist and untwist, and lay them out in their proper colors."

Oliver nodded. His stomach began to growl, but stood next to Tate at the long table and reached out for a hump of twisted colors. The silk was soft and easy under his fingers and rippled like snakes as he pulled the mass toward him. At least the work was fairly easy; at least he wasn't in the mines.

～

WHEN THE CHIMES FROM ST. JAMES'S CHURCH ECHOED through the streets and alleys to sound the noon hour, Tate put down the spool he'd been working on, and took off his apron to hang on the peg. Oliver followed suit.

"We'll go to dinner now," said Tate. "We can leave the ribbons, as long as we shut the door." He seemed to find this funny, probably because he'd been right about the delivery not coming till the afternoon and Henry had been wrong.

Oliver watched him close the door and wondered how long that particular battle had been going on. Then he followed Tate up the short staircase and into the passageway, past Mr. McCready's office, and down the stairs to the kitchen.

At the bottom of the steps and against the wall was a small table with a basin and towel. Oliver did what Tate did, rolling up his shirtsleeves only a little way to his elbow, as there was no sense flashing his scar about, and washed his face and hands and wiped them on the towel that Tate had just used.

Mrs. Pierson waved them both to sit down; Oliver noted he was to sit on the bench seat along the wall and away from the warmth of her stove. It was obvious that the head of the table was reserved for Mr. McCready, and the seat on the side near the stove was for Henry. Superiority was no doubt perpetuated downstairs as well as up.

"Mr. McCready will be down directly," said Mrs. Pierson, checking everything on the table as the boys sat down. She spoke in a clear voice; the kitchen was her domain, so, of course, she was in charge. When her eyes decided everything was just so, she went to the bottom of the stairs. "He's just locking up, I expect."

Tate didn't serve himself, so Oliver didn't. But he watched

while Mrs. Pierson brought over the kettle of soup, and the slatternly looking hired girl, who seemed to have popped out of the scullery with her hair half-tucked, carried over a hefty plate of buttered bread. Then she darted over to the stove and returned with a bowl of boiled and buttered potatoes.

Oliver kept his hands in his lap. He felt slightly ill from standing for so long and then from sitting as the smell of food poured over him. Was he as weak and useless as Mr. Grimwig had always seemed to think? Even without always expressing it, those wide-apart eyes and the scowl of disbelief had said it: Oliver was not truly kin, did not belong, and should be put out on the street before anyone was forced to eat his own head.

Why did he have these mean thoughts now, when he was being served a dark, rich stew into the china bowl in front of him, and was being handed a plate of bread and butter from which he could take as much as he wanted? The girl poured cups of tea for everyone at the table, and then Mrs. Pierson went to the sideboard and fussed with what looked like a large pudding.

A wind whipped down the stairs and through the kitchen area, banging the windows in their panes.

"Not another storm," said the girl, rather boldly, since no one had asked her. She tucked up her hair under her cap, but the cap was askew and so her hair slid down her neck.

"This one will bring ice, mark my words," said Mrs. Pierson.

Tate and Oliver waited in silence. Oliver watched the steam of heat curl off the platters of food until finally Mr. McCready and Henry came down the stairs. They washed at the basin, and Mr. McCready took off his suitcoat, hanging it on a peg. Henry hung his apron and the two of them took their places at the table.

"Good afternoon, boys," said Mr. McCready, dipping his head.

His brown eyes flicked around the room, as if looking for something amiss. But they found nothing, and he smiled at them all. He seemed calmer now that the day was underway, and Oliver began to think that Mr. McCready's irritation had passed.

"There was a good bit of work done this morning, which I am glad to see. I hope those ribbons won't take too much longer."

He looked at Tate as he said this, and Tate shook his head, seemingly unworried.

"A few hours, Mr. McCready," he said.

Oliver nodded his agreement.

"Good. Let's continue that. Are we ready, Mrs. Pierson?"

"It's all on, Mr. McCready," said Mrs. Pierson. "I hope the new boy will be well satisfied; it's not cooking he's used to at home, to be sure, but I do my best." She wiped her hands on her apron and stared at him, as if daring him to disagree.

Mr. McCready bowed his head, and the boys, Mrs. Pierson, and the girl did likewise. Oliver followed suit and listened as Mr. McCready said a quick grace.

"Amen," said Mr. McCready, raising his head. "Well, tuck in, then."

"Yes, sir," said Tate and Henry at once.

Oliver opened his mouth to echo the agreement, but he was seconds too late, and his voice hung in the empty air. Tate smirked, but no one paid any attention to him as they picked up their knives and forks and began eating.

Cutting his piece of bread and butter in half, Oliver dunked it into his stew. The first bite told him it was delicious, with just enough salt to make his stomach jump up and down and demand more. He had yet to make it through his first afternoon, but this meal just might see him through. Besides, didn't it take a fellow a bit to get used to work when he'd not been doing it for a while?

When they were all mostly through their stew and bread and butter, Mrs. Pierson cut them each a large serving of pudding, putting each slice in a bowl. The hired girl poured the steaming yellow custard over each serving and then handed them around.

"Pour more tea for the lads, girl," said Mrs. Pierson.

"They've got enough; they've got full cups already." The girl's tone was sullen.

Oliver kept his attention on his plate and didn't look up. No one he knew would have permitted a servant to talk to them that way. But it wasn't his place to determine; perhaps the rules were more lax here; perhaps Mrs. Pierson liked it when—

"Just pour it and then you can go check the fires; make sure there's enough coal on hand."

Oliver made himself not pay any mind as the girl slopped the tea in the cups, picked up the coal scuttle, and stomped past them to where a little door in the wall led to the coal cellar.

Chewing on the last of his slice of bread and butter, Oliver leaned back to let Mrs. Pierson take away his supper plate, and then picked up his spoon to attack the pudding. It was a yellow sponge with jam swirled in, sweet and heavy and moist. Mrs. Bedwin had preferred to make light, airy puddings, but this one was better. It filled the corners of his stomach and let him know that he'd make it till supper.

"It appears as though the new boy enjoys your cooking, Mrs. Pierson," said Mr. McCready, from the head of the table.

Oliver looked up to see Mr. McCready wiping his mouth with a napkin.

"Nothing like honest work for a healthy appetite," said Mrs. Pierson. She looked as though she was trying to appear stern, and if Oliver let himself, he might think that she meant to say the word *honest* to make a point. As if a boy such as Oliver wouldn't know the first thing about honest work.

But there he went again, imagining that Mr. Grimwig had gotten to each and every person in the household. Mr. McCready might have told Mrs. Pierson about Oliver's past, but then again, as he'd thought before, Mr. McCready didn't seem the gossiping type. He wouldn't feel the need to explain why he'd taken an orphan, ex-pickpocket, and ex-member of a thieves' gang into his house. No, he would make his decisions and expect Mrs. Pierson to accept them.

"Was it enough, then?" She was looking at Oliver as if her greatest enemy was a hungry boy and she the only soldier in the ranks to combat it.

"Yes, Mrs. Pierson, it was very good." His voice sounded small and meek to his own ears, and he mentally kicked himself. If he wanted to make a new beginning, then he had to start acting like a young man brave enough to be on his own with a job to do. Not some milksop orphan who had barely enough backbone to stand up with.

"You spoil these boys," said Mr. McCready. He put his napkin on his plate and pushed back his chair to stand up.

"And why not?" she replied, jerking her chin at him but in a friendly way, as if this were an old, comfortable argument. "With mine fully grown and all?"

"No reason at all," said Mr. McCready, in kind. "You boys bring up your cutlery and plates. Put them in the right place; no tossing, do you hear?"

"Go on, then," she said, making motions with her hands. "I've got to get that girl on the washing to take down to the laundry and a joint to get on for supper."

Oliver's mouth began to water all over again. Uncle Brownlow's cook had done well enough, but with an invalid in the house and Mr. Grimwig not being the most active of men, their evening suppers had been light, soups and toast, perhaps some cheese. To be able to look forward to a proper meal at the end of the day was good news indeed.

Henry and Tate did exactly as they were told, and Oliver did as well. A full belly made him feel very obedient. Or perhaps it was Mrs. Pierson's stern eye and manner, standing eye-level with the boys' collars and breast buttons. Checking them over before they went upstairs. She stopped Oliver when he came up in the line to place his empty plate and bowl and utensils in the correct location.

"You've got a bit of potato, here," she said, taking the edge of a cloth to wipe it off. "There, that's you, then. Off you go with the others."

Oliver nodded his thanks and washed his hands in the basin. He used the comb and the looking glass to neaten his hair, without really taking time to look at his own reflection, and went up the stairs to the warehouse where Tate and the ribbons waited. His stomach was full, and although the back of his legs ached a bit, he found he could keep going for a while.

He joined Tate in putting on his apron, looking up at the windows, which were whitish-grey with snow. The warehouse felt even colder than it had before dinner.

"It's only till teatime," said Tate, tying on his apron.

"Beg your pardon?"

"Until teatime. Mr. McCready doesn't like it when boys drag their feet at the end of the day. So Mrs. Pierson, she makes us tea. Puts in extra sugar."

"Really?"

"Keeps us on our feet, he says. For those end-of-the-day customers, we're all bright and bushy-tailed, ready for them. Instead of dragging about. That's what Mr. McCready says."

It sounded sensible and even kind. So maybe, with the good food and the work not being overly difficult, except for all the information to remember, this might be the best decision he'd ever made. For all he was so exhausted and his feet ached and his wrists hurt, as though someone had twisted them, this would be a good place for him. He knew it.

EVEN WITH THE NICELY HOT AND SWEET CUP OF TEA THAT Mrs. Pierson brought out to the warehouse at mid-afternoon, by the time supper was served, Oliver could only see objects and people through a blur. It was as though he were looking through the glass windows of an old church, windows had been in place for centuries and sagged at the bottom of the frame, leaving bubbles and a thinness so stretched it could not be seen through. Yellow light or grey, depending on the weather, might ooze through, but it was all shapes and blobs and the hiss of the fire in the stove.

He heard someone speaking to him.

Oliver blinked and looked up. He realized he was hunched over his plate, both hands on the edge of the table, and that Henry and Tate were bustling to the counter with their plates and knives and spoons. The girl was grumbling as she poured a bucket of water into the large kettle on the stove, and Mr. McCready and Mrs. Pierson were both staring at him.

"I'm—" He jerked his head up, not sure what he'd been going to say. "Sorry?"

"Are the ribbons done?" Mr. McCready was asking Oliver directly now, and not Tate.

Oliver nodded. They'd worked at it for hours, and halfway through Henry had come in and reminded them to spool the ribbons on the new wooden spools. Which meant that Oliver and Tate had had to unwind and then rewind all the ribbons all over again. But they'd looked very nice on the new spools, and even Henry had been well satisfied when he'd come to check on them.

"Yes, sir," he said now.

"Well, on with you," said Mr. McCready, waving grandly. He took a sip from his cup of tea and then said, "The lads and I will shut up shop, and tomorrow you may learn that as well."

"Thank you, sir," said Oliver, standing up. He reached into his pocket. "I got a penny today," he said. "As a tip. Mrs. Acton's maid gave it to me." Too late, he remembered Henry had gotten a penny as well, and would Henry think Oliver was trying to get him into trouble? Henry had not mentioned his penny at all.

"You keep that," said Mr. McCready. "Mrs. Pierson, get one of those empty boxes, you know, the one that matches come in. Oliver can have that for his tips."

"But I'd give it to the church on Sunday." Oliver stood steadfast, wanting to make his point clear. He wasn't the sort of lad to take off with money that didn't belong to him, but he was too tired to think it through clearly.

"Oh, for heaven's sake, Mr. McCready, give him an early night. The boy's done in." Mrs. Pierson shook her head as if at the foolishness of overworking a poor lad on his first day. "Here's a box for you. I'll take your plates."

As Mrs. Pierson handed him a small rectangular wooden box that smelled slightly of sulfur, she gave him a pat on the arm. Then she took up his plate and cutlery. "The girl will bring up some water for you to wash; you go straight to bed, mind."

Oliver climbed the stairs, eyes half-closed, clutching his box to his chest. He could hear the girl stomping up the steps behind him. Once in the room, he hung his apron on one of the pegs near the bed nearest the window and watched as the girl poured the steaming water into a tin pitcher that sat on a table opposite the beds.

She lit the three candles, one by each bed, then growled at him and slammed the door behind her. He could hear her angry steps down the stairs and wondered blearily if she hated him or the position. He couldn't imagine anyone turning their nose up at working in a good household such as this.

He sat on the bed, putting the box on the floor, and struggled with the laces on his boots. He caught the vague scent of soap and boiled onions, and felt odd whistles in the wind against his neck as it snuck in through the thin panes. The small dormitory beneath the eaves didn't resemble his old room back at Uncle Brownlow's, which seemed years away now. But the room was nice enough, though cold; the candles burning by each bed made dappled shadows across the slanted ceiling.

Oliver made himself get up, and, unpacking as quickly as he could, put the case under the bed. He placed his books and letters from Aunt Rose in the box at the foot of his bed, and closed the lid. He hung his nightshirt on the peg on the wall and lay back across the bed.

Looking at the shadows and felt the thin pillow behind his head, he thought about his old bed. He folded his hands under his head and let his stockinged feet loll on the woolen blanket. It was thick enough, but nothing compared to his silk counterpane beneath which he used to sleep. He could feel the rough cotton of the sheet; it was durable but nothing fine, nothing such as he was used to.

But he was not in his old bed. In fact, his old bed would probably never be made up for him again and, in essence, no longer existed. If it ever had. He'd never been kin to Uncle Brownlow, a fact that Mr. Grimwig enjoyed reminding him of as often as possible. *You're on loan to us,* Mr. Grimwig had said once, *and as soon as we're able, we'll be sending you back.* As though he'd been a book from a shop or a rented seat in a park. To let, for hire, return for deposit.

He made himself stop and turned his head to bury it in the pillow. There was only one pillow and one thick grey blanket. Oliver enjoyed having two pillows, three if he could get them, with a few little ones thrown in lest his head ever think of touching the mattress. He wanted a fluffy eiderdown and soft flannel for his bed. Though he could do with one pillow and had slept many years without any, was it a sin, then, to want more?

It wasn't. Besides, compared to his first ten years of life, his current residence was a palace. He had a whole bed to himself and his own chair next to the bed, a box for his books, his own pegs on the wall. He currently shared the use of a washbasin with only two boys, and there was a couch to lounge on that they might share with him. He had hot meals during the day and water to wash in and a job to go to. Clothes to wear. Sturdy boots. A window that, mostly, had no holes. A penny in his pocket, and four pounds, ten shillings, as well. He had a brand-new scarf, bright green. Why should he complain?

Because for the last five years he'd lived as a young princeling, and he had only to voice a whim to have it answered. Or, at least, seriously conferred upon until he could be convinced that, indeed, sliding down the banister was not an occupation for a young gentleman. Nor was playing with the tinker's children. Or that eating a hot roll in the street was no way to set an example. All imparted to him in Uncle Brownlow's soft tone, a brown-eyed smile, and a pat with a large, gentle hand. A hand, which never, not in all the days that Oliver had known it, had ever been raised in anger. Only in love.

*Do you miss me, Uncle?*

He and Uncle Barlow had never been apart. Except for that time, short by the sun but long in Oliver's memory. The time he never wanted to think about again. And he certainly didn't want to think about Jack—

He screwed his mind shut to the memories and threw his arm over his eyes. If he could cover himself to the light, then he could cover himself to the memories and hold them at bay. Till his death day, if need be.

Too tired to wash or even read, he breathed in and out, watching the flicker of candlelight from under half-closed eyelids. In and out, till his breath seemed to flow, as though it were a river, solid and slow, focusing his mind on it, on the still-ness beneath the push. On the current, pulling him into dark-ness. Wondering if it would ever take him somewhere good. Toward the blue.

HE WOKE SOMETIME LATER WITH THE CANDLE BESIDE HIM guttering out all on its own; the other two candles on their respective chairs were already properly out. He could see the humped shapes of Henry, closest to the door, and of Tate in the middle bed, the one nearest Oliver. He wondered for a moment if Henry had, at one point, made Tate sleep in the bed closest to the window, or if it had remained empty until Oliver's arrival.

Well, that was between Henry and Tate, wasn't it? Oliver made himself let the thought go and stood up, the floor almost icy beneath his stockinged feet. He slipped off his waistcoat and had a quick wash with what was left of the cold water in the pitcher and dried his hands and face on the used towel. He fumbled around on the wall for where he'd hung his nightshirt and wondered how much noise he was creating, and how grumpy it would make Henry and Tate if he actually woke them up.

Standing there for a moment, he heard the snow slapping against the windows, and realized he was shivering. As he took off his trousers and shirt, he folded his clothes roughly and placed them on top of the box, knowing that they would have wrinkles in the morning. But the wrinkles would be covered by his apron, and in the morning, Henry and Tate would thank Oliver for not waking them up with his bumbling about, trying to hang things on pegs in the half dark. He bent to blow out the candle, then he slipped between the sheets, which were clean and thick and heavy.

He'd been lucky. Mr. Grimwig probably hoped that Oliver would be miserable, but so far he was not. He tipped his head back; the pillow was thin, but what of it? That he'd ended up here, somewhere nice, was almost a miracle. The river came. And then sleep took him.

## ❧ 10 ❧

# A COLD DAY TO OFFSET GRIEF

The next morning, Tate had to shake Oliver awake, and, with muscles protesting even the smallest movement and eyes half-closed, Oliver struggled into his clothes and boots. But when he was buttoning up his waistcoat and rolling his sleeves halfway up his arms to wash, he saw that Henry and Tate were waiting for him at the already open door.

"There's no hot water to wash up here," said Henry, in a tone that indicated that Oliver should have known that.

"Sometimes the girl forgets," said Tate, giving Henry a piece of his elbow. "So we wash downstairs. Sometimes."

His throat was still too closed from sleep to reply, so Oliver only scrubbed at his eyes with the back of his hand and followed Henry and Tate downstairs to the warm kitchen. There, they washed at the basin on the stand against the wall, with Oliver last in line, as was the order of things. He didn't want to look at himself in the mirror, but in spite of that effort, he caught a glimpse of his hair pressed to his skull and large circles beneath flat blue eyes. It was to be expected, perhaps, that he looked so tired, as yesterday had been his first day. He knew he could catch up to Henry and Tate's energy and speed, if given the chance.

But as the god of beneficence would have it, when Oliver

127

turned around, there was Mrs. Pierson in her dark, wide-skirted dress and a bright, clean apron and cap. She was busy at the stove, stirring something in a saucepan while she added what was perhaps sweet milk from a pitcher. The kitchen was warm and smelled wonderful, and as Henry and Tate sat in their usual places, it occurred to Oliver that there was, indeed, a place for him at the table, and he felt the shock of the change in his life all over again.

When he sat down, he realized Henry and Tate were, really, only half-awake themselves. Henry yawned at him, and Tate slumped on an elbow, as if he were a young boy at home and not really expected quite yet to behave with good table manners. Breakfast was more relaxed altogether, it seemed, as Mrs. Pierson came over and ladled each of them porridge in their bowls. The porridge was golden with some spice, heaped high in the bowl, and on the table was a pitcher of cream, a yellow bowl of butter, and a blue bowl with lumps of sugar in it.

"You boys start with that," said Mrs. Pierson, observing to make sure they took at least their fair share. "I've got to be finishing making the eggs and sausages myself, after having built my own fire and heated my own water on top of everything else, since the girl didn't show today."

"Can we help with anything, Mrs. Pierson?" Henry said this as he shoveled in the first mouthful of porridge.

As Tate straightened up to attend to his breakfast, he nodded to show his agreement with this idea, and so Oliver nodded as well, though his mouth was watering and he felt he might strike someone if they attempted to take him away from the bowl of porridge in front of him. He piled on the butter and sugar and laced the whole of it with plenty of cream.

"Well, you're a good lad, that's what you are. All of you are." Mrs. Pierson put down the ladle and pot from which she'd served the porridge and looked about her at the kitchen. "After you've eaten, if Tate would carry the slops down and wipe the stairs, and Henry could help me with the bedding, perhaps

Oliver could get coal and take care of the fire in Mr. McCready's office and in the warehouse?"

It was a lot of work for one person, and he was glad to help if Mrs. Pierson needed assistance. And while Oliver didn't relish getting his hands black with coal dust, at least he wouldn't be carrying slops or making other people's beds.

"I'd be most willing, Mrs. Pierson," said Tate brightly, as if the occupation, while beneath him, didn't bother him in the least, though Oliver knew it had to.

"And I as well," said Oliver, watching while Mrs. Pierson bustled at the stove to finally bring over fried eggs and sausages, which she piled on the plate in front of each boy.

"Very well and thank you, and mind, here comes Mr. McCready now; he'll be wanting some fried bread with that."

The heavy tread sounded on the steps, and when Henry and Tate straightened up to more polite postures, Oliver did likewise. It wasn't as if they had been being disobedient; more, it was apparent that there were different levels of decorum for different occasions: one for Mrs. Pierson at breakfast and another one for when Mr. McCready was present.

"Ah, there we are, Mrs. Pierson. Thank you for the fire this morning. I'm dreadfully sorry about the girl; you should give her a good talking-to about her punctuality or she will lose her place." Mr. McCready sat down and pulled his napkin into his lap as Mrs. Pierson served him tea and fried toast all at once. "Good morning, boys," he said.

"Good morning, Mr. McCready," said Henry and Oliver. Tate's mouth was full, so he nodded in place of that, and Mr. McCready went on with his breakfast as if everything was in good order.

When the boys had finished, they excused themselves and went to attend to their morning tasks while Mr. McCready dawdled over his tea and flipped through pages of the newspaper from the day before.

Oliver went to the short door that led to the coal cellar and grabbed a bucket full of coal. He knew he should have gotten the proper copper scuttle, but he didn't know where it was, and he wanted to keep up with the other boys when they started on their regular shop-related duties.

He went up the stairs to Mr. McCready's office first, trying not to scatter coal dust on the stairs as he went, but then Tate would be following soon behind to wipe the stairs down. Still, it wouldn't do to make extra work on his first—no—second day. Mr. McCready's office was narrow, and it was only by lifting the bucket up high that Oliver was able to avoid leaving black marks on any of the furniture.

As he knelt down and opened the stove, he knew he should scrape out all the ashes and blacken the stove before he lit a new fire. And while he could easily put the ashes in the bottom of the bucket, the stove being a small one, he didn't know where the blacking was or the stove brushes. Besides, the girl would black the stove next morning, so perhaps it wasn't up to Oliver to set everything to rights, but only to light a good fire.

This he did, getting smudges of black ash on his skin all the way up to his wrists. He managed successfully to open the damper before the smoke started to fill the room, and afterward, as he stood up brushing his hands together, he felt well satisfied with himself.

The stove in the warehouse was much easier since the opening was bigger, and there was a vent in the bottom for the ashes. Oliver placed the large pieces of coal on the floor and then put the bucket beneath the stove and pushed the ashes through the vent. Clouds of dust flew up, but that couldn't be helped.

There was plenty of room in the stove for coal, and the fire was easy to light and didn't smoke at all. At the very last moment, he remembered the vent, and had to push the coal away to pull the lever to let the ash fall into the bucket, after which he had to poke at the coal with the iron poker to make the fire more even. Then he closed the front of the stove and stood up, looking down at himself while at the same time praying that he'd not gotten any ash or coal dust on him, as he'd quite forgotten his apron.

There were no black streaks on his brown uniform, luckily, so he went over to the pegs in the wall to pull down an apron that looked slightly used, tying it on to be ready for the regular shop chores. Henry was soon there, putting an apron on as well, and together they went outside into the icy air.

In the sky above the high-walled yard, the clouds hung low and the morning air was so still that when he and Henry breathed out, the puffs of air coming from their mouths wreathed around their heads, dappling bits of beaded frost in their hair. As they walked around to the front of the shop, frost glittered on everything.

"It is cold," said Henry, as if agreeing with Oliver's unspoken observation, while he demonstrated how to take down the shutters. "But it's only for ten minutes or so on a day like this."

Oliver nodded, gasping at the weight of a single shutter that Henry seemed to carry with such ease. He followed Henry, slipping a bit on the icy stones in the alley, then staggered across the yard, quick as he could on Henry's heels, following him into the warehouse where the shutters were placed.

"These go just inside the warehouse door so no one can take them and they won't get smashed by horses' hooves in the yard."

"I see," said Oliver, shivering in the stillness of the warehouse. The fire he'd lit seemed to have gone out, and indeed, none of the heat had reached as far as the doorway.

"Two more trips, then," said Henry, going back outside, though his lips were blue with cold. "Tomorrow, it'll take you six trips instead of three, since you'll be doing this on your own."

Oliver could only nod; his whole face was stiff, and his shoulders and back shivered up and down until they ached. The air outside in the yard was now coming down with frost that settled on the top of the tall brick fence and the open wooden gate, looking like sparkles of frozen diamonds on every surface. Grabbing the next shutter that Henry handed to him, Oliver almost ran through the clouds of glittering air to be done with this part of his morning chores; it was dreadful, so dreadful that he longed to be back in bed, at home, under his comforter, waiting for the maid to bring him hot tea.

But no. Henry insisted they perform their usual duties of scraping ice from the windows and sweeping the steps to the front door, and clearing the pavement of any snow and scattered debris. By the time they returned to the warehouse to change out of their dirty aprons into clean ones, Oliver was shivering from head to foot, his teeth clacking in his mouth so loudly that Henry turned to look at him.

"You'll get used to it," Henry said, not completely without sympathy for Oliver's plight, perhaps because he recognized how hard Oliver had worked. Or at least it was to be hoped.

"Go on down to the kitchen," Henry said now, as he led Oliver out of the warehouse and into the passageway to the shop. "Mrs. Pierson will let you warm yourself by her fire and perhaps, if you look pathetic enough, she'll give you a cup of tea. After that, go out and build the fire in the warehouse again, and help Tate for the morning. We might go on deliveries this afternoon, if there are any."

Oliver did as he was told, his brain numb from the realization that he had a whole day of working ahead of him; he was already exhausted, and it wasn't even noon. But Henry and Tate seemed content enough, so the situation had to get better. It must get better. He would just have to keep putting one foot in front of the other and keep moving, doing as he was told and stopping for a breath when he could.

As he clomped down the stairs into the beautifully dry warmth of the kitchen, waves and waves of comforting and good smells enveloped him.

Mrs. Pierson called to him. "Is that you, Oliver? I rather imagined you might be down."

When Oliver's feet hit the flagstones, Mrs. Pierson was

there, guiding him to sit in Henry's chair, which was nearest her stove.

"You sit down now, and drink this. It's always hardest on the first few days, I know that. But Mr. McCready doesn't want his boys to look at any moment as if they might collapse; it's important to keep up appearances, you see."

Oliver sat down and curled his fingers around the mug of tea in front of him. The mug was hot in his palms, and steam rose from the tea. His legs vibrated against the edge of the chair, blood pounding through them, making him glad of the waves of warmth that oozed from the stove and began to soak into him.

"You finish up that tea, Oliver," said Mrs. Pierson, turning back to her stove. "And tell me whether you fancy pudding with jam or pudding with currants for dinner? Or both?"

Taking a long gulp of hot tea, Oliver sighed. There was only one answer to that question. "Mrs. Pierson, whatever you make will be fine, I'm sure of it." And then, feeling a dash of boldness amidst all the comfort and warmth running through him, he added, "Though you might want to make extra, as I'm sure to be rude and ask for seconds."

Behind him, he could almost hear her smile.

BACK IN THE WAREHOUSE, TATE SHOWED OLIVER HOW TO open the damper in the stove just a bit more to make a better draw and keep the fire from going out. He demonstrated the use of the poker and the cloth that hung on a nail in the wall to open the stove when he was going to put more coal in.

Then he walked Oliver through the shelves, pointing as he demonstrated the way the shelves were organized, not alphabetically, but by content—buttons here, ribbons over there, collars in the middle where the dust was less likely to seep in to befoul them. And as far up the shelves as it was possible to go were the beeswax candles, packed in wooden boxes and tightly bound with canvas and rope.

"Why with canvas?" asked Oliver. It wasn't likely that the candles might spill out, not when they were packed in solid wooden boxes.

"Well," said Tate, brushing his hands on his apron. "Truth be told, the mice might like to eat the candles, but especially rats, if they can get at them."

"Rats?" asked Oliver, somewhat stunned.

"Perhaps a few," said Tate, shrugging as though this were completely ordinary, though Oliver could hear a small bit of mirth in Tate's voice, as if he were amused by Oliver's shock. "Don't you mind the noise if you hear them scratching in the attic. There's far more filth and dirt outside for them to scrabble through, so they are never up there long."

"I see."

Oliver tongued the inside of his teeth. The townhouse had never had a single rat or mouse that Oliver knew of, and any that had managed to creep in would not have lasted long. He struggled to keep his mouth closed, to keep from bragging that he'd never known of any rat or mouse under any roof where he'd abided, but that wouldn't be fair, not to Tate, who was doing his best to be informative.

"There you go," said Tate. "That's the spirit. Now, over here is the pole that we use to open and close the windows, as need be. They're closed at night, but sometimes, even if it is cold, we open them in the afternoon, to keep the air fresh. That keeps the mold from growing on silk ribbons and woven patterned shawls and the like. Do you see?"

"Yes, I see," said Oliver again. He struggled to focus on what Tate was saying and prayed for the noon hour to come.

THE MORNING, GRATEFULLY ENOUGH, SPED BY, AND MRS. Pierson's dinner was as filling as breakfast had been, with the added benefit of jam pudding with custard cream to pour over the top. As promised, Oliver asked for a second helping, which Mrs. Pierson was serving to him even as he was requesting it. The indulgence she paid him was kind; indeed, her kindness was given to any at the table who wanted more pudding. And, moreover, the food was excellent.

The afternoon seemed somewhat easier than the day before. Oliver was able to help Tate sort through more boxes and sweep the warehouse, and though he had to go and wipe the stairs with an oiled cloth, as Tate had been unable to get to them, Oliver didn't grumble. Besides the fact that Tate had not mentioned that Oliver had not correctly lit the warehouse stove the first time, the work appeared to be shared as was needed, with a sense of fairness and balance that made him feel easier about doing someone else's chores.

Then, just before supper, as Oliver was carrying in a box of hat pins for Henry to stock the shop with, he heard Mr. McCready in the hall.

"It's so cold and icy, we'll shut up shop now, I think. Don't you agree, Henry?"

"Yes, sir," said Henry from around the corner. "There's barely anyone on the streets right now, so no one will be coming in the shop unexpected."

Feeling joyous, Oliver assisted Henry with the brisk job of hanging shutters in the half dark of the street, shivering the whole while but concentrating on Mrs. Pierson's cooking and the hot supper to come. He helped Tate lock up the warehouse and bank the warehouse stove and hurried into the shop to help Henry sweep the floor and wipe the counters. Then he trotted down the stairs to wash in the kitchen with Henry and Tate before sliding into place for Mr. McCready to say grace.

After the *amen* was said, Mrs. Pierson served up a thick stew with noodles in it, which was accompanied on the side by stewed tomatoes and rice, which Oliver appreciated even more, seeing as how she'd been on her own all day without any help. Dessert was a baked crumble, filled with rhubarb, and served with hot custard.

Oliver ate until his stomach was quite full, and he thought he was as content as ever he could be, even if part of him longed for the familiarity and comfort of the townhouse.

"Would you boys care for any more? Mr. McCready?" Mrs. Pierson held out the remains of the pan of crumble, as if loath to save it for another day.

"No, I am quite replete, Mrs. Pierson, as you well know, because the colder it gets, the richer your food, for which I know we are all entirely grateful."

With a sense of satisfaction swirling around him, Oliver smiled to himself. Boldly, he took his finger to make a last swipe at a bit of custard that lingered on the rim of the empty bowl in front of him. Sucking on the taste of custard on his skin, Oliver looked up. Everyone was watching him; he'd quite forgotten where he was and had lapsed into manners that befitted a stable hand.

But Mrs. Pierson only smiled as she patted him.

"I'm glad to see that at least *someone* enjoys my cooking," she said, as though peeved by everybody else's collective lack of appetites and appreciation.

"We all do, Mrs. Pierson," said Mr. McCready, accompanied by Henry and Tate's nods. Then he added, "We'd starve without you, you know that."

"Well, that's good, then," said Mrs. Pierson, mollified. "Now up you get, clean your places, and bring down your letters and lessons and whatnot. It's far too cold to linger upstairs, isn't that right, Mr. McCready?"

"Yes, indeed," he said. "Now do as Mrs. Pierson says, and come back down with your things. We'll keep the fire going down here till bedtime."

Somewhat befuddled, Oliver did as he was told, but as he

followed Henry and Tate up the many flights of stairs to their room, he determined to make a clean breast of it to them.

"I don't have any lessons; what do I bring?"

"Oh," said Henry, as they got to the top floor and he opened the door. "You finished with lessons, then? Well, bring whatever you have, letters or books."

As Henry and Tate preceded Oliver into the room, the still air icy and chill from being unoccupied for the entire day, he stopped. He was being told to bring his books down so that he could read in the warmth of Mrs. Pierson's kitchen. He was being *told* to do it, and it was like a gift, a miracle, to be told to do the very thing he actually *wanted* to do.

Without a moment's more hesitation, Oliver walked straight to his box and pulled out the thin volume that contained Boswell's biography of Dr. Johnson. That had been another gift from Uncle Brownlow, and though Oliver had read it twice already, it would make comfortable, familiar reading in such a new place.

With the book under his arm, Oliver followed Henry and Tate back down the stairs to the warm kitchen, where Mrs. Pierson had wiped the table and made a pot of tea, which she casually placed on a thick mat in the middle of the table, with fresh cups and spoons, and a bowl of cut sugar and a jug of cream nearby. In small bowls, all set in a row, were the remains of the crumble, slightly cool now with the custard thickening on top, but Mrs. Pierson had put them out as if she'd known that no one would be able to resist having just one more bite. And she was right.

Oliver settled in his seat and accepted a mug of hot, sweet tea. As he began to read, he absently reached for a bowl of pudding, putting the spoon in his mouth as he leaned over his book and absorbed the words.

Across from him, Henry was reading letters and asking Mrs. Pierson for some sheets for reply, as the paper the letter was on had already been crossed. Tate was sitting next to Mr. McCready, using a slate to take notes from the book he was studying. It looked like history, and even then Oliver didn't envy him one bit. He had his book and a hot drink, and his stomach was full, and he was warm all the way through.

Perhaps, since today hadn't been as difficult as the day before, tomorrow would be even better. All the activity of the day pointed to it, so he was hopeful and sank into his book until Mr. McCready announced it was bedtime.

This sent the boys washing hurriedly at the bowl in the kitchen in the cold, leftover water. Then, led by Henry with a single lit candle, they hurried up the stairs to the icy, dark attic room to change as fast as they could into their nightclothes.

"Leave your stockings on," said Tate, pointing at Oliver as he struggled with his boots.

Oliver took this advice gratefully and wished Henry would give him the candle so he could put his book in the right place. But Henry kept the candle near him and blew it out as soon as he was ready for bed, so there was nothing to be done about it at this point except place the book all anyhow in the chest at the foot of his bed and to change for bed as fast as he might and slide beneath the woolen blanket.

As soon as his head was settled on his pillow and Henry's and Tate's were settled on theirs, he heard a scratching noise from overhead.

"Is that—?"

"Yes," said Tate, in rather dark tones. "There must be hundreds of them up there by now, coming in from the street on account of the cold, you see."

"Don't mind him, Oliver," said Henry, his voice somewhat muffled from beneath his blanket. "There are two or three at most; Mrs. Pierson wouldn't hear of rats in her attic, so there simply aren't that many."

"There might well be thousands, Oliver," said Tate, his voice coming through the dark in a way that made Oliver's heart pound. "All scrambling around up there with their yellow teeth clicking and their sharp claws scratching."

"*Tate*," said Henry. "Honestly, sometimes you are so full of nonsense I cannot understand how you make it through the day."

With a small laugh, Tate turned in his bed so that his voice was close to Oliver's ear. "I'm only messing, Oliver, it's just for fun."

Fun as may be, but the thought of rats running along the beams over his head kept Oliver up for some time after the other boys had fallen asleep. But though he heard one or two sounds, which might have been rats, the other noises were merely the familiar groans and creaks of wood shifting as the building around him settled into the cold night. He fell asleep eventually, somewhat tense, but willing himself not to be, mindful of his new situation and the luck which had come to him in getting it.

# RELATES HOW OLIVER, HARD AT WORK, IS DISTRACTED FROM HIS TASKS

Halfway through the next morning, Oliver started to feel as though he'd gotten the rhythm of it. After breakfast, Oliver was sent to clean the steps, and again before dinner. These tasks were interspersed by jobs of counting and sorting with Tate. The work was never-ending, it seemed, but Mr. McCready had given him a nod or two, and a *well done, there*, so Oliver imagined everything was well and that he was doing a good job.

Then, after a robust dinner, in the brisk, grey-lit afternoon, along wet, cobbled streets, and sometimes in a light snowfall, he and Henry bundled up and delivered packages. They walked all over London, to the river and back, going through Newgate and Cripplegate and Aldgate, each one of lumbering grey stones grown darker with wear and time and coal soot. They even delivered to some of the fine houses around St. James's Park, where Henry was courteous enough to explain to Oliver how each residence preferred their deliveries.

Sometimes, Henry would stand back and let Oliver have a go at it, to later tell him what he'd done wrong or right, in perfectly reasonable tones so that Oliver felt courageous enough to ask him a question or two. Without Tate around, Henry was still acting as though he were in charge, which he was, but he was less bossy and snappy, so the afternoon went well.

At night, Oliver sat with the boys and Mr. McCready in Mrs. Pierson's kitchen, with candles lit and the stove banked and warm, to look at his geography book and thumb through the poetry he'd also brought down. And though Henry and Tate raised their eyes at his selection, they didn't ask what he was reading, nor did they mock him.

AFTER DINNER ON WEDNESDAY, WHEN OLIVER WAS REPLETE with roast chicken and boiled potatoes, he washed and followed Henry to the shop. Henry was busy tying on a clean apron, looking quite settled in his plans to attend customers at the counter that day.

"Aren't we going for more deliveries, Henry?" asked Oliver. When Henry looked up at him, tying the last knot behind him by feel, Oliver said, "It's good weather out and there are plenty of deliveries to make; I see the list there on the counter."

Mr. McCready, who was opening the door to admit some lady customers into the shop, seemed to hear Oliver's question and he nodded at Henry, who turned to Oliver.

"Today is the day, Oliver," said Henry. "You're to make deliveries on your own. I've watched you; you're efficient with customers and have a good sense of direction. Here's the list; get the deliveries together and do your best."

There was nothing to be gained by protesting that it was too soon; in addition to which, Oliver felt a flutter of excitement at the thought of it. He was going to be trusted to perform shop business on his own, and on his third day. This was quite an accomplishment, and he wished, suddenly, that he had Mr. Grimwig right there so he could very carefully explain just how wrong Mr. Grimwig had been.

When Uncle Brownlow had been alive and they were in the City, he and Mrs. Bedwin had flinched at any idea of Oliver being on his own. It wasn't that he himself couldn't be trusted; it was the City that couldn't, and thus he'd mostly stayed at home.

So really, this was his first taste of freedom in the City. Except for the trips to the taverns, and those didn't count, as the outings had always been furtive, with him being always afraid of getting caught. Oliver shook his head, clearing it of unproductive thoughts. He was well on his way to a future that wanted him, a future that any respectable person would approve of.

"Do Mrs. Acton's delivery first, mind you," said Henry. He pushed several small bundles across the top of the counter at Oliver. "It's only candles and soap, and some needles, but she's asked for you specially, so do be on your best behavior. You're to go to the front door from now on. Remember, it's your job to keep our delivery customers happy, and she's one of our best."

It was with his chin held high and a sense of pride that Oliver took the list and gathered and bundled the items together, putting them in the basket with Mrs. Acton's purchases on top of the rest. He went downstairs to doff his apron, put on his cap and coat, and let Mrs. Pierson fuss over him a bit as she arranged his scarf around his neck and tucked it into the collar of his jacket so it would be warm and look nice. He even let her pat his cheek, as Mrs. Bedwin might have done on such an auspicious occasion.

He went back upstairs, grabbed the basket, and practically sailed out of the front door. It was blustery and cold, but not overly so, and for once, it wasn't snowing. Besides, he was well wrapped up in his coat and scarf and on his own in London. He felt truly prepared for his first solo delivery; he was a real apprentice at last, so he barely felt the weather.

As he walked along the lane to the corner where Oxford Street would take him to Mrs. Acton's, he noted some shopkeepers weren't as alert to the niceties of scraping snow and ice from their windows, nor of laying grit on the pavement in front of their shops. It was this common courtesy, as Mr. McCready had repeated often, that allowed potential customers to linger in front of the shops, and then, finally, most likely, come in.

Oliver had seen it demonstrated in the haberdashery. If customers came in, they browsed. And if they browsed, they purchased. There was not one lady in a hundred, Mr. McCready had intoned, who could resist a lilac sachet or a set of brass buttons or anything refined that her eye fell upon. Mr. McCready, it seemed, was well convinced of the fickleness of a woman's mind and insisted on arraying his shop as if he were waiting for a magpie, or any bird who liked to gather bright things.

But Mr. McCready's insistent practice of keeping the pavement clean, well, Oliver saw the sense in it now, for he found himself hurrying, head down, watching where he walked on the slippery, un-gritted pavement. Others as well, top-hatted gentlemen and ladies with sloped bonnets, even the beggars—and there were a few—scurried over untended pavements in front of more slovenly shops and lingered in a convivial throng in front of those shops whose pavement had been cleared. Who knew so much could be manipulated by the deft removal of a little snow and ice?

Oliver hurried, stopping on the corner of Oxford Street for only a moment to linger at the frosty window of a bookshop, through which the spines of books were arrayed on a small table. He spied a few titles that looked good; some he'd read, others he'd heard about. In particular, there was a new French version of *The Arabian Nights,* though he couldn't imagine why anyone would want to read it in French when the English version was already so handy. There was also an old copy of *Dr. Johnson's Dictionary*, a book of poems by Byron, which he'd never been allowed to read, along with poems by Thomas Grey, and even a battered version of *Moll Flanders.*

There would be time, perhaps, later, to tarry and touch the pages. Not that most apprentices could afford to spend their pay packets on books, but as he was to own his own bookshop one day, there was no better time to start collecting his stock of books. The bookshop's location on Oxford Street promised to bring with it fairly dear prices, however, so Oliver shuffled past it without going in and thought to find a better place more suited to his current salary. Besides, the day might be nippy, but it was glorious to be out and about among the movement of the City.

It took him a good twenty minutes to make it across London, with views of frost-covered spires and the smoky tip of St. Paul's from time to time poking above the line of roofs and bare trees, to where Mrs. Acton lived, all the way up past Russell Square. As to why she couldn't have taken her purchases with her when she paid for them, it had been explained to him in quiet tones by both Mr. McCready and Henry: *A lady does not want to be burdened with packages. Especially a lady of rank and breeding.*

Unsaid, of course, was the fact that for a lady of such breeding, and of course, wealth, having fripperies delivered at some cost—and to be seen having such deliveries—only elevated her status the more. Oliver knew to be thinking such thoughts was vulgar, so he didn't speak them aloud. But he thought them, just the same.

When he arrived at Doughty Street, he stopped a moment to admire the row of townhouses made of cream-colored brick, the tidy stone pavement swept free of snow in front of each house. As he walked up the stone steps at Number 14, he noted with new awareness that the steps were not only white and gleaming, they were entirely dry, which bespoke of recent, perhaps hourly, cleaning.

Had he been delivering meat or milk, he would have gone down the stairs to the kitchen area, but Mrs. Acton's request had been clear: he was to deliver to the front door. So he walked directly up and clapped the well-polished knocker against the brass plate, and heard, in short order, footsteps within.

When the door opened, he saw it was a maid, different from

the one before, dressed in afternoon black with a white apron and cap, as befitted a good house such as this one.

"Can I help you, sir?" she asked, looking up at him.

"I have a delivery from McCready's Haberdashery, miss," he said. "It's the items Mrs. Acton ordered."

The maid stared at him a moment, her mouth open. Just as Oliver began to wonder if he'd mumbled, she blushed hotly from cheek to ear. Taking a step back, she ducked her head, exuding clumsiness where only a moment before had been grace.

"Won't you step in a moment, sir, while I get the mistress?"

Oliver stepped in, and as the maid turned away, kept himself from frowning by sheer dint of force. Surely he'd not been actually flirting with her? But no, he'd kept his voice as level as he could, hadn't held her eye in any bold manner, hadn't done anything to incite such a reaction. And yet, there it was. That blushing, girlish reaction he often got, that made Mr. Grimwig call him vain and accuse him of causing it on purpose. But he never had; he could swear to God he never had. At least not on purpose.

As he waited, he looked at the front parlor through the open doorway. He wasn't able to look for very long or focus on any one item within when Mrs. Acton came down. She was dressed in an afternoon gown with plaid flounces trimmed with black velvet. Her hair was done up, as though she were planning to go out, though Oliver didn't see any other evidence of her outdoor things being prepared for her.

"So you are the new boy, Oliver Twist, at the haberdashery?" she asked. When she reached the landing, she stopped, though her hands remained on the banister, arrayed as if she were posing for him. "I saw you from my window when you were last here, when you were kind enough to deliver my silver buckles."

"Yes, ma'am," he said with a little bow. "I've come to deliver your order. Beeswax candles, I believe, and other items as well." He held out the package, which was tightly snug with string.

She'd need a penknife to open it, though he supposed her maid would have one.

Mrs. Acton came down and took the package with fluttering hands, barely glancing at it, and held it out for her maid to take. "Take these, Jane, and see that they're set out and properly trimmed by prayer time." Then she looked at Oliver with a little smile such as he was unused to receiving from ladies he did not properly know.

"Did I order any ribbons, young man?"

"No, ma'am," he said with what he hoped was a responsive and responsible air. "But if you had, they'd be all ironed and organized, per Mr. McCready's instructions."

"What a good lad," she said, coming down off the last step to stand quite close to him. "You must be chilled from your walk. Won't you stay and have some tea? Or tea and cake? Young men always want something hot and sweet after a cold walk. Jane, go and fetch tea and cakes and bring them into the parlor. Leave the door open, please; it'll be more proper that way."

Well, it would be rude to refuse a lady, now, wouldn't it? Mr. McCready would say so himself. Oliver very well knew the standing order of keeping the customer happy, so he nodded his head and tucked his cap under his arm and loosened his scarf as he followed where Mrs. Acton led.

Jane hurried off, and Mrs. Acton placed her hand on Oliver's arm and escorted him into the parlor. Right away, he could feel the warmth of the fire, and saw the small table covered with a fine, white cloth. Upon it were cups and saucers of good china, silver teaspoons, a silver creamer, and a bowl of white sugar.

The parlor was even more grand once he was within it, done up in the latest style with dark red walls and a thick red rug on the polished floor. The room was crowded with severely dark furniture, and there were ornaments all around, including a group of china shepherdesses on the mantelpiece, a brass dog by the fireplace, a large painting of a country scene over the mantel, and a wide peacock feather fan that spread out behind a vase of fresh roses.

Over on the sideboard was a large collection of silver plates, arrayed to show how shiny and of what good quality they were: a platter that leaned against the wall, a pitcher with a curved handle, a set of knives, all of which were carved in loops and swirls in the old-fashioned way. Beneath every object was a circle of lace or something crocheted to add additional elegance. There wasn't a speck of dust on any ornament or thing; all were shining as if they'd recently been polished, for all it seemed they were too grand to ever get used. Oliver wondered how long it took the maid to dust such a room.

"Come now, and sit beside me," said Mrs. Acton. She sat on the small floral settee and patted the cushion next to her. "Jane will be along soon. I hope you have a taste for sweet things."

Oliver did as he was asked, putting his cap and scarf on the arm of the settee next to him. He was puzzled that if he was asked to tea, why no servant had offered to take his cap and scarf. But this curiosity was outdone by the fact that Mrs. Acton shifted closer on the settee and patted his knee. Her eyes were bright, the pupils enormous, a hectic flush colored her cheeks.

"You do enjoy sweet things, don't you, Oliver?"

She was close enough that he could smell her breath, which was sweet, as though she'd recently drank something that contained floral water. Or maybe it was her hair that had the scent. He only knew that the air smelled like attar of violets all around his head, and he thought if he could just shift away, even if only for a moment, he could get a clear breath of air.

"Yes, ma'am," he said. He felt hot under his collar, as though he were suffocating from the force of her attention.

Luckily, Jane came back into the room carrying a large silver platter, and behind her, a footman carried a silver tea urn. The footman put the urn on the table, and as he went away, Jane placed the tray on the table. Oliver saw that the tray had held a vast and fine array of sandwiches and the sweet cakes.

"I'll serve, thank you, Jane," said Mrs. Acton, and was silent for a moment as she watched Jane depart.

Without asking him for his preference, Mrs. Acton poured a cup of tea for Oliver, putting in two lumps of sugar and a large dollop of cream. As Oliver took the cup and saucer from her, he felt her fingers linger on the backs of his hands and tried not to jerk away.

"It's so nice to have a young man to tea," she said.

Her smile was so bright that Oliver knew there was definitely something amiss. No woman would take on so, not with a lad so much younger than her. Even if age weren't the matter, she had a wedding ring and Oliver was only the apprentice boy. It suddenly occurred to him he should not be stopping to have a cup of tea while on the job, let alone in such an intimate way with a lady of such recent acquaintance.

"Drink up, now, Oliver, and tell me how you're getting on at the haberdashery. Is Mr. McCready as good a master as I hear tell of?" She curled her fingers under her chin and coquetted up at him through her lashes.

To keep from speaking, Oliver took a quick gulp of tea. He liked sweet things, that was true, and while the tea was sweet enough, it was not very hot, and the taste was stewed, as though it had been made and kept on a sideboard until his arrival. That wasn't Jane's fault, surely. Oliver took another swallow of tea and didn't let his eyes wander to the plate of sandwiches and cakes.

"Well?" she asked.

"Mr. McCready is a very good master," said Oliver. "I'm learning many things as an apprentice."

"I'm sure," said Mrs. Acton with a little curl to her lips that Oliver couldn't even begin to understand. "Have a cake, Oliver; you must be hungry after that long walk all the way from Soho just to bring me my candles."

There was something in her tone, her manner, that made Oliver want to fidget. Then he caught sight of Jane, passing in the hallway outside the parlor; her expression was fixed but disapproving, though whether of her mistress or of Oliver, he didn't know. Yes, it was very easy to determine that the whole interaction was somehow inappropriate. Should Mr. McCready hear of it, Oliver was sure to be sacked.

Oliver put his cup and saucer, with half the tea still remaining, back on the silver platter.

"I must be going, Mrs. Acton. I have other deliveries to make, though it was quite kind of you to—"

"Must you go?"

Oliver stood up, and Mrs. Acton stood up also, clutching at him, pressing her bosom against his arm. He was almost made immobile by this action, never having been so close to a lady, or any female for that matter, before. She smelled good and was soft, as all ladies must be, but there was something wrong with the way she was looking at him.

"Mistress," said Jane, from the doorway. "Is there anything else I can get you?"

Jane was speaking to Mrs. Acton, but her eyes were on Oliver —large, enormous eyes. Oliver knew that this was his chance, perhaps his only one, to make a graceful exit.

"I must go, Mrs. Acton. Thank you for the tea. It was very nice. Let us know if you need anything else from the shop."

Oliver snatched up his cap and scarf in a cold sweat and, without putting them on, strode out of the parlor, brushing by Jane, giving her a grateful look as he did so. He grabbed his basket and let himself out the front door, not wanting to tarry, to hear whatever other unpropitious things Mrs. Acton might say. She should not be saying them, and he didn't want to hear them.

He hurried down the stone steps and, once on the pavement, paused only a moment to put on his cap and wrap his scarf around his neck and adjust the basket on his arm. The wind was cold, and he started down Doughty Street, away from Mrs. Acton's and on to his other deliveries, wherever they might be.

On the corner of Doughty Street, he scanned the list of addresses and to determine his next delivery. It would be a good ten-minute walk to Craven Street, an address that he knew to be by the river and which sounded vaguely familiar somehow. Best of all, it would take him well out of the neighborhood and force him to walk very fast, which would help clear his head and settle him down. He began to walk briskly, head held high as though he were—as he was—a valuable, responsible apprentice with very important deliveries to make.

His delivery to a bonnet maker on Dean Street—his last—confused him somewhat, as there were two Dean Streets on the map of London in his mind. He was easily able to figure out that the first Dean Street was near St. James's Park, and the address actually was to a church; the second Dean Street was quite close to the shop, and the address was that of a bonnet maker who had urgently needed new pins for the bonnets she was making.

That she could have easily walked to the shop to get the necessary articles was less important than the display of having the owners of nearby shops getting a good view of her having them delivered to her. Oliver held his tongue about this and only inquired as to whether she'd need anything else delivered, and when she said no, Oliver walked back to the shop, faintly out of breath and very glad to be on what was beginning to seem like familiar ground.

ON THURSDAY MORNING, AFTER BREAKFAST, AND AFTER HE'D already taken care of the pavement in front of the shop, Mr. McCready sent Oliver out again to brush the dusting snow from the pavement and to make things as tidy as could be, given the weather.

Oliver wanted to linger in front of Mrs. Pierson's kitchen fire first, but he did as he was told without balking, using the broom to push the snow into the gutter, the bustle of the street bumping past him as though he weren't even there. The day was snapping with cold, pressing through Oliver's shirt as though his shoulders were bare.

In spite of the weather, Wardour Street, and on into Broad Street, was full of shoppers and buskers and dogcarts, their wheels bumping over the refuse poking up beneath melting clumps of snow, with everyone getting out as though there'd never be another day where it didn't snow. The bells from St. James's Workhouse bonged out the hour through the fog that was already thick across the rooftops, the air choked with the smell of sulfur and sending spots of black coal soot down on Oliver's newly cleaned stairs.

Oliver picked up the bucket and cast the grit around. He'd have to sweep it up again in the afternoon, once if not twice, but in the meantime, potential customers would enjoy the sensation of walking without sliding on ice, which would then draw them into the haberdashery. Or so Mr. McCready often said.

He was just gathering his gear, gripping the cold handle of the bucket in one hand, when a passerby bumped into him, hard, with a sharp, rude elbow. Oliver tightened his face as he looked up to determine what he should say, whether it should be *pardon me, madam, miss,* or *sir.*

But instead of any of these to be spoken to, it was Jack Dawkins, resplendent in a top hat and a thick coat, different from the one he'd worn before, with a double row of shiny buttons down the front. And, of course, Jack wore Oliver's scarf of brilliant scarlet red around his neck.

Oliver did not doubt for one second that the rest of Jack's getup, in addition to the scarf, was stolen, or at the very least, acquired by less than legal means. In spite of this, Oliver's heart sped up and his breath caught, but he wasn't sure whether he was surprised to see Jack, angry about it, or rather that he was pleased to see a familiar face.

"Hard at work, I see," said Jack, already laughing, eyes alight, his teeth sharp. "Like a proper servant."

Oliver's potential spark of pleasure died as quickly as it had come and gave way to the heat that rose behind his eyes. Jack was there, unwelcomed and unannounced, and, what's more, mocking him. Oliver had hoped that their wretched meeting in the Green Dragon would have been the last, but here Jack was again. Just like a bad penny.

Two customers, quality ladies with fur on their cloaks and bonnets and all over their muffs, came out of the shop. They looked out of the corners of their eyes at Jack and then hurried past, as though he was dangerous, and perhaps he was. This was dreadful. If Mr. McCready caught Oliver lollygagging at his duties, that would be bad enough. But to have Jack spotted there at his side, making intimate conversation with him as though they were a pair of idle gentlemen? That would be a disaster.

"You don't belong here," said Oliver, low. "You should go back to wherever you came from." He wished he could pretend to keep working, but he'd already cast the grit, and so now the task was finished.

"That's what I come to tell you," said Jack saucily. "Where I am these days, an' it's at the Three Cripples now."

Though Jack's presence was disruptive as he stood there in the street, Oliver could only stare because Jack was vibrant and more alive than anything Oliver had seen in days. In comparison, he made McCready's Haberdashery seem worn and dull. Oliver had to fight against a sudden visceral response to the flash in Jack's eyes.

"It ain't much, but it's home. I'm signed up for some jobs, an' I got a fence an' everythin'"

It was with this declaration that fighting the draw of Jack's bright plumage became much easier.

"I don't care where you are," said Oliver, determined to make Jack go away. "And what's more, I don't care what you do there. Now, you need to leave before my master sees me with the likes of you."

Rather than being injured by such rudeness, Jack showed his

teeth in a smile that wasn't truly a smile, his eyes looking Oliver up and down.

"'Tis a free country, ain't it? I gots as much right to be here on this pavement as you."

As benign as this remark seemed on the surface, there was something in Jack's tone that made Oliver clench his fist around the handle of the bucket. He hefted the broom as though it were a spear, ready to strike if Jack came closer.

But Jack didn't move. He eyed Oliver, taking in the tenseness of his hands, looking at Oliver as though examining him for flaws. Then he cast a glance over Oliver's shoulder, at which point he stepped back and tipped his hat, a shiny new top hat he couldn't possibly have actually *purchased*—

"Looks like someone's lookin' for you," said Jack. "I'll come back another day, an' why not? I'll have more to tell you then, show you my takings, share it with you, like we did in the old days."

Oliver heard the door to the shop open and turned to see Mr. McCready looking at him and then over his shoulder. Oliver looked around and, to his dismay, saw what Mr. McCready was seeing: Jack, sashaying down the street, with a flicker of red scarf and all the dash of a man who owned the earth he walked upon in spite of the worn-at-the-heel boots Jack wore.

Mr. McCready gestured for Oliver to come closer, rubbing his hands together to stave off the cold. Oliver did, holding his tools in his hands so as not to leave them in the way of any ladies or gentlemen who might want to use the pavement.

"Who was that?" Mr. McCready asked from the top step, looking down at Oliver. While he looked comical with puffs of air coming out of his mouth, his forehead was wrinkled, which made him look grave.

"No one," said Oliver, shaking his head. He swallowed. "Just someone looking for directions; he wanted the nearest bakery, I think."

"You don't want to be hanging out with the lower orders,

Oliver," said Mr. McCready, idly rubbing the brass edge of the door with his fingers as if attending an invisible spot. "It brings down the tone of this establishment and everyone who works here, and we can't be having that. Are you finished here?"

"Just about, sir," said Oliver, casting a glance to see that all was done. Yes, the steps were scrubbed and polished, the refuse pushed into the gutter, and grit spread about. "Yes, sir," he said.

"Then bring in some coal for Mrs. Pierson; the girl's gone early, someone sick at home, I believe, but then, when isn't there? She's entirely unreliable, that girl."

"Yes, sir," said Oliver. The task was actually beneath him, but he'd hauled coal for Mrs. Pierson before and was willing to do so again.

"Be sure to wash before you sit down to dinner; she won't appreciate her good cooking being flavored by coal dust," said Mr. McCready. Then he shut the front door behind him, only to turn and open it with a little jangle as a pretty miss and her black-garbed governess hurried up the stairs. "In you come, ladies, where it's nice and warm and out of the wind."

Oliver watched them go, tracing their outlines through the wave-patterned windows. Henry came up to the pair at the counter, his apron gleaming through the glass as though it were made of snow, and tipped his head to the ladies with a little bow. Henry was perfect at the job, that was plain to see.

Well, that was all right. Oliver could learn a great deal from all at the haberdashery; it might not be books, but it was buying and selling and dealing with customers, and counting up money and going to the bank. It would work out well. All he had to do was pay attention, mind his temper, and do everything that Mr. McCready asked of him. Then one day, not too far off, he could start making inquiries as to how one started a bookshop. Then, on that day, he would really be on his way.

AT THE NOON HOUR, OLIVER QUICKLY BROUGHT SOME COAL from the cellar for Mrs. Pierson and washed at the basin along the wall just as quickly. The kitchen was warm with the glowing stove and the smell of boiled potatoes and salt. After Mr. McCready said a quick grace, Mrs. Pierson served up hot boiled beef and potatoes and bread and butter.

It was simple fare, but Oliver ate through the pile of his first helping and then looked hopefully at Mrs. Pierson. She *tut tutted* a bit at him but dished out more for him, trying not to look pleased that he was enjoying her cooking so much.

"This afternoon," said Mr. McCready between bites of beef, "I need Tate to attend to the pavement out front while Henry shows Oliver how we do the count-up. I want to make a deposit in the morning and to be able to rely on more than one apprentice for that task."

"That's quite an honor, Oliver," said Mrs. Pierson. She was stirring something in a pot on the stove. When she brought it over to the table, Oliver saw it was only stewed rhubarb, but at least there was warm custard to put on it.

"Tate's helpless with money," said Henry around a mouthful of potato. He didn't say it with true meanness, but Oliver knew it could have gone unsaid. "He can't remember the difference between a pound and a guinea, and he wouldn't know a half-penny if it bit him."

Tate just rolled his eyes at this.

"But he is good at keeping track of stock," said Mr. McCready. "He's got a memory longer than Moses. He can remember what anyone bought, when they bought it, and in what part of the warehouse anything was stored."

"He still can't even remember how many shillings are in a pound," said Henry, making his point quite boldly, as though he was trying to maintain his status as being more useful than Tate.

"That's not a concern, seeing how he works mostly in the warehouse." Mr. McCready shook his fork at Henry. "So just never you mind; he's good at what he does, and I know I can leave him to it."

The argument was one that Oliver sensed was an old topic that bestirred Henry to speak out in that way or to make Tate ignore Henry. But Mr. McCready felt he had it well in hand enough to get up from the table without another word about it, and Mrs. Pierson bustled about as if the matter were all settled.

## 12

# AN INAUSPICIOUS SECOND VISIT
# FROM A CERTAIN LOW
# ACQUAINTANCE

After dinner, there were no deliveries to be made. Instead, under Henry's watchful eye, Oliver helped with the count-up. He enjoyed the feel of the coins under his hands as they thunked on the pad of leather Henry had put down to protect the glass on the counter. Oliver wrote amounts on a scrap of paper and then added them up, double-checking as he went. Henry looked at the final total and gave Oliver a nod.

"This is to the penny," Henry said. "And you've a nice hand as well; Mr. McCready will be pleased."

As was Oliver himself.

Later in the afternoon, Mr. McCready and Tate went with Oliver out to the high-walled cobbled yard that abutted the warehouse and that led through the gates to the alley.

"This is where the flats and carts and delivery wagons come to unload," said Mr. McCready with a wave at the yard and the small shed against the brick wall. "It is also where the drivers water their horses, and unfortunately, where the horses relieve themselves. Though no customers come back here, it must be kept spotless."

He turned to look at Oliver and Tate, but mostly at Oliver, who was still the new boy.

"Go get the shovel and bucket from the shed, Tate; later you can show Oliver where they are kept."

As Tate raced to do this, bringing back the large, broad-bladed shovel and a heavy wooden bucket, Mr. McCready continued.

"The tone of the establishment must be kept up," he said. "It is not an elegant task," he said now, handing Oliver the shovel and bucket. "But it is a task that must be done. Henry has been elevated above it by dint of his being a full-time front shop boy; you and Tate must share this task now."

Oliver looked over at Tate, who shrugged his thin shoulders as an invisible wind tufted at his thin hair. He made a face, a not unkind face, because though it was still his responsibility, it was not, at present, his turn. Oliver determined not to be thrown off course; as a gentleman who owned a bookshop, he would never be called upon to perform such a duty. But as the newest apprentice in the lot, he could be asked to do any number of things. Shoveling horse manure was one of them.

"Don't forget to sluice the cobblestones with water, Oliver," said Mr. McCready. "And carry the muck into the alley."

"Yes, sir," said Oliver.

He took the shovel and bucket and hefted them in his hands as Mr. McCready and Tate headed into the warehouse where they would no doubt review stock and determine what the next week's order should be. Except for counting money with Henry, which had, ostensibly, been to test Oliver on his arithmetic, Oliver had yet to be a part of what it really took to run a shop, and he was itching to do it. Shoveling manure and rinsing horse urine wasn't what he'd had in mind when becoming an apprentice.

But he began, keeping his face still, not showing his disdain for the lowness of the task. First, he shoveled the leavings in a bucket, the cold air racing down his neck. He grimaced when splats of urine and manure got onto his apron, but there was nothing to be done about that except mutter under his breath in dismay. But at least the muck wasn't on his trousers.

After he'd scraped up the horse leavings, he carried the bucket through the gates and into the alley, and tossed everything from the bucket into the narrow gutter in the middle that carried an ever-present trail of water that came from a dripping pump at the end of the alley. Even in the coldest weather, the ditch ran and steamed, cutting through the ice and iced mud, smelling dank and fulsome, like a dark bite of something rotten.

Most of London smelled that way; he was used to it. In his old life at the townhouse, when the girl, or sometimes the lad who tended the fires, carried slops and dumped them where they ought to go, Oliver had only to avert his nose whenever an unpleasant smell chanced his way. But that association had been from a distance. Now he was right in the thick of it, doing his best not to get any on his boots, for he had no doubt Mr. McCready would consider the boys cleaning their own boots a task that would teach them responsibility.

It took three trips getting buckets full of water from the ice-cold pump in the alley, and many stern scrapes with the shovel to get the cobblestones looking somewhat less fouled. He discovered, however, that there was no way to get horse manure from the cracks and dips where his too-large shovel could not go. He tapped the cobblestones with the edge of his shovel and considered. No, he would not be scooping that out with his bare hands.

"Here's the lad, the very lad I come to see."

Oliver whirled, shovel and bucket in hand, to see Jack standing there between the open wooden gates to the courtyard. How was it that Jack not only seemed to always catch him off guard but with a bucket in his hands as well, working as though he were a common laborer?

"What do you want; what are you doing here? I thought I told you this morning—" He snapped, startled to be caught by Jack's ease as he stood there, a colorful spark in a grey and cold afternoon, as though he were a bright-feathered bird from some hot jungle country, flitting about, winging from place to place, with nothing to do, and no responsibilities.

"It's no use," said Jack. He was dressed as he had been that morning, with Oliver's red scarf tucked high under his chin, demonstrating the same jaunty air. "You know I'll always find you, an' anyways, I'm stoppin' only on my way to the palace, to have tea with the Queen, you see."

"Jack, stop it. Just please go away." Oliver's heart was pounding with wondering when Jack would start tormenting him about the dark splats on his apron.

"Actually, I just wanted to say thanks, as one mate might to another." Though Jack pushed his hands in his pockets and tipped his head back jauntily, he seemed somewhat more diffident now, as if needing less to impress and more to simply be there with Oliver in his sights.

Oliver wanted to send him away, directly, before Mr. McCready came out wondering at the delay in Oliver finishing his assigned task, whereupon he would spot Jack. And not just on the pavement where he might have a right to be, a simple passerby, but in the yard, on haberdashery property. Besides which, what on earth would Jack want to thank him for? There was no need for Jack to linger, no reason at all.

"Say what you have to say and go." Oliver said this low, trying to be threatening. It wouldn't do to encourage Jack.

"For not peachin' on me earlier."

"What on earth are you talking about?"

Oliver cast a look over his shoulder at the doorway to the warehouse, at the windows above the courtyard. No one was watching, so he had about a minute. He turned back to Jack, who was bundled and warm against the snow and smiling at Oliver, and who had missed none of Oliver's covert glances.

"I listened to you talk to Old Grumbly, an' I heard. Or didn't hear."

"*Jack.*"

"You never mentioned my name. You'd never call no peelers,

now would you? If you were serious about it, you would have. So thanks for that."

Oliver felt his whole body jerk with surprise. Yes, he'd protected Jack, but why on earth would he do that, when with one shout it would be all over? For Jack was surely lying about being here legally; Oliver had never heard of anyone returning from being deported, so Jack must be lying. But Oliver had had lied about Jack and who he was, as Jack said, lied while explaining it to Mr. McCready, never mentioning at all that he knew Jack.

"I knew you wouldn't break the code," said Jack, satisfied.

"I didn't do you any favors," said Oliver, keeping his voice low, wanting Jack to understand this. "Next time, I'll shout it out at the top of my lungs, so will you stay away? Otherwise, I will have the constable, I *swear* it."

Jack just smirked.

"I might come by an' I might not," he said. "But I've been lined up for some jobs at the Three Cripples, like I told you, an' all the while waitin' for the gang to come back. I'm pretty sure that if they were to come anywhere, they'd come there. So you should—"

Now, instead of just thanking him for a favor between old friends, Jack was trying to pull Oliver through a doorway into Jack's world, where Oliver simply did not want to go. Oliver felt hot along the back of his neck. He did not want this; he did not *need* it.

"Look, you," said Oliver, pointing the handle of his broom at Jack. He was almost close enough to touch Jack with it, but not quite. He didn't know what Jack would do if Oliver actually hit him. "I told you. Bill Sikes died while trying to escape the law. Nancy died by Bill Sikes's hand. Fagin was hanged at Newgate. The gang is scattered to the wind, gone."

"Well, they might come back," said Jack, nonplussed. "They might do, if—"

"They're *not*, Jack. Will you listen to me?"

Oliver knew he was raising his voice, that it echoed in the yard, that surely someone in the shop might hear him. But it was as if he couldn't help it. Just the sight of Jack was enough to make him feel hot inside and out, anger boiling up into his head, filling his lungs with a shouting rage that for so long he'd kept locked up inside. His astonishment battled with his frustration; why wouldn't Jack see reason?

Jack was frowning, something a little hurt and lost in his eyes, but Oliver didn't let that stop him.

"Fagin and his people are not going to come swaggering into the Three Cripples. They are dead, gone, and scattered, and the sooner you realize that, the sooner you can move on with your life. Take advantage of the reprieve given you, if indeed it has been given you."

"Got nowheres else to go," said Jack. He swallowed and straightened up and narrowed his eyes at Oliver. "An' neither, from the looks of it, do you. Besides, there's nowheres else I'd rather be, so you better be good to me."

The door from the warehouse was partly open, spilling a little bit of light from the glow of the potbellied stove onto the cobblestones of the yard so recently tended to by Oliver himself. Oliver turned to check, but no one was standing at the door, looking to see the source of the shouting that echoed off the bricks in the alleyway.

In a moment, if Jack left, and no one had seen him, then everything could go back to the way it was. Oliver could step into the relative warmth of the warehouse, and continue on with his pretty good life, whereas Jack would have to trek back to the Three Cripples. Oliver had never been to the tavern, but he could picture in his mind—a filthy, decrepit huddle of a building, where only thieves and pickpockets and the dregs of the street would have cause to assemble.

When Oliver turned back around, with a last flicker of the red scarf, Jack was gone, leaving only traces of his footprints in the snow to signal he'd been there at all.

"Oliver."

Oliver whirled. Mr. McCready stood just inside the warehouse door. He was only an outline in the relative smudge of the daylight, but he must have seen Jack. *Had* seen Jack as he scampered away, leaving Oliver to deal with the mess Jack had left in his wake.

"Come here, Oliver," said Mr. McCready. His voice was stern, but then, it had a right to be.

Carrying his tools, Oliver walked over to the doorway of the warehouse, through which he could see Tate, busy with his counting, his *never-ending* counting, working away. Oliver didn't think Tate would run telling tales to Mr. McCready, as he didn't know about Oliver's injunction against speaking to lower orders. But then, Tate might simply have said something to Mr. McCready, based on the odd fact that Oliver had been seen talking to a strange boy. In the yard, no less.

"Well, Oliver," said Mr. McCready. "Do you have something to say to me?"

Standing there, Oliver felt faint and cold, now that he wasn't moving.

"You have been spoken to about this, Oliver, and I have asked you a question that you are beholden to me to answer."

The snow was starting to flurry a bit, and Oliver shivered. He opened his mouth, but there was nothing he could say, nothing about who he'd been in his past and why he would even consider tarrying with the likes of Jack Dawkins.

Mr. McCready's brows began beetling together, and Oliver realized he had to say something.

"It was a young man," he said. "He'd lost his way; I was giving him directions."

"Is this the same young man with whom I saw you talking this very morning when you should have been working?"

"It was, but—" Oliver felt hot now, the whole of his neck under his collar damp as a steam house, the smells from his stained apron thick in his nose. He could not even begin to create a story around this; he'd been warned, and now it was too late. "He came by again; I don't know why."

"You will cease letting him hang about the premises, Oliver. Do you understand this? I am running a business, not a boy's home. Moreover, he looked quite disreputable. Do you actually want to bring down my shop? Don't you realize it will send away customers who don't wish to mingle with the lower orders?"

Mr. McCready loomed tall and angry; his mouth was bunched in a scowl, and Oliver knew that he himself was in the wrong. It wouldn't do, at this point, to explain that Jack Dawkins recognized no boundaries drawn by God or man; he came and went as he pleased. And should Jack be confronted by Mr. McCready, Jack was less likely to listen to him than he was to Oliver. It wasn't Oliver's fault that Jack had come by, but he couldn't say that, couldn't explain it that way.

"Do you have nothing to say for yourself?"

"He's an old friend," said Oliver, finally. "We lost touch long ago. I don't know why he's coming around now, but I told him to stay away." He shrugged his shoulders with a sigh; Mr. McCready was a decent man, and as such, had probably never known the type of street person with whom Oliver was very much acquainted. "I'm sorry, Mr. McCready."

"If I see you with that young man, or any person of that ilk, and believe me, I will know it, then I will have to punish you. It will mean a whipping, is that clear?"

"I won't let it happen again."

"See that you don't," said Mr. McCready, still stern but mollified. His anger died away so quickly that Oliver realized that Mr. McCready wasn't a cruel man. Just, it seemed, one who was very invested in being an honest shopkeeper; he was steadily middle-class, and he didn't want anything to disrupt that.

"No, sir."

"Finish up here, then, and help Tate with the new shipment; he's just cut open the binding, and it's in a muddle as usual."

Mr. McCready left Oliver in the yard, standing beneath the

white curtain of light snow, and closed the door to the warehouse behind him, blocking off the light and the streaks of warmth.

The next time Oliver saw Jack, and he knew he would, he needed to make Jack stay away. But Jack was not only persistent, he did not care what Oliver wanted. Were Oliver to explain it with even the slightest bit of increased force, it might very well make Jack just that much more insistent. There was almost no way Oliver could win this.

# 13

# DESCRIPTIONS OF JACK'S DELIGHT REGARDING OCCURRENCES AT THE THREE CRIPPLES, AND THE REPERCUSSIONS WHICH OLIVER MUST BEAR ALONE

W hen business picked up on Friday, there were again deliveries to be made in the afternoon. Pleased, Oliver bundled up against the cold as he waited for Henry to fill the basket. He was eager to be out and about, even with the frost thick in the air and the dark smuts from smoking chimneys turning the snow black and grey.

The deliveries took him from Soho down to the river straightaway, where brisk curricles and hansoms on Prince's Street attempted to run him over, as though he weren't there. The street was alive with the high-pitched shrieks of thin wheels against the cobbled stones, and bright with freshly painted green ironworks and polished brass knockers and door knobs.

The packages for the white townhouses along Weston Street by Hyde Park were small and carefully wrapped by Henry. Oliver got a penny at almost every door, with the copper coins weighing down his trouser pocket and jingling about, making him wish he could have at least gotten his change purse back from Jack before he'd sent him away that last time.

For his final deliveries, he walked boldly up the Strand, amidst the hustle of black-coated businessmen and the groups of bewigged lawyers standing just outside a tavern, and past the sweet young miss in a bright blue bonnet with a cloak to match, who smiled at him as she tucked her hands into her fur muff. He paid none of the sights any mind, but got through the deliveries quickly, making his way up to Oxford Street, and, finally, past Russell Square. By the time he'd reached 14 Doughty Street, his face was numb with cold.

When he trotted up the snow-dotted steps and tapped the brass knocker, it was Mrs. Acton herself who answered the door. She was dressed in an outfit that looked as though it was made of white froth, something Mrs. Bedwin might have described as a morning dress, even though it was afternoon.

Mrs. Acton floated as lightly as foam through the doorway to Oliver. With a start, he realized she was outside on her own front step, out of doors dressed in that way, with her cheeks as rosy as though she were already next to the fire.

"Are those my deliveries? Are those my ribbons at last?" she asked. "One can never have enough ribbons, so I'll be sure to order more that you can deliver to me."

Oliver nodded and took out the last string-tied brown parcel from his basket to hand to her. Her fingers curled around his arm in a possessive way as she attempted to pull him inside.

"Come, take off your coat and tarry a while. Mr. McCready surely won't need you at the shop so soon?"

Oliver stepped back as lightly as he could, keeping his smile painted on. Her hand fell away from his arm, and though it felt as though a weight had fallen away from him, his chest felt tight.

"I'm sorry to say, Mrs. Acton, that I must get back, even with such a kind invitation."

Mrs. Acton frowned, her pale skin wrinkling as she did so, and it was then that Oliver noted how she smelled like fresh flowers, and how her hair was done up loosely in a trailing pink ribbon, as though she were just preparing to go to bed, rather than to meet visitors in her front hall. As she saw him looking at her, she smoothed her features and tried again, petting his arm and leaning in close.

"Oh, won't you stay, young man, just for a while, a quarter of an hour—"

"No, ma'am," he said, trying to make his voice stern as he had with Jack, hoping that this time it would have more of an effect.

He pulled away far enough so that her hand was forced to drop from his arm, though her fingers seemed to leave traces of perfume in the chill air. He saw the sparks in her eyes, though they couldn't be tears, not with her mouth in a smile again.

"I'm so very sorry, but I must go now." As he said this, his face felt tight. With a tip of his head, he put his cap on and backed away. The maid was off making tea, he presumed, so unfortunately there was no one to witness his refusal, regardless of how firm it had been. With a parting glance to her, he dipped his chin. "Good day, ma'am."

The air on the street was icy after the warmth of her doorway, so he tightened his green scarf around his neck and tucked his hands in his pockets as he strode down the pavement, his empty basket banging against his hip in his haste. That wasn't the way it was done, of course; a gentleman made his way along a street with dignity and grace. But he felt rattled, knowing that he shouldn't have gone in and had tea with her that first time. He wasn't a gentleman of leisure to be consorting with ladies.

Oliver reached the corner, ignoring the crossing sweeper with his thin body, valiantly sweeping the street against the falling snow, his thin boots flopping around his feet, mud ground into his trousers up to the knees. Oliver looked the other way, and just as he was about to step into the street, he careened into a body.

"Such a rush you're in, Nolly."

Oliver looked up.

It was Jack. *Again.* He looked bright and warm, green eyes sparking, features replete with that smile and sharp teeth, that top hat tipped back on his head, as though it wanted to fly off at any moment. He made a complete contrast to the highborn pedestrians, the gentlemen in shiny top hats and somber black greatcoats, the ladies, their fine wool cloaks trimmed with soft fur, not to mention the tidy street, and the clean, white rows of townhouses upon whose slanted roofs not even the smallest smut ever dared land.

"I told you to leave me alone. What are you doing here? How did you find me?" Oliver asked, half-glad at Jack's presence for a moment before irritation set in.

The last thing he needed was to see Jack. He was trying not only to make a good impression, but to keep it. But who knew how long that would last, with Jack coming around. Mr. McCready had already threatened a whipping over Jack; the only thing saving Oliver was that they were far enough from the shop that Mr. McCready might never hear of it.

"I followed you, of course," said Jack, his smile getting broader, as if he enjoyed the teasing almost as much as he enjoyed Oliver's reaction to it. "An' anyway, I've come to bring you news, news that couldn't wait."

"I don't wish to hear any news you might carry," said Oliver, with what he thought was haughty dismissal, even though talking to Jack was preferable to ruminating about the street sweeper.

Oliver looked across the street to where the sweeper had finished, and, leaning his broom against his thigh, was holding up a soot-blackened hand for the penny he had just earned. The gentleman whose path he had cleaned held his head high, however, and walked on as if the sweep wasn't there.

Fighting the impulse to give the urchin a penny from his own collection of change jingling in his trouser pocket, Oliver instead turned back to Jack and looked at him with what he hoped was implacability.

"It's just that—" Here Jack stopped. There was something in his voice that Oliver had not heard recently, not in some long years, not since the day they'd met in Barnet. The memory teased him, and he wondered, not for the first time, what Jack had been doing so far from Fagin's hideout, as Barnet was some miles from Saffron Hill. "I've been lookin' for some of Fagin's gang—"

"I don't care who you're looking for!"

Oliver felt his shoulders go up; talking about Fagin's gang was bad enough, but looking for them? It was beyond his ability to comprehend why it would be important. Besides, passersby were starting to look at them, their confusion evident that a well-dressed apprentice lad was standing in the middle of the pavement in earnest discussion with a person of such obvious ill repute.

"I don't want to know anything about that, can't you understand? Please go away, Jack, *please*."

"*Please*, is it now?" Jack asked. His eyebrows twitched, as if he were keeping himself from laughing outright, but only barely. "Such fine manners you have when there's somethin' you want."

"I only want you to go away." Oliver lowered his voice and stepped closer to Jack in the hopes of making their conversation more private and perhaps more effective. "To leave me alone and stop following me!"

"Such an ugly frown on such a sweet face." Now Jack did laugh, tossing his head back, giving his hat a little jerk to keep it in place. "So I'll tell you quickly an' save your face from freezin' that way."

Oliver turned on his heel and started walking away.

"Leave me alone, or I'll call the constable and have you arrested." He meant it this time. He really did.

"I'm at the Three Cripples, havin' my dinner," said Jack, calling after him. "An' in he walks, one of Fagin's gang!"

Oliver froze at the corner of the street. All of Fagin's gang was dead or disbanded, either of which, to hear Jack tell it, was tantamount to the same thing.

"What of it?" Oliver asked over his shoulder as he waited for a curricle and its prancing horses to move past him so that he could cross. He had no desire to remember anyone from that time.

"Don't you see? How grand this is? You said that no one would ever come, an' now they have! His name's Morris Bolter, an' he says he knows you."

Jack's voice, so bright and charged with energy, was right over Oliver's shoulder now. Oliver turned, barely missing Jack with the edge of his gloved fist.

"I told you," said Oliver, through gritted teeth, trying not to think of where he'd heard that name before. "I don't *care* about anyone from Fagin's gang. I don't *know* anyone named Morris Bolter, and I wouldn't care if I did."

"He knows all about you," said Jack, so close his breath brushed across Oliver's cheek. Jack smelled like onions from his dinner and the stale beer he must have drank. "Told me about those blue eyes an' that rosy mouth of yours. Told me about your thing for washin' an' how you had an appetite like a sailor, an' how you once attacked—"

"I don't care, don't you understand that?" It was beyond him why Jack simply wasn't listening, not to mention that Jack's closeness was prickling on his skin. "Those days are long in the past, and I've moved on. *You* need to move on. Why aren't you off stealing silver and picking pockets, or whatever it is you're doing these days? Or, I shouldn't wonder, you've already got small boys stealing *for* you."

He meant to hurt Jack, and maybe he had, for there was a pause before Jack burst out laughing, right there on the street, where anyone could see the raw display of his wide-open mouth. But it was of no concern to Jack that anyone might see a fine young gentleman such as Oliver Twist consorting with a street thug such as Jack Dawkins.

"You know me too well, Nolly," Jack said, shaking his head, causing his hat to slip a little. He straightened it with one bare hand and then smoothed his lapels, tugging on the edge of Oliver's red scarf. "I'm lookin' to start a new gang, although, right enough, that might take some time. There's a couple of lads at the Three Cripples who are lookin' at me with interested eyes, I don't mind tellin' you, but it's Morris, he's the one, he's got all these *stories*—"

Jack's voice rose on the last word, as if this fact, associated with that particular person, were the shining star in all of this, and Morris the best thing about it. Jack's remark and his obvious admiration for someone with such a sullied reputation snapped Oliver's patience right in two, and he actually grabbed Jack by the lapels and gave him a good shake.

"Don't you understand? I do *not* care. Not about the Three Cripples, or this Morris Bolter, and especially not about *you*." Oliver's voice rose to a high pitch, enough so that passersby were looking at him with widened eyes that told Oliver exactly what they thought of two lads having an altercation on the pavement. Well, one of those lads was going to end on his backside, and it wasn't going to be Oliver.

"You keep on and I'll call the constable, right now, I'll do it, I swear." He put his hand over his heart to emphasize his intent that he, Oliver, was going to do this thing.

But Jack just smiled and put his hands—bare, cold, knuckle-scarred hands—over Oliver's brown gloved one. Jack held on tightly, fingers curved, pressing Oliver's hand against his own chest. Oliver looked down, closed his eyes, and tried to jerk away from the pressure of Jack's hands. Oliver opened his mouth to shout—yes, he was positively going to shout for the nearest constable.

"Sir?" came a voice. "Sir?"

Oliver's eyes snapped open. He turned his head just as Jack let him go, and he in turn let Jack go to look at the owner of the voice. It was Jane, the maid from Mrs. Acton's townhouse. The door to the house was closed, but there was the maid without even a shawl to keep off the afternoon chill. She had an envelope in her hand, which she held out to Oliver.

"It's from the mistress; she wishes you to take it to your master."

Jane was blushing again and looking at Oliver. She purposefully did not look at Jack, not that Oliver could blame her. He would have done anything at that instant to not be associated with Jack; perhaps Jane felt that if she didn't look at Jack, the meeting between the three of them had never happened. She only need report to her mistress that she'd delivered the note, and that was the end of it.

"Thank you," said Oliver.

He took the envelope, which seemed weightless in his gloved hand. Both he and Jack watched the maid scurry off. Then Jack smacked Oliver on the shoulder.

"She's a pretty one. Been flirtin','ave you?"

"You can just shut your mouth."

Jack took a step back, eyes widening a bit in surprise. Then he smirked.

"Yes, sir, young master, sir." He doffed his hat and, curving his other arm around his waist, bowed low, his oily hair spreading out, the hat and the hems of Jack's coat almost sweeping the ground. "I only live to be at your service."

With his mouth pressed tightly against anything else he might say, Oliver stuffed the envelope in his pocket and marched off. He didn't look to see if Jack was following. It wouldn't matter. Jack knew where he lived and would come around, and then it would turn into a disaster. The only hope Oliver had was to stop Jack before he came in the yard again, or God forbid, came into the *shop*—

"Till later, then, Nolly," said Jack, in the distance.

Oliver didn't turn his head to acknowledge this. Instead, he marched along, head down, concentrating, trying to pretend that the meeting had never happened. There would be no one to tell Mr. McCready about it, no one in this part of town, and he certainly wouldn't mention it. God willing, that would be the end of it.

~

THE LIGHT WAS GROWING PALE AND BLUE, THE SHADOWS LONG as Oliver hurried back to the shop. That his path was downhill most of the way did not help, for ice had formed, freezing the runoff from the noon melt. He had the note from Mrs. Acton, and he'd tell Mr. McCready that Mrs. Acton had mentioned perhaps wanting more ribbons. That request might make a future sale, something Mr. McCready would approve of.

Checking his pocket with his hand, Oliver slipped down the cobbles as he stepped away from the Strand to cut across Leicester Square. The traffic was busy, and he had to duck between flashing carriage wheels and the wide skirts of ladies on their way home from taking an airing with their maids, showing off their fine garments. They rather enjoyed walking slowly and grandly. With far too much skirt and not enough hustle, they were making him later than he already was. Surely it was coming on to suppertime; he could not imagine what Mrs. Pierson would say, let alone his own stomach, were he to miss out on her good cooking.

Somehow, he made it in time, slipping across the yard and in the warehouse door just as the bells from St. James's Workhouse started tolling. As he came up the stairs and opened the door to the shop, he heard footsteps leading down to the kitchen. He put the basket on the bench, and hung his jacket, scarf, and cap on the peg in the hall and stuffed his gloves in his coat pockets. Rubbing his palms on his trousers, he took the note from his jacket pocket and headed down the stairs with as much calm as he could manage.

The kitchen was warm, and the smells of cooking filled his nose almost immediately. Mrs. Pierson moved between the stove and the sideboard, her skirts swirling. The girl was nowhere to be seen; Henry and Tate had already taken their usual places. A second after Oliver realized that Mr. McCready was also not among them, he felt the step on the stair behind him. He had a sense of those broad shoulders and then Mr. McCready's voice.

"Running late, Oliver?" he asked. "Never mind, those streets can get treacherous and busy this time of day. Is that a note for me?"

Oliver turned slightly to hand it to him and then slipped onto the bench seat next to Tate. He held his breath as he did this, hoping no one had noticed that he'd not taken the time to wash. But Mrs. Pierson was busy handing around the platter of fried cod and potatoes, and as always, the bread and butter. This time, there was a dish of pickles in the center of the table. His stomach growled and demanded that he hurry and start eating.

"I'd have gotten to the peas if that girl hadn't taken off early," said Mrs. Pierson, scooting the hot dishes around the table, making sure that each boy had some food close at hand.

"No need to worry, Mrs. Pierson," said Mr. McCready. "The boys have plenty to eat here and should learn to eat what's put before them."

"Are you saying I spoil these boys?" she asked, holding her hands to the apron over her stomach as if quite shocked.

"As is your duty, Mrs. Pierson, as is your duty."

"And in doing my duty," said Mrs. Pierson, "there's apple pudding for dessert."

Oliver looked up; he could see the pudding on the sideboard. As always, there was a pitcher of pouring custard next to it. It was probably full to the top, and she could make, as she always said, more if need be. He waited for Mr. McCready to say grace, then pulled his full plate to him and picked up his knife and fork, preparing to dig in.

He barely noticed Mr. McCready standing up, Mrs. Acton's letter in his hand, but when the whole table froze, Oliver forced himself to pay attention. He had his fork halfway to his mouth, but at the expression on Mr. McCready's face, he put it back on his plate with a clink.

Mr. McCready glared at Oliver, eyes narrow, his face turning white, and in his hand, the letter almost shook. Then Mr. McCready put the letter on the table next to his plate.

Oliver could see the careful dark script that seemed to go on for quite some time. He couldn't imagine an order for ribbons and lavender sachets or anything else Mrs. Acton might want could take that long, or require that much close writing.

"Oliver, put your knife and fork down and look at me."

Oliver looked up as he was told, but he didn't understand.

"Why, whatever is the matter, Mr. McCready?" Mrs. Pierson stared at Mr. McCready, hand half over her mouth, the other on her bosom. She could see the letter as well as Oliver could, and the way Mr. McCready now picked the letter up again, it was obvious that this was the source of his agitation.

"I don't wish to—" Here Mr. McCready stopped. "It is not right to keep secrets, not when it affects my business. This is a letter from Mrs. Acton. It concerns Oliver's meeting in the streets near her home. A meeting with a young man she describes as a low, disreputable person wearing a top hat, a great-coat, and red scarf. She states, Oliver, that you were talking with him as if you knew him, the very individual whom I specifically stated you were not to have any dealings with."

Everyone in the kitchen turned to look at Oliver. Tate and Henry were wide-eyed, and Oliver supposed that not much of this type of drama ever happened in the kitchen at McCready's Haberdashery. Mrs. Pierson looked mortified, as if on Mr. McCready's behalf.

"Are you quite sure?" she asked, her voice coming out faintly. "Perhaps she misunderstood the meeting, perhaps Oliver—"

For one moment, he felt he loved Mrs. Pierson, perhaps almost as much as he had anyone, for coming to his defense as she had, even though she'd only known him a short time. Perhaps she liked him because of the fine manners Mrs. Bedwin said he displayed, or maybe even because of his pretty face. Or his appetite for her cooking. It didn't matter, because—

"Do you deny it, Oliver?" asked Mr. McCready, breaking into

Oliver's thoughts. "Did you meet with some person you did not know, and Mrs. Acton mistook it for an acquaintance? Or was it truly, as I have forbidden, that you were talking with same young man as has been coming around to detain you from your work?"

Mr. McCready stopped to fold the letter with quick, angry motions of his hand. He placed the letter on the table, as if not caring that her fine writing paper might become smudged with grease. Then he looked up at Oliver with blazing eyes.

"Is this the young man, the *same* young man, whom your dallying with will most *assuredly* bring down the tone of this shop and send customers away, just as Mrs. Acton says she will take her custom elsewhere. For, as she says—"

Mr. McCready unfolded the letter again, just as quickly, and scanned it for the exact quote he wanted.

"She says she cannot bear to associate with a shop that allows its workers to mingle with—And then she almost actually states that you were *impudent* to her, though I imagine she's just trying to add insult to injury there. No, I believe she saw what she saw, and what I'm waiting for you to do, Oliver, is to either deny or accept these accusations."

Oliver could hardly breathe. He'd had no idea that Mrs. Acton would take his refusal of a cup of tea and a slice of cake so badly. Of course, it was more than that. He'd refused her the second time because she'd pawed at him the first time. But then, after refusing her, Oliver had marched right out into the street and gotten into a heated discussion with a lowlife, an ex-convict, no less. In comparison, that would make Mrs. Acton feel very insulted indeed, so no wonder the letter.

As well, the crux of it was that the accusation was quite true, though he couldn't have imagined it getting reported this far, this fast. Then again, he'd carried her letter in his pocket and delivered it with his own hands. He might as well have put his own head on the block; ice filled his lungs as he realized he'd unwittingly engineered his own doom.

"Do you deny what she states, Oliver?"

Mr. McCready was standing there quietly, at odds with the terror climbing in Oliver's breast. Why had he not called for the constable the very first time Jack had come up to him, at the very first words out of Jack's mouth? *Leave you be, Nolly? That's all anyone's ever done, is leave you be.*

Well, he was paying for it now, that laxness, that acceptance, allowing Jack to stand there and talk to him, wasn't he?

"Oliver, don't add sullenness to your list of sins. I only want you to answer me."

This made it worse; Mr. McCready had warned him. If only Oliver had stopped Jack that first time or run in the other direction or *something*—

"I see you are not denying it. Well, then, come with me now. Mrs. Pierson, make sure the boys eat and help you clear the table afterward."

Mr. McCready began walking around the table, and when he got to where Mrs. Pierson was standing, he gestured with his hand.

Oliver, feeling numb all over, let Mr. McCready grip the back of his neck and push him up the stairs and down the small passageway to the warehouse. It was freezing cold and dark, and Mr. McCready only let Oliver go long enough to light a candle, the one that stood at the end of the long deal table where Tate worked.

Mr. McCready took down a switch that had hung on a handle from one of the long beams. Oliver had seen it there but had not thought anything of it. It would never be for him, he'd been sure, because he was going to do well here. At least that's what he'd thought; now he knew differently.

Looking at Oliver gravely in the half-light, Mr. McCready said, "I will give you one more chance to say what needs to be said. Your apology will take you a long way in my good graces. But you must apologize, ere you lose that way."

Oliver felt as though he was already lost. Mr. McCready had helped to place him here, in this house. His intentions had been good, and Oliver himself had agreed to it. He had felt, even at the time, that it had been a good choice, and he knew now that only he himself was to blame for the predicament that he was in.

"Do you have an apology, Oliver? Or even an explanation?"

"No, sir," said Oliver, low.

Mr. McCready started, eyebrows rising, as if Oliver had struck him.

"I mean, that is—" said Oliver. "I'm sorry for today, but I don't have an explanation." He wanted to add that he deserved what was coming to him, but he didn't quite have the voice for it. Moreover, he did not want to bring Jack back into the conversation. Mr. McCready had been reasonable and generous, and Oliver had only let him down.

"Then I'm afraid, Oliver," said Mr. McCready, looking somewhat cross, "that I must deliver punishment, as promised."

Oliver's stomach dropped, as though it had fallen down an old well with no water at the bottom.

"You will come to the table now," said Mr. McCready. He stood to one side and swished the switch once in the air, checking to make sure that the damp had not softened it.

Oliver walked to the table and bent himself over it. Part of him hoped that this would impress Mr. McCready; the other part hoped he could distract himself from the squirming of his gut by clenching the edge of the table. He hadn't been beaten in years; it was hard to breathe.

A hand landed on the small of his back and pressed down, and Oliver had to open his mouth to get in enough air. The snow spat against the windows in the silence, and somewhere a door opened and closed, leaving an eternity between.

The whipping started with three quick strokes across the backs of his thighs. The blows vibrated all the way down to his bones, and Oliver cringed away. He felt Mr. McCready's body blocking his way and tried to force himself to stop quivering. He failed.

"Do not make this more difficult by trying to get away, Oliver," said Mr. McCready.

Oliver did not answer; prolonging the whipping by being openly defiant, when he'd already brought enough shame on the shop, would make it worse. Mr. McCready started again, bringing the switch down on two or three spots only, six more times, making it feel as if Oliver's skin had split in a burst of heat, as though someone were pressing burning iron against him.

When Mr. McCready stopped without ceremony or announcement, Oliver wanted to cry. He was shaking so hard his teeth rattled. Hot lines vibrated in an uneven path in his brain. He clenched and unclenched his fists, arms curled around his head. He wanted to stay there forever and sink deep, deep into the cool, scarred wood of the table.

But Mr. McCready yanked Oliver up by the collar, jerking so hard that stars flashed in front of his eyes.

"You will go to bed directly," said Mr. McCready, releasing him with a shake. "You will not get any supper, and on the morrow, we will make a new start. The matter is done now, and you will no longer consort with—"

Mr. McCready paused, and in the light of the single candle, his face was soft around the edges with concern.

"Is he someone from your past, Oliver? Is that it? Someone you knew when you were—?" Mr. McCready stopped himself and began again in more confident tones of instruction. "You should know that he will only hold you back. Your past is an angry, monstrous thing; you must do your best to escape it. And this person, this acquaintance of yours, is really not your friend."

Oliver's knees felt weak and his thighs throbbed. The care and comfort Mr. McCready lavished on his boys was worth a great deal. And he was right, of course, in that hanging about with the likes of Jack Dawkins would do Oliver's business prospects no good at all. But how Mr. McCready had deduced that Jack was well-known to Oliver was beyond him. There had been three brief meetings, only two of which Mr. McCready had seen with his own eyes, so how had he guessed it?

Oliver wanted to confess it all, tell the whole story, but Mr. McCready was already waving Oliver away, hanging up the switch, and moving toward the stairs.

When they got to the main landing, Mr. McCready motioned Oliver to go up the stairs.

"You'll go to bed without supper, young man, and perhaps you'll be able to think upon the direction your life had better take." Then he went down to the kitchen, leaving Oliver in the darkness of the closed shop.

Oliver trod slowly up the stairs, finding his way through the gloom and into the slanted dormitory. There, he used his hands to find the matches and candles, lit one, and stood there, smelling the sulfur and the sparking wax. As he watched the paraffin start to melt beneath the golden sliver of light, he realized he had not called the constable on Jack, yet again, though why, he could not fathom. His brain was too tired, and the backs of his thighs ached with every move he made.

There was no water to wash with, as both jug and basin were dry. With the lack of a girl to help, Henry and Tate would most likely wash in the kitchen before they came up to bed, so Oliver would have to sleep as he was, coated with sweat and the dust and ash from the street. And with Jack's touch, the mere brush of his hands, having left the faint smell of beer, still pulsing through the back of his hand.

He didn't want to look down at his legs, so he got out of his clothes as fast as he could, his teeth chattering in the chilly air. But, just as he put on his nightshirt, he did look, and could see that the backs of his thighs were a swarming red, with darker lines across the swellings. There'd been nine blows in all; none of them had broken the skin, but even so, he had to look away.

He thought about reading till the boys came up and the lights went out; his books would help relax him and make him feel more as if everything was as it should be. But exhaustion fell on him like a blanket of wet clay. The candle guttered as he moved to his bed. He yanked back the sheet and the two wool blankets and got into bed and lay down on his left side.

Pulling the covers up to his chin, he looked at the light flickering shadows on the wall and the panes of glass in the window. Yes, he had to move and tend to the candle; Mr. McCready didn't want the boys to leave anything burning. Wincing, he rolled over and blew out the candle, which sat on the chair beside his bed, and then rolled back, clasping the scar on his left arm to settle himself in the dark; darkness into which leaked Jack's voice. *I'm at the Three Cripples. One of Fagin's gang has come an' he says he knows you. He's the one. He's got all these stories.*

Oliver shut off the thought as fast as he could. But something echoed there, something, a memory that he couldn't quite pin down.

Of course, Jack would want to know stories; he was always ready to hear those. Ones about great criminals dying nobly or, even better, getting away with it. He could imagine Jack's glee at finding a member of Fagin's gang, but except for Charley Bates, Oliver couldn't remember any of their names, and certainly not anyone named Morris Bolter. Who, evidently, knew Oliver well enough to know about his penchant for cleanliness and his great appetite for food. No, Jack was teasing him, making it up for a lark. Which was Jack's way, and always had been.

He sank his head into the one pillow and tried to breathe slowly and not think of anything. But this absence of thought allowed the pain from the whipping to seep in, the great throbs echoing as his heart beat. He'd deserved the beating, almost as assuredly as if he'd asked for it. Which didn't make it hurt any less; it hurt a great deal.

Had he grown so soft, then? Although, when he was little, a whipping like this would have sent him sobbing into a howling ball on the ground, so maybe he was tougher now, could stand it more. Or, which was more likely, the switch Mr. McCready had held in his hand was not as harshly felt as his disappointment.

Oliver sighed. He must do better in future. He would do everything that Mr. McCready said. The instant an order was given him, he would obey it. If Jack came around again, Oliver would be shouting for the constable and marching right up to Mr. McCready to report the incident. Yes, that's what he would do. He swore it. This whipping would be the last he would ever receive at Mr. McCready's hands.

## 𝕩 14 𝕩

## LESS DRAMA AND VIOLENCE ARE
## CALLED FOR BUT ARE
## DIFFICULT TO ACHIEVE

I n the morning, after wincing through getting dressed, Oliver followed Henry and Tate down to the kitchen. He felt sore all over, and the visits from Jack and Mr. McCready's disapproval nagged at him. But in the midst of this wash of emotions came the confusion of watching Henry and Tate line up in front of Mr. McCready, who was already seated at the table for breakfast.

Henry, as usual, was first in line, He held out his hand, into which Mr. McCready unhesitatingly pressed a shiny shilling. Tate was next, curling his fingers around the coin with a smile, and then, indeed, Mr. McCready nodded that Oliver was next.

"Well done, lad, keep up the good work," Mr. McCready said, handing Oliver a coin.

In that small moment, with the coolness of the shilling in his hand, Oliver received his first pay. In spite of this small victory, Oliver felt the remains of the previous day's whipping as well as the glimmer of temper he imagined was still in Mr. McCready's eyes.

Oliver put the silver coin in his pocket, meaning to tuck it away in his tip box when he had a chance. But as the girl had not brought up any hot water, the boys lined up to wash in the kitchen.

Since Oliver was the last boy in line, by the time he'd washed his face and hands, splashing water and soap all over the wash-stand and the slate floor, and dried his face on the towel, he looked up to see the entire of Mr. McCready's household already seated and waiting for him. No one said anything as he limped to his place beside Tate on the bench seat. Then Mrs. Pierson began serving up hot toast and butter, honey and bowls of porridge, and a tray of baked eggs.

"I don't know as yesterday's doings have brought this house down forever," she said. She scowled at Oliver, her eyes a little moist, as if she weren't quite sure whether or not she was angry. "But it seems to me that a good deal less violence and drama would be better to be getting on with. Wouldn't you agree, Mr. McCready?"

"Yes, indeed, Mrs. Pierson, and thank you," said Mr. McCready. "Would you happen to know if the tea is ready yet?"

Mrs. Pierson nodded and shoveled a baked egg onto Oliver's plate, plus an extra one for good measure, and then quickly walked to the stove where the kettle was just boiling.

The extra egg almost made Oliver feel worse than the night before; he'd upset Mrs. Pierson, and *still* she was feeding him. Which only strengthened his resolve to shout at the top of his lungs the moment Jack again turned up. Which he would, knowing Jack.

AFTER BREAKFAST, OLIVER FOLLOWED THE BOYS UP THE STAIRS to put away their respective shillings and quickly followed them back downstairs, where Mr. McCready was already behind the counter. Henry went to unlock the doors as Oliver put on his apron and hustled outside in the cold air to take down the shutters. While he was grateful that he'd actually received his pay, his heart was pounding with the thought that Mr. McCready might still decide to send him packing.

And indeed, upon his return inside, Mr. McCready was waiting for him with his hands on the glass countertop.

"And you, young Oliver. You were quite indulged this morning. Mrs. Pierson thinks a great deal of you, I'd say."

Oliver didn't know what to say to this. So he nodded and tried not to look prideful. Which was hard, when his stomach was comfortably full of Mrs. Pierson's good cooking, and he'd had an extra piece of buttered toast, as well.

"I do feel, however, that some extra work is what you need to keep your mind and body occupied."

Extra work was not what Oliver needed, not when every movement of his trousers brushed the backs of his legs, irritating the welts and bruises there. But he nodded his head and kept his mouth shut. Whatever Mr. McCready had in mind, it wouldn't be beyond his ability to bear, surely.

"There's a delivery due this morning. You will unload it yourself, without assistance."

"Yes, sir," said Oliver.

Anger bloomed in his belly. He'd already taken his punishment and apologized, so why the additional work? Perhaps it was because he'd not been able to explain away his meetings with Jack, or perhaps it was because he'd not begged to be let off or shown as much meekness and contrition as was called for. But it was hard. He'd spent so much of his life standing up and facing misfortune, without letting anyone know—No, he had to stop. Mr. McCready wasn't the enemy; Mr. McCready only wanted the best for him.

"I'm sorry about yesterday, sir," said Oliver now, instead of everything else he wanted to say.

"I know, Oliver," said Mr. McCready. "Now, to your work, and we'll speak no more about it."

As if to prove how normal a morning it was, Mr. McCready turned to Tate, who was standing close by, pretending very hard that while he was eavesdropping, he was really only waiting for his orders.

"Tate, would you double-check that box, the one with the spools of thread that came yesterday?" Mr. McCready consulted a list on the counter. "I feel almost certain the count is low, but before I talk with the manufacturer, I want to be sure. Can you do that?"

"Yes, sir," said Tate, and he hurried off, ducking down the stairs to the warehouse like a rabbit disappearing into its burrow, and Oliver took a grateful, deep breath and followed him.

THE GATES WERE HOOKED WIDE OPEN TO ADMIT THE DELIVERY wagon, and Oliver stood alone to greet it. Normally, there would have been at least two boys to attend to this particular task, but this time there was only Oliver.

With the horses' shod hooves striking sparks on the cobblestones, and with creaks of wheel and harness, the cart finally stopped, half-turned in the yard, the back end sticking out in the alley, taking up a great deal of room all the way around. The driver covered the two dray horses with a blanket each, and as Oliver began unloading, the driver climbed back on his bench behind the horses' rumps, watching him. He had a flask in his hands that he sipped at from time to time. Oliver imagined it was gin, though, at the same time, he wouldn't lower himself to ask for a dram to help keep him warm while he worked.

Carrying each slatted crate from the cart to just inside the door of the warehouse made him almost warm enough in the weak sunlight trailing through the mist that Oliver soon doffed his jacket but kept on his apron and cap. He still felt cross about everything, with the driver watching, and no one to help him. There seemed to be hundreds of crates with rough edges that left splinters everywhere, and wooden flecks on his apron and under his skin. In truth, he knew there to be only about twenty or so crates, although, yes, the splinters were real enough.

He'd jabbed himself with a splinter along the fleshy part of his palm and it ached with each trip through the open door, the little one, so as to keep the chill off Tate, who was at his counting next to the deal table. Oliver wondered if he could chance going into the workshop to ask Tate if he might use the gloves that Tate wore when there was rough work at hand.

The gloves went with a workman's coat, a rough, stained thing of heavy wool that he'd seen Tate burrow into when he'd grown cold during his counting. The coat was so ugly that Oliver did not even want to touch it, but he was thinking about it differently this morning. The wool of the coat might protect his arms, which were now scratched and red and bleeding in streaks. But each time he went into the warehouse, he didn't look at Tate, and Tate didn't look at him, and he didn't want to be accused of slacking merely to have the questionable comfort of a grotty coat.

There were several crates at the far end of the wagon, so Oliver ducked through the gates and walked close along the wet and dripping brick wall of the alley till he could reach them. Just as he stopped, well out of eye and earshot of the driver, he felt a movement behind him and casually looked, thinking it was some pedestrian with the foolish notion that walking through the alley would provide a better passage than walking along the street.

"Ho, there, Nolly," said Jack. "You look like you're limpin' a bit. Been in an accident, have you?"

Oliver froze. He saw Jack there, and in spite of all his promises to himself, simply froze, with a slatted wooden crate in his hands, though at least it wasn't a bucket this time.

"Go away, Jack." His voice held no inflection, and his lungs felt as though they had no power. "You're not wanted here."

"But I've more to tell you," said Jack, moving close.

Oliver's red scarf was still in evidence around Jack's neck, although it was now becoming smudged along its fine woolen edges. There was a flash of blue silk inside Jack's coat, which meant that Jack had managed to procure a new waistcoat, by stolen means, no doubt, and suddenly Oliver was sick of thinking about Jack and how he took everything and anything he wanted without working for it.

Now Oliver moved. He threw the crate down to the cobbles and watched out of the corner of his eyes as it exploded against the mud and ice. Then he slammed into Jack, pushing him against the far wall of the alley, smacking his head hard enough against the icy brick to send that fine hat of his tumbling into the mud. He brought his face close to Jack's and thought about yelling for the constable, of alerting the driver so that he could go and fetch Mr. McCready. But first, he wanted to make his point that he wasn't afraid of Jack, and, moreover, didn't want anything to do with him.

"You listen to me, Jack Dawkins," said Oliver. He felt so *fierce*, and he wanted Jack to cower, to shrink away from him and listen. He grabbed Jack by the lapels of his jacket, and shoved hard, holding Jack against the wall, looking into his green eyes, shaking Jack till his dark hair sprawled across his forehead, making him listen. "I don't *care* where you've been or where you are or who you've been talking to. I simply don't care, and I want you to leave me alone. Do you understand? Leave me *alone*."

Jack chuckled, though Oliver sensed he was trying to catch his breath, that he was not quite comfortable, and maybe his head ached a bit.

"But it's a funny story, an' don't you want to hear it? The things Morris has to tell about you—an' about me, he was there when I was arrested!"

"No story from any friend of yours would be funny, Jack. No one is laughing. I'm certainly not."

Oliver was about to release his hold on Jack and shout at the driver for assistance, for he knew there was nothing that Jack would listen to better than the shrill of a peeler's whistle. When Oliver did let go, Jack shoved him with the flat of both palms against Oliver's chest. Down Oliver went, his feet slipping on the ice as he fell with a slam into the ditch in the middle of the alley. He was soaked through with icy mud; the clawed edges of the ice cut into him, into his bruises, making him yelp as he tried to roll free.

Jack was over him, pulling him up to press him against the near wall of the alley. Oliver shivered, dripping and cold, blood pounding under his skin so hard that for a moment all he could see were black spots in front of his eyes. He clenched his hands at his sides, not wanting to reach out for something to hold on to, feeling at any moment that he was going to topple over, right back into the icy mud. And then he grabbed on anyway, to the first thing his hands could find.

When he could blink enough to clear his vision, there Jack stood, standing close but not touching him, even though Oliver was clutching Jack's lapels. There was something overly still about the way Jack watched him, as if waiting for Oliver to move as an animal waits for prey. His eyes darted to the open gates to the yard, his ears listening to voices on the street. Wary for any movement that might spell danger to him. Of course. Jack was always on the lookout for danger, and never mind what trouble he'd caused Oliver.

Jack must have taken the pause for hesitation on Oliver's part because he smiled and stepped closer. He pressed his bare hands over Oliver's with a sudden, quick movement that jolted Oliver all over. He tried to cover his wince as best he could, but Jack's eyebrows came together.

"Just come an' meet him," said Jack. "I promise I'll stop comin' round an' gettin' you into trouble with your master. He won't whip you n'more."

It was too much to imagine how Jack had so quickly got to the heart of the problem when Oliver had never told him.

"Don't squinch," said Jack, taking one hand up and rubbing his thumb along Oliver's brow. "It makes you all bumpy an' ruins those pretty looks of yours. One visit an' that's all. Upon my word as a gentleman."

"For what *that's* worth." Oliver let go of Jack's lapels, trying to calm his breathing, and smacked Jack's hand away.

From the cobblestone yard, Oliver heard a shout, sharp in the misty air. "Oliver! What's keeping you?"

Mr. McCready had obviously been alerted to the delay by the presence of a cart so long idle in his yard. He had come to look for his newest apprentice boy.

Oliver cast a look up the alley. The passage from the yard into the alley was blocked by the cart. For Mr. McCready to find Oliver, he would have to come out the front door of the shop and walk all the way around. But if he did so, he'd find Jack as well; Oliver needed to get Jack to go away.

"Get out of here, Jack, for the love of God," said Oliver, his jaw tight. He knew Jack might keep his word if it suited him, and then again, he might not. But for the time being, it would keep Jack away and Oliver out of trouble. "I'll come, I'll meet him. But after that, no more, Jack. No more visits, no more pennies, and give me back my scarf! And my change purse!"

Oliver reached out, but Jack danced back, his eyes laughing as he brought his hand up and held it over his scarf as though he were holding his hand over his heart.

"Yes, yes, an' no," said Jack. "It's mine now. Nine out of ten of the law an' all that."

It was ridiculous the way Jack misquoted everything, as if he'd heard it and deliberately turned it around to annoy Oliver. It was as if he enjoyed watching Oliver get riled and seemed always to know exactly how to get the desired results. It made Oliver's head hurt; he pushed his palm hard against his temple, trying to stem the low throb that was developing.

"Am I givin' you a headache?" asked Jack, trying for innocence as he picked up his top hat from the damp stones and shook it off before he put it on his head.

"You *are* a headache," said Oliver. He swung backward, freeing himself of the pull of Jack that he didn't understand.

"Oliver! Oliver *Twist!*"

Mr. McCready sounded closer now. Oliver looked at Jack, who had not moved.

"Please," he said. His voice sounded as young as a child's, and he didn't like how that made him feel. He swallowed, and tried to gather some air in his lungs, to make it come out stronger. To make it come out as though he meant it. "I need to get back to work."

He turned away from Jack and heard booted feet making their way out of the yard and into the alley. But as Mr. McCready appeared around the corner, and into the space between the cart and the gate to the yard, Oliver didn't dare look back to make sure. Either Jack would be gone and there would be no need to speak of it, or he would not, and no explanation that Oliver might offer would be enough.

Mr. McCready stopped, mouth open, and for one instant, Oliver thought Jack had not left. But then Mr. McCready came up to the mess of the crate that Oliver had thrown down. There were many narrow paper boxes of hat pins, now spilled all over the ground, and of those, some had opened and spilled their bright, colorful contents into the icy mud.

"Whatever has happened?" asked Mr. McCready. He wasn't really talking to Oliver. He was already bending down and reaching for a pile of pins that had come loose from its box. Then he looked up at Oliver. "Why is the crate smashed?"

"I slipped, sir," said Oliver, taking the easy road. And it felt easy, so incredibly easy, to lie about this. "It was the ice, and I, well, I'm sorry, sir."

Mr. McCready straightened up, pins in his hand, mud dripping from his fingers. As he looked at Oliver, Oliver knew he would see what was most obvious to see. That the crate was broken, and Oliver was quite rucked about, muddy, soaked, and dripping. Anyone in the world would conclude the truth of what Oliver had just said, rather than imagine the lie.

"Get these pins, Oliver, and I'll get Tate to clean up the rest of this mess. We need to get this cart out of here; there's another delivery due any moment."

The disaster of having to pay one driver to wait while another backed out of the yard was, of course, very much to be avoided. Oliver gritted his teeth and kept his mouth shut.

"You're bleeding," said Mr. McCready. "Never mind those pins now. Get Mrs. Pierson to bandage up your wrist, and brush off those trousers before they are permanently stained."

Oliver looked down at his hands, palms up. His left wrist had been sliced by the ice. Not deeply, but enough to leave a jagged tear that had bled over the heel of his palm. Now that he was looking at it, it began to sting, blood oozing in the cold air to drip down to his boot tops. All at once, his head began to weave back and forth and his body followed obediently, spiraling into a sense of what he had done to himself. He'd cut himself wide open so that he was bleeding in the alley, had smashed a crate of perfectly good hatpins, and he had *still* not called the constable on Jack.

"Oliver." The voice came from some distance. "Oliver, are you all right? Here, we'll get you inside first. Tate. *Tate!*"

He felt a warm arm around his shoulder and the sudden shield of Mr. McCready's chest. Then he heard the scurrying footsteps of Tate, running but trying not to slip on the ice. As they went into the yard, and Tate came over to them, Mr. McCready let Oliver go, motioning to Tate to *hurry now, hurry*. Out of the warehouse door came Mrs. Pierson, her hands over her mouth at, presumably, Oliver's state.

"Oh, *no*," she said. "Whatever have you been up to?" She held up her apron and skirts above the mud in the yard and gestured to him, almost violently, in the cold. "Come away in, this instant. What a disgrace you are! And you're bleeding all over those trousers."

But her voice sounded only mild and scolding rather than that she was truly angry with him. Not to mention the look on her face bespoke of her intention to straighten him up, to get his trousers brushed. And, moreover, to *feed* him. For the first time in what seemed the whole morning, Oliver felt his chest and shoulders relax. This he could bear; a little clucking and fussing would not come amiss right about now.

AFTER SUPPER, WITH HIS WRIST BANDAGED, OLIVER STOOD IN his nightshirt in the kitchen, waiting with a thin towel as Tate finished his bath. Henry, being the senior boy, had been first to use the cleanest, hottest water, and had already gone up to bed. When Tate stripped to bare skin and got into the slightly used water, Oliver was shocked, but pretended it didn't matter. Because even though he was used to having hot water brought up to his room for his own private Saturday night bathing needs, he knew most apprentices were lucky to have any water at all to wash with, and sharing bathwater was only to be expected.

So he kept his mouth shut and rubbed at his scar while he waited for Tate to finish and thought about whether or not he should take off the bandage Mrs. Pierson had wrapped around his wrist. It would be better, perhaps, to give the wound another washing, and so, while Tate put his nightshirt back on, seeming unembarrassed by his mostly naked state, Oliver concentrated on unwrapping the bandage.

By the time Tate was thumping up the stairs, Oliver had slipped out of his nightshirt and was in the fast-cooling grey water. It wasn't that anyone was there to see his scar, or stare at his state of nature, it was just that it was easier to jump in the water fast enough so that he did not have time to think about how it had so recently been swirling about other bodies, other naked limbs. At least there was soap, and he had his own towel. More sharing than that, he could not have borne.

~

THE EARLY BEDTIME OF SATURDAY NIGHT WAS FOLLOWED BY A slow Sunday morning, with Mr. McCready and the boys showing Oliver how it was done. They ate, mostly in silence, the cold breakfast Mrs. Pierson had prepared the day before, which was followed by attendance at St. James's Church just down the street. Mr. McCready took Henry, Tate, and Oliver with him to St. James's; Mrs. Pierson, who was off for the day, went to her own church, St. Anne's, where apparently her family all went.

Oliver sat on the hard bench of the pew, turning the penny that Mr. McCready had given him for the collection basket over and over in his fingers. It was nice to be able to sit in a pew amidst the somber folk and listen to someone talk without feeling as though there was anything he should be doing or worrying about. And, as well, Jack was hardly likely to come to church services, whatever the temptation.

In the afternoon, when church services were over, Mr. McCready and the boys shared the cold lunch that Mrs. Pierson had left for them. The boys went out somewhere, and Oliver was left on his own. He went upstairs and took out his book of poems by Dr. Johnson. He read on his bed on his stomach, turning the pages slowly beneath a vague patch of sun that came and went through the window as the clouds tumbled past.

## 15

# OLIVER KEEPS HIS PROMISE TO JACK AND FINDS THE THREE CRIPPLES INSALUBRIOUS

I t wasn't until early the next week that Mrs. Pierson determined that Oliver's wrist could be unbandaged. Up till then, she'd insisted he be kept close by, so any deliveries were local and quick. But Mr. McCready insisted, with equal force, that Oliver do his regular tasks around the shop, and so, for a few days, the warehouse was always swept and the coal bins by each stove kept full, even though the girl was being entirely unreliable again.

Oliver was willing to pitch in, not only to keep himself busy but to be useful enough to make up for his as yet undiscovered dalliance with Jack the week before. In addition, he was grateful to hear, while listening to Mr. McCready talk to Mrs. Pierson, that Mrs. Acton's upset had been taken care of, which was important, as she was the shop's most particular client.

As Oliver walked toward the front of the shop, Henry waved him over.

"Mr. McCready wants you to make deliveries today, Oliver."

Henry handed over a list, which Oliver took and scanned. Then he looked at the basket, full to the brim with string-tied brown paper parcels.

"These addresses are as far as Russell Square," said Oliver.

Then he realized what it meant, and to which part of London his deliveries would take him. The thought of actually going to see Jack made his stomach squirm. As to what Mr. McCready would say, were he to find out, was actually making him feel queasy. But he'd made a promise to Jack, and he, Oliver, was a man of his word.

"No," said Henry. He tapped the string-tied parcel at the top of the basket. "That's *Regent* Square, and it's uphill all the way, so you better hurry."

Oliver nodded as he hefted the basket. He tucked the parcels in so it looked as though there were more packages than there actually were. He needed the time, and Henry would support that he sent Oliver off with a full basket, were anyone to ask.

At Henry's nod, Oliver, with jacket and cap and scarf firmly in place, was out the door, pushing past customers in a rude way, turning abruptly away from St. James's Workhouse to avoid going past the high iron gates. He used his shoulders to slip through the traffic on the street, dodging carts and wheeled barrows, and hurrying past the beggars and the coffee vendor.

He made his way up Oxford Street, then went into the dodgy back lanes and muddy alleys off Tottenham Court Road, where he ought not to go, not if he wanted his pocket to remain unpicked or his person to remain unassaulted. But he must have been too early for most who would do him ill, and he managed to slip through to where the streets widened out, and Regent Square appeared, tidy and quiet, before him.

He went as fast as he could to get the deliveries made before it got too late to go to the bottom of Saffron Hill, where Jack said the Three Cripples was located. When Oliver was through and his basket empty, he headed down Grey's Inn Lane. And when he got to the bottom of the slope at Holborn, it started looking as though it would lead to somewhere less than amiable. Ill at ease and not a little lost, he stopped at a corner tavern and asked for directions to the Three Cripples.

The proprietor did not even pause as he continued to pull mid-morning beer and ale.

"What you want is to go across to Field Lane, and take a left, and when that ends, then up you go on Saffron Hill. It's right there."

"Saffron Hill?" asked Oliver. He couldn't imagine that Field Lane simply ended up being Saffron Hill.

"You follow this bit," said the proprietor with a sigh, as though Oliver were the most troublesome of fellows. He pointed out the window, gesturing the way the street went uphill. "And then, when you get to Field Lane, keep going up; the Cripples'll be on your left, you can't miss it."

With the directions all dizzy in his head, Oliver backed out of the tavern. He followed the directions, feeling blind, feeling as though he would miss the tavern in spite of, or perhaps because of, the directions. When he got to the downward slope of Holborn, with the sounds and smells of Smithfield Market just beyond a street or two, there was a dark, narrow lane to the left. Of course, it would be the very direction he needed to go that would be so nasty, where the light went dim and the smells combated those of the market.

He went up the lane, as instructed, and as he walked, the narrowing street was lined by row upon row of handkerchiefs, hung on strings, an all-too-familiar sight, even if the memory was long in the past. In spite of the fetid scraps in the street and the gutter of mud, he passed a pie shop, which was a bustling spot of activity. There was even a short line out the door and the wafting smell of hot meat and onions almost smacked him in the face.

He kept walking, and suddenly, it was there, the Three Cripples. It was almost at the near end of the lane, somewhat tall, with narrow windows peeking out from beneath the rough-edged roofline. The last coat of paint had been years ago, and the window casements were sooted dark and had not been cleaned within recent memory. The sign that hung below the eaves was a rough shield shape with faded green paint. The three blotches on it barely resembled anything approaching three figures, let alone crippled ones.

Smoke from coal fires tended to bring coal dust down in thick layers, so if the tavern keeper had not enough hands to fortify against it, then layers of grime were the result. But other shops and doors and windows along the lane looked in far worse shape; at least the Three Cripples looked as though it had active customers, upright ones, rather than the skulking, filthy shapes that he tried to ignore as they passed behind him or lounged in doorways that looked like they'd not been opened in years.

Oliver knew, with a surety, that he ought not to be here at all, not in this neighborhood, and especially not with the goal of visiting Jack Dawkins. He should be able to deal with Jack's stories and threats another way, shouldn't he? But he didn't have another way, and anyway, here he was, at the Three Cripples.

As he opened the door, the smell of beer and damp hit him along with the thick reek of an untended cesspit. He stepped into the large room, which had a long, rough wooden bar taking up most of the center, with a scatter of tables and chairs set about in rough clumps. The windows, which would barely let in any sunlight at all, were it shining, had short seats and low tables attached to the wall beneath them. A small fireplace jutted out from the far wall, and on one side was a doorway leading to a small room, and beyond that was a passage and two other doors, one of which was opened and seemed to lead to a kitchen, from the smells and sounds that were coming from it.

While no one was looking at him directly, he sensed they were looking at him askance. He was dressed too fine to be where he was, and while he thought he had the right Three Cripples, perhaps he didn't. Maybe there was another one? Besides, Jack was nowhere to be seen. Oliver felt the stirrings of panic at the thought of actually going up to the bar to talk to one of these rough men to inquire after Jack.

The door opened to admit more customers, all roughly garbed in stained woolen jackets and thick boots, their caps and hats tucked low over their eyes. A small wind whisked around Oliver's heels, carrying the scent of their labor, the odor of long-unwashed grime on their skins.

Oliver wondered if he should stay or go.

Go. He should go.

He turned back to the door and pulled it open. It sagged badly on its hinges, and he struggled to keep it open so he could slip out just as more customers came in.

"Come in, then, if you've a mind to."

Oliver turned around, and there was Jack. His face, dirtier than Oliver had last seen it, was streaked with old sweat, and his eyes were narrow, as if speculating why Oliver had given in to his threats. But he looked pleased somehow, somewhere behind his green eyes, as if content Oliver had come to see him at last.

"Close the door, then," said Jack, coming up to do it for him. Casually, as if Oliver's visit was not his first, nor was it likely to be his last.

"Want some cider?" asked Jack. "It's on the house. Or gin. You'd rather that, I reckon."

Oliver looked at Jack, holding his empty delivery basket between them, standing in the flow of working men that continued their passage, snaking like a river, in and out of the door. Jack's voice seemed overly friendly, and those eyes appraised him, not ready to be truly welcoming until Jack was good and ready.

"Been making deliveries?" asked Jack, moving in close and reaching out to run both hands over the trim of Oliver's lapels. It was a move that felt familiar, and Oliver stepped back. "They'll be missin' you, them that gave you them togs, you think?"

"No," said Oliver shortly, though the statement didn't surprise him. "They won't. I'll be going in a moment."

Of course he must go; even Jack couldn't stop him. The men with their elbows at the bar were starting to eye him as though he was a prize bullock at a fair.

"Comin' all this way just to leave your card, eh?" Jack tipped back his head with a laugh, then settled for giving Oliver a rough pat. "You're here; you might as well wait, as Morris'll be along any time now."

Jack led Oliver into the first room off the main room, a small alcove that had a table and a pair of bench seats in the corner near a small coal fire. From the rooms down the corridor beyond, Oliver could smell yeasty bread and grease that said something was frying. Jack sat near to the fire, facing the open doorway. Oliver noticed a clay pipe oozing smoke as it sat in a small, round dish on the table, and the sight of it brought back a rush of not altogether unpleasant memories from the past.

Oliver sat across from him, and Jack gestured with wide arms, smiling honestly now.

"There, that's better, ain't it? An' there he is! Morris, the man of the hour. Come, Nolly, say hello to our new friend."

Oliver couldn't imagine who Jack might know that knew him and had also been in Fagin's gang; it just didn't make sense. But his curiosity overrode his irritation, and so he turned slowly in his seat and looked.

The man coming through the low doorway had long arms and legs that poked out of a once fine jacket and trousers. His hat was off, but he touched his forehead to Oliver, fingers brushing hair that was like dark straw above glittering eyes. He came close, standing near enough to Oliver that his tin-smelling cologne and the sour smell of unwashed linen overpowered the smoke of the coal fire. Oliver's mind formed a question, as though it were trying to solve a puzzle.

The man smiled, showing an eyetooth lapped across a fore tooth and, with a lopsided grin said, slowly, "'Ello, Work'us."

"Noah," said Oliver, not believing it, though his stomach felt as if it had warded off a blow, and he cringed inside, imagining that more blows were to come. "Noah Claypole."

"His name's Morris Bolter," said Jack, almost laughing, as if Oliver were playing a joke on him. "Like I told you. Morris Bolter from Fagin's gang. The one I told you of."

"Yes, I know," said Oliver, not heeding his own rudeness as shock ripped away any semblance of manners he might hope to hold onto. "Morris Bolter, as you said, but this is Noah Claypole, for all he's anyone else."

"Same as was," said Noah, his voice the same as it had been many years ago, mocking, slippery, but much deeper now. He towered over Oliver as he always had, only now he had the breadth of a man across his shoulders. "One an' the same, actually. Bolter is me workin' name, as it was when I worked for Fagin."

"Then it's true," said Oliver.

One look at Jack told him that Jack had no problems with not knowing all of Noah's aliases; he was too proud that he'd been right and that Oliver had been wrong about one of Fagin's old gang having come back. No doubt he'd be rubbing it in with much salt later.

"Of course it's true, Nolly," said Jack. "An' here I was tellin' Morris, I mean, Noah, all about you, when you'd already met. What a laugh it is!"

"Work'us an' I met, right enough, and you an' I, Jack, almost met that day in the courthouse, though you probably don't remember it."

Noah looked a little smug at Jack's pleased expression. Oliver could tell right away that Noah had a great many of these little story tidbits that he had been, and would be, feeding to Jack, little by little, to keep him hanging on.

"'Course, I don't know as what the record books say," said Noah, his chest expanding. "But I was there, right enough, an' didn't I run straight to Fagin to tell him all about it? I reckon I did, an' he was as pleased as he could be."

"You'll tell me the story, won't you?" said Jack. "We'll have drinks an' talk around the fire. That's what gentlemen do, ain't it, Nolly?"

Jack reached across the table and gave Oliver a generous smack on his shoulder. Oliver jerked away, gritting his teeth, not saying what he wanted to say, that Noah wasn't fit to be anybody's friend. But Noah, the lout, professed to know Jack's story as well as his own, and that was something Jack simply would not be able to resist.

"How do you two know each other?" Jack's eyes were on Oliver now, fully, glinting green and brown all at once in his excitement. "I'll wager you never expected to meet each other here, then, eh?"

So it was true then; Noah had been feeding Jack stories, little by little, leading him on like a fish on a hook. Oliver felt his eyes grow hot at Noah's smile, which always had, now that he recalled, the ability to get him worked up with a mere twitch. Then, when Oliver's feathers were well and truly ruffled, Noah would throw on a comment or two and watch Oliver explode into temper, which would always get Oliver into trouble.

*"Work'us," said Noah, as a tear rolled down Oliver's cheek. "What's set you a-sniveling now?"*

*"Not you," replied Oliver, hastily brushing the tear away. "Don't think it."*

*"Oh, not me, eh?" sneered Noah.*

*"No, not you," replied Oliver sharply. "There, that's enough. Don't say anything more to me about her, you'd better not!"*

*"Better not!" exclaimed Noah. "But you must know, Work'us, your mother was a regular right-down bad 'un."*

*"What did you say?" inquired Oliver, looking up very quickly.*

*"A regular right-down bad 'un, Work'us," replied Noah, coolly. "An' it's a great deal better, Work'us, that she died when she did, or else she'd have been hard laboring in Bridewell, or transported, or hung: which is more likely than either, isn't it?"*

Noah's smile now showed that he'd not forgotten this power he'd once had, and Oliver made his heart settle in his chest and vowed that he'd not let Noah get to him. Not yet, anyway.

"We met," began Noah in the wake of Oliver's silence, "at Sowerberry's undertaker shop, back in Hardingstone. Oliver was brought to tend to the shop while I learnt the funeral business.

Then, after he was promoted to mute, ahead of me, mind you, Oliver ran off, an' I figured, soon after, that dead folks were of no interest to me, in spite of the money to be made. We're both well shet of that place, ain't we, Work'us?"

"What?" asked Jack. "Why do you call him that?"

"'E's a workhouse boy, ain't he?" said Noah, nodding in Oliver's direction. "But 'e was such a mite of a thing when he came in, I 'ad to shorten the word just to match his stature. But didn't he grow!" Noah tossed back his head to laugh. "Just like the missus said he would, grew right out of his station, an' that's the last we saw of him. Won't they be surprised to know I found you 'ere."

"You won't be writing them," said Oliver, the words clipped off. "Besides, they already know where I am and what's become of me."

"No, no," said Noah, reaching out in what he probably thought was a friendly gesture, thumping Oliver on the chest. "If I was to tell them where you were, I'd have to tell them where I was, an' I'm afraid I can't do that."

"Why?" asked Oliver with a snap. "Because you made off with the master's silver?"

Jack roared at this. Roared as loudly as Charley Bates would have done, and at something completely illegal, and for one moment, it was as if the spirit of Fagin's gang was alive and dancing right there around them.

"What a treat," said Jack, gesturing, as if to draw them closer to each other. "I propose we toast this with a round of beer!"

"My friend, you are too generous," said Noah. "But I must be away, as I am expected in court soon to bear witness to some horrible, though not capital, crimes."

"Come by later, then," said Jack, giving him several stout pats. "The beer will be as cold as ever it lasts. An' you an' your old mate can catch up, an' tell me stories of your adventures in the coffin business."

"Indeed, I shall, an' I shall look forward to it." Noah gave

Oliver a slanted smile and a wink. "You an' me in front of the fireplace, just like old times, Work'us?"

Oliver had clamped his mouth so firmly closed that he could not speak. But Jack was watching, so hopeful and expectant, that Oliver made himself nod. He didn't know why he had stayed this long or listened to even one word of what Noah had to say. Perhaps Jack's world was so different from the haberdashery shop that it invited, by mere curiosity, further inspection.

"Don't mind him, Noah," said Jack, emphasizing the new name with a nod. "He's a little wound, comin' in here, steppin' like he were a thief comin' into a den of peelers and traps, instead of the other way around!"

This lively statement earned Jack a roar of approval from Noah, who also delivered more thumps to Oliver's shoulders. Oliver could only scowl and didn't stop, even though something flitted across Jack's eyes. Surely Jack knew that all was not right. That Oliver and Noah were not friends, never had been. Never would be.

Jack shook Noah's hand and watched him go, turning to Oliver with a broad smile.

"Fancy you knowin' him, Nolly. Why did you never say?"

"You said his name was Morris Bolter," said Oliver. His mouth felt stiff; in fact, all of him did, with the shock of Noah's return. "I only ever knew him as Noah Claypole."

This made Jack nod, as if the sense of it were all very clear to him now.

"Still, it's strange, ain't it? That our paths all cross here, at the Three Cripples?"

It did seem rather strange, though Oliver let this thought distract him for only a moment. The immediate concerns of whether or not this visit with Jack and Noah would suffice outweighed the more philosophical question of how different rivers of time could carry twigs from different mountains to the same gritty pond.

Jack waved over a serving of beer, still smiling, as though

pleased that Oliver was wrong, that Fagin's gang was coming back to the Three Cripples at long last. Back to Jack.

Oliver stood up to leave, but was stopped as a man came into the alcove to stand beside their table. He was tall, his broad shoulders stretching the thick cotton of his shirt near to the breaking point. His stained waistcoat gaped open from a missing button. He had a scarf around his neck, as many working men did. But what stood him out was the mass of curly, dark hair that hung low over his eyes, and a broken tooth when he smiled.

"Who's this, then, dear Jack, as has come visitin' amongst us?" The man's voice was ragged, as though he'd been punched in the throat one too many times.

"This here's my friend, Oliver Twist," said Jack, and while Oliver wanted to object to the term, he didn't; the man was looking at him too hard, with sharp eyes that probably saw how Oliver twitched and tried not to shift away. "I've known him since before I was hextricated, you see, and now, well, he's come by to visit, ain't you, Nolly?"

Oliver nodded. He didn't hold out his hand to shake because, in this sort of place, with these sorts of people, it simply wasn't done. Greetings were shouts and slaps on the back, an elbow in the ribs. At least that's what he'd seen in his travels, such as they were.

The man held out his hand; Oliver could see calluses along his fingers and the edge of his palm that spoke of handling tools.

"Cromwell, they call me. Never had a first name, though I might pick one sometime."

There was nothing for Oliver to do but shake the hand in return. Cromwell's skin across his palm felt like worn wood left out in the sun, and he pulled his hand away as fast as he was able. The feeling reminded him of the time he'd been with Bill Sikes and Toby Crackit on a job to rob a house of all its silver plate.

"Well, I'm off, then," said Cromwell with a toss of his curls. "Jack, you come by later about that job. An' bring your friend, if he's interested. There's plenty we could do with such a pretty face as that."

Jack nodded his assent and smiled at Oliver as Cromwell left.

"A beer for you?" Jack asked. He seemed to take it for granted that since Oliver was there, he might stay awhile.

"No," said Oliver, all at once feeling the boundaries between their respective lives as clear as daylight. "I've got work to do. For unlike some, I've a job, and a station in life that I aim to keep."

Jack took the pot of beer that was served to him, but he was scowling now, and Oliver realized he might have made a mistake in making Jack angry. And just when he was on the verge of getting Jack out of his life forever.

"And I'm sure you have more important things to do as well," said Oliver. He tugged at his scarf and adjusted his cap. "More important than entertaining the likes of me. It's just that—"

Oliver broke off, not knowing quite how to put it. Though he questioned his own gentleness with Jack, he could not afford to have Jack stomping through his life, breaking it apart just as Oliver was building it up.

"You're not to worry, it's my word," said Jack, after a swallow of beer. "I've given it. Won't go back on it, even if you are an arse."

Oliver nodded and turned to go. But Jack tugged on his jacket, just once, as if to make Oliver stay. Picking up his empty basket, Oliver made himself pause to hear what Jack wanted to say. It wasn't his fault that Morris Bolter turned out to be one of the few people Oliver hated with every breath in his body.

"You're always welcome, though," Jack said, and for once he seemed in earnest. He evidenced no winking or smirking or larking about as though the whole thing was one big joke. "For some hot gin an' sugar, a break from that fancy life of yours. I could show you my tattoo, an' we could be swappin' stories, an' that. You reckon?"

"I doubt it," said Oliver. He kept his voice low. "But thank you."

He tipped his cap at Jack and then turned to plow his way through the crowd that had assembled in the main room. The faces in the throng of men all turned to watch him, as though surprised to find him there. And if that was so, then they were as surprised as he. For though he must have been in or near the Three Cripples at some point when Fagin held him, he did not remember any of it. And now, he felt he might not forget it.

## ❧ 16 ❧

## THE CONSEQUENCES OF A
## BROKEN STOVE

For several days, Oliver felt something sharp in his chest at the memory of Noah Claypole and his oily smile, and of Jack, so happy that Fagin's gang was, in his mind, getting back together again. Everything at the shop, however, and in spite of Oliver's distracted thoughts, went on as usual, with work in the warehouse, cleaning the front steps and pavement, and making deliveries. Each night, at the table in the warm kitchen, with Mr. McCready and the boys, and Mrs. Pierson bustling about, Oliver would try to read from his book of poems, or even one of the children's books, but his eyes would close as the candlelight started to gutter while Tate and Henry muttered at each other and scratched on slates, and Mr. McCready scowled at the newspaper.

When it started to get cold again, and his chance to get out of the shop abated, he worked with Tate in the warehouse, creating new record books by lining ledgers with a piece of lead and a ruler to make the lines straight. Tate admired Oliver's workmanship, though he wouldn't yet let Oliver write in any of the record books regarding the stock. That was Tate's job, and he was very jealous of his position.

Oliver looked at Tate and thought, suddenly, how different he was from Jack. Or from himself. Or from Uncle Brownlow, for that matter. Uncle Brownlow, who was unfailingly polite to one and all and who never reflected even the slightest bit of jealousy toward his fellow man.

Sadness came at Oliver, a slamming weight, and seemed almost too much to bear. He hadn't felt this way for days, so why now? Why this sudden, dark grief? He paused at the bottom of the warehouse stairs as though adjusting his apron and turned away toward the wall, telling himself that now was not the time. To cry over Uncle Brownlow and that life he once knew was to lose touch with that life; while the memory hurt, it was still fresh. And mixed with that was the recent dredging up of Noah Claypole, somebody who Oliver had never expected to see again in his life. Then there was Jack; Oliver had no idea what to do with his uncertain feelings about Jack.

He took a deep breath and turned back toward the warehouse, toward the balm that untold hearts before him had found, that of industry. Thankfully, there were always shelves to dust, floors to sweep, and the pavement in front of the shop to keep clear of snow and dirt. Tape to hold up stockings had to be rushed to Henry in the shop, and the lady patrons who braved the cold, as always, needed something desperately, something they could have done without, but would never suffer themselves to do so: corset strings, a new hat pin, garters for their husbands.

For all of his deliveries, either quick and close by or most of the way across London, Oliver took particular care with any deliveries to Number 14 Doughty Street. He did not want to see Mrs. Acton again, let alone be put in a position where he'd have to detach her claws from his arm. Mostly, he did not want to give her any excuse to complain to Mr. McCready about how he'd behaved with her. She'd proven herself to be flighty and cruel, so when there were packages for her, Oliver made sure to go down to the kitchen area to make his deliveries.

And, as ever, with relaxing regularity, deliveries came through the tall gates at the back of the yard, and the goods were accounted for as they came off flat-bedded wagons or high-sided carts. Horses stomped over the cobblestones in the yard, chipping the edges and leaving their droppings and puddles of urine. Oliver poured himself into tending to all of it, wanting to be exhausted at bedtime.

AT THE END OF THE WEEK, OLIVER WOKE TO THE COLD AND the sound of rain smacking on the windowpane. He got up and washed his face in the cold water in the basin, not rolling up the sleeves of his nightshirt as far as the scar, as always, so that neither Henry nor Tate would have any questions to ask. Then he hurriedly dressed in the chill air and tagged behind Henry and Tate down the stairs to the kitchen to find Mrs. Pierson red-faced, hair trailing in wisps against her cheeks, quite unlike her. There was dust on her chin and on her white starched apron. The stove was boiling with smoke that filled the room. Standing next to her, Mr. McCready pressed his mouth tightly together as he listened to her through her tears.

"Last night was bad enough, with that girl taking off the way she did. I let it go and did the washing up myself. But *today*? She never even showed up, so by the time I came down, there's no stove lit, no hot water going, no breakfast set out for me to cook, and so now it's only me with all the shopping and cooking *and* cleaning!"

"I'll get you a new girl," said Mr. McCready, in a tight way that told Oliver that he was struggling to keep his voice calm. For if he lost his temper, then Mrs. Pierson would surely lose hers, and they would lose a cook and a housekeeper, something Oliver couldn't imagine was easily replaceable in the middle of winter.

"It won't be enough!" Mrs. Pierson's voice rose as Oliver had never heard it. "I've been struggling with stiffness and aches and pains this past year, so it's not enough! You may sack me if you will, this moment if you must, but I cannot abide those stairs another day. Let alone carrying coal and cleaning three fireplaces and hauling hot water, day after day—"

She broke off, clutching her handkerchief to her mouth.

Oliver looked at Henry and Tate and they at him, and none of them dared move, let alone laugh, not while smoke loomed over the room. Presently, Oliver determined to open the door to the kitchen area, which he did. The smoke eased out while the colder air from the street rushed in.

Mr. McCready looked like he wanted to comfort Mrs. Pierson somehow, but one didn't actually touch a housekeeper, let alone hug her. At least not in Mr. McCready's book. Had this been his old nurse Mrs. Bedwin sobbing into her handkerchief, Oliver would have run to her without a thought and wrapped his arms around her and begged her not to cry and for her to tell him what was wrong and what he might do to fix it. The memory was so strong he could almost feel Mrs. Bedwin's pillowy bosom beneath his cheek, and the edges of her white muslin pelerine against his skin. *Tell me what I can do to aid you, my dear Mrs. Bedwin, and I shall fix it at once.*

"Oliver."

Oliver snapped to attentiveness, focusing his eyes on Mr. McCready, though it took him some seconds longer to force the image of Mrs. Bedwin away and concentrate once again on Mrs. Pierson. Who, though just as respectable and as kind, would never have the creamy, grandmotherly softness of Mrs. Bedwin.

"Oliver, pay attention and close that door. It is quite fresh in here."

Oliver blinked a few times and then did as he was told, all the while sensing Henry and Tate shuffling from foot to foot, seeming at a loss as to whether they should sit down or depart.

"My dear Mrs. Pierson—Henry, make her a pot of tea—do sit down, Mrs. Pierson."

Mrs. Pierson sat down, something Oliver had rarely seen her

do, even in her own kitchen. She sat in a chair at the end of the table, her respectable black skirts fanned out around her, and her apron crumpled in her lap. She wiped her eyes with her handkerchief and seemed to compose herself.

"There won't be any tea, because the stove won't light. 'Tis broken!"

"The stove won't light?" Mr. McCready seemed astonished by this, in spite of the roiling smoke.

"It's been broken for weeks now," said Mrs. Pierson in a cracked voice.

"But it worked just yesterday."

"That girl had a knack, which is why—"

"But why did you not tell me the stove was broken, Mrs. Pierson? And how long has it been thus?"

Her handkerchief now soaked, Mrs. Pierson buried her face in her apron and sobbed anew. Henry and Tate inched toward the stairs. Oliver remained frozen where he was, mesmerized. He'd never seen anyone collapse in this way.

"Because I broke it just after Christmas, and I didn't want you to dismiss me."

Mr. McCready's mouth flew open and, for a moment, no one said anything. Indeed, Oliver didn't know what could be said. But the situation was desperate, even he could see that. Mrs. Pierson was the best cook, bar none, with a sure hand at roasting a chicken or making a crust for an apple tart that melted on the tongue. If McCready's Haberdashery lost her, they would be hard pressed to find another like her.

Mr. McCready sat at the table next to Mrs. Pierson, and reached out to pat her arm, but then, at the last moment, pulled back.

"My dear Mrs. Pierson," he said, as gently as he might to one of his most timid customers. "That stove is not the youngest of its kind, I'm afraid, and even the stoutest of metal can suffer wear and tear."

Mrs. Pierson used the edge of her apron to dry her eyes. She looked at him, a little color coming back to her streaked face.

"But who will fix it? And what about—"

"I will send for a blacksmith to fix the stove."

"What if it can't be fixed?"

"Then we shall get a new one."

"And the stairs? What about them? I can't take all those stairs any longer."

"We'll get you a hired girl. A respectable one from the Collins Agency, you know the one."

Oliver wondered if there had ever been a risk of saying good-bye to those mouthwatering pies or if this had been a ploy of Mrs. Pierson's all along. For there seemed to be a small glint in her eyes; the cold kitchen and lack of anything to eat—the whole of it was too grand a tableau for a woman who planned her day's cooking and cleaning as though she was an army general. It was a grand scheme indeed to get what she wanted; if not a new stove, then a working one. And not just some help, but a reliable girl, a top-notch girl from a top-notch agency.

"Those types are too haughty for words," said Mrs. Pierson. But she was sitting up straight now, tucking her dark hair back under her cap. She almost seemed to smile as she said, "Too haughty to take orders from a common housekeeper and cook, and with hands too fine to clean a stove, let alone light it. I've seen girls from that agency; too haughty for words, I tell you."

"We'll get you a boy as well," said Mr. McCready. "He can take care of the lower sort of work."

Oliver could see it as if it had already been done. If Mrs. Pierson had a hired girl from the Collins Agency, and a boy as well, she would be able to lord it over her friends and other housekeepers along the lane. Not only that, she would be able to drop it in casual conversation after church.

"I put it to you, Mrs. Pierson: you shall dress in your best, this very day, and with a clean face, go to Collins and select the girl yourself."

"But what about breakfast?"

Mrs. Pierson looked up, as if suddenly seeing the three apprentice boys standing there amidst the wreck of the cold and ash-dusted kitchen. Apprentices she looked after going hungry? *Perish* the thought. Mr. McCready looked up at them also, regarding them each with a solemn eye.

"We have a reputation to uphold, Mrs. Pierson. No girl is too fine for this establishment. You go and sign up whomever you please. And in the meantime, Henry and Tate and Oliver shall have—"

"There is no food, Mr. McCready," said Mrs. Pierson. She stood up, tucking her handkerchief into her apron pocket, from which she pulled out a piece of paper. "There is only what can be cooked, which nothing can be. The last of the loaf of bread went at tea time yesterday, and this is my shopping list. There is simply nothing to eat."

She held out the scrap of paper, as though it were a ticket of admittance.

Mr. McCready stood up at this, almost smiling. He reached into the pocket on the inside of his jacket and pulled out his change purse, from which he counted some coins.

"Boys, come here." When they did, he handed them each a tuppence. "You'll have coffee and bread on the street till the stove is fixed today."

To Mrs. Pierson, he handed a five-pound note before putting his wallet back in his inside jacket pocket. "This is for the groceries and the girl; if she costs more, put it on account. Have the girl help you with the shopping on your way back from the agency."

"And the coal?" asked Mrs. Pierson smartly as she folded the bill in her hand. "Who will carry that?"

Oliver's mouth was watering at the thought of coffee and buttered bread from a street vendor. Mrs. Pierson's bread was, of course, miles above the rest. But there was something about sipping hot dark coffee from a metal cup while standing in the street as a cold wind whistled past. It made the coffee warmer and more darkly rich somehow. And the buttered bread, slightly coarse and so sweet, between sips of dark coffee. Then, of course, the last time he'd stood at a coffee vendor's was with Jack when he'd stolen Oliver's pennies.

Jack had smacked his lips over that stolen repast, his mouth glistening with butter, puffs of coffee-flavored steam exuding from his mouth with each chomp. He'd only laughed when Oliver had reached for his red scarf; Oliver had known he'd never get it back. But the memory of the smell of the hot coffee and Jack's still-new presence had struck him all the days since, and as it did now, in the midst of such a domestic ruckus.

"Henry and Tate will put a sign in the window, keeping the shop closed till noon. And then they will go to Mueller's down on Broad Street and tell him of the stove and hire his services."

Again, Mr. McCready's words broke through Oliver's reverie. His empty palm reflected the fact that Mr. McCready had not given Oliver tuppence, as he had Henry and Tate.

"And what shall I do, sir?" he asked, thinking that Mr. McCready might have him sort through the new stock in the warehouse. The little box stove there worked, at least, and the peace and quiet might be nice.

"You and I shall tend to the matter of a boy," said Mr. McCready. "We'll go to St. James's Workhouse over on Poland Street; they'll like as not have something."

Oliver nodded, though his feet felt cold, as though someone had dropped him in the icy water of the Thames.

It didn't take him but a moment to recall that the workhouse at St. James was the closest. He'd passed it sometimes when making his deliveries, and when he couldn't avoid going past it, he averted his eyes. His only picture of the place was from sideways glances: the severe, dark-grey roofline and the dark-green paint on the pointed iron gates, the semicircular sign above the gate, iron letters spelling out the name.

He looked up at Mr. McCready, mouth working as he tried to

come up with a single thought that he could turn into an utterance that might excuse him from such an errand.

"Caps and coats and scarves, boys," said Mr. McCready. He gave Mrs. Pierson a slight nod. "Get the finest girl you can hire, Mrs. Pierson. Come along, Oliver, we've a boy to find."

Feeling numb from the waist up, his feet frozen and heavy, Oliver followed Mr. McCready up the stairs to the small back hallway. There he gathered his cap and his brown coat and green scarf, which still felt new and stiff against his neck, but at least it was warm.

They stepped out the front door and shut it firmly behind them; the day was quite rainy and almost cold enough for snow. With the rain beating down on the top of his cap, Oliver shivered. A low dread began to fill him as they headed toward the lane where St. James's steeple broke above the sharp, slate-covered roofs. The bell began tolling nine o'clock, and with each tone, Oliver shuddered. He'd lived all of his life within earshot of one bell or another, but this was the first time he'd felt that the sound was something fearsome, marking, rather than the hour or a call to prayers, a call to some more awful fate.

"You look a trifle pale, Oliver. Shall we stop for a bite to eat?"

They were passing the Crown and Mitre on Broad Street, a higher class tavern than the Three Cripples could ever hope to be, and just then the door opened to push out the smell of something hot frying, pork perhaps, and the smoky warmth of pipes being smoked. Mr. McCready led the way in through the push of people, mostly gentlemen in dark coats, not waiting for Oliver's reply.

Perhaps he did not need one, for it appeared that if one was with the master, one didn't breakfast on mere coffee and two slices of buttered bread. Perhaps, also, it was the emptiness of Oliver's stomach that was filling him with such unease. Usually by this hour, he was well finished with his breakfast. His unusual sense of fear, then, was hunger and nothing more. He told himself this.

A pleasant woman in a starched apron and cap led them to a table near the fire and brought two china cups of coffee without being asked. Oliver lifted the cup with both hands and took a tentative sip. Since it was early in the day, the coffee was newly brewed, so it tasted sweet with sugar rather than being bitter.

Mr. McCready ordered cold meat and whatever bread was just come out of the oven. Then Oliver and Mr. McCready both sipped their coffee, holding onto their cups with both hands, warming their fingers. They shared a silent moment, enjoying the cheer of the fire and the convivial company of the warm room.

The food came, slices of cold ham and twisted, crusty bread so warm the butter dripped off the slice that Oliver prepared for himself. As he stuffed it in his mouth, he thought that this surely was much better than standing in the street drinking from a metal cup. Better and warmer and surely more respectable. But he was enjoying almost none of it.

"This workhouse boy," said Mr. McCready, cutting up slices of ham with a clink of his knife on the plate. "He can do the rough work so you won't have coal dust all over you when you go out for deliveries. What do you say to that?"

Oliver tried to keep his face a complete blank and to keep eating. But he felt the blood rushing around inside of him, doing something harsh that made him want to spit out what he had in his mouth. His fingers and toes had gone numb besides. He did not want to step foot inside a workhouse, let alone go to one to acquire a boy to do the rough work. He knew how it would go, *exactly* how it would begin, and afterward, how it would be. Workhouse boys were grimy little creatures, despised by all and pitied by none.

Mr. McCready was a genial enough man when things were going as he wanted them, but Oliver knew the truth of it. The orphan they acquired would be scrawny to begin with. He would do all the drudge work and be subject to the most basic of care, if that, and Mr. McCready wouldn't think anything of it.

That's simply how workhouse boys were treated and, after all, the workhouse always had plenty more to spare. Not to mention that Oliver would be required to look at that face, where he would see his own past, twisting along a long, scarred string, leading right back to Hardingstone and Mrs. Mann's baby farm, and to Dick, who he'd last seen weeding in a garden. He'd done his very best to forget about Dick, with his angled face and thin shoulders and a heart so good it shone from beneath his rags. Oliver shuddered all over.

"Oliver, I'm speaking to you."

Oliver could only look at him as he forced himself to swallow the tasteless mass in his mouth.

"I must say, I would have expected you to be more excited about the prospect, for it will, in a way, take you up a notch up in the shop. You'll no longer be the newest boy, eh?"

"Yes," said Oliver, though his voice sounded faint to his own ears. "It's just that—"

He paused, thinking of a way to make it comprehensible to Mr. McCready, but he could not explain how he felt every time he passed the gates of a workhouse. Or how it made him tense up to see a small boy or a young girl in the street who, by their clothes and demeanor, were instantly recognizable as being very poor and probably hungry. Each time, Oliver had to fight against the hope of doing anything about it.

It wasn't just the chimney sweeps or the crossing boys or boys hauling carts much too large and heavy for their skinny arms. It wasn't just the beggars, or those faded, grey-faced girls selling useless trinkets from trays slung from their necks. It wasn't even what they did or didn't do—it was *all* of them, the look in their eyes, their sunken cheeks and unwashed faces. He didn't want to be around it at all, and up till the time of Uncle Brownlow's death, he'd been able to avoid anything that smacked of his old life. Until now.

"I sense you are uncomfortable with workhouses, Oliver," said Mr. McCready. His gaze was steady and his eyes solemn as he put down his knife and fork. "Mr. Grimwig indicated to me you suffered badly at the workhouse you came from. And I imagine you still suffer mental anguish at the death of the guardian who took you from that life."

Mr. McCready took a sip of his coffee and scanned the room with its dark-coated customers. They were mostly men, but there were two black-garbed women at the table near the window, partaking of a small meal of meat pies and sliced fruit.

"I am coming to realize that you are loath to have anything to do with our business this morning, the way your brow looks as though it were lowered by some oncoming doom. But not all workhouses are fully bad, Oliver. Don't you see? They do a great deal of good for the indigent and the poor. If we take a boy, surely he'll be treated better among us. And, with food and useful work, surely he will be a more productive member of society?"

Oliver wanted to stand and shove the table back and shout that Mr. McCready didn't have any idea what he was talking about. Because if Mr. McCready thought workhouses did a *great deal of good*, then Mr. McCready might as well be living with his head in a barrel. Workhouses did nothing good, nothing of the sort. They stripped the soul and beat hope out of the body, and starved and smacked and locked up any gentleness till all that was left were the bones and some rude, leftover animation to keep those bones going till they dropped.

But though his heart was beating fast, Oliver kept his hands in his lap and his jaw stiff. He looked at Mr. McCready as steadily as he could.

"Must I go, sir?"

"Yes, Oliver, you must. For who knows more about work-house boys than you? I need your keen eye. Finish up, and then we'll be off."

Oliver felt Mr. McCready's eyes on him. He made himself eat and respond to a polite request for the salt.

"All is well, Oliver?" asked Mr. McCready, at one point.

"Yes, sir," said Oliver, trying for an assuredness that would stop Mr. McCready from looking at him in that way and asking Oliver questions he couldn't possibly respond truthfully to. "It's just a little strange, going back like this."

"Indeed, it must be," said Mr. McCready.

## ❧ 17 ❧

# TREATS OF ST. JAMES'S
# WORKHOUSE AND THE ORPHAN

Oliver wanted to drag his feet as he walked beside Mr. McCready, but it wouldn't do. If Mr. McCready noticed Oliver's reluctance, it would give a lie to Oliver's assertion that he wasn't troubled by this errand to acquire a likely boy.

What was doubly disconcerting was the fact that Mr. McCready and Mr. Grimwig had exchanged words about Oliver, which he'd not known until now. Whether that exchange had been by post or in person didn't matter; either way, Mr. Grimwig would have cast Oliver in a less than sterling light. Even more unnerving was the fact that Mr. Grimwig had noticed Oliver's fear of workhouses, and seen it enough to understand it, and communicate it to another person.

Yes, Oliver was conscious of having crossed over to the other side of the street, however broad or narrow, rather than having to pass in front of the gate to *any* workhouse. And yes, he'd skirt quickly past blind beggars. He ignored every ragged woman, there was one on every corner it seemed, who held out her little one, bundled in a hemp sack, tiny bare feet exposed, stained with mud and blue with cold, and begged with a loud voice devoid of shame and broken with worry. Or the little girl in her shabby broken bonnet who he'd seen often on the corner near the haberdashery; he'd ignored her too. Ignored her proffered silk flower drawn from a basket, a tumble of purple and pink against the grey snow where she'd set it down.

Besides that, all the beggars smelled—of dirt from the streets, from barefoot walks through overflowing basement cesspits. With mud dried on every part of their sparse clothing, they all had the dark tang of unwashed skin spotted with sores. A penny's worth of good soap and hot water would have done miracles for many, but Oliver had none to spare. Never did, never would. But still, they looked at him, speculative and with hopeful eyes, begging him to search his pockets, his heart.

He'd rushed past them all, never handing out so much as a farthing; he'd been in the same circumstances, and look how far he'd come. Let them all pull themselves out of their respective gutters, as Oliver Twist had.

St. James's Workhouse loomed in front of them before Oliver was properly ready. The building rose, grey and hard, above the walls surrounding it, and from behind the wrought-iron gate, which was spiked with a half circle above proclaiming the name. There were more iron spikes embellishing the top of the stone wall that ran all the way around the workhouse grounds, walls to keep people out or in at the parish's pleasure, it didn't matter the reason why. The spikes made a boundary between the two worlds, between hopelessness and hope, though the hopelessness continually oozed into the street, reaching Oliver in a way that he'd known for nine years of his life before leaving it behind.

Mr. McCready rang the bell-pull at the gate and waited, looking down at Oliver with a benign smile. All was well with Mr. McCready, of course; in his mind, he was performing a duty that had a dual benefit to the world around him. The first was relieving the parish of its obligation to a pauper, and the second was providing his newest apprentice with a trial by fire that could only prove to be to his benefit. Oliver could see this in Mr. McCready's eyes, in the cordial way he greeted the stiff-collared porter at the gate, in the polite way he announced their business there.

"We've got a number of likely lads," said the porter. "Come away into the office and we can discuss the particulars."

Oliver's whole body felt tight as he followed Mr. McCready and the porter across the cobbles of the forecourt, his eyes briefly alighting on the female paupers all around. They were dressed as he once had been, in brown uniforms, but it was not the same as the rich, deep, warm brown he now wore. No, the pauper's brown was faded, as if even the dye had been too meager of strength to do more than stain the cloth. Their faces were thin and pale, their unwashed hair covered with grey caps.

Oliver raised his eyes to look once into one face, but it was too upsetting. After a fleeting second of seeing that hopeless, *hopeless* hungry expression, he had to look away. Thereafter, he kept his eyes down, looking only at the hem of Mr. McCready's greatcoat or the steepled clasp of his own hands. It was safer. It provided no chance for any pauper to look back at him.

Once inside the building, the porter led them down a short, dark hallway to his office, which was a small room with two tall sash windows crossed with bars on the outside. There was a shelf with around ten books and a large table that served as a desk. The porter invited them to sit in the two chairs across from him.

Once seated, Oliver pulled off his cap and let—no, *forced*—his mind to wander. He didn't want to participate in the conversation about a boy. *A likely lad*, the porter was saying, *of about ten years or so, the going rate, five pounds, of course.*

Suddenly, the whole outing felt as though it resembled a sale of flesh from the devil. He clamped his jaw shut, feeling his stomach roll. Not wanting to think of it now, not wanting to remember it as it had happened then.

*"Dear me, he's very small."*

*"Why, he is rather small; he is small. There's no denying. But he'll grow, Mrs. Sowerberry, he'll grow."*

*"Ah! I dare say he will on our victuals and our drink. I see no saving*

*in parish children, not I; for they always cost more to keep than they're worth. However, men always think they know best. There! Get down stairs, little bag o' bones."*

The memory felt as though someone had slapped him right across his face, bare skin stinging with the echo of those words. Mrs. Sowerberry had never liked him, and while it seemed at the time that nobody had, she was so intent with her hatred and scorn that she had never hesitated in letting him know it.

The porter clapped open a ledger, and Oliver started in his chair. His eyes were riveted as the porter ran his finger down the page.

"Yes, this is the one," said the porter. "Martin, aged ten. Christian name, Gregory. As for the parents, well, the mother dropped him off last summer and never came back for him. He's not as rough as most; he should do for you very nicely."

Mr. McCready took his wallet out of the breast pocket of his suitcoat and unfolded it. He crinkled the five-pound note between his fingers a moment before he handed it over. The porter took the note, laid it on the desk, and pulled out a sheet of paper. He picked up his pen and dipped it in ink, then looked at Mr. McCready as he tapped off the excess.

"We'll make it for three months to ensure he suits. Will that do, Mr. McCready?"

"Will that do, Oliver?" asked Mr. McCready, breaking through the cloud around Oliver's head. "Oliver?"

Oliver blinked and ran his fingers across the brow band of his cap. Telling himself that he'd not lost all feeling in his hand from clutching the cap too tightly.

"Looks a bit reluctant, sir," said the porter.

"Oliver? You have been asked a question, and you would do well to answer it."

Now Oliver had to look up and focus to take in the expectant faces of the porter and Mr. McCready. To see the five-pound note, a shining, gold-edged white bit of thick paper on the dark blotter on the porter's desk. To see the sensible, plain wallpaper framing the sash windows that looked out into a small yard surrounded by walls of grey stone. The meager light could barely get in through the glass, and beyond that, there was another wall of stone through which no one could get out.

His throat went dry, and the two faces in front of him began to swim in a hazy way, back and forth. He felt Mr. McCready's hands on his shoulders and realized Mr. McCready was standing in front of him. He felt a light tap on his cheek.

"Oliver! What's wrong with you, are you ill?"

Oliver heard the question from a distance, as though his whole body was falling through air, toward the sound of Mr. McCready's voice and then away from it at the same time. He felt the rush of cold as wood slid against wood, and he realized that the porter had opened the window. Oliver took a deep gasp of air and tried to narrow in on Mr. McCready's voice.

"I had the windows closed against the morning chill," said the porter. "It does get somewhat stuffy in here; I do apologize."

"It's nothing," said Mr. McCready. "Oliver, are you all right now?"

Oliver sat up and nodded. "Yes, sir, it was just the close air. I'm all right now."

His face was turning hot at the thought that he'd almost fainted simply because he was sitting in the porter's office of the St. James's Workhouse, waiting for an orphan to be brought to them so they could take him home and put him to hard labor. Starve or feed him as they would. Cheap at any price.

The porter opened the door, bringing another waft of air, this one redolent of dust and damp and laundry soap too strongly applied. Oliver wanted to itch as he remembered that feeling of stiff wool prickling his skin after the laundry was done. But he didn't; young gentlemen didn't scratch themselves in public, so he sat stiffly, hands clamped on the edges of his seat.

The workhouse matron appeared; Oliver knew it was the matron from her enormous starched cap and broad white apron, the chatelaine of keys dangling from her waist. By her hand she pulled a small boy, dressed in workhouse brown. Oliver had a glimpse of untidy dark hair and enormous brown eyes before he made himself look away.

"This here's Martin Gregory," said the matron, her voice curling stiffly around what she probably presumed were cultured tones. "He ain't got much to say, but he should be of some use to you."

She let go of the little boy's hand and shoved him in their direction. The boy came right at Oliver, it seemed, for the boy's thin garment brushed Oliver's knee and the tiny hand almost rested there.

Oliver lunged to his feet and stepped away, shuddering, brushing imaginary dust from his cap.

"Go along with the gentlemen, Martin, and do as you're told, for I certainly don't want to see you back here."

Martin nodded, eyes wide with trepidation. He held out his hand, held it up for someone to take.

Oliver's eyes grew hot, and he looked away and promised himself he'd pretend the orphan wasn't even there.

Orphan? What orphan? There was only the shop and Mr. McCready and the lads, Henry and Tate. There was Oliver himself, working hard at being the best apprentice shopkeeper London had ever seen. And Jack, there was Jack, of course, causing trouble as he always did.

Oliver focused on shared moments with Jack, and they sprang brightly in his mind. Jack and his snapping grin were a perfect distraction, and they allowed Oliver to follow Mr. McCready and the small figure he towed by one hand. Out of the porter's office, across the yard, and through the gate. It was only then, when his boots hit the paving stones outside the yard, that Oliver felt he could draw a deep breath once more.

～

THEY ARRIVED AT THE HABERDASHERY JUST AS HENRY AND Tate did, and Mr. McCready motioned for them all to go down to the kitchen. Mrs. Pierson awaited them, gesturing to the newly fixed stove. Then, with several *tut tuts* and *my mys*, she called for the new girl. The new girl came forth, a round and rosy-faced, sensible thing with a dark blue dress covered with a white apron; her shining golden hair was tucked under a starched white cap.

"This is Lucy. She's as stout as a mountain pony," said Mrs. Pierson, politely trying to hide her smile and failing. "Get that tub now, and let me know if you can't find that cleansing soda."

The girl went down the corridor to the laundry, fetched the tin bath and put it near the stove, went out again, and carried in two buckets of hot water with no more effort than she might have taken to lift a sheet of paper to write a letter.

Mrs. Pierson pulled the orphan by the hand into the middle of the kitchen.

"Come along, you," she said, and began unbuttoning his shirt collar to divest him of his garments. "Let's get these lice and this dirt off you before you track it all through the house."

Oliver escaped up the wooden stairs to the ground floor. He took off his jacket and cap and pulled on his apron. He went out to the chilly warehouse and turned to Tate, who'd been following him.

"It's my turn to clean the yard from where yesterday's wagons and horses have been," said Oliver, grabbing the shovel and the bucket.

"What?" asked Tate, not hiding his surprise that Oliver was volunteering for the most loathsome of tasks even though it wasn't his turn.

"Yes, I'm going to do that and sweep the warehouse, and then I'll help you count stock."

"You're going to—but what about—?"

"I'll do everything else, but I won't go past the kitchen for more coal for the warehouse, Tate, you understand?"

Tate nodded. He didn't look as though he was going to protest, let alone question Oliver's demands. It had been an easy day for him already, Oliver knew, and no apprentice worth his salt would be likely to complain about more of that continuing.

∽

OLIVER SCRUBBED AND SWEPT AND COUNTED AND DID NOT allow himself to think. By the supper hour, when Mrs. Pierson actually had to come out to the warehouse to call him in, Oliver felt he'd worked off most of the tenseness in his shoulders. He followed her in obediently and doffed his apron before clattering downstairs. But as he washed in the basin by the wall, he caught sight of everyone already seated around the table, looking at him, somewhat puzzled at his tardiness as he sat down.

As Mr. McCready said grace, Oliver bent his head and clasped his hands. Out of the corner of his eyes, he saw the orphan, who sat on a tall stool next to the sideboard, a meager plate of food at his elbow. His face and hair and brown clothes were much cleaner than they had been before, but his eyes were still wide. He did not involve himself with grace, but instead was looking at Mr. McCready's back with some apprehension. Certainly it had been made clear to him his standing in the haberdashery.

When Mr. McCready said *amen*, Oliver spared a glance at Mrs. Pierson, noting that her mouth was down-turned with displeasure. She served them her good, hot food, apron twitching, serving ladle clanging against china, and it was then Oliver realized why the room was filled with nothing but silence.

First, there was a spare seat at the table next to Henry, but it was obvious by the rigid line of Mr. McCready's back that the orphan wasn't to be allowed to sit with the master and his apprentices. Fair enough; Oliver didn't know of any master, fair or cruel, who would allow a mere pauper such liberties.

But second, the orphan wasn't to eat as the rest of them did.

The orphan had, Oliver could see, a single slice of unbuttered bread and a bowl of the stew Mrs. Pierson had served to them all, but other than a mug of plain water, that was it. He had no boiled potatoes, no buttered peas, no steaming pile of carrots.

Likewise, it was easy to presume that the orphan would not and would never be allowed to partake in the pudding and custard that were always the delight of anybody who'd ever been privileged to sit at Mrs. Pierson's table. Hence Mrs. Pierson's displeasure. She lived to feed, and to be denied that, especially to one who could benefit so greatly from it, well, that was tantamount to having to go hungry herself.

Oliver made himself concentrate on his own plate and on the good food there and not on the orphan. Who although he was apparently trying to be as unobtrusive as possible, his skinny elbows tucked at his sides, nevertheless tore into the plain bread and drank the stew from his spoon noisily, in big gulps, as if he'd not been fed, not properly anyway, perhaps for years.

When the orphan finished, he set the bowl back down on the sideboard with a rude clunk. Mrs. Pierson jumped up, spoon at the ready to give him a second helping. Oliver felt something in his chest loosen as he watched her.

"No, Mrs. Pierson," said Mr. McCready, holding up one hand firmly. "He will eat what he is given and nothing more. He is only a workhouse boy, after all."

"What about scraps?" asked Mrs. Pierson, her voice sharp, as if the orphan had been begging for hours, and she come to her last reserve of politeness. "Surely we can spare a bit of potato peelings and bacon grease, as there is only so much I can sell."

Mr. McCready studied the table, looked at the plates and cutlery.

"If the boys leave anything on their plates," he said carefully, as if wanting to make himself quite clear, "then the orphan may have that. But nothing else, mind."

"Very well, Mr. McCready," said Mrs. Pierson. She nodded, smoothing her apron as she put down the serving ladle, which she'd not been allowed to use, on the table next to the soup tureen. By her frown and crinkled brow, it was apparent to everyone that she was not happy about it.

Oliver looked down at his plate. His stomach was tight even at the thought of the sweet pudding to come. Beneath his carefully laid cloth napkin, his knees were shaking. But in spite of this, he picked up his knife and fork and proceeded to eat everything in front of him. Every bite. Even the peas, and he loathed and despised peas.

～

WHEN IT WAS TIME FOR BED, THE NEW GIRL, LUCY, HAD LEFT enough hot water in the pitcher in the boys' attic room that there was no squabbling over the basin. They each took their turn.

Oliver went last because he was still the new boy. But for the first time since his arrival, when Oliver poured Tate's leavings into the slop bucket, there was enough hot water for him to have an entire basin to wash with. He used it all, and a great deal of soap besides, and dumped that in the slop bucket, and saw that there was still more water available.

The lack of hot water had never been anything that any of them had ever wanted to complain to Mrs. Pierson about. Not only were they mere apprentice boys, and, as such, not obliged to expect anything so luxurious as enough hot water, they all knew, unspoken, that with the aid of only one unreliable girl, not to mention all those stairs, Mrs. Pierson had been doing her best. Plus, as Oliver had once or twice surmised, Mrs. Pierson's cooking was far too good to risk complaining about anything else.

Oliver sat on the edge of his bed and took off his boots as he looked at the box where his books were stored. But he was too tired to read, so, shaking his head, he undid his suspenders and took off his trousers, pulled on his nightshirt, and crawled into

236

bed with his stockings on. He listened to Tate and Henry disagreeing, albeit drowsily, about something that had happened that day, but to Oliver's gratitude, there was nothing said about the orphan. Of course not. To them, the orphan was beneath their notice, worthy of little regard.

He would do the same; he decided this as he shifted on his narrow bed, pulled the blankets up, and began his nightly ritual of ignoring the skinny draft of cold air that whispered past the casement window.

It seemed that sleep would never come, but eventually Oliver fell asleep and dreamed, the images startlingly clear, even after all this time, of Dick's face. Dear, sweet Dick, that large collar flapping away from his workhouse-thin neck. His sparse auburn hair, that narrow face, thinned from want. Spindly fingers clutching at Oliver's arm as they both crouched in the dark, backsides sore from a recent thrashing from Mrs. Mann. Both of them too weak to stand, the space too cramped for them to be able to lie down.

*"I'm so hungry, Oliver. Tell me that you spared a bit of dinner in your pocket."*

*"I don't have anything for you,"* the dream Oliver had said, his teeth gritted against the bear's claws ripping the inside of his stomach.

Then the images had shifted, as they did in dreams, to that morning when Oliver had run away from Mr. Sowerberry. Dick had been in the garden, weeding at an ungodly early hour, probably as punishment.

Dick was stick thin, his face grubby. His fingers turned into skeleton bones as he reached for Oliver's bundle, the bundle that was suddenly full of thickly buttered bread and sweets and a jacket potato and bowls of porridge, hot and drizzled with honey. But Oliver said no to Dick and broke off his finger bones, one by one, prying Dick off him, breaking the small, thin bones of Dick's neck—

Oliver started and sat straight up in the dark. His head pounded, the memories of the nightmare clinging to him as he gasped and clutched at the bedclothes, trying to focus on the darkness above him. For the dream had never happened in spite of it feeling so real. Yes, he'd stopped to see Dick and had said good-bye; he should have asked Dick to come with him, but hadn't. And when Dick had assured Oliver he was dying, the much younger Oliver had left it at that and walked off to seek his own fortune, and never mind Dick's fate. Then Dick had died, and it was, at least partly, Oliver's fault.

He should have insisted that Dick come along, should have dragged Dick behind him. Maybe it would have slowed Oliver down to the point where he would not have met up with Jack Dawkins, and the whole nasty, sordid business with Fagin and his gang never would have happened.

But then, Oliver would not have been nearby when Jack and Charley had picked Uncle Brownlow's pockets. And then, he, Oliver, would not have ended up as Uncle Brownlow's cosseted ward, and discovered the serendipitous fact that Uncle Brownlow was an old friend of Oliver's dead father. Such was the turn of the wheel that circumstance begat circumstance. But did it follow that Dick had had to die so Oliver could be given his inheritance? That Dick's life had been the price for Oliver's current good fortune?

Oliver pitched forward in his bed and scrambled out from beneath the bedclothes. His whole body was so hot, as though with a sudden rush of fever, that the floor felt like solid ice beneath his stockinged feet. But that was good, the chill shiver that went through him; it helped clear his head. He ripped off his stockings and paced in his bare feet, willing the icy boards to distract him.

He went over to the washstand and plunged his hands into the last of the water in the pitcher, now quite cold, and splashed his face with it. All of this in the stone-cold darkness, breathing through his teeth, desperate not to wake Henry or Tate, either of whom might exclaim in surprise, which would bring Mr. McCready from his peaceful, law-abiding slumber across the hall to inquire about the disturbance and who was the cause.

Perhaps he might not be overly surprised to find Oliver as the source of disquiet in the middle of the night. And that discovery, in turn, might encourage him to send Oliver packing into the street without so much as a reference, leaving him there to starve, to turn into a ragged beggar with skeleton-thin arms and sores on his face and a belly full of emptiness. Fit for the nearest workhouse and nothing more.

Oliver froze, grabbing his left arm, clamping on the scar so hard it went numb. He had to quiet himself before he woke Henry and Tate; he had to shut everything off before he came apart in bleeding, sobbing pieces. How could the presence of a single orphan under the same roof be so disquieting? It shouldn't be. It wasn't. Oliver couldn't let it. *Wouldn't* let it.

He took a deep breath and pressed his hands, now drying in the chill air, to his hot eyes. Took another hot breath, feeling fully now the cold rising from the floorboards. His teeth were chattering. He clamped them tightly and did not let them chatter. Did not hop from foot to foot to ease his freezing skin. Did not hurry as he climbed back into bed, which was now cold, no body warmth remaining. There was nothing the matter. An orphan was only an orphan, after all, and it had nothing to do with the likes of Oliver Twist.

## OLIVER'S TREATMENT OF THOSE
## WHO ARE BENEATH HIM

I n the morning, after he'd received his second week's pay, Oliver galloped upstairs with the other boys to stow the shilling away. Then he raced back down to the kitchen for breakfast.

He didn't see the orphan during the meal, but that didn't matter to him. If the orphan had already been dismissed and sent back to the workhouse, then that was a good enough way to start the day, and not question anyone about it.

But when he went out into the yard to open the gates to the alley for the delivery wagons, there the orphan was. Shielded from the cold by one of Mrs. Pierson's oldest shawls, the orphan was picking up bits of smashed crockery from the cobblestones and putting them in a bucket.

It happened sometimes, on a Friday night, when men were drinking and spirits got high, that they tossed things about. It amused them to hurl items into yards, simply, Oliver assumed, to hear things smashing against stone. It was probably similar to the feeling he'd had in the country when he'd thrown rocks down a gully just to listen to the breaking sounds. So he understood that these men, drinking, didn't care what a mess they made or whose property they destroyed.

At the same time, it left the orphan picking up shards of very sharp pottery with his bare hands on a cruel, frosty morning. Oliver felt his lips curl, and as the orphan looked up, he turned his face away.

He had to concentrate on his own morning tasks and open the gate, so he walked forward, more warmly dressed than the orphan in thick stockings and the warehouse coat. He even had a scarf around his neck for the brief jaunt into the cold weather. With eyes averted, he walked past the orphan as if he weren't even there. And truly, he wasn't. An orphan was nothing, amounted to nothing. Was of no account.

When Oliver got to the gate, he tugged the scarf away from his neck and wrapped it around his hand. Bare metal was cold, and any dampness might freeze his skin to it, so he was careful. He pulled the bolt up from the rivet in the ground then undid the upper cross bolt and then, finally, the latch in the middle. He swung both gates open, pushing them apart. He did up the left side first, as he always did, attaching the iron hook through the eye bolt in the high brick wall, and then he did the right one.

He turned around, and the orphan was right there, not two feet from him, mouth open as if to speak.

Oliver couldn't begin to imagine what the orphan would have to say to him. In fact, the orphan shouldn't even dare speak to him at all. Oliver was a working lad, on his way up in the world, and the orphan was at the bottom of the heap.

Oliver held his head high and marched right past the orphan and his too-heavy bucketful of broken crockery, thinking somewhere in the back of his mind that the orphan probably only meant to ask what he might do with the leavings from the night before. Well, it was none of Oliver's concern, was it. His boots clicked on the cobblestones as he hurried into the warehouse with an eye out for the sort of work that would keep him out of the way of the orphan.

DURING THE NOON MEAL, OLIVER KEPT HIS EYES ON HIS PLATE and ate everything Mrs. Pierson served him, even though his nerves felt jangled and sore. He'd been helping Tate in the warehouse, while at the same time trying to make it look as though he was not concerned about bumping into the orphan. Which, alas, happened more than once, as he would come around a corner of shelves to find the orphan there, with a broom in his hand, or a cloth, or whatever it was he was working with, and jump out of his own skin. With big, scared eyes, the orphan would look up at Oliver as if Oliver might not see him and would walk right over him. As if Oliver could do anything else but notice that the orphan was there.

Right after dinner, Oliver went upstairs to grab his coat and cap, and, tossing his scarf about his neck, hurried out to the warehouse where Mrs. Pierson said Mr. McCready had gone. He intended to inquire if there were any deliveries that needed doing right away, for he needed to be out and about in the City, far from the haberdashery.

As Oliver pounded down the warehouse steps, Tate was already bent to the stove, poking at it and eyeing the coal scuttle, with Mr. McCready at his side.

"Oliver, come here, lad." Mr. McCready waved him to come closer, which Oliver did with as much haste as he could without actually running.

"Yes, sir?" he asked.

"Here," said Mr. McCready. He held out a long sheet of paper with Henry's writing on it. "Evidently, Henry took a great many orders yesterday while we were out and only now saw fit to tell me. I want you to tend to this directly. Collect the order for each delivery and wrap it. Can you do that? And then deliver them before it snows."

Oliver took the list, trying to hide his pleasure. The list would keep him busy all afternoon and would put Oliver in places that the orphan would never go. Oliver would be out in the streets of the City, free as a bird in his green scarf and his brown jacket and cap that announced to the world that he was the delivery boy from a very important shop.

"Yes, sir," he said. "I'll get on that right away."

He heard a hesitant step behind him, more of a shuffle, and a clang as someone put down a too-heavy bucket.

"Sir," said a very small voice indeed, and Oliver saw Tate's start of surprise.

Shaking this off, Oliver hurried up the warehouse stairs to the shop. He'd gather the items quickly. Then he'd be off. With luck, he wouldn't have to talk to anybody at all.

AFTER GATHERING THE ITEMS FOR DELIVERY, OLIVER WAS alone at the deal table in the warehouse, packaging all the bits of ribbon and pins and collars and sweet soap powder and samples of cloth, and a bobbin stand for a new customer who lived way out in Burton Crescent near Tavistock Square. This took Oliver the good part of an hour, after which he tucked all the paper-and-string bundles in the covered basket. By the time he finished, there were enough to items to make both lids stand up, and the basket was quite heavy.

He took down his green scarf and wrapped it carefully around his neck as he entered the shop. Then, as he put on his cap and was shrugging on his coat, Mrs. Pierson mounted the stairs from the kitchen. She came to Oliver and helped him with his buttons.

"It's such a cold afternoon," she said, snugging the scarf higher under his chin. "We don't want you frosting that pretty face of yours, now do we?" Her voice sounded stern, but she helped him set his cap on his head, fussing over him as if he were one of her own. "There, now. You hurry back and don't be late for supper. I'll have apple tart waiting."

"Yes, Mrs. Pierson," said Oliver, trying not to grin too broadly at her. She might think he was mocking her for fussing over him, and he didn't want that, for Mrs. Pierson's apple tart was so good that it might have been made by the angels themselves.

"Now, then," she said, turning to look behind her. "Get along with that, you, in Mr. McCready's office as quick as you can. Heavens, why are you just standing there? Get along, now."

To Oliver's dismay, the orphan appeared at Mrs. Pierson's side like a small, smudged ghost. He had the coal scuttle in his hands. It was full to the brim, and much too heavy for those small shoulders to bear. Oliver hefted the wicker basket in his hands; it was heavy, too, but no one saw him complaining, did they.

In order to avoid brushing past the orphan, Oliver turned and hastened out the front door, leaving it to bang shut behind him, though he didn't stop to check it. He needed to be very far from the shop just now. It was better to be out of doors, even if it was starting to spit icy rain; he didn't think it would turn to snow, but it was cold, just the same.

Thank goodness he'd have a hot cup of tea and a nice meal, not to mention Mrs. Pierson's apple tart, waiting for him when he got back. And perhaps, as sometimes was the case, one of the nice maids he saw along his delivery route would take him into the kitchen and offer him a hot drink. He'd be fine; the day would turn out fine, in spite of the weather.

WHEN HE FINISHED WITH HIS DELIVERIES, ABSENTLY THINKING of the meal that Mrs. Pierson would keep warm for him even if he was late, Oliver headed down Doughty Street, his basket swinging empty on one arm. When he got to Grey's Inn Gardens, he could smell the foulness of the dust heaps along the side streets. He turned left, since that way was relatively free of traffic and pedestrians, and when he got to the street where all the leather shops were that sold their wares of boots and belts and harnesses, he realized where he was.

He'd trekked all this way to one of the nicer parts of London to discover himself to be only two streets over from the warren of Saffron Hill, where the windows went unwashed, and the steps were rarely scrubbed, even though they were tracked with mud all the year round. Where rooftop tiles went slipping into muddy, fetid gutters in which bare-legged children searched for scraps. One more block would take him directly to the Three Cripples, the exact place where he ought not to go.

He kept going in that direction anyway, thinking that maybe, perhaps maybe, he could inure himself to the sights and sounds of the less well-to-do, indeed, the poorest of the poor. So that by comparison, the orphan might seem very well off. Oliver would try it. It might work.

At the top of Saffron Hill, he headed down into the streets of dank air where the houses and questionable shops almost met across the street at their rooflines, and where crumbling walls were sometimes held up with the shaved trunks of felled trees. Where, if the cold didn't freeze it solid, a narrow river of thick brown water ran constantly in a ditch in the middle of the lane. Where the smell of cesspits overflowing into the ground below rose and smacked him in the face.

Covering his nose with the back of his hand, he hurried downhill, passing filthy shops where dark-coated men lurked, and open doorways of leaning, chipped wood that displayed strings of handkerchiefs, of both tawdry cotton and dappled silk.

He kept walking as fast as he could past the old bone-and-rag shop with its mildewed piles and stacks of rust and iron until he at last came upon the door to the Three Cripples. The door banged open as someone exited, and then three men went in. Oliver slipped in with them, hoping to use them as cover, not that it was likely that anyone he knew would be there to witness what he was doing.

For it was one thing to visit Jack upon the threat of Jack

coming into the haberdashery, but it was another to do it of his own free will. As if his time was his own and this was not the very worst thing he should do. But there was the orphan and all the beggars and sweepers, with their grimy hands reaching out for the smallest coin, passing just at the edges of his vision, and they simply would not *stop*.

The air of the Three Cripples was, as it had been before, close and still and dashed with smoke, as if no one ever thought to clean the grate free of ash and soot, let alone open a window. Now that he wasn't so rattled, as he had been during his first visit, he could see that the walls, once light colored, were patchy with smoke stains and streaked with damp. The mantelpiece over the main fireplace was cluttered with unwashed glasses and pots, with candle wax dripping down in slow, off-white streaks.

Oliver skirted the crowd of men at the bar, who were hastening to order their mugs of beer that served in place of a meal, and made his way to the open door that led to the alcove off of the fireplace, presumably reserved for the better type of guest.

He was lucky, for there was Jack Dawkins, sitting where Oliver had seen him last, on the bench seat nearest the fire. Though Oliver's red scarf was nowhere to be seen and his coat was off, Jack was fully resplendent in his silk-embroidered and grease-spattered blue waistcoat and his shiny, worn top hat. He had his sleeves pushed back and his clay pipe in his mouth, looking for all the world like a gentleman at home, warming himself beside his hearth.

Indeed, there was a coal fire glowing in the grate, sending out waves and waves of acrid, smoking warmth that drew Oliver in. He realized his teeth were chattering and his hands couldn't feel the basket that hung from his fingers, but he didn't think it was the cold alone, no, not merely the cold that had him shaking.

As Oliver approached the table, Jack looked up and fanned a deck of cards between his fingers in an almost graceful way. His hat slipped forward, and he sent it back on his head with a jerk and then smiled at Oliver. His lips curled as though he were smirking, ready to mock Oliver at the first opportunity.

"My eyes," said Jack, his eyes sparking, amused. "Will you look at this. Of his own free will, yet, the great one comes to visit us."

When Oliver didn't say anything, Jack tipped his head and doffed his hat, waving it over the seat opposite him. He placed the hat on the table because, of course, he knew it would irritate Oliver.

"You are most welcome, Oliver Twist." The way Jack said this did sound mocking, but in that funny, shaded way Oliver remembered as being only one flicker away from being either kind or mean, as determined by Jack's mood and the circumstance.

Oliver sank onto the bench seat opposite Jack and laid his cap and scarf and basket beside him. He decided that he'd draw less attention when it didn't look so obvious as to how out of place he was. And, in spite of himself, it was good to sit for a moment, to not be moving. To take in the warmth and feel his shoulders relax.

He watched as Jack took a draw on his pipe, holding it with one hand, then laid it aside in a little clay dish as the smoke twirled up from his mouth.

"All this way, then, just to see me, Nolly?" Jack asked, his eyebrows going up.

"No," said Oliver, knowing that his presence needed some explanation, at least. "I was a few streets over, making—" He clamped his mouth shut. It was none of Jack's business what he'd been doing. "I was in the neighborhood, that's all. It was raining."

He saw it in Jack's eyes, even though Jack didn't say it aloud: *It rains all the time, and you're all over London every day. So why today?*

But instead Jack shouted for two beers, and when the drinks were delivered in plain tin pots, he looked at Oliver, as though he expected Oliver to refuse to imbibe at such an hour of the day. And in such a place.

With a hot feeling in his breast, Oliver picked up the pot nearest to him and took a large mouthful, rude as a sailor, swallowing a great, greedy gulp. The beer stung his throat, but he kept it down anyway, looking at Jack, his eyes narrowed.

"So, then," said Jack, shuffling the cards in one hand while he took a drink of beer, bringing the mug to his mouth with the other. "Care to join me in a game? Somethin' simple, whiskey poker, perhaps, or there's a new game out called black hearts. Shall we have a go? We can play for pennies, or ha'pennies, if you ain't got any pennies. Or sticks if you an't got any ha'pennies."

It was on the tip of Oliver's tongue to say it, *playing cards is a sin*, but then, so was being in a place such as this when it was still before evening, and truly, as an apprentice, his time wasn't his own. That he was sitting there, lollygagging on his master's time, that was the sin; playing cards would just make it worse.

His thighs tightened as he attempted to get to his feet, but he overbalanced and tumbled against the edge of the table, tossing his mug enough to make it spill beer in shiny circles on the black-scarred surface of the table.

"Steady on," said Jack, his hand going out as if he meant to keep Oliver from falling over. "The beer got to you, then? Don't drink much of it, I reckon, being the teetotaler that you are."

Which was a lie. Jack had seen Oliver quaffing gin not so long ago, so he knew Jack was truly mocking him now.

The expression on Jack's face, however, said something different. His dark brows were lowered, and he looked thoughtfully at Oliver.

He took another puff from his clay pipe and laid it by again in a small pot and slowly, as though tasting it, let the smoke go out of his mouth. As though it were nothing that Oliver was here in the middle of a working day with almost no explanation at all, as jittery as a high-strung horse. As if Oliver in a tavern, spilling his beer, was an ordinary, everyday event.

"This here's patience," said Jack, shuffling the cards twice before putting them in a stacked pile between them with their worn edges all lined up, the gold and black pattern on their backs shining dully. "It can't be much of a sin because you don't play to bet, or even to win. You plays it just to pass the time, like. When you're on your own an' waitin' till the time is right to meet your fence or the fella who's goin' t'melt down all that silver you just stole into a nice, sellable blob. Like I been just last night, but you don't want to hear about that, eh?"

Oliver frowned, but Jack just smiled, as though teasing Oliver was something he did every day, and that talk of fences and stolen silver and how to melt and sell it was a common conversation between them.

He watched Jack's hands, deft and grime-knuckled, turn up the cards, one-two-three, and pull out the aces to lay them in a row when they came up, placing the other cards, as the numbers and colors, black and red, came up so as to be in sequence as Jack laid them on their respective piles of spades, hearts, clubs, and diamonds. The pattern was simple and somewhat mesmerizing, and it was surprising that Jack didn't cheat, not even when Oliver could see the necessary card directly beneath the one that showed on the top of the pile.

"It's just to pass the time, see. Do you see, Nolly? Not quite so much the sin as you might like to think."

"No," Oliver agreed. "I suppose it isn't."

"You want somethin' to eat?" asked Jack, shuffling the cards again. "Somethin' to help you keep that beer down?"

Without waiting for an answer, Jack waved his hand, presumably at someone behind Oliver, and presently, a girl brought over two bowls of stew and a plate of bread and cheese, which she placed between them.

"Eel an' potato," said Jack, picking up a dented spoon, starting in on the oily-looking broth in his bowl without waiting for Oliver.

Oliver would not eat anything made of eel, not that Jack knew that. Instead, he picked up a corner of cheese and brought it to his mouth. He could tell, without even tasting it, that the cheese was old and dry, fit only for hog swill. He didn't quite know what to do, but found his hands crumbling the cheese back onto the plate.

"Typical," said Jack, his mouth full of stew. He shook his head. "You an' that fussy mouth of yours."

Of course, Jack was right. There was many a mouth that would be willing to eat cheese like that, even if it was old and moldy. Or who would take the dented spoon that now rested on the table in front of him and eat the stew, whether or not it contained bits of eel.

He ducked his head, feeling ashamed; he knew what it was like to be so hungry you could eat dirt. Jack, of all people, didn't need to remind him of that. Shouldn't have had to. It made him a little cross as well; he'd come up in the world and was above having to eat what was put in front of him if he didn't enjoy the taste of it. He had money in his pocket, tips from his deliveries made that very day, and he could walk into any shop and order a real meat pie, if he fancied it.

He opened his mouth to give Jack this very return and found himself saying something quite different indeed.

"Mr. McCready bought an orphan yesterday," said Oliver, low, as though to himself.

He was so very glad that Jack kept his attention on his food. In fact, Jack was practically slumped over his bowl, both elbows on the table, one hand propping up his head, the other using the spoon to shovel the stew in as fast as he could. He had the worst manners Oliver had ever seen, but focusing on his anger at seeing Jack's bad manners felt better than the feeling of shame from a moment before.

"An orphan," said Jack, his eyes on his bowl, only pausing in his shoveling to take a large drink of beer.

"From a workhouse," said Oliver. Now he wanted Jack to look up at him, to understand what Oliver meant without him having to explain it; he could barely explain it to himself. But

Jack just kept eating, so Oliver had to manage on his own. "And I can't stand the sight of him."

"Me either," said Jack with a grunt.

He picked up the bowl and tilted it to his mouth, using the spoon to scrape the last bits into his open mouth. Then he set the bowl down, and with a sigh, wiped his mouth with the back of his forearm, looking at Oliver while he did this.

"Can't stand their skinny little faces an' their dirty hands clasped in prayer, lookin' up at me like I'm the last stop before hell's fires." Jack's eyes glittered as he finished saying this, and Oliver felt he was being told something he didn't quite understand but should. "Makes me want to smack 'em right into next week."

"And then I had a nightmare about Dick."

"Who's that, then?"

Oliver's face flushed, and he told himself it was the heat from the coal fire finally getting to him. He should have known better than to attempt to tell the story of Dick to Jack.

"Never mind." He shoved the bowl of stew at Jack. "You eat it, then," he said.

He trying to stand, and found the table getting in the way again. The bench seat was nailed to the floor, and he couldn't shove it back at all. He grabbed his cap and basket and began to slide out sideways, fingers grasping the edge of the table, tucked back so that his fingers wouldn't go into the pool of beer and quickly cooling stew.

"Hey, now, Nolly, don't be cross. You know I'd never be so mean as that. Why, I'd give 'em a penny if I had it, you know I would."

Jack stood and put his hand on Oliver's arm just as Oliver wrenched his basket free from the confines of the bench seat. Oliver clapped his cap on his head and glared at Jack, willing him to let go. But Jack didn't, and so Oliver had to yank his arm free and try to push past Jack, who stood up and let him pass, though not without some attempt at delay.

"Say, did I ever show you my tattoo?" Jack started unrolling his shirt sleeve to peel it back, looking down so that Oliver had a good view of the back of his head, the hair tangled and flattened, as though Jack had only an hour ago arisen from bed. Then Jack looked up. "I got it on board the *Bertha May* when I was exported, an' you know what it's of?"

"No," said Oliver, gritting his teeth and shoving Jack out of the way. "No, and I don't care. Only thieves and whores have tattoos." Although, truth be told, Oliver himself had a tattoo of sorts, if one counted a scar left by a servant's bullet. Not that he was about to tell Jack about it; Jack would just want to see it.

"Well," said Jack, letting Oliver get by him, as though it were of no consequence to him. "I'm not a whore, by any stretch, but I *am* a thief, ain't I? An' an ex-convict, I'm proud to say, so you might amend your list a bit there, don't you think?"

With fury exploding in his stomach at the seeming futility of talking to Jack about *anything*, Oliver pushed past all the customers in the Three Cripples and wondered, as he slammed the door open, why on earth he had thought this was a good idea. Not only was the thought of eel stew making him feel like vomiting into the nearest gutter, he'd gotten black smudges on his trousers somehow, and his scarf smelled like dank smoke.

Mrs. Pierson was sure to fuss over him when he got back to the shop, and how was he going to explain his tumbled state to her, let alone catch sight of the orphan without wanting to burst out shouting? He had no idea.

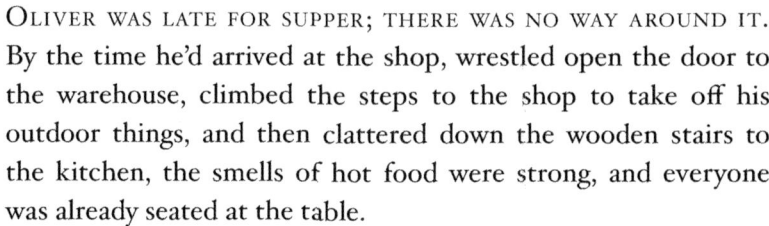

OLIVER WAS LATE FOR SUPPER; THERE WAS NO WAY AROUND IT. By the time he'd arrived at the shop, wrestled open the door to the warehouse, climbed the steps to the shop to take off his outdoor things, and then clattered down the wooden stairs to the kitchen, the smells of hot food were strong, and everyone was already seated at the table.

As his feet touched the stone floor, everyone stopped, spoons and forks halfway to their mouths, which were open in surprise, even though, by now, Oliver's lateness to meals was becoming a commonplace event. Even the orphan looked taken aback in an almost comical way, as if Oliver's keeping him from his stale bread and simple broth were the worst sort of manners.

"Oliver," said Mr. McCready. He wiped his mouth and laid his napkin back in his lap. "You're quite late. I'm assuming you have an explanation? Regardless, I'm quite tempted to make you go without supper, to teach you—"

"Oh, dear me, Mr. McCready," said Mrs. Pierson, coming up to the table to serve Oliver without waiting for leave. "On such a cold day as this, can't you see the boy's had a struggle, making all of them deliveries this afternoon? Henry said there was one as far as Burton Crescent; he's done in."

She was dishing up a bowl of something that resembled potato and cheese and onion, all melted together. She plunked that down on the table at Oliver's empty chair, and then got slices of cold ham and boiled celery.

"Bread and butter's just there, Oliver; now you wash and catch up with your supper, so we can all start on the pudding together."

Oliver looked carefully at Mr. McCready, but it was obvious even to him that the decision was already made.

"The streets were very crowded today," said Oliver, generally, to no one, as he washed his hands.

When he sat down, he put his napkin in his lap, and tried to pretend that he and Mrs. Pierson weren't, essentially, disobeying Mr. McCready and doing as they pleased. She to feed him, and he to eat.

Another glance told Oliver what he already knew and didn't care to think about. That the orphan had finished his allotment of bread and broth and was now staring at Oliver's plate as he ate.

Which Oliver did, as quickly as he could, determined that

there'd be no scraps for the orphan. He ate so fast that by the time Mrs. Pierson served up the jam tarts, his stomach hurt. Still, he ate his share of pudding anyway, telling himself he needed the food and that his stomach wasn't uncomfortable. And that no one in the room could smell the smoke on him or could tell where he'd been by the smudges he saw on the edges of his palms. He'd washed very carefully, so his only hope was that everyone was concentrating on the tarts and not on him.

THAT NIGHT, BEFORE BEDTIME, HE LIT TWO STUBS OF CANDLES and ignored Tate's remarks to Henry about it and tried to read one of his books while lying in bed. He had picked out *Aesop's Fables*, but he knew all the stories by heart, and the words merely danced on the page as though they wanted to take flight.

Attempting to concentrate didn't help; his stomach ached, and in his mind's eye, he could see the orphan on a coarse blanket on the kitchen floor. Perhaps he was pressed close to the warmth of the cast-iron stove; even as the heat faded away, it would be better than nothing. Perhaps he had two blankets. Perhaps he had none.

Oliver got up to put his book away in his chest, ignoring Henry's irritated sigh and any remark that Tate might make, and blew out the candles. The smell of burnt wax lifted in the cool air; Oliver inhaled it, thinking of sleep now, concentrating on that.

The dream came again, of Dick in the garden, his thin garments hanging off white bone, his hair falling across empty eye sockets. When Oliver woke up, he was sitting, breathing hard, staring into the darkness. He had tried to forget about Dick all these years, to forget about walking away, leaving poor Dick in the garden. But it seemed that the idea of Dick, and what Oliver had failed to do to save him, was not about to be left behind.

## ❧ 19 ❧

## OF CRUELTY

After the dark dreams, with images of Dick crowding into his sleep, going to church with Mr. McCready and Henry and Tate on Sunday was hardly enough to calm the twisted feeling in Oliver's breast, however peaceful the service might be. The rows of pews aligned beneath the arched roof, the graceful glow of oiled wood, the smell of fine candles, and the dim light coming in colored streaks through the decorated, lead-lined windows—none of it made even a dent into Oliver's unsettled state.

Even Sunday afternoon, though it allowed for the leisure of reading and resting by the kitchen stove, left Oliver so troubled that by the time he'd reached his bed, his sleep was as sketchy as if he'd spent the day in battle. By the time Oliver was dressed and in the shop on Monday morning, he was exhausted and heavy-eyed.

He stood at the edge of the long counter in the shop, looking for Henry's list, desperate to not be in the warehouse where the orphan was sweeping. The broom was far too long for the orphan's tiny frame, and Oliver had lasted all of five minutes watching him before he had left off sorting boxes and crates and snuck inside. Then he heard the voice behind him.

"A moment there, Oliver."

Oliver turned. "Yes, sir?"

"The deliveries can wait, Oliver, my boy," said Mr. McCready, coming up behind him. "I know the sun is peeking through the clouds and fog, but it'll be more worth your while after dinner, yes?"

Oliver tapped the counter, watching his prints smear across the glass. Henry would have to take vinegar and cloth to those later, but it would make him look busy and efficient, so perhaps he might enjoy it.

The shop was quite quiet, as though with the weather picking up, every customer had somewhere else to be. Subsequently, there was almost nothing to do. All the work was in the warehouse today, where Tate was the king of the roost, counting boxes and buttons and sorting through starched collars and ordering the orphan around. Tate wasn't cruel, necessarily, but he was lordly, pointing and commanding in a way that had the orphan scampering and stammering.

"Why don't you go back and help Tate?" said Mr. McCready. "I fear he's determined to start spring cleaning early."

Spring was weeks away yet, but Oliver was feeling the same restlessness that Tate probably was, the push of some energetic sensation that had Henry buffing the brass fittings at the edge of the counter, almost needlessly, with puffs of his breath and a brisk cloth.

"Oliver?" Mr. McCready's hand rested for a moment on Oliver's shoulder.

Oliver didn't jump under the touch, but instead gripped the edge of the counter to distract himself from his irritation.

"Yes, sir," he said, and made himself let go of the counter's edge. He turned and Mr. McCready patted him with some heartiness.

"You can make deliveries after dinner, Oliver," said Mr. McCready kindly. "And that's a promise."

"Yes, sir."

Oliver made himself step from the relative warmth of the shop and into the sunnier, albeit chillier warehouse. The sun came and went as wafts of cloud scudded along and whispers of fog tumbled against the glass, as though fighting against being burned and blown away. For a moment, Oliver stared at the high, narrow windows. Tate could be heard beyond the set of shelves, muttering to himself; Oliver imagined that at any moment, Tate might start barking out more orders to the orphan.

As for the orphan—

Oliver scanned the room, looking at the high windows, the brick walls. He looked at the deal table along the wall, piled with the half-sorted boxes Tate had abandoned, with ribbons spilling out, corset tapes stacked awkwardly as though ready to fall, given even the slightest push.

"*Martin*," came Tate's shout, finally. "Put some more coal on the fire, damn you, before my arse freezes off."

It wasn't as cold as it had been the week before, so Tate probably didn't really need more heat. There were bits of red glowing gently through the slits in the stove, but Tate was too far from the stove, trapped in the box of cold air between the shelves, that was all. Had he been near the stove, he would have been warm enough. He merely sounded as though he was enjoying giving orders.

The orphan, for his part, was under the table with an old blacking brush and a cloth, taking the grit and cobwebs from the space between the floor and where it almost met the wall. It would take the orphan a good few moments to extricate himself, so when Tate shouted Martin's name again, Oliver strode over to the stove, intending to perform the task himself.

But the orphan, as if seeing Oliver's boots go marching past him, crawled out from beneath the table and scurried to the coal scuttle, reaching out for the door of the stove with his bare hands. There was a charred cloth on a nail in the wall next to the stove or, indeed, the door could be opened with the fire poker, with the curved end shoved under the latch. Perhaps the orphan hadn't been taught this, or, knowing Tate's tendency to over-speak things, the orphan had been taught and had just forgotten.

The orphan's skinny, chapped hands were just at the handle when Oliver grabbed the orphan's collar and yanked him away from the stove door. With the back of his hand, he landed a good, solid slap on the side of the orphan's face, a blow so hard to the bone that a bruise blossomed there, even as the orphan went sprawling to the stone floor. Arms and legs spread, crying piteously, the back of his jacket torn by Oliver's tug on the cloth.

"Mind what you're doing, you," said Oliver, his voice storming out of his chest. "Or do you want to burn yourself? That handle's red hot."

Crying in earnest now, the orphan attempted to sit, looking up at Oliver with big, dark, teary eyes. The orphan's hand went to his mouth, and shaking, came away; there was blood on his chapped lips. Tate had meanly ordered the orphan about, but only he, Oliver Twist, had sent the orphan to his knees. Though he'd been trying to protect Martin from a bad burn, he'd struck the boy so hard, he was crying. *Bleeding.*

Oliver was no longer the newest boy in the shop. And now he was no better than Noah Claypole, who would, if he were here, howl with amusement at Oliver's fall from grace.

Tate came out from between the shelves and approached slowly, looking at the orphan and then at Oliver, his eyes wide and wary, as if Oliver might strike him next.

"On your feet, Martin," said Tate, and while he pulled the orphan to a standing position with some confidence, his voice was shaking. "There's work to be done, eh?"

"Where's the shovel and bucket?" asked Oliver, trying to stand firm against the waves of white that swam past his eyes, the way the brightness of a sudden shard of sun made him feel blind and sick.

"'Tis already done, Oliver," said Tate from somewhere beyond the white.

"The broom, then, and I'll sweep." Desperation rose in his chest.

"Martin's already attended to that, just now. As you well know."

Oliver sensed rather than saw Tate push the orphan in the direction of the shelves, and then Tate came up to Oliver. Close enough so that Oliver could see his face, his forehead wrinkled in lines of confusion.

"Will you sort collars, then, as you started? While I clean the shelves." Tate sounded almost gentle, and Oliver had to bite the inside of his cheek lest he burst out shouting at Tate as well, as that type of behavior Mr. McCready would definitely not tolerate.

"Yes," said Oliver.

Without saying anything else, he pushed past Tate and marched on numb feet to the table and stood there for a few breaths till his head cleared. As Tate fussed with the stove, Oliver let the clanks and clunks of iron against iron and coal against iron pull him back to the very spot where he was. In the warehouse, sorting collars, tucking the corset stays away from the edge of the table. To help Tate avoid additional work, Oliver grabbed the first stack of collars, cleared a space on the tabletop, and began to sort.

Oliver kept his head down and didn't allow himself to listen to Tate and the orphan working some feet away, nor to lift his head or to stop working till Mrs. Pierson called them for dinner. Then he washed, last in line, and didn't dare look anyone in the eye. Not even when Mrs. Pierson *tutted* over the orphan's state.

"What have you been tumbling in, then?" she asked.

"Nothing, ma'am," said the orphan, in a voice very small and soft.

"Leave him be to eat his dinner," said Mr. McCready, setting his napkin in his lap. "Workhouse boys are used to hard work, and he'll not thank you for softening him up."

Oliver felt himself flushing hard and couldn't tell if Mr.

McCready was looking at him markedly or not. Didn't want to find out. Didn't want to eat Mrs. Pierson's good cooking. But he didn't want her to start *tutting* at him either, so he made himself take a bite and keep it down.

~

THE AFTERNOON HAD TURNED WINDY, BUT IT WAS STILL bright, so after Oliver had swept the melted snow and dirt from the front steps and pavement, the order of the day was deliveries. And as Mr. McCready handed him the delivery list, Oliver felt that he himself had been delivered. For if Mrs. Pierson kept the orphan close by, or if Henry felt he needed more coal, then Oliver would be far, far away, and would not have to reconcile himself to any of it.

Mr. McCready helped him gather the packages and tie them up.

"You look unwell," said Mr. McCready, stuffing yet another brown package tied with string into the basket. "If you are, I will select one of the other boys to go."

"No, I'm all right," said Oliver, putting on his coat and cap and scarf. He pulled the basket over his arm before Mr. McCready could make any more remarks that might keep Oliver around the shop. "Some fresh air will do me good, I think."

Fresh air, indeed. Being out of the confines of the shop would be almost like being free of the insistent cloud hanging inside of his head. It might follow him out of the shop, but the streets of London would afford him a great deal of distraction. Oliver almost ran out of the store.

In the scattered sunshine as it struck the snow-clad stone and brick, the air moving on Wardour Street was almost overwhelming. Oliver breathed it in and hurried up the wet lane into the main thoroughfare. Cabs and carts and butcher's floats clattered along the cobblestones, spraying slushy snow and mud as they went.

He dodged between them, heading toward his first delivery just on the other side of the Strand with as much haste as he could muster. But being an apprentice boy from McCready's Haberdashery did not mean he could shove and push his way through the crowd. The clothes he wore stood out and resembled a uniform, the brown trousers sensible, the brown jacket thick and well made. With the green scarf, he was a walking advertisement; any ill usage of potential customers on the street would not reflect well on the shop.

He made his deliveries quickly; they all seemed to be clustered around a group of tall and grandly fronted hotels just where the Strand turned into Fleet Street. His last delivery was at a fine house where he could see through the open curtains a gathering of well-dressed folk and a woman in a flowing dress and veil that indicated that there was a wedding party going on.

Oliver handed over a small brown parcel to the woman who answered the door. By her silk gown, it was easy to see that she was the mistress of the house, and, with her hair coming out of its bun, she looked quite distracted but happy.

"Here's a shilling for you," she said.

His attempt to hand it back to her was met with a quick slam of the door.

A shilling was far more of a tip than he'd ever received and seemed out of measure with the amount of work he'd done for it. But Mr. McCready said that tips could be kept, so he slipped the shilling into his pocket and stood there, listening to the sound of happy chatter and laughter coming from beyond the door. He would only disturb them if he were to attempt to return the shilling, so he turned and hurried down the steps.

He cast his eyes up and down Fleet Street at the thronging crowd, the hustle of skirt, the brisk pace of the sandwich men. He could go back to the shop, of course, and hang about, hoping for more deliveries. Or he could enter the warehouse and face the disaster that had become the orphan, hoping all the while that no one had told Mr. McCready what he'd done.

It was early yet, and he wasn't wanted back in the shop. What's more, no one was expecting him. With his hand in his pocket, he traced the edge of the shilling. The wind whipped around his head, bringing with it the blowy smells from the river, which was not many streets off.

His feet were pointed in a direction that might lead to disaster, but he could hardly go back and face the mental confusion he'd left behind at the haberdashery. He determined he was hungry; there was a pie shop, one that he'd passed on his way to see Jack that first time, the one with good smells, just on Dean Street. He would go there, get a pie to eat while he stood in the street, and then he would go home. He refused to allow himself to remember how close Dean Street was to the Three Cripples.

THE PIE SHOP BENEATH THE BRIGHT SIGN SAYING *ABIGAIL'S Pies* was as busy as when he'd last seen it, and it took him a good five minutes of standing in line before he was at the counter. A slightly frowsy older woman with her hair straggling from beneath her mostly clean cap slapped the counter in front of him with a flour-dappled hand.

"Sixpence," she said. "Cheese and onion, or sausage and onion, or egg, leek, and onion. We're all out of sausage and cheese."

"Sausage and onion," he said, his mouth watering. He handed her the shilling, and she handed him back sixpence change, which, as he shoved it in his pocket, would make a better story to Mr. McCready than to say that he'd been tipped an entire shilling.

The woman behind the counter shoved the pie at him.

"Next!"

Oliver stepped away, out into the damp and windy street, with his empty basket over one arm and the pie in both hands. Pausing just outside the door, he took a bite, and the flaky crust fell over his lips almost lovingly; the filling was still warm. He only hoped, as he chewed and swallowed, that it wasn't actually made of horse or cat or something; the neighborhood around the shop was dodgy at best.

Within minutes, the pie was finished, and his stomach felt more settled than it had all day. Oliver licked his lips and wiped his hands on the sides of his trousers. When he resettled his basket, he realized where he was. Of course he'd known, he'd always known, right where he was. Just a turn to the left and up the street and there he'd be, at the Three Cripples. Though why he imagined he might want to go there was beyond him.

But as he thought about going back to the shop, where he worked for a respectable man and made an honest living and had hot water to wash in and a clean place to sleep, his whole body stiffened up. The *orphan* would be there, with half of his face blotted dark by a bruise delivered by Oliver's own hand. Tate would be there, with looks out of the corner of his eyes, as if he didn't quite know what Oliver might do next, but that it wouldn't be anything polite. As for the rest of them—

Oliver shoved his hands in his pockets and walked up the lane, making the brief left and marching right up to the door, opening it before he could think twice. The smell of beer whipped him in the face again, and the brisk skiff of wind he brought with him made the customers at the bar turn to look at him, with annoyance at the cold, and as if he didn't belong.

He stood there a moment, refusing to let his out of place feeling send him back the way he'd come, and then Jack strode through the door at the far end of the bar with two pots of beer in his hand. His hat was, for once, not upon his head while he was indoors, and he'd doffed his blue waistcoat as well, leaving him in only his muslin shirt, with the buttons opened at the neck, showing the press of bone beneath skin.

"Nolly!" Jack gave a jerk of his head. "We're just havin' a drink, so come on then. I'll get them to bring some gin an' sugar for you."

Oliver nodded, wondering who the *we* was that Jack spoke of, and as he stepped through the door to the little room with the coal fire, he saw that, yes, of course, it was Noah. He had shed his coat to reveal his stained plaid waistcoat. Rolling up his sleeves, he was just sinking back in the bench seat when he caught sight of Oliver.

"Nolly, me lad!" said Noah heartily, as if they were the best of friends, and Oliver's whole body jerked.

"Only I calls him that, mind," said Jack, in a way that had Noah blinking at him in surprise. Jack bent to put the pots on the table, casual, as if he'd said nothing remarkable.

"Work'us it is, then, come an' have a sit. We're celebratin' my pay packet, an' we invites you to share."

Of course, someone such as Noah would think to celebrate getting paid by spending it instead of putting it by, as any sensible person would do. But then, perhaps for Noah, there was always more where that came from. It was none of Oliver's business, at any rate, where or how Noah made or spent his money.

Instead of saying anything about it, Oliver merely took the bench seat across from Noah, and since Oliver had stolen Jack's spot, Jack shoved Oliver in toward the wall to take his place on the outside. This put Oliver in the corner, somewhat trapped, but this was probably a good thing, as he couldn't be seen from the door or the window. Not that anyone he knew would come through the doors of the Three Cripples, now or anytime soon.

"Bring us some gin!" shouted Jack, turning his head away from Oliver. "Warm gin an' sugar, for my friend Nolly, here!"

"Gin, is it?" asked Noah with a smirk. "Never thought I'd see the likes of that, our very own Work'us drinkin' gin."

"Yes," said Jack, turning back around to grin at Noah. "He likes it best of all, an' mind you," here Jack leaned toward Noah, giving Oliver a wink, as if it were all fun, "he can put back many a tot, as many as a sailor, before he starts any singin'."

Where Jack had got that idea, Oliver didn't know, as Oliver

couldn't even sing a note, but it made Noah and Jack laugh very hard indeed, almost spilling the beer in front of them.

The gin arrived in a tall tin tumbler, accompanied by a small jug of warm water and a little bowl filled with clumps of sugar. It was a strange feeling to have had this ordered for him and to be prepared to drink it while Noah and Jack looked on, but he'd had the worst day possible, the worst day in his experience at McCready's Haberdashery. Not that he was about to tell Noah that, or even Jack, but he wanted this drink. He wanted the relaxed feeling in his bones that it would bring him.

So, pretending he was alone at the table, at least for the moment, he plopped a bit of sugar in the gin, grabbing it with his fingers since there were no tongs to be found, and then swirled the gin and sugar around, waiting for the lump to melt a bit. Then he poured in a little of the hot water and swirled the tin tumbler around some more.

He took a sip and saw that Noah and Jack were watching him, Noah with that sneer he wore when thinking about how to bedevil Oliver, and Jack, his brows quirking down, as if something confused him. Oliver looked away, took another big swallow, and felt himself loosen from the inside.

"You'll be wantin' fried onions an' potatoes with that," said Jack.

When Jack shouted for the order, Oliver didn't stop him. He had sixpence, and lord knew how much Noah had in his pockets, and yes, he was hungry now, very hungry, if you please, in spite of the pie he'd just eaten. Fried onions and potatoes would be perfect with the sweet gin.

"So tell us the story about me," said Jack.

He grabbed the plate of potatoes and onions from the serving girl and plunked it in the middle of the table. She let go a fistful of forks that clattered in a pile.

"You mean the one where you was announced to be hextri-cated," said Noah, as he grabbed a fork and speared a potato, which he shoved, whole, into his mouth. "Where I saw it all, 'cause I was there, right an' proper like, on Fagin's orders?"

"That's the one."

"But I've told it *three* times already."

"Not to Nolly."

Jack looked straight at Oliver, and Oliver could see that Jack was proud of this event, that he wanted to brag about it as though it were something right and proper. The fact that Noah had actually been there, in the very courtroom, on the very day of Jack's trial and at Fagin's behest, would only add fire to the fuel.

"C'mon, Noah, be a dear lad an' tell the story."

"Fine, but this is the last time, you hear me, Jack? The last time!"

Jack nodded, concentrating on the chunk of potato he was slicing through with the edge of a fork.

Oliver took some potato, tucked it close with a bit of onion, and started eating. The grease the potato had been fried in was old, but there was plenty of salt to make it taste fine. And he considered, as he ate, that Noah would tell the story as many times as need be, with as many embellishments as were wanted to keep the story fresh.

"So there I was," began Noah, spitting a bit, "in the back row, keepin' low like, behind some old dame who smelled like a tannery, an' along comes Jack Dawkins, as ever was, resplendent in his gentleman's top an' tails, struttin' like a peacock, wavin' to one an' all."

"Tell the part where I demand me rights," said Jack, leaning forward on his elbows.

Jack's muslin shirt became half-rucked on his shoulders, exposing the naked skin of his chest. Jack seemed not to notice this; however, Oliver began to grow quite warm by the fire, somehow drawn in by the shimmer of the buttons against the muslin. Bestilled by the contrast between pale skin and white cloth, the curve of muscle as Jack turned his head, as Jack looked at Oliver and winked.

"I'm gettin' to that, if'n you'll shut the hell up," said Noah, getting riled.

Jack just smirked, and Oliver took another sip of his gin and sugar and let the warmth of the liquor do its work. He was fairly sure half the story would be untrue, but as it was, it was beginning not to matter nor he to care. Besides, Jack was there, so Oliver was pleased with the company, even if Noah was taking most of Jack's attention.

"'Where are my privileges?' I shouted to the magistrate!" Jack almost shouted this now.

"Yes, yes, you shouted it an' then you lectured the court on their responsibilities to you an' to your schedule that day, an' if it would please them, could you have the names an' records of all of them who were on the bench accusin' you."

"An' then the whole place busted up laughin'!" Jack pounded the table, eyes sparkling. "An' all of this for a tuppenny-ha'penny snuffbox."

Jack was laughing so hard at this, at the recollection of it, even though Noah hadn't yet finished the story, for surely there was the judgment and sentence to come, that Oliver couldn't help but smile himself.

Jack was so bright, a vibrant thing, so alive and moving and so very distracting. It was easy for Oliver to forget his own troubles, in that moment. And he could remember the Jack he knew then, and imagine him cocky, demanding the attention of one and all in the courtroom and imposing his will on them. Or trying to; Oliver couldn't imagine that the magistrate had been even slightly amused, however much the spectators in the gallery had been laughing.

"An' the witnesses," Noah continued. "They brought the very gentleman in to testify, an' a high toff he was, too."

"Could have bought another snuffbox easy," said Jack. He

shook his head. "What was it to him, then, eh? Even if it was made o' silver."

Oliver opened his mouth, thinking just then to remind them both that private property was protected under the law, whether it be a twopenny-halfpenny snuffbox or the crown jewels themselves.

"That's when you told them you wouldn't besmirch yourself talkin' to the witness an' announced to the place that you was to breakfast with the Vice President of the House of Commons that very mornin', an' could you be on your way. Which is when they committed you!"

This last was presented in a shout, and both Noah and Jack pounded the table and roared and ordered more beer to make up for what they had spilled. Oliver allowed them to order him another gin and sugar, which he politely sipped while they swilled their drinks, getting it over their collars and cuffs.

"C'mon, Nolly," said Jack, giving him a shove with his bare elbow. "You're all long in the mouth, like someone's just pulled a tooth from you. Tell ol' Jack what's wrong with you, an' I'll cheer you up, quick as you please."

"It's the orphan," said Oliver, feeling it slip out of him before he could stop it. "They're being cruel to him at the shop, and I—"

He was about to mention Dick one more time, to see if by explaining it to Jack he could understand it himself. He wanted Jack to help him make sense of the guilt that was eating at him, and maybe it would be good to say it out loud. But Jack interrupted him.

"Why are you so worked up about this lot? Is the poor, wee mite bein' buggered?" asked Jack. "You'll not want to worry about that, my pretty. Boys get buggered every day."

This sent Noah to snickering into his beer, and Oliver felt that the gin was starting to wear off. Still, the room was warm and close and exactly what he needed to chase the images of a skinny-faced orphan from his mind, so he took another long drink of gin, and then swallowed, considering his question.

"What's buggering?" he asked.

Noah spat out a whole mouthful of beer, mostly on himself, as he howled and pounded the table. Jack, ignoring Noah and his spasms of laughter, was serious and almost kindly as he looked at Oliver.

"You can't save the world, Nolly," Jack said.

"I can, my little corner of it," Oliver said.

He gripped the edge of the table and fought off a sudden light-headedness. He shouldn't be at the Three Cripples at all, let alone drinking, let alone having this conversation. Let alone visiting Jack Dawkins, ex-convict. Let alone sharing a drink with *Noah Claypole*, of all people.

The worst of it was the lie; he couldn't save the orphan because he himself was the one being cruel. But he couldn't confess it now; Noah was wiping his eyes about whatever *buggering* meant, shaking his head as if he couldn't believe that Oliver didn't know.

"I should get back to the shop," Oliver said.

He tried to scoot past Jack out of the bench seat, looking around for his basket, when Jack grabbed the sleeve of his jacket and did not move, so Oliver was stuck.

"But you'll come again?" said Jack. "I'll show you my tattoo next time. I got it durin' a ceremony in the bush; them blacks're awful clever with a needle."

"I thought you said you got it on board the *Bombay Mary*?" asked Oliver. He was sure that he'd heard the story about the tattoo differently last time.

He stood up and moved along the bench so Jack would have to move out of the way. Jack just shook his head and looked up at Oliver with a little smile as he leaned back, but not far enough to give Oliver a clear space. Their bodies pressed close for a moment, thighs and knees bumping. Oliver froze, blinking as a sudden warmth moved up his belly and into his chest.

"No, no, it was them already there, in Australia, that did it. You couldn't get a tattoo as clear as mine on a movin' ship, now could you?"

Oliver nodded, pretending not to be irritated as he lurched free of the bench, beyond the reach of Jack's hand as he bent to grab his basket. He supposed that what Jack said was so, but why on earth Jack couldn't stick to the truth the first time was beyond him.

"Good day, gentlemen," said Oliver, tipping his cap at them.

"Always with them airs an' graces o' yours, eh, Work'us?" asked Noah, shaking his head as Oliver pulled himself together.

"What's it to you, then?" Oliver asked, his reaction breaking through the ease the gin had created.

"Nothin', as always," said Noah, smirking at him.

For a second, Jack looked confused, as if he couldn't possibly imagine that Noah and Oliver were not friends. Oliver could see how in Jack's mind they were all one happy collection of Fagin's boys, and surely, being such, they would want to band together and hold down the fort until more of them arrived. The likelihood of that was very small, but Jack had proved Oliver wrong once already, and so might again.

Tucking his basket in the crook of his elbow, Oliver made his way out of the throng that had collected in the Three Cripples and into the street. It was much later than he had supposed, with the sun now fully behind the clouds that were building over the dark, jagged rooftops of the City.

Church bells started clanging the hour; it was five o'clock, then, and Oliver began walking as fast as he might, given the traffic and the slippery streets. If he didn't make any wrong turns, didn't get held up at any crossings, then he'd be back at the shop within the half hour. No one would know where he'd been or whom he'd been talking to. But only if he hurried.

## ✤ 20 ✤

## CONSIDERS HIS IMPETUOUS
## ACTIONS AND PAST REGRETS

By the middle of the week, the bruise on the orphan's face began to fade, though no one asked any questions or seemed concerned in any way as to where it had come from. The orphan himself had not said anything about it, though, truly, he never said much of anything at all. Oliver told himself that Martin was getting used to the hard work, and that everything would work out before too long.

Besides, the shop had a new, very well-to-do customer on Charlotte Street who wanted a shawl delivered to her right away, which distracted everyone.

Oliver planned carefully for this delivery; the area was a fancier neighborhood than the one where the shop was, and just a little bit more elegant, with wider streets, and newer paving stones. There were a great many more street sweepers, as well, who were less dirty about the face and who were, perhaps, a bit less fractious about their task of sweeping the walks, as there were plenty of stately and well-dressed gentlemen for every sweep to attend to.

Even as Oliver crossed the street, a penny flipped past his head, and the sweep caught it. He was grateful that a penny was all it took to have the street free of debris, to save himself from having to spend too much effort cleaning his boots.

The delivery of the shawl was to a very fine townhouse, but then Oliver had expected that, given the address. What he didn't know was whether deliveries should be made to the front door, so as to make an impression, or down to the kitchen area in a more circumspect fashion.

Since the townhouse was in the middle of the block, there was no side door for him to linger by while he attempted to figure it out. He stood there on the pavement, with the basket over his arm. He studied the sparkling windows, the newly scrubbed steps, the fresh paint on the railing down to the kitchen area, while the rain soaked into his cap.

Just then, the white cap of a parlor maid peeped out from behind the thick curtains in the front window. The door opened, and the maid stuck her head out, just a little way.

"Go down," she said. "I'll meet you there."

Oliver nodded and then hurried down the iron stairs to the kitchen area, and tapped lightly on the wooden door. It opened to admit him to the wide, clean kitchen. The parlor maid came up to him and took the package, opening it with the cook's knife to examine the silky, patterned shawl, before refolding it to take up to her mistress.

The cook, who was talking to someone who looked like a housekeeper, gestured to Oliver to sit and warm himself by the fire. Oliver did so, doffing his cap and loosening his scarf, reaching out for the hot cup of sweet tea that was urged upon him.

The parlor maid, the cook, and the housekeeper all flitted about him as if they'd nothing better to do than urge another cup of tea on him after he'd drunk the first one, and then a slice of yellow cake. It was as if he'd just crossed some frozen tundra and would surely perish without some sustenance.

The cook even patted his face, saying, "How soft your cheeks are, you're as fair as an angel."

But this attention wasn't the same as that paid to him by Mrs. Acton, with her fingers curled around his arm, expecting him to say or do something a bit more daring than he usually did when making deliveries. No, the cook was more like Mrs. Pierson or even dear Mrs. Bedwin, cooing and petting and mothering as though there were no tomorrow. As if he were the dearest, sweetest creature on earth. He dropped his chin and smirked a little bit, then held his cup out for more tea.

As tea was being poured, he saw the scullery maid coming from the laundry with a basket full of lumpy white cloth. She was thin in the face, with straggles of hair coming from beneath her faded cap. He could tell it was an effort for her to hold the basket of white things away from the soot-dusted fold of sacking she had tied around her waist.

He'd heard Mrs. Pierson complain a time or two about how getting clothes clean got the ones being worn so very dirty; it was obvious that the scullery maid was having the same problem. Being so very thin, her arms were shaking under the weight of the basket, and, in a second or two, she was going to drop it and spill the clean linen all over the stone floor.

Then it happened. Just as everyone's back was turned, Oliver saw her shift forward to heft the basket a bit better on her hip, and three white lumps fell to the floor. She looked at Oliver from beneath her loose hair, her eyes wide.

He didn't know whether she was ill used or just having a bad day, but he had only a brief moment to decide what to do. Did he draw the attention of the parlor maid, the cook, and the housekeeper to the incident? Or did he distract them? But why should he help a mere scullery maid? What was it to him if she had to wash the whole lot over again? Henry and Tate would have fallen about laughing had they been there, as would any apprentice.

But before he could make up his mind, the cook caught him staring and turned before the scullery maid could scoop up the washing and put it back in the basket.

"What are you after?" snapped the cook, getting red in the face as she advanced on the girl, who looked too startled to speak. "Flouncing about as though you weren't the least scrap of flesh in this kitchen? Pick that up and get back to your work before I have a good reason to lock you in the coal cellar for the night."

The cook slapped the girl in the face, leaving a red mark, dark beneath the skin over bone, and bringing quick tears to her eyes.

The scullery maid trembled as she bent to get the once-clean laundry, crying hard enough to leave silver-white splotches on the brick floor. Her hands shook as she tucked the cloth in, and were white as they gripped the edges of the basket. Without lifting her eyes, she turned and hurried down a small white-washed corridor, where, he assumed, there was a room strung with rope for drying before the ironing.

Unsettled, Oliver put the teacup back on the saucer and stood up, holding his hands out for his cap, his scarf, and his basket. The back of his throat tasted bitter, not because he hadn't been able to help her, but because he'd been unable to decide. In the end, he might as well have announced her mistake, as he had done by looking her way so intently. She wouldn't be thinking kindly of him, and all the attention of the rest of the female staff wouldn't change how badly that made him feel.

Worst of all, he could not bring himself not to care.

He took his coat and scarf, now mostly dry from being next to a warm coal fire, and put them on. Then he took up his basket and put his cap on and said thank you to the ladies. With their waves and good-byes, he made his way up the stairs, telling himself he wasn't shaking.

When he got up out of the kitchen area and onto the street, it was as busy as before, even with the slanted, freezing rain coming down that caused the gentlemen to hurry to their carriages or under their umbrellas, pushing past him as if he wasn't even there. He stood like a dolt in the middle of the pavement, his empty basket under one arm, hearing the chimes sound the hour from a nearby steeple.

As Oliver tucked his chin into his scarf and scurried through the back lanes to Oxford Street, he realized that he could have taken the time to go to the Three Cripples to see Jack, but he wasn't going to. He was soaked through, and, besides which, Jack would not only be completely unaffected by Oliver's struggle, he would laugh and slap Oliver on the back, as though the whole thing was a lark performed for his amusement. But it wasn't.

None of this was amusing, not any of it. That Oliver had struck Martin to the floor, and that it had not been as cruel a blow as the cook's to the scullery maid, didn't matter. It had been a blow against someone who was not only defenseless, but who would be punished for fighting back. A blow was a blow, and through his cruelty to Martin, Oliver was no better than a common cook. He was worse, in fact, for he had been through it himself, and knew, *knew* what it was like to be on the receiving end of that senseless, blind brutality.

To finish matters off, Oliver had, since the orphan's arrival, been pretending, when he could, that the orphan wasn't even there. To be treated as though invisible? That was the height of cruelty. No one deserved that. Oliver certainly never had, no matter what the man in the white waistcoat might say, and the orphan—Martin—certainly didn't.

He and Martin were both workhouse boys, bundled and tossed into the world without a hint of caution. Even if between them there had not been any other connection, under the skin, they were of a kind. In realizing that, he could no longer go on treating Martin as he had. If he did, if he *did*—

At the corner of Soho Square, where the streets started bending toward the river, Oliver stopped, feeling light-headed. Normally, he would have put it down to hunger, though certainly his body was accustomed to that.

But Martin—so small for ten years of age. Oliver had seen him at mealtimes trying not to stare at the amount of food on the table once his own meagre food was gone. Trying and failing. With all the work he was doing, as much as any boy in the shop, he must be—he was—*starving*.

And it wasn't right. Oliver knew that, knew it in his heart. If he didn't change his approach to Martin, he would lose everything kind and good that was inside of himself. Yes, Martin reminded him of people and events better left forgotten, but the boy did not deserve to go hungry for it.

Oliver swallowed and took a breath, collecting his thoughts as the rain dripped from his cap. It was pouring now, and ice was starting to come down like shards of silver, slipping down his neck through his sodden scarf. It was time to go back to the shop; he started walking, heading directly there instead of delaying along the way, as he normally would have.

UPON HIS RETURN, HE HUNG UP HIS DRIPPING COAT AND SCARF and hat in the warehouse, and went straight down to the kitchen to wash, wanting to be the first person at the supper table. Which he was, and he felt slightly warmer as he slid into his seat and accepted the cup of hot tea that Mrs. Pierson gave him to drink while waiting for Mr. McCready and the boys.

She didn't give Martin any tea; Oliver felt himself flush, cheeks red, and wished he could put it down to the warmth of the kitchen versus the damp cold of outside. But it wasn't. No, it was Martin's glance his way, and his obedient stillness on his tall stool, which wobbled a little as he balanced his thin elbow on the sideboard. Waiting. Just waiting.

Oliver looked away, even though he'd told himself he wasn't going to ignore Martin, and concentrated on the sensation of a hard fist pressing on his empty stomach. He tried sipping his tea, but it had gone cold, or maybe there wasn't enough sugar in it, he didn't know. It didn't taste as good as it ought to have done.

Tate and Henry soon came quickly down the stairs, squabbling about the warehouse door, as usual, much to Oliver's relief. They washed, and then sat at the table. Henry scraped his chair, drowning out anything Oliver might think to say, and particularly, anything he might want to say about the fact that Martin was still watching him. Normally, even with an audience, Oliver would have snapped at the orphan—at Martin—to mind his own business, but he only tucked his head down and kept his mouth shut.

Mr. McCready arrived at the table, and as soon as he'd said grace and *amen*, Mrs. Pierson hurried to serve them their supper, even more eager to feed them, perhaps, on account of the cold weather. Then, finally, Oliver could cut open one of Mrs. Pierson's perfectly baked kidney and bacon pies, salivating before even a single crumb of it was in his mouth. As he chewed, he watched Henry and his perfect manners, then looked up. Martin, with a bowl in his lap, was eating something cold and leftover with both hands, and though he was looking at Oliver, he didn't say anything. But then, he wasn't allowed to, not at mealtimes.

Oliver looked at the wall, at Henry and Tate eating, at Mrs. Pierson fussing over their plates, anywhere but at Martin. Then he looked at his own plate. In addition to the savory pie, there was a pile of buttered peas, which Oliver had never cared for but made himself eat for Mrs. Pierson's sake.

He'd seen the orphan and his thin, sallow face just that morning scrubbing the stone floor that led to the larder and boiler room, soaked to the skin, his wrists and thin arms red from the washing soda. It was obvious, even from where Oliver was sitting, that there were no peas in Martin's bowl.

As Oliver put his cutlery down, Tate looked up, knife and fork in his hands, and watched Oliver push his plate away.

"I'm quite full, Mrs. Pierson," said Oliver, slowly. "Or would you see that as a ruse to leave more room for your sponge pudding?"

Mrs. Pierson preened a bit at this, then jumped up to grab

Oliver's plate as if he might, at any minute, change his mind. Before anyone could say anything, she scraped the remains of Oliver's plate into a low-sided bowl and handed it to Martin.

"Waste not, want not," said Mrs. Pierson. She watched for a moment while Martin grabbed the slice of pie with one hand and scooped up the peas with the other, and then turned back to the table where everyone was looking at her.

Mr. McCready looked a tad thunderous, but there was nothing he could do, not really. By his own edict, leftovers were to be given to the orphan.

She took all their plates and handed out the sponge pudding. Across from Oliver, Tate took a few spoonfuls that were dripping with custard. Then, looking at Oliver, Tate pushed his bowl away from him.

"I cannot understand it, Mrs. Pierson," said Tate, his mouth quivering, as if he was struggling not to smile. "I am so full, even your pudding can find no room."

Henry only shook his head when Tate looked at him, and Oliver imagined this game was too foolish for such an up-and-coming young man as Henry.

Mrs. Pierson's eyebrows flew up, and she grabbed Tate's plate and rushed it over to Martin, who was looking at her with a shocked expression. But it was too late for Mr. McCready to object; the sponge was gone in the orphan's mouth before Mrs. Pierson barely had time to get back to the table.

Oliver finished his pudding, not letting himself look at Tate. He felt shivery and hot inside at the realization that Tate was only doing this to amuse himself. It might be fun for a while, but if they bent Mr. McCready's rules to breaking point, then the rules would change, and the orphan would again know hunger and want. Martin would be the one to pay, even though it wasn't his fault that Tate enjoyed a joke. Or that Oliver's soft heart could no longer be guarded while the orphan looked so pale and shivered as he went about his daily tasks.

"That's quite enough, Mrs. Pierson," said Mr. McCready.

"Finish up your work, boys. And you, Martin, bring more coal; I cannot imagine why you think there is sufficient to bank the fires."

They returned to their tasks, Henry and Mr. McCready to the front shop, and Oliver and Tate to the warehouse. It was colder today, so Oliver poked the fire, putting in bits of coal with his bare hands, using the charred cloth to close the door tightly.

Martin came with a scuttle of coal to fill the box next to the stove and went away quietly. Oliver tried not to think upon it and instead focused his efforts on drawing up more ledger books for Tate, using a square piece of lead and the edge of a ruler to make the lines straight.

"No one does it the way you do, Oliver," said Tate as he took the prepared ledger from him. "You've got quite the hand, ever so tidy."

"Thank you," said Oliver.

When he owned a bookshop, he would be able to sit at a desk keeping records all day. A man who owned a shop had workers to haul coal and sweep horse droppings from the yard, and he never had to dirty his hands with the more mundane work.

It was just before the supper hour on Friday when the air turned cold. The snow began to come down in thick flakes, like lather from a wrestling match, cutting through the fog and making the ground quite white within minutes. Oliver had just finished loading boxes onto the shelves and was looking at his finger where a splinter had gone in. He worried it with his teeth for a moment and then thought about leaving it in place and pretending it wasn't there.

"Splinter?" asked Tate, untying his apron as he walked past Oliver.

Oliver nodded, halfheartedly thinking about getting a

penknife and digging at it, and watched as Martin came from the shop, carrying a bucket of ashes down the stairs.

For the past few days, Oliver, at most meals, had explained to Mrs. Pierson that he'd been too full to finish what was on his plate, so, subsequently, Martin had had more to eat. Tate had, for a little while, joined in for the joke of it, giving Martin his pudding both at dinner and supper. Now Tate had stopped doing this, probably because going without a sweet at the end of the meal wasn't as amusing as he'd thought it would be. And though Oliver had wanted to punch Tate for being so fickle, he didn't. At the very least, there was a little more food for Martin, who, indeed, had a bit of color in his face, now, and more energy in his walk.

Still, Martin was currently leaving a trail of ashes behind him as he walked down the wooden stairs to the ash bin in the warehouse, but it was easy to see that he wasn't aware of it. Without considering it, Oliver straightened, his mouth open to say something, trying to think quickly so that it didn't come out harsh as it might have done only days before.

But then there came a roar from the shop, and Mr. McCready was on the heels of Martin, smacking him to the stone floor before Oliver could get out a single word.

"What are you doing, leaving hot ashes to burn a wooden floor? Have you no sense?" Mr. McCready stood over Martin as he curled up on the stone, holding the side of his head where Mr. McCready had boxed his ears. "I'll teach you to be so careless."

Mr. McCready grabbed the switch from beside the door. He came back and hauled Martin up by his collar, much in the way that Oliver had once done, but Mr. McCready's grip was sure and the collar stayed true. Which meant that Martin was half choking as Mr. McCready held him and began thrashing him.

Oliver could hear the switch whistling through the air, and the sharp sound it made as it cut through skin and cloth. Martin, through low-pitched cries, couldn't even breathe enough to scream out loud, and the switch kept coming down.

"Stop." Oliver heard this coming out of his own mouth, more of a croak than anything else. Tate stood nearby, eyes wide in astonishment.

Oliver cleared his throat and heard himself say it again, in clear, ringing tones that belonged to someone altogether quite different than the person he felt himself to be.

"*Stop*. Stop *hitting* him."

The switch froze in midair, and Martin hung from Mr. McCready's grip, a dark purple bruise on his face. The switch had torn through Martin's thin trousers; Oliver saw the lash marks and counted them, vivid red pulses, the same marks his own skin had so often felt.

"What did you say to me? Are you speaking to me, Oliver?" Mr. McCready's voice thundered as he pulled Martin to a standing position. "How *dare* you. I run this shop, and the boy is in my care. You will apologize at once, do you hear?"

"When heaven's trumpets sound," said Oliver.

"What?"

"I said I will apologize *when heaven's trumpets sound* and not before." The words came out as a roar, as though a wild animal had been woken by seeing the orphan being thrashed with such violence unbefitting his small stature.

"What on earth—" Mr. McCready's mouth fell open, shock coloring his cheeks.

"He's only little," said Oliver, swallowing, feeling some of the fire die away inside of him. "And it was an accident, him spilling the ashes. The bucket's too big for him to carry, and it's been filled to the brim. What else would happen but that he would spill it? You shouldn't treat him so cruelly."

Everyone in the warehouse was looking at Oliver, their eyes wide, frozen in place, as though Oliver had begun speaking in tongues or had grown an extra head. Either of those would be more likely than that he would speak up on the orphan's behalf.

Oliver knew this; he'd been nothing but cruel to Martin since the day he'd arrived, the gift of the leavings from his plate notwithstanding. To see him now, thus, in defense of Martin, he could understand their confusion. But to stop Mr. McCready from doing what he saw as his duty? They would only conclude that he must have gone quite.

Mr. McCready let the orphan go with a shake. Martin shuddered, wiping his face with the back of his hand, and looked up at Mr. McCready with wet eyes.

"You sit over there on that bench beside the steps and you will stay out here until I give you leave to come inside. Do you understand?"

Martin nodded and went to sit down, wincing with each movement, sitting there with the weight of his body on the welts. It was a cruel thing to do, but of course, Mr. McCready never did anything by accident.

"And you." Mr. McCready turned on Oliver, pointing the switch at him. "I will give you one more opportunity to apologize. You are *not* the master here and you will *not* dictate to me—now apologize at once!"

"No," said Oliver. "I will not."

Anger suffused Mr. McCready's face with color, and Oliver could see the confusion in his eyes, the wrinkled brow. Oliver was a disappointment, he knew that. Mr. McCready probably felt that his trust in Oliver had been misplaced; any warnings Mr. Grimwig might have shared were probably coming to the forefront of Mr. McCready's mind.

But Oliver could not apologize, not for this. The orphan was a tiny mite of a thing, put to tasks that would have left Lucy, the sturdy hired girl, breathless. Oliver could no longer stand aside and see it done. Not even if, particularly not if, he'd been party to it from the beginning.

"No," he said again. "I will not. And this cannot go on."

This stopped Mr. McCready; the switch lowered in his hand. "What are you on about?"

"He needs more food; he needs more rest." Oliver could hardly believe he was saying this out loud, let alone to Mr.

McCready. Yet something in his heart insisted on it. "Let the girl take some of his tasks; she can manage those buckets better than he."

"Are you telling me how to run my shop?"

Mr. McCready's brows lowered, and he went white, and Oliver knew he'd misspoken. It was one thing to defend the orphan, but to give Mr. McCready direction? Oliver was an upstart orphan himself, who, in Mr. McCready's eyes, had overstepped his station. But it was too late to back out now.

"Yes," said Oliver. He jerked his chin up, stood his ground.

"I've spent my last ounce of compassion on you, thinking you'd shape up to be a proper clerk, but no," thundered Mr. McCready. "In spite of my best efforts, the workhouse has left its stamp all over you. Now, get over here."

Mr. McCready gestured with the switch to the table. As Tate scurried out of the way, pressing himself against the wall on the other side of the stair from the orphan, Oliver walked over to the table. He wanted to march proudly, head held high, but he knew he barely lifted his feet. The whipping he was about to receive was the least of it. Oh, yes, it would hurt, for days, perhaps, but he'd let Mr. McCready down in the worst way, and that hurt more than anything.

His face quivered as he bent over the worktable, and he hid his head in the circle of his arms. There was trying to save his little corner of the world, and then there was this. When the switch came down across the backs of his thighs, Oliver's whole body jerked, as if he was being ripped apart from within, but he did not make a sound. Would not, clamped his mouth shut, pressed his forehead against the rough boards as the switch came down again, cutting through the air, whistling, biting through to his skin. Finally, at the tenth blow, he was gasping, sweat on the back of his neck, as Mr. McCready hauled him up by his collar.

"You will go to bed without supper while I think of reasons not to dismiss you," said Mr. McCready through gritted, bared teeth. He let Oliver go with a shake, much as he had done with the orphan, to whom he pointed with the end of the switch. "And *you* will stay there till I give you leave to get up."

With dignified steps, Mr. McCready replaced the switch on the hook and pushed his hair back from his forehead. He gestured for Oliver and Tate to precede him up the stairs. When they reached the landing, Mr. McCready stopped.

"There will be two less for supper," he called down the stairs to Mrs. Pierson. Oliver could hear her confused voice as she replied, but could not make out the words.

Then Mr. McCready cuffed Oliver on the back of the head to send him up the stairs to the boys' dormitory. "I don't want to see you until morning."

"Likewise, I'm sure," said Oliver, shocked to hear himself, but he kept his voice low, almost a whisper as he limped up the stairs.

The risers seemed interminably steep, and the narrow walls pressed in upon him as though to stop him on his way. Halfway up, he paused on the landing, leaning against the wallpaper to breathe slowly, in and out, waiting for his heart to slow down. Waiting for the hot, burning layers all along the backs of his legs to stop feeling as though they'd just been given stern jabs with a hot poker.

By the time his lungs had stopped heaving and the pain in his thighs had abated a little, he made his way up the stairs to the boys' room. He went to the washstand, dipped his hands into the pitcher of leftover cold water from yesterday, and pressed his palms to his face. Had he been in anyone's good graces, Mrs. Pierson might have *tut tutted* over him and given him some sweet honey to distract him from his ill-usage, and maybe brought a cold cloth, with drops of lavender pushed in, for his forehead as he lay on his bed.

But he had none of this, only the cold water, which he drank, lifting the pitcher straight to his mouth. When that was gone, he put the pitcher back in the bowl and turned to the row of beds.

They were neatly made up, as they had been every day since

Lucy and Martin had been hired. The floor was shining, the bedsteads dusted. The room was a model of industry and comfort, at least the type of comfort an apprentice shop boy could expect. From below came the smells of supper, wafting up, speaking of boiled potatoes and butter, meat frying, and something sweet for afterward.

Shaking this off, Oliver thought about getting a book, but this would mean bending down, and he was not up to that. There was nothing for it but to shed his clothes, put on his nightshirt, and struggle under the covers. He had to lay on his front, with his arms tucked under the single pillow, so he did this, clasping his left arm with shaking fingers, blinking against the semi-gloom of the late evening room, some reflected light coming through the curtain, from a link boy perhaps, or a fire from the alley, lit by some vagrant, made up of old crates that Oliver and Tate had left there.

He had thought he would have to deal with Henry and Tate when they came up after supper, answering their foolish, probing questions. But when he next opened his eyes, the room was dark, and he could sense the breathing humps that were Henry and Tate, tucked in their beds, already asleep. They'd come up to bed hours ago, it seemed, and it was so dark and still and cold that Oliver knew it was the middle of the night.

He'd woken up from another dream about Dick, full of tangled, messy images of bone and mud, and a sharp wind whistling through his clothes as he tried to find his friend. The hunger lingered on a smudge of memory right behind his eyes. Oliver was cold all over, and the backs of his legs hissed at him whenever he tried to move.

Would Mr. McCready send him packing in the morning? Or would he have some kind though disappointed lecture for Oliver, one that would make Oliver feel worse than he already did? Would he again demand an apology, and could Oliver give it? He couldn't change the world, but surely he could do something to protect this one orphan. Just this one.

He imagined what Jack might say if Oliver were to tell him the tale of the day's happenings. He could imagine, as well, the look of confusion that Jack would give him, as if to ask, *Why should you care? Why would you go to such ends?*

Oliver knew it was true; one orphan or a thousand, the story was the same. They all lived hard lives and were loved by no one. It was his own story, and the fact that he'd escaped it to start another life was a miracle of coincidence and dumb luck, all floating on a river of circumstance, such as the one that had carried Noah to the Three Cripples just in time to help Fagin with his machinations. How odd was that, how improbable?

Noah, for his part, would just shake his head if Oliver were to tell him. Not only did Noah not care about any humanity, save his own, he didn't understand why anybody would feel any different than that. Looking out for himself had always been Noah's credo; to do anything else was to cause himself too much expense and bother. Let the other man fall on his face, for what did Noah Claypole care? He would only mock Oliver if he knew what Oliver meant to do, which was to stand up to Mr. McCready in the morning to ensure that Martin was not overworked. That he be treated better.

What would Oliver do to gain that aim? Would he then apologize? It would be a burden to apologize, but perhaps he should. If Mr. McCready didn't sack him on the spot, that is.

His eyelids were starting to feel heavy, so he kept them shut instead of trying to blink to keep himself awake. He let the darkness take him where it would, with blurred images of Dick's face, that last morning in the garden, and of Jack, cocking his head to stare at Oliver that first day in London. Staring at Oliver, ragged and haggard from walking seven days on almost no food, looking at him with an expression that, in retrospect, had been calculating. Looking at Oliver as if he was a bright new toy that Jack had just found, something for Fagin to use as he would.

Oliver had no doubt that Jack had had no part of the deal between Monks and Fagin, though Jack had, to be sure, gained from the introduction of the very young Oliver to the kindly old gentleman of his intimate acquaintance. Money, perhaps? Or extra recommendations as Jack moved up in the ranks? Oliver would never know.

How might it have been different had he taken Dick with him to London, those many years ago? Would that he had taken another turn that day or kept going or stopped sooner. Then he never would have met Jack. Though, in truth, it wasn't Jack's fault, or even Noah's, that put Oliver where he was now. In serious disgrace and at the risk of losing everything. But what price was too high if he answered to his own heart?

The last thought, which draped itself about his mind as a well-worn velvet cloak, was replaced by the question as to what on earth Jack had been doing in Barnet, so far from his normal stomping grounds. Oliver had wondered that, on and off, through the years; it had never occurred to him he might take the opportunity to ask.

## 21

# THE CONSEQUENCES OF
# OLIVER'S PASSIONATE NATURE

Oliver awoke to the stumblings and mutterings of Henry and Tate as they squabbled over the hot water that Lucy had just brought up. He heard her steps going down, and Mrs. Pierson's loud shouts for something or someone, and he knew he had to get up. Face the day. Face his workmates. Face Mr. McCready.

For their parts, Henry and Tate merely nodded at Oliver, as though yesterday had been an ordinary day. Which it had not been, though whether or not Tate and Henry had talked to each other about it, Oliver didn't know. They were not unkind boys; it was not in them to torment, or in Tate's case, to tease overly much. They both knew the grace of their stations; to become ill-mannered was to chance losing them. For as anyone could see, a McCready's Haberdashery boy was a cut above an unemployed ex-apprentice.

"Water's yours, Oliver," said Tate, as he finished pouring his slops into the bucket. "Better hurry to breakfast; you must be starving after yesterday."

"Yes," said Oliver.

He made himself get straight out of bed and go to the basin to wash. But he forgot and rolled the sleeves of his nightshirt too far, exposing his upper arm and the jagged half circle of ridged flesh. Both Henry and Tate stood there with open mouths and wide eyes. They might have heard about what had happened, perhaps, but now they had the evidence of it with their very own eyes, that Oliver came from a very bad background.

"Not looking's just as bad as staring," said Oliver, his heart racing, trying for some levity as he imagined Jack might at a moment such as this. Though why he felt that being like Jack was ever a good thing was beyond him. Jack might laugh when he told him, if he ever did.

He made himself finish washing, as if this were any ordinary day. He went to his bed to put on his clothes and to put himself in order, straightening his suspenders, tying his boots, taking down his brown waistcoat from its peg. All the while feeling the stiffness of the whipping from the day before. It began in the back of his neck, as if all of his muscles were joined together, locked in iron. He had to roll his shoulders before he could pull the waistcoat on.

He could go on this way, feeling angry, or he could apologize; Mr. McCready said he might, if he was able. Mr. McCready always kept his word and let bygones be bygones once reparations had been made.

Straightening his waistcoat and adjusting his shirt collar, Oliver followed Henry and Tate down the stairs. They all clomped, of course they did, in spite of the many injunctions against it, both by Mr. McCready and Mrs. Pierson. But with the good smells of a hot breakfast, even Oliver could not help but hurry.

In the kitchen, Mrs. Pierson was alone, with the table half-set and she with her hands dirty with coal.

"Can I assist you, Mrs. Pierson?" asked Henry, gallantly.

"You can load this coal and deal with this fire while I finish up this porridge."

"Has the new girl gone off already, Mrs. Pierson?" asked Tate.

He took his seat with a little smile, as if he were on the verge of finding the whole disarray of the morning extremely funny.

"No, the master wanted extra hot water, and so I sent her up." Mrs. Pierson looked directly at Oliver as though yesterday's events had never happened. "Oliver, be a dear boy and go and find that orphan. I've called and called, but there's been no answer."

Oliver nodded, glad to be of use and out of the kitchen while it was so unsettled. He checked the laundry and the scullery and the storeroom, all only a little way off the kitchen, but still a viable set of rooms where an orphan might hide and sulk. He even checked the door to the larder, but it was locked, and only Mrs. Pierson had the keys. A quick check of the coal cellar revealed the same. Martin was not in the most obvious places.

Feeling a moment of pure concern followed by an odd sensation of dizziness, Oliver climbed to the main floor and walked around the quiet shop, gloomy on account of the shutters still hanging on the outside of the windows. The room was clean and empty, with not even a scuff mark or a bit of dust to indicate anyone had been there since yesterday. The whole of the shop was entirely silent, with only the barest of noises from above and below to indicate anyone was nearby.

Oliver determined to go to the warehouse, though with no fire lit, it would be cold this hour of the morning. When he opened the door, he could smell the smoke from the fire the day before, though the icy cold air through the opened upper windows felt clean and brisk against his face, and the morning's church bells came through on the damp breeze. He stood at the landing with one foot on the top stair, and scanned the warehouse, the narrow spaces between the shelves, noting that the small door inside the big door was firmly shut and locked from the inside.

Thinking to kneel next to the deal table under the window to look for Martin there, he went down the stairs, and as he descended he heard a small stuttered sound. When he turned to look for the source of it, he saw Martin, tucked against the wall on the bench, his knees pulled up to his narrow chest.

Martin's skin was white, and he hadn't even the strength to shiver nor, it seemed, the sense to reach up and take down the warehouse coat to wrap around him. That Mr. McCready had neglected to bring Martin in after his punishment was obvious. The night had been cold enough to leave frost along the edges of the windows, and was cold enough still. Oliver could see his own breath cloud in the air.

Oliver rushed over to Martin. As Oliver knelt on the cold stone floor, Martin gave several hitching gasps, and when he turned to look at Oliver, he could barely open his eyes. They were dim, clouded over, and his lips were blue. When Oliver touched the orphan's face, it was as cold as Uncle Brownlow's face had been when Oliver had kissed him good-bye. Colder, even, because inside of the small frame was a beating heart; the contrast was too horrible to contemplate.

Oliver stood, pulling the small boy into his arms. Martin, still and cold, huffed a breath, a small, icy movement of air against Oliver's neck, and then went still. There was no respite from the panicked thud of Oliver's heart as he hurried as fast as he was able with the bundle in his arms, up the wooden steps to the shop and then down the stairs to the kitchen, where Mrs. Pierson's freshly lit coal fire waited.

"What in heaven's name—" Mrs. Pierson broke off as she watched Oliver kneel on the stone floor, unfolding Martin into the slow warmth that circled in waves around the cast-iron stove.

"Why, Oliver, has he been in the warehouse all this time? On such a cold night?"

Oliver looked over his shoulder, but only for an instant. Mrs. Pierson had her hands to her face, mouth open, a soundless heaving of her bosom. Likewise, Henry and Tate had stood up from their places at the table, frozen, as though uncertain what was going on.

Oliver turned his back on all of them and watched his own

hands reach out, feeling numb and mindless, as though he were observing himself do this from a long distance away. There was no feeling in his fingers as he stroked Martin's face, touched his temples, chafed his wrists.

He gathered Martin's hands in his own, the small fingers with permanent grime scoured into the knuckles. Martin's hand was still, so still, and the fingers did not clutch back. They merely slid from Oliver's hands like small, boneless ribbons.

There was a silkiness to Martin's hair as Oliver pushed it away from Martin's forehead, which Oliver, to his horror, realized was damp from the frost melting in the warmth of the room, and not from the boy's skin. Martin's eyes, a milky blue, were open but did not flicker, nor did the narrow chest rise and fall. Between the moment Oliver had lifted Martin from the warehouse floor and this, the orphan had breathed his last.

"He's not breathing," said Oliver, barely able to speak the words. "He's—he's *dead*."

"Nonsense," said Mrs. Pierson. She gave Martin a nudge with the tip of her black shoe poking from beneath her skirts. "Get up, you wretch. There's work to be done, so none of your lolly-gagging."

Oliver touched the skin beside Martin's eyes, but Martin did not even flinch. Oliver wanted to shove the cold body away from him, but he thought of Dick and gently cradled the back of Martin's head as he laid him down on the stones. The warmth of the fire was quite close now, but though it dried the dampness from Martin's hair, his skin was growing cold.

Oliver stood up.

"Leave him be," he said to Mrs. Pierson, to the room. "He's dead, so leave him be."

Mrs. Pierson's hand flew to her bosom, face white as she took a step back.

"Why, Oliver," said Mr. McCready, as he stepped into the kitchen from the stairs. "How dare you speak to Mrs. Pierson

295

so? Apologize at once and avoid further disgrace. And you, boy, get up from the floor now, and get to work."

"The only place he'll be going is a pauper's grave," said Oliver, utterly confused why they didn't seem to care what had happened to Martin. "Don't you understand? He's *dead*."

"There's no need to carry on so," said Mrs. Pierson.

"No, indeed," said Mr. McCready. He came fully into the kitchen, moving past the boys and Mrs. Pierson to come right up to Oliver. "Besides, there are plenty of orphans at St. James, thus we can easily acquire another."

*"Another?"* Oliver felt the roar rush from his chest as he said this, his voice a live thing with no master. "You left him in the warehouse, and he froze to death, and you imagine you can simply acquire another? And then another after *that?"*

Mr. McCready's eyebrows rose, color rising in his cheeks, as if it were horribly inconsiderate of Oliver to stand up for a dead orphan.

"He was never sturdy, Oliver," said Mr. McCready in the same tone he'd used with Mrs. Pierson the morning the stove had broken down. A tone meant to be soothing and pleasant, but which only made Oliver's blood pound quicker still. "Some of the warehouse boys, why, a stiff breeze would knock them over. I'm quite sure the workhouse council and the beadle will under-stand that."

"There might be an endless supply of small boys with nothing to eat and nobody to speak for them," said Oliver, his face hot, his jaw clenched, teeth bared, "but they are not made available for you to abuse and neglect as you please. They are not yours to dispose of at a whim—how dare you, how *dare* you—"

Up to that moment, Oliver had been the obedient boy that everyone expected him to be, the sort of boy that Jack had mocked him for being. But something was moving thickly inside of him, like huge timber beams on a ship tossed at sea. Oliver reached out and only meant to push Mr. McCready back, as far away as possible, from Martin's still form on the floor. Instead, he slammed Mr. McCready in the middle of his chest.

Mr. McCready stumbled back, mouth open in astonishment. All the breath in Oliver's body left him as though it had been sucked out by the silent, gaping roar that seemed to fill the room.

Oliver reached out his hand and grasped the handle of the cast-iron frying pan that was warming on the stove, in preparation, no doubt, for thick slices of good bacon, and hefted it in the air. He had one split moment of thought, a whispered caution, one that almost stopped him, but momentum had built up in his body. He swung the pan in the air and slammed it against Mr. McCready's head.

Mr. McCready jerked upright for a second, his whole body tightening, his shoulders stiff, and then he toppled to the floor, blood pouring in a red wave, forming a lake across the stones.

The iron pan vibrated against Oliver's palm. He dropped it and stepped back from the blood that splashed up and hit the edge of his boot.

Mrs. Pierson, her shrieks ringing in Oliver's inner ear in dull echoes, ran to the door that led up to the street. He could hear her yelling, yelling for the constable, shouting at someone passing by on the damp street above to go and fetch the constable.

As Oliver looked at Henry and Tate and they at him, the moment became as frozen and still as a pauper's grave, as Dick had been placed in, as Martin shortly would be. The thought of it shuddered through Oliver, leaving him trying to breathe, gasping gulps past which no words could be eased. He could not explain that striking Mr. McCready was not what he meant to do, let alone—

"You murdered him," said Tate, hardly above a whisper. Of course it was Tate who would speak first; Henry remained silent, his expression tightening, as though with some deep disdain for Oliver that he hardly had expressed until that moment.

"No," said Oliver, protesting against not only the accusation but also against the hot tumble in his belly that rose to his chest, threatening to choke him outright. "I only meant to—"

Mrs. Pierson stumbled back through the door, the air of the frosty morning leeching the warmth out of the room. She clutched her apron and skirts out of the way, and Oliver could see, through the narrow top of the window, a pair of booted feet clattering on the top step.

Oliver skirted the pool of blood turning to brown on the floor as it dried by the heat of the stove. He scrambled up the wooden steps to the first floor, mouth open, panting, arms aching with emptiness. He'd left Dick behind so callously. He'd failed Martin, leaving him to all the misery of abject neglect. And now this.

The air was sparking with black dots in front of his eyes; he could barely see as he headed along the narrow corridor on the ground floor and went through the door that led to the chilly warehouse. Without thinking, hands and limbs numb, Oliver grabbed the warehouse coat and threw it on, noting the dull flowers of red and brown on his shirt bosom as he pulled the jacket over it.

He could barely manage the lock on the small wooden door that led to the courtyard; it was stiff with cold. Oliver bent close and breathed on it, his fingers tugging all the while until it loosened and shot open beneath his hands. He could hear shouting from the kitchen; he had to hurry, or they'd catch him.

He knew, his heart thudding painfully against his breastbone as he stepped through the opening and into the cobbled yard, that there was only one place he could go. Only one person he could turn to. So he started running.

## ❧ 22 ❧

# THE FLIGHT; OR AT THE THREE CRIPPLES

A s Oliver flung himself up the alley that led to Soho Square, he thought he could hear the clink of sturdy hobnail boots on the muddy cobbles of Wardour Street and the shrill, ear-piercing whistles of constables on the alert. But that sound was soon dampened by the ragged breaths in his own throat, the pounding of his heart as he ran through Soho Square, churning up chunks of black snow in his wake.

When he skidded into Oxford Street, he skulked at the corner, clutching his arms around himself, gazing numbly at the traffic going past. It was too wide and well-traveled a street, and he was already too visible, particularly in the grime-stained warehouse coat with the splatters of blood on his shirt. He looked as out of place in this respectable street as Jack had in front of the haberdashery.

Oliver crossed the street as quickly as he could, jumping between overloaded, slow-moving wagons and spinning carriage wheels, keeping the jacket clutched around him. Then he ducked into an arched alleyway between two fine buildings, behind which lurked narrow lanes of mud-stained rookeries and leaning, half-timbered houses that were so old the bricks had crumbled through the whitewash, leaving red stains, as iron might, in weeping trails beneath the rudely shuttered windows.

With a bleak gasp, Oliver made himself head up the slight slope along the narrow lanes, ducking under timbers propped in the middle of the oozing, muddy streets, his sturdy boots splashing in half-frozen mud, getting it on his trouser legs. Not caring. Not letting himself care, as he ran along the grime-painted back streets that, though parallel to Oxford Street, were as different from it as the white flakes of snow were from the muddy, moving boil of the Thames.

His boots slipped on the mud and half-melted snow that seeped between the cobblestones. Panting, he only partly realized where his feet were taking him, but at least the whistles of the constables seemed to have faded from being directly behind him to several streets over, so that was something.

Spars of sunlight half-banked off brick walls, heating them and melting the snow, bringing a fulsome smell that swirled up around him. He pushed past it and kept moving, running till he thought his heart would burst. Then he stumbled as he turned a corner, reaching out for the edge of a cold, wet window ledge to steady himself.

Surely he was not lost. He couldn't be this confused about where he was going, not after having been the best delivery lad McCready's establishment had ever known. Surely the tavern was just beyond this narrow lane, which was thick with drapes of handkerchiefs and shabby goods for sale. Surely the Three Cripples was just ahead on the left.

He made himself walk normally and calmed his breathing, though his heart was pounding, till at last his feet found a familiar intersection, and his nose told him that the leather-working shops near Saffron Hill were just along on his right. And that if he kept going on Charles Street until it met with Saffron Hill, he would get there.

What would he do if Jack wasn't at the tavern? Or if Noah Claypole *was* there and the only person known to Oliver? It was bad enough he'd sunk so low that the Three Cripples might be his only refuge. Or maybe, seeing as they were merely thieves and housebreakers, the customers at the Three Cripples might not want a murderer in their midst. So what was he to do then?

He kept walking anyway, and when he arrived at the Three Cripples, his hands shook as he put them around the door knob. He was not only unexpected but also uninvited, and overwhelmed by his actions of that morning. The way his head ached and the welts from the whipping from the day before—how had he fallen so far that such a low place was the *best* that he could do?

As he pulled on the knob, the brown door, streaked with street-splatter, came open, sagging slightly, as it always did, letting in more than a smattering of weather, as it always did, so that the seats and tables by the door, swathed in damp, were usually occupied by those low enough not to demand better.

He stepped into the steamy, hop-laced air of the Three Cripples. The crowd was very thin; it was early, even for regulars. Oliver scanned the tables and then peered into the little alcove where a coal fire was often burning in the afternoon, and where he'd found Jack on previous visits. He told himself it was foolish to expect to find Jack there, just as Oliver had last seen him. As though Jack had nothing to do but wait for Oliver, tipping back his chair and tapping his clay pipe against the scarred, dark surface of the table.

Jack wasn't there, but then neither was Noah, so that was a small blessing, at least. He recognized no one, but if sanctuary was not to be found at the Three Cripples, then he had nowhere else to go. Maybe he should turn around now, walk out, find the nearest constabulary, and admit his guilt.

Oliver stood there, feeling almost naked without his hat and scarf. As the barkeeper looked him up and down, Oliver became conscious of his bare hands, the filthy coat he wore. And, beneath that, the bloody streaks that he knew must be drying into an impenetrable brown; nothing would get those stains out.

"What you want?" asked the barkeeper.

The barked question from the bar startled him, and he jumped. When he opened his mouth, he hadn't the faintest idea what to say.

"We ain't open yet."

This was a lie. Even Oliver knew that. Any fool could see the two men huddled over their pints beside the window. Any fool could see the man with his long coat, which almost hid his filthy trousers, popping back a tot of gin as he stood near the bar. It might be early, but the Three Cripples never really closed.

"I'm looking for—" Oliver began, but then he stopped. It was as if to say it, to say Jack's name aloud, was to take the final step in admitting why he was here, even if only to himself.

"'E's Jack's," said a man, as he came out from the back room wearing only a shirt and a greasy wool scarf around his neck. He grunted the words out. "Seen 'im 'ere, 'e's Jack's."

Oliver blinked; he'd only met Cromwell once, but perhaps it didn't matter, he recognized him now. Cromwell now had Oliver's ticket into a safe haven, however temporary, if only he could open his mouth and clear his throat and inquire as to where he might find Jack.

"Jack!" Cromwell bellowed the name, raising his voice to the ceiling; in the relative quiet of the tavern, the shout echoed in the air.

After a moment, where Oliver looked at the bartender and was stared at in return, there was the sound of a door slamming. It came from overhead, from somewhere within the upstairs warren of the tavern. Footsteps came trundling along the hall and halfway down the stairs. And then there was Jack.

His shirt was untucked, his chest bare, his hair rumpled. He was yawning from sleep and looking so familiar in the morning gloom of the tavern that Oliver almost started forward. But he stopped himself. It wasn't guaranteed that Jack would want to harbor a murderer.

"Jack, your mate's 'ere." Cromwell barked, waving his hand at the bartender, as if to indicate that this was no longer any of his concern. Then he jerked his thumb in Oliver's direction, as though Oliver weren't the only out-of-place figure in the whole of the tavern.

Jack woke up slowly and then fast, as Oliver remembered, and it happened now. He nodded at nobody, rubbing his fingers hard in the corner of his eye, the gesture a memory from when they'd shared rough blankets in Fagin's den. All of this flooded over Oliver as though it had spilled out of Jack in this one, unguarded gesture.

And still, Jack had not seen him. Expressions moved across Jack's face, and Oliver tried to discern what each of them meant. And from that determine whether Jack would be serious or whether he would joke or whether he would dismiss the whole thing as beneath his notice.

As soon as he focused on Oliver, Jack's eyebrows went up and he hurried down the rest of the stairs, smiling, barefoot in the cold morning.

"Nolly? What you doin' here, then? Hell, it ain't even noon."

Oliver almost smiled in return, but didn't.

As Cromwell walked over to the bartender, Jack walked right up to Oliver. Seeming unfazed by the rough coat and absence of the gentlemanly hat and scarf that marked Oliver as an apprentice at a very well-to-do haberdashery. Jack reached out to touch the edge of the collar of Oliver's shirt.

"You look at bit done in, Nolly," said Jack, almost cheerfully, as if, indeed, Oliver's being down-and-out was a good thing. "Come upstairs, then," said Jack in a relatively normal voice, though it might have been too normal, especially for a chilly and mostly empty tavern.

Jack paused, really looking at Oliver, missing nothing. Jack's eyes narrowed. That he could see all the evidence was easy to believe, even if he didn't yet understand any of it. Jack caught Oliver's eyes with his own and held them, looking, watching.

Oliver opened his mouth, panting, unable to speak, while the memory of yesterday, and that very morning, overwhelmed him. He struggled with the words he needed to say, must say. To explain it to Jack and to himself.

He'd never thought he was a person so evil as to take someone's life, but he *had*; the lake of blood had spread around Mr. McCready's head with the ease of spilled water. Oliver's life had dragged him to this spot, and so there he stood, unable to say anything nor tear his eyes away from Jack's.

"Nolly?" asked Jack. his brows lowered, confusion making him look cross.

As Oliver took a breath to try again, the constable's whistle shrilled just beyond the door. It was too much to hope they were after a common pickpocket, not when they'd been hot on his heels all the way from McCready's Haberdashery. Not so early in the morning. Not in this slanting, freezing winter rain. Not if they didn't have to.

"Are those for you?" Cromwell asked, turning his head toward the door, eyes narrowing.

Oliver nodded.

"An' you brung 'em 'ere?" Cromwell strode toward Oliver, forcing the words out through gritted teeth. "They're already lookin' at us, they're always lookin', an' you brung 'em 'ere?"

There was a pounding at the door, and before Oliver could even begin to stammer an explanation, Jack whistled to the bartender and jerked his chin at Cromwell.

"I'm puttin' him away," snapped Jack. "You lot carry on."

Jack grabbed Oliver by the arm and hauled him up the wooden stairs he'd just come down. The smell of rot and damp barely pierced the panicked thudding of Oliver's heart as he scrambled up into the gloom and dark after Jack. Jack, who pulled on him hard and didn't let go.

At the top of the landing, the narrow passage went to the left, and Jack practically ran, yanking Oliver past battered brown doors, through the fetid, still air that bespoke of windows shut tight against the cold night, to the end of the corridor. Jack stopped and pushed, not at the door at the very end of the corridor, but at a wooden panel on the wall. It opened upon a small space, about half the height of a man and not much wider than that. It gaped at Oliver like a dangerous, open mouth.

"In," said Jack, pulling on the scruff of Oliver's coat collar. "Get in an' stay down. An' keep your yap shut till I whistle, you got it? Otherwise, the peelers'll have us all if they're chasin' you an' find you here. Got it?"

Oliver nodded, and Jack pushed him in the hole, almost knocking Oliver's head against the low lintel, not even waiting till Oliver was settled before he moved his hand along the wood panel to close it.

"Wait for my whistle."

The panel closed with a scrape and a slide, leaving Oliver in the small space. He tried to settle himself, shaking, blinking as his eyes teared up, ice thumping in his veins. Bracing his back against the cold brick wall, he tucked his knees up. The walls were so close, he could barely get his arms around his knees. He could only tip his head low, chin against his chest, and close his eyes against the darkness.

Dimly, through the cracks in the wooden floorboards beneath him, he could hear faraway voices, none of which he could recognize as Jack's. He waited, teeth chattering, listening to feet walking across creaking boards, doors slamming, the feet coming closer, as though they were mounting the stairs. Then footsteps, several pairs, came down the corridor toward him, and he could now hear the distinction between different voices. Among them was Jack's, seemingly sleepy and, uncharacteristically, almost bored.

"Yeah, gents, here's the rooms," said Jack's voice, yawning. "But 'tis early yet for the likes of us.

"The likes of you?" asked a voice, stern and careful.

"We keeps a tavern," said Cromwell, and Oliver's whole body jerked with a start when he heard it. "Drinkin' ain't a sin yet, is it?"

"No," said the voice in a crisp way that made Oliver sure the constable was only two feet away and so very close. If Oliver so much as shifted, the man would be able to hear the brush of cloth against cloth. "It's not a sin, although serving drink before time is not legal."

"Them two men rows a skiff on the river," said Cromwell. "T'other works the new ditch along Fleet. Surely it's nothin' to anyone to give them a bit of comfort against the cold."

"Ditchin's hard work," added Jack, his voice sounding as though it came directly from the other side of the wood panel.

Another pair of footsteps approached as doors were opened and closed. Several low voices muttered in protest. Cool air eased up through the floorboards, bringing the scent of fresh river mud, the tang of beer, the funk of an unaired room.

"Everything seems in order, sir," said a new voice, as though in response to an unasked question. "One of them below reported seeing someone of the description hurrying past the windows."

"And?"

"He seemed indifferent, sir, as though he couldn't be bothered to tell us more than that."

"We'll keep up the search, then."

"What's he wanted for?" asked Cromwell. "This fella you're lookin' for."

"Not that it's anything to you," said the first constable. "But with the *wanted* posters going up this very day, everybody will know. There's an apprentice lad who's wanted for assaulting his master."

There was a silent moment as this notion sank in, and then the footsteps started off.

"Take several men and go north of Holborn and search there," said the first constable. "I'll take the rest and head toward Smithfield. And get those posters up as quick as you might."

"Yes, sir," said the second constable.

Oliver's heart started to pound so hard that he couldn't hear anything else. Only his heart and the ratchet-like clicking of his teeth. The darkness behind his eyes grew, and he struggled to remain where he was, struggled not to move, struggled not to shout or leap to his feet and claw his way through the wooden panel.

He had murdered his master and everyone in the Three Cripples, Saffron Hill, even the whole of London, would know the truth inside the hour. The constables were after him. If they caught him, he'd be hanged, just as he'd been born to, just as the man in the white waistcoat had predicted so many years ago, the day Oliver had turned nine. That was the day he'd met Mr. Bumble. The day he'd been separated from Dick, and the day his life began moving from one misery to another, until he met Uncle Brownlow.

He hugged himself hard and breathed deeply, telling himself he was too old to be afraid of the dark, although he was not too old to be afraid to die. He couldn't be certain that Jack, in his irritation, might not simply throw Oliver into the street for the constables to take. And wasn't Noah an informer? If Noah found out, if Noah saw the wanted posters that told of Oliver's awful deed, surely he'd be first in line for the reward money. Whether or not Jack helped Oliver, Noah must never know, must *never* be told.

Oliver waited in the darkness for a long time; he didn't know how long. Just that his knees began to feel stiff, and he longed to stand and stretch out, to take a deep breath. The wood beneath him and the bricks behind him were cold, and some unseen draft soaked through the thick warehouse jacket and his good woolen trousers. Even in his sturdy boots he felt it, creaking and freezing till he began to lose feeling in his toes.

A faraway door slammed, and he heard footsteps racing up the stairs. He wanted to move, but Jack had said to wait for the whistle, so Oliver waited. Soon he heard it, piercing and low, not hesitant but quick. Then it came again, making Oliver think he must whistle in response to answer it. But before he could lick his dry lips, the panel slid back, letting in a stream of warm air, and the outline of Jack. Jack's hand reached for him, yanking him out of the small room. Jack hauled him toward the farthest door, the solitary door at the very end of a very narrow corridor.

"I've got him," said Jack, over his shoulder, and Oliver had a brief glimpse of Cromwell and the barkeeper crowding the landing at the top of the stairs. "I'll take care of this."

"See that you do," said Cromwell. "I don't want them constables sniffin' about more than they already do. And get 'im a different shirt, that one's got blood on it. An' can you do nothing to rough up 'is edges? Take 'im, Jack, an' do somethin' about that. We can figure out how to use 'im later."

"Got it," said Jack, tugging on Oliver's jacket as Cromwell and the bartender disappeared down the stairs.

Oliver wanted to protest that he wasn't going to be used by anybody, least of all a criminal, but he'd laid Mr. McCready low, left him bleeding on the flat stones of the kitchen floor, so maybe he deserved to be used.

"Jack," said Oliver, as he went where Jack was dragging him. "I want to go home."

"You can't," said Jack. "But don't worry, he won't want much, you'll be all right with us. Just do as he says, and you'll be safe."

But Oliver felt so far from safe—so very, very far.

Pulling a key from his trouser pocket, Jack unlocked the door and turned the small brass knob that glinted against the scratched and stained wood. The key and the lock seemed too feeble than to do more but keep out an errant passerby; if anyone wanted to get in, they could. But once Jack had pushed Oliver into the low gloom, he could understand why it wasn't important.

The room contained only a low bed under the slanted ceiling, a small, old-fashioned clothespress, a square wooden table, and a single chair. There might or might not be a candlestick on the shallow mantel above the small fireplace, but since Jack did not move to light it, Oliver could not be sure. The room smelled dank and closed and faintly of Jack; his scent spread all over Oliver, now that he was standing still.

Oliver went over to the far wall and slid to the floor in the small space between the long, narrow window, which let in a little light, and the clothespress in the corner, upon which was heaped a pile of garments. The clothes were possibly Jack's, or, more likely, stolen, waiting to be sorted and sold. But it didn't matter. Jack loomed over him, kicking the door shut with his heel, blocking Oliver's movement, leaving him no chance to stand up or move aside or to do anything but look up at Jack.

"Care to share, then?" asked Jack, voice tight, eyes sparking in the half dark. "Why'd you come here, bein' a murderer, knowin' it'd bring the peelers down on our heads, gettin' us all hanged on account of associatin' with the likes of you?"

Oliver struggled to push himself away from the wall; he could think a great deal more clearly if he could but stand and talk to Jack man-to-man, not cowering in the corner. Because he'd not meant to, had never meant to—

Jack hauled Oliver to his feet, suddenly, and pushed Oliver against the wall. Oliver planted a bold hand in the middle of Jack's chest to hold him at bay.

"Do you think I wanted to come here?" Oliver asked, rage pounding in his head. "Do you think I *wanted* to kill him?"

He swung his fist at Jack and clocked him right on the jaw. Jack staggered back, slapping a hand to his face. His eyebrows rose in surprise, just as Oliver realized he'd struck the solitary person who might not only have the ability to hide him, but who might also have cause. Jack himself could as easily turn Oliver in as anything else, and Oliver knew he'd been foolish to let his temper get away from him.

"You must have done," said Jack, tightening his lips, snarling. "Otherwise, you wouldn't've."

"I didn't *want* to." Oliver almost shouted it. He pressed his back against the cold wall, knocking his head against the frame of the high, narrow window. "But he left the orphan, locked him in the warehouse all night. He froze to death, he—Martin's *dead*, don't you understand?"

Oliver stopped, eyes hot, fully expecting Jack to burst out with a derisive laugh and deliver some comment about how it was an orphan's lot to die in the freezing cold. And what of it? Orphans died every day.

But Jack was silent, brows furrowing as his green eyes scanned Oliver up and down. Oliver could see Jack's expression in the low gloom, and that he was calculating the risks and thinking about what needed to be done.

Oliver looked down at himself. The warehouse coat, with half of its buttons missing, had fallen open. There was a slash of blood across his shirt bosom and larger spots near his collar, and the placket was dirt-smudged where he'd clutched the orphan to him. The evidence was all over him; all Jack needed to do was to shove him out into the street and shout for the law.

Then Jack surprised him.

"Get them things off, quick now, afore the peelers determine to have another go at us."

Jack came at him, hands divesting Oliver of his coat and throwing it on the bed. Without asking permission, he pulled Oliver's shirt out of his trousers and over his head, leaving Oliver shivering, bare-chested and half-naked. And before Oliver could stop Jack, he'd knelt and tossed the shirt on the low coals of the small grate. He poked at the cloth with a metal rod that served as a poker and breathed on the coals till the cloth caught. Warmth plumed into the room for a bare second and then faded away.

Then Jack stood, turning, walking toward Oliver, purposeful and focused, as though Jack were intent on assault. Oliver took a small step backward as Jack approached, folding his arms across his chest, partly from the air, chill against his bare skin, and partly to hide the scar on his upper arm.

But Jack didn't stop; he came right up to Oliver until they

were toe-to-toe, so close that Oliver felt the path of Jack's breath on his bare neck. He shivered as Jack's hands landed on his waist, pulling on the tabs of his trousers. With his fingers splayed wide, Jack half turned Oliver to better get at the buttons of the tabs, when he stopped. There was a quiet pause as the edge of Jack's fingers crept above the wool of the trousers and onto Oliver's waist, where they rested, still and warm, on Oliver's icy skin.

"When'd you get these, eh?" Jack asked. Both of Jack's hands moved up, circling Oliver's bare waist, fingertips tender as they avoided the welts that curved around Oliver's back.

Oliver shivered at his touch. He did not want to think about anything else now, let alone talk, but Jack wanted an answer.

"Yesterday evening," said Oliver, for what did it matter now? He was a murderer, so a thrashing from his master was hardly of importance by comparison. "Mr. McCready had hard words for me after I—well, I objected to his treatment of the orphan, and then he—" Oliver stopped, flinching as Jack's finger traced the curve of a welt. "Never mind it; it doesn't matter."

Something flickered across Jack's face, but then he was all business again, tugging at the waistband of Oliver's sturdy brown trousers.

"Take off them boots an' get out of them trousers."

"Do you have a shirt? Let me put on a shirt first." Oliver didn't even pretend he wasn't embarrassed, as Jack was likely to mock him in any case. But he wasn't about to willingly stand in front of Jack halfway to being in a state of nature.

Jack surprised him again by nodding. He reached around Oliver, bumping him out of the way, and dug through the pile on top of the clothespress to pull out a shirt. Straightening up, he pressed the shirt into Oliver's hands.

"It's one of mine. It's not exactly clean, but that don't matter. Be quick about it. An' if you're goin' to be stayin' with me, at any rate, you'll be givin' up them fancy manners of yours. Otherwise, you'll stick out, plain as a Chinaman in Trafalgar Square."

Jack was helping him, but Oliver still wasn't sure why. Maybe

Jack would have sheltered anyone for whom the constables were searching. *We look after our own*, Jack had once said. But did that mean Jack would now consider Oliver to be one of his own?

Oliver pulled the shirt over his head, and became enveloped in Jack's scent, coal soot and sweat blended together. The shirt was of thick linen, ragged along the cuffs and with a long burn mark along the collar. No doubt, being so thick and fine, the garment was stolen. But it also hung halfway down to his knees, which meant he could keep most of his modesty as well as cover the scar.

Jack knelt at Oliver's feet, and pushing up the bottom of his trousers, grabbed his ankle. Oliver tried to pull his foot from Jack's reach, but Jack just looked up at him with that smirk, as if he knew everything that Oliver was thinking.

"Quit your fussin'," said Jack. "These boots, your whole kit; a peeler an' anybody else for miles could spot you as bein' out of place. Like I said. You stay here? My lodgin's, my rules."

Oliver became still, heart thumping as Jack forcibly removed his boots and threw them against the door. They clattered and fell with a thud, and Jack stood, reaching for Oliver's trousers again.

"I'll do it," Oliver said. He held up both hands. "I will, just let me alone."

Jack paused, eyes glinting, but at the ready, it seemed, to divest Oliver of every stitch if he didn't do exactly as Jack wanted. Oliver fumbled with the buttons, hastily, and pulled the trousers off, feeling the bite of cold air against his thighs through the linen shirt. Then he threw the trousers at Jack, who caught them and fingered the sturdy cloth, heedless of the recent intimacy of Oliver's skin against the wool.

"These'll bring a price," Jack said. His mouth pursed in a thoughtful line, and Oliver could almost see the pennies stacking up in his eyes. Jack bent to gather up the boots. "I'm goin' to get you a different coat an' hat as well as trousers, so you can be one of us, instead of one of them."

Never mind that the warehouse coat was shabby and worth nothing; Oliver never wanted to see it again. He was struck by how the whole of the exchange reminded him of the last time he'd been taken up by Fagin's gang, how Jack and Charley had taken every valuable piece of clothing off of him, and how Fagin had given him worn, thin brown garments to wear.

And then how Fagin had locked Oliver up for days at a time till he thought he might go mad. Had gone mad, in a way, with nothing but books about killing and death to distract him from the shadows of the day and the darkness of each night. Would Jack, as well, keep him prisoner until Oliver proclaimed himself willing to join in his law-breaking acts? But then, Oliver was already a murderer, so what did it matter?

Jack plopped down on the low bed, dumping his bundle beside him while he pulled on stockings and tied up his own boots. Standing up, he shoved Oliver a little out of the way to dig for his coat and hat, then took up the bundle of Oliver's clothes and boots again.

"Lock the door, an' stay here, quiet like, till I gets back."

"Will you whistle?" Oliver asked, half-naked, shifting on his stockinged feet as the cold leached up through the floor.

"Lord, no," said Jack, looking at Oliver from head to toe. "But do lock the door after, an' don't answer unless it's me."

# 23

# A NEW HAT REPRESENTS A NEW LIFE, ONE THAT HE IS HESITANT TO ACCEPT

J ack swung the door wide as he stepped through it and slammed it shut behind him, leaving Oliver alone in the room, naked except for his stockings and a stolen shirt.

Oliver flipped the latch, thinking again that the thin, faded brass was not very much to keep anyone at bay who might be determined to make their way in. The confines of the room pressed on him. His eyes darted around, taking in the half gloom, ears ringing with the racket of the street beyond the thin glass, wheels rattling hard on the cobbled road, shouts, the raspy bark of a dog. He'd barely escaped being taken by the constables today, but would tomorrow promise the same?

To stave off the fear amidst his rampant thoughts, he stepped over to the small fireplace and knelt in front of it. The grit from the floor bit into his bare knees, and the scent of the rotten tallow candle on the mantle was stronger now. Lifting the metal rod, he poked at the charred ribbons of his shirt, which lay smoking and dark on the grate.

Bits of orange and blue made starry paths against the coals. The warmth oozed slowly toward him, but was wicked away by the cold before it had time to do much good.

Besides lacking in fuel, the grate needed a good cleaning, a stern blacking. The soot had built up around the mouth of the fireplace enough to absorb the heat and send smoke into the room. Not that Jack or anyone at the Three Cripples probably cared. Not since Jack probably used the room only to sleep in, and not much else—

Oliver realized he was shaking, not so much from cold as from the panic that threatened to overtake him and send him running, half-naked, into the streets. He scooted back from the useless warmth of the fireplace and sat on the low bed, which was shoved under the long, narrow window just beneath the eaves. Grease and age made the bedclothes stiff, and the dirt on the surface of everything was making Oliver's skin itch. But he stayed where he was, teeth chattering, each jagged, jumpy breath burning in his throat.

As his eyes became accustomed to the scattered light from the window, he looked about the room at the scarred wooden mantel with the tallow candle, and what looked like a clay bowl for Jack's pipe. Over the mantelpiece, on a series of nails hammered into the wall, hung a curved string, where Oliver supposed Jack might dry his stockings. Or, more likely, hang stolen handkerchiefs in a row where they might more easily be sorted. Other than that, the room was bare; Jack probably carried anything he needed on his person, in his pocket, or in his hatband.

Oliver concentrated on this, the mundane reality of Jack's rough ornaments rather than the panic rattling in his belly. Would he stay here? Could he? With Jack? But where else could he go? Jack was the only person he knew who would not instantly turn him over to the law. He shuddered all over and buried his face in his hands. He sank to his knees, unable to pray, curling and uncurling his stockinged feet, telling himself it was too late to cry, that this moment had been his destiny all along.

Then, startled by a creak of wood in the hall, he looked up and saw the scarf, the red scarf that Jack had stolen from him and which Oliver had not seen around Jack's neck recently. The scarf was a tad unraveled at the edges, but it was still bright and soft where Jack had arranged it in loops across the slat of wood that served as the headboard of the bed.

Oliver reached up, stroking the cheery red wool, his fingers leaving a slight streak just in the center. He drew his hand away. He didn't know what the scarf was doing there, laid out as though it was a favored piece of finery, but if he was to take it back, then Jack would have something to say about it. And Oliver was not, at that moment, up to a heated discussion about what belonged to him and what belonged to Jack.

IT WAS A GOOD HOUR, BY THE CHIMING OF THE CHURCH BELLS from nearly every steeple, before Oliver heard footsteps beyond the door. His teeth had been chattering for some time, and he vaguely remembered pacing back and forth across the floor before he'd sat down on the bed, wanting to be anywhere other than where he was. For what kind of life would this be, consorting with thieves and pickpockets, living with Jack?

He thought again of the portly man in the white waistcoat at Hardingstone Workhouse, and his dire predictions of Oliver's future hanging. Then of Noah's taunts about how bad blood, Oliver's gift from his mother, would always come to a bad end. And finally, of Mr. Grimwig, who'd never trusted Oliver from the very first, and who had been proven right, along with the rest of them, those forgotten workhouse wardens who'd muttered or scolded or tormented him. They'd all been proven right, whereas anyone who'd been the least bit gentle with him, even for the barest second, had been proven wrong.

So maybe he deserved it, this bitter point, this dark and dreary place. Maybe he'd truly been meant to be one of Fagin's boys from the very moment of his birth. Maybe he had all the evidence to support that and nothing to support anything else. He nodded to himself, determined to manage that much, to be one of Fagin's boys, even if everything, every kindness and civility he'd ever known must be shoved to the most remote part of his memory.

He scratched the back of his neck, out of nervousness or, what was just as likely, the family of lice now making their way from the patched bedclothes and up his spine. Then he heard Jack's footsteps, and his heart quickened. But it was odd—how did he know the footsteps were Jack's?

"Nolly," said the voice that went with the footsteps. "Nolly, open the door."

Oliver leaped from the bed, sending dust to furl the air, and opened the door. He stepped back as Jack barreled in with a bundle of clothes under one arm and a pair of battered black boots slung over his shoulder, dangling by their laces. He pushed past Oliver to lay everything on the table with a thump.

He turned to appraise Oliver.

"Been rollin' in the soot, have you?"

"I was sitting by the fire," said Oliver, as calmly as he could manage, but he knew the quaver in his voice gave him away. "And then on the bed."

"These are for you," said Jack.

Oliver went over to the table when Jack stopped him.

"Here," said Jack. He licked his thumb, and before Oliver could imagine what he was doing, felt the pressure against the line of his jaw.

"Just a bit of blood there," said Jack. "But nothin' nobody could see."

Oliver hesitated before wiping his face with the edge of his sleeve. Jack seemed so matter-of-fact about it, as though Oliver's showing up looking rumpled and suspicious was something Jack dealt with every day. Though maybe he had dealt with things like it when he'd been deported to Australia, and when he'd been part of Fagin's gang. Oliver didn't know, didn't want to ask.

He ran his hands over the bundle of clothes. If he put the articles on, he'd be that much further from everything he knew.

And yet, if he didn't separate himself from his old, safe life, it would all catch up with him and everything would be over. In spite of these dark thoughts chasing around in his head, he unfolded the pair of wool trousers from the bundle and put them on. They buttoned all around a front flap, and the buttonholes were dark with grease.

"Thank you," Oliver said with a nod as he tucked his shirt in.

"Such manners you have, ever so," said Jack. There was an edge to that laugh, as Jack must be fully aware that if he couldn't hide Oliver well enough, he too would be brought down.

"Now, I'm goin' t'do somethin'," said Jack. "You won't like it by half, but it'll keep you safe, this, what I'm about to do. Got it? Now, sit down."

Oliver could only look at him, his hands fisted on his thighs. He wanted to move, to run, but he couldn't even imagine to where or how. He had no money, and he couldn't go to Aunt Rose, not like this. Not today. Not ever.

"Nolly, I have to do this." Jack's exasperation was laced with some worry. He turned the wooden chair to face the dusty fireplace and patted the seat.

Oliver sat down and looked at the lumps of grey ash that choked the grate.

From his pocket, Jack pulled a short knife. It was probably the one he used to cut his supper or to shave pieces of wood if he was the least bit inclined to light a fire. He came at Oliver, holding the knife to one side. He moved between Oliver's legs , pushing them apart with his own legs, and ruffled his hair.

"What are you doing?" Oliver asked, shocked at Jack's nearness, the casual intimacy of their thighs touching. He jerked his head back and looked up at Jack.

"Helpin' you," said Jack. "It'll grow back, never fear. You'll have the golden locks of an angel again inside of a week."

Jack put his hand on Oliver's head. The heat of his fingers on Oliver's scalp ran through him with a shock. The smell of the grease in Jack's trousers, Jack's sweat, the grit of his life that was pressed into his skin—all of this surrounded Oliver as he bent his head forward.

Tugging, Jack pulled strands of hair away from Oliver's scalp and cut through them with the knife. There was a *scra-scra* sound, more tugging, and Oliver closed his eyes and pretended he didn't care. The cutting made his skin shiver, whispers of hair falling on his cheeks and down his collar, though it seemed Jack paused after every other cut to toss the strands in the smoking fireplace.

Finally, the cutting stopped, and Jack pulled Oliver's head till his forehead rested on Jack's belly. He ran his hand over Oliver's nape, the palm of it cupping a circle along the back of Oliver's skull, the touch, without the thickness of hair, close and warm.

"Now there," said Jack. "You look a wee bit rougher, so that'll please Cromwell."

"I don't care to please him," said Oliver, lifting his head, feeling some stirring of anger in his breast as he looked up at Jack.

"You'll care to remain hidden, so let me do this next bit, with no fussin', mind you."

Oliver stared at his knees, seemingly the only safe place to look at in this entire encounter. Jack put the knife back in his pocket and bent to the grate. He showed Oliver his hands, black and dusty, and before Oliver could open his mouth, Jack was between his thighs again, tracing his fingers along Oliver's jaw, past his ear. He ruffled the edge of Oliver's hairline, pushing his fingers against Oliver's scalp and through what was left of his hair. Oliver shuddered; no one had ever touched him like that. Not in his whole life.

Jack backed up a little way and took both of Oliver's hands in his, looking for all the world like a courtier bending to kiss his lady's hand. But he didn't kiss anything, only used his thumbs to smudge the back of Oliver's hands, pressing between the veins, moving the bones around, leaving smears that pretended to resemble work-worn grime.

"It'll only work if you keep your hands to yourself an' not wash 'em," said Jack, still holding Oliver's hands in his. Then he leaned forward, his face close to the hollow of Oliver's neck.

"You've got the hands of a gentleman, you have," said Jack, breath whispering against Oliver's skin. "An' you smell like a spring mornin' compared to the lot down there. Soap an' water, I expect." Jack drew back, unexpectedly, smiling down at Oliver. "I could be quite the draw for the ladies, too, if I ever determined to take up bathin'. So much maintenance, though."

Oliver's skin felt jumpy and, alarmed, he brought his hand to his neck, uncertain what to do with this intimacy, so sudden and uninvited. Uncertain what to do with the whisper memory of Jack's mouth so close to his skin.

"That's the ticket," Jack said, and Oliver realized he'd just smeared more soot on his own skin, which was to the good if he was to survive any of this.

"It won't work," said Oliver, his lips numb, completely undone by all of this. "They'll find me. I was born to hang, that's what the man in the white waistcoat said. He said it several times."

"Who's that, then?" Jack stepped back, as though surveying his handiwork.

"The man in the white—oh, never mind. He's long dead now."

It was too hard to explain, with his hammering heart and the echoing of voices from below sounding like a faraway storm that was about to reach him. The man in the white waistcoat had taken one look at young Oliver and pronounced him bad, oh, many years ago, when he was nine. No older than Martin had been, just yesterday. So very small—

"I think I'm going to be sick," said Oliver, standing.

"No," said Jack. "You're goin' to get drunk, an' *then* you're goin' to be sick. Gettin' drunk first makes anythin' worth it."

Jack held up a jacket and helped Oliver into it, as gravely as any manservant. The jacket didn't quite fit in the way he was used to. It was dark blue and made of fine, thin wool, much finer than the warehouse jacket, with a high, old-fashioned collar and cuffed sleeves that were too long. It had down the front a double row of shiny buttons, too tarnished to be genuine gold, of course, and a set of cut-off tails, resembling a gentleman's finery, trimmed back.

"It's too fancy, Jack, it's—" Oliver stopped himself, unable to continue, because when he considered his outfit the way that a criminal might, he could see how it might look to the police. And why was that so easy?

"It is fancy, but it's the last thing a bloke on the run would wear, eh? It's a distraction, that's what it is. Here's a kerchief for your neck."

The kerchief was a rusty black and, as Oliver, with trembling fingers, attempted to tie it into a turn of cloth that resembled a cravat, Jack shoved his hands away and stepped near to tie it for him. With his head bent to his task, Jack was so close that Oliver could see the faded freckles across Jack's cheeks, the thin white scar next to one eye, and feel the breath from Jack's mouth. See the way he held his tongue against the inside of his cheek as he folded and looped the cloth.

When Jack was done, he handed Oliver a hat. It was unlike his apprentice cap in every way; it was a top hat, just like the one Jack wore, except that this one was brand new, the silk still shiny, a smooth circle beneath his hands as Oliver petted it. Being a fancy type of hat, so new and so bold, it would probably separate him from his old life better than the rest of the outfit put together.

As Oliver adjusted the top hat on his head, he saw Jack smiling at him. It was then that he understood, at least part of what was happening to him. Oliver was here, in Jack's lair, in Jack's world, and whether Oliver had come of free will or because he had nowhere else to go, to Jack, Oliver's presence in the room was a good thing and worth smiling about. For the briefest of seconds, that thought pushed away Oliver's worries; to Jack, this was a good day.

Oliver looked down at himself. He quite resembled one of those men who loitered on the street corners looking for day work, or who lurked in the doorways of taverns hoping to find a score of some sort. He now belonged to the lowest level of quality, but if that was the only way he was going to escape the hangman's noose, then so be it.

As Jack opened the door, the runaway galloping feeling came back into Oliver's chest, leaving a numb spot where his heart was and roiling fear in his belly. It was obvious that Jack didn't expect Oliver to stay in the room all day, and it was likely that going downstairs constituted more of Jack's plan of distraction. Being there, amidst the crowd of regulars in the Three Cripples, would be the best disguise possible.

With a jerk of his chin, Jack looked at Oliver, appraising the results of his work.

"Tie up your boots an' come down; Cromwell wants to see you."

"Why? What does he want?"

"He owns the Three Cripples, as you well know. I'm sure he'll want to make certain arrangements."

"But I'm here with *you*." Oliver could already feel the darkness of Jack's world taking over, and he wasn't nearly ready for it yet.

"Shouldn't worry," said Jack. "He just wants his pound of flesh, an' that ain't so much to pay when there's an alternative lurkin' about."

This was true; the alternative was so much worse. They hanged murderers, plain and simple, and Oliver had seen what that fate had done to Fagin, how it had shattered him. Oliver knew he'd be broken like a snapped twig if they sent him to Newgate to await that same fate.

"Yes," he said. "Just let me—" He needed a moment before he could bear facing any part of Jack's world. He'd met Cromwell and had been greeted with grunts and assessing looks; he could imagine what Cromwell would want, but did not know how he, Oliver, could ever manage to provide it.

Jack nodded. "I'll tell him." And he was gone.

The warmth of the fire was flickering down, sucked out by the coldness of the room, and Oliver told himself his hands weren't shaking, his teeth weren't gritted so tightly he could feel the blood pounding through his jaw.

## 24

# AS IT WAS IN THE OLD DAYS

When Oliver had finally calmed his fingers enough to lace up the new, scuffed boots he'd been given by Jack, he managed to make his way down the stairs, his heart hammering. A man he did not know him past Jack's alcove. They went down a short white passage to a small room behind the bar, where there was a little fire choking in its grate. The room held a table and chairs; the table was thick and heavy and almost too big for the room.

Oliver saw Jack out of the corner of his eye just outside the doorway; Jack didn't come in, so Oliver sat in one of the chairs on his own. It seemed that the man himself, Cromwell, was going to make Oliver wait. Someone brought Oliver a pot of beer, but he couldn't bring himself to touch it.

Oliver's stomach was growling by the time Cromwell's frame filled the doorway of the room. His head was bare and his black neckerchief was still undone, though it was getting toward noon. Whatever he'd been doing, Cromwell looked relaxed and smudged, and to Oliver's surprise, he had a small smile to share.

"So, then, young Oliver," Cromwell said, as he took a seat across from Oliver. He looked at Oliver and nodded, as if admiring Jack's handiwork. "In a spot of trouble, then, are you?

Want to be stayin' on with us? That'll cost you, but first I want to know what you did."

Cromwell folded his arms on the table in front of him, his sleeves rolled up to display the thick muscles of his forearms. The table was not so wide that he couldn't reach Oliver if he wanted to. If Cromwell's goal was to intimidate, then Oliver, had he been able, would have congratulated him on his success.

"An' if you lie," said Cromwell, pointing a finger at Oliver, "then I'll know it, an' believe you me, you don't want me catchin' you at that. So 'fess up, then."

Oliver opened his mouth but couldn't speak. Cromwell shoved the pot of ale at him. Oliver took a sip of ale and then licked his lips.

"I murdered my master," he said, wanting to get it out. The horrible confession seemed unreal, even as he said it.

Cromwell's eyes crinkled up as though he didn't believe Oliver and was going to laugh in his face at any moment.

"An' 'ere I was thinkin' that they were lyin', that you'd stolen from the till an' gotten into it with one of your mates or some-thin'." Then, without hardly changing his expression, Cromwell snapped out, "So you killed him. Why? Speak up, you."

"He—he locked the workhouse boy in the warehouse, and he died, come this morning. Mr. McCready didn't seem to care, so I—"

"You killed your master out of spite? *You?*" A flicker crossed Cromwell's face, as though he was trying to assess how this could possibly be true. "You sit there lookin' like an angel, all sweet an' rosy an' well fed, an' you tell me this?"

"It's true!"

Cromwell laughed at him, mouth open, teeth flashing, and something in Oliver's breast sprang up, hot and insistent.

"I hit him in the head and he fell to the floor, bleeding."

"Hit 'im? With what?"

"A frying pan. An iron one."

Now Cromwell bent forward and howled while he pounded

the table, spilling his beer. Oliver got up, pushing back the chair, intending to leave, to march right out into the street. He'd thank Jack for his hospitality, he'd find a way out of London, and then nobody would be able to find him.

But Cromwell sprang from his seat and blocked Oliver's exit. His shoulders loomed as he bared his teeth, the smell of the street thick in the air around him.

"You've got a temper on you, boy. Wouldn't know it to look at you, sweet as you are, but I'm tellin' you, you'll do as you're told around 'ere, temper or no." He bent over Oliver, his fist next to Oliver's face.

"You're not my master." Oliver barely managed it with Cromwell's mouth so close to his, so close that Oliver could smell the beer on his breath.

"Oh, yes, I am. I very much am, an' you raise one 'and to me an' you'll find yourself floatin' down the Thames."

Oliver's heart pounded, but he made himself stay still, glaring as Cromwell brushed his clenched fist against Oliver's face and then gave him a shove into the passage. Jack waited there with wide eyes, watching and careful, but Oliver could see he was somewhat undone by Cromwell's threats, even if they weren't directed at him.

Cromwell grabbed Oliver by the collar of his shirt and escorted him to the alcove, where he shoved Oliver onto the bench seat with his back to the main room.

"I want you should stay 'ere, all day, like nothin's wrong, you got it?"

Oliver rubbed the back of his head, nodding. He could sense that Jack was nearby, but didn't turn his head to look. Jack had done nothing to stop Cromwell and had not spoken up on Oliver's behalf. But the feeling of irritation was soon overridden by the chill, sharp bite of fear; Jack and the Three Cripples was Oliver's only escape.

Oliver spent his day sitting in Jack's alcove with his back to the door, in the seat closest to the doorway. After Cromwell had gone, Jack slid into the seat across from him.

"Unless someone comes right through an' looks you in the face, no one'll take any notice of you. Why, you look just like a regular customer." Jack added this last as if it were a good thing, seeming a little proud as he took Oliver's hat off and put it next to his own on the table. He smiled as though well pleased with the obvious success of his ruse, though Oliver didn't return his smile.

It was a mad idea, all the way around, just sitting there like a coney, and it made Oliver edgy. But Jack insisted on it, and brought Oliver a bowl of stew that he couldn't eat and beer that he wouldn't drink, and made him stay there. Oliver was beginning to feel as though he'd been nailed in place when more customers came in. Heated sweat and wet wool, filtered with smoke and the effluvia of the cesspit in the cellar, smelled dank in the chancy heat of the coal fire. But as the tavern filled with noise and movement, Jack began to relax his vigil.

The din of the Three Cripples crowd grew, the stamping of feet, the click of a glass, the call for another round. Any time a figure passed in front of the light or stopped at the door to speak to Jack, Oliver found he couldn't bear to turn and look any of them in the eye, lest they be the one to come and, as Jack might say it, put the finger on him for Mr. McCready's murder.

Uncle Brownlow would be horrified, and even old Fagin would have been astonished to find Oliver sitting there with the shadow of a man's blood on his hands. As for Bill Sikes—what would he think of Oliver now? Would he, upon finding out, stand back and tip the brim of his hat as a sign of respect? And since when had Oliver fallen so low that respect from a housebreaker and murderer would be welcome?

Oliver looked at his hands. They were filthy, but still were much cleaner than the tables and the floor. Cleaner than Jack's hands. And cleaner than the neck and hands of the boy that brought another pot of beer that Oliver simply couldn't bear to drink.

Shaking, Oliver brought his hand to his face, wishing he could get a basin of hot water and some soap and wash all of this off. Then he touched his hair and scrubbed through the stiffness of it, feeling the curve of his scalp, feeling exposed. He raked his fingers through the bristle, till, finally, Jack reached out across the table and touched Oliver's face.

"It'll grow, by-and-bye," Jack said. He brushed a stray lock from Oliver's forehead that he'd forgotten to cut, and patted his cheek gently.

Oliver made himself be soothed by this, although the feeling of comfort lasted only a moment, and then it was gone.

WHEN THE AFTERNOON CROWD PUSHED IN AND THE MAIN room was a throng of men in coats and boots, Noah arrived. He came right through the open doorway to the alcove and stood at the end of the table. The firelight glittered on the sheen of his fancy suit and on the spots of frozen rain on his hat as he held it in his hands. He was grinning, looking down at Oliver, mouth open, tipping back on his heels as if this sight, Oliver hiding from the hangman's noose, was the best joke in the world.

"Oh, how the mighty are brought low," Noah crowed, eyes shining as he looked at Jack, as if wanting him to join in. Then he looked at Oliver again. "So proud, so proper, an' yet 'ere you are. An angel-faced murderer, all ready for the 'angman's noose." He slammed Oliver on the shoulder.

"We'll keep him from that," said Jack. "Never you mind him now, Nolly, we'll keep you from that."

Oliver knew Jack would do his best, but given what Noah did for a living, it wasn't a sure bet that he wouldn't take it upon himself to hand Oliver over to the law.

"I see you've 'ad your 'air cut as well, no longer lookin' such a swell, more like one of your everyday street weasels."

Oliver jerked, stopping himself from brushing his hand along his head, which he'd done several times that very hour, bringing a shade of soot to layer his trousers.

"You did 'im in with a fryin' pan, I 'ear," said Noah, smirking. "How your old, dead mother would be proud, so very proud."

The invisible leash that had held Oliver in one spot broke with a snap, and he lunged out of his chair, reaching for Noah's throat. Noah, unprepared, stepped back, mouth open, hands flailing as he lost his balance. Oliver shoved him against the doorjamb.

Oliver wanted to roar with the loss and the futility of everything he'd done and tried to be. He drew his fist back and hooked it, just under Noah's chin. Noah's jaw clicked, and Oliver punched him again, making his nose bleed. Then he slammed him in the neck, cutting off Noah's breath, making him tumble to the ground, clutching his throat while Oliver stood over him, legs spread, heart thumping.

"You'll not speak of my mother to me," said Oliver in a voice that was thick and almost not his own. He glared down at Noah, who looked up at him, gasping. "I told you once, don't *make* me tell you again."

He probably should not have struck Noah, but he didn't care. It felt good to best Noah, as he had that day so long ago.

Then Oliver was grabbed from behind and turned around by a pair of hard fists. Cromwell's grime-drawn face was sweaty and angry.

"He had it coming," said Oliver, fury still gritting his teeth. Noah deserved to be beaten.

"Boys, boys," Cromwell said, giving Oliver a shake, but it wasn't a hard one. "You'll be mindin' your manners and not makin' such a fuss in my tavern. Take it outside next time."

Cromwell let him go, and Oliver watched Noah struggle to his feet. As Noah left, no one stopped, nor tended his passing.

Only Cromwell followed him into the main room, toward the front door, to make sure Noah left.

The irony of it was that, at the Three Cripples, fighting like that was a scolding offense; whereas at Mr. McCready's, there would have been discipline and shame. As for murder, here it got laughed at, and Oliver knew, as he should have known, that coming to the Three Cripples was a mistake. But at the moment, it was a mistake he couldn't undo.

"Come on, then, Nolly," said Jack.

Oliver tried to focus, waiting for the heat in his veins to simmer to something less fiery before he spoke.

"You've had a day, then, haven't you." Jack's voice was almost soft. He got up and touched Oliver's face with his fingers, making Oliver jerk his head back. "Come here to me, now, an' sit closer to the fire. You're all flushed, but your skin is cold."

Oliver didn't want to be soothed, but Jack's touch was so gentle that he did as Jack asked. Jack slid along the bench seat and pulled Oliver down on it to sit next to him.

He was shivering as he sat down, yet the fire seemed unable to reach him, and his blood rattled against his bones. A serving girl brought in a plate of food and a tumbler of gin, placing them on the table with rude thunks. Oliver inhaled the smell of salt and grease, the tang and the heat of juniper.

"It'll be all right, Nolly, it will. You won't miss that life so very much, not for long, I promise."

Oliver looked at Jack, at the freckles across his blunt nose, at the smudges around his chin, on his collar. He could smell the sweet funk of unwashed skin, see the grime beneath Jack's nails as he touched Oliver's wrist. Jack was sitting so very close, but that was a damned sight better than Noah standing over him, mocking. Or Cromwell, bristling and threatening.

"Yes," said Oliver, though he didn't really understand what he was agreeing to.

He reached for the plate of food; it held slices of beef, roasted, and bread, scraped with dripping, and boiled eggs; there was enough for a fighting cock, and Oliver's stomach rebelled. Instead, he took a sip of sweet, warm gin and reached for the bread. The dripping on the bread was crisped with grease and salted, and that was fine. It went with the gin. He flicked his gaze up to Jack, who was watching him.

"There's enough for two," said Oliver. He could barely stand to think of eating all of it, even though his stomach was growling and empty, and he was still shaking.

"Yes?" asked Jack. He pulled a slice of beef from the plate and ate it with his fingers as the skin around his eyes crinkled with pleasure.

It took Oliver back to those times in Fagin's den, when food was spare and shared. He didn't know if Jack remembered those days, or even if the memory of them ever ghosted across his thoughts. But he didn't feel bold enough to mention it. Especially not now, when Cromwell was no doubt just beyond the door, or had listening ears nearby.

Oliver pushed the plate with the remains of the dipping bread at Jack, using the edge of his hand that already held a slice.

"Here," he said. "You can have the rest."

"You're ever so sweet to be so generous," said Jack, with a lilt that told Oliver he had meant to tease him about his manners, but that the sharing had undone him. Though, as Jack probably had enough to eat these days, Oliver could not figure out why Jack would be so pleased. But he was.

Jack ate with relish, his shoulder brushing Oliver's, and he seemed also to relax on the bench near the fire. Being there, as they'd sometimes done in the past. Not saying anything, just sharing a meal with the acrid warmth of the low coals layering the air around them. And, as Oliver polished off the gin and sugar and warm water, he realized he was too tired to pay attention to any more of it, that he needed to rest, and was it yet time to crawl under some blanket and block out the day?

He watched as Jack ate mouthfuls of the beef and boiled eggs, a flush of color coming into his cheeks. He didn't ask to share Oliver's gin, though he did call for a pot of beer, which he drank in several large gulps, wiping his mouth with the back of his hand afterward, looking at Oliver as though measuring him.

"You look ready for nighttime prayers, then, Nolly. Prayers an' bedtime stories an' all that." His eyes went unfocused for a moment, as if he were remembering something, then he looked at Oliver, blinking.

"I'm beyond prayers," said Oliver, feeling the shortness of the statement badly balanced by the enormity of the truth of it.

"You're floggin' yourself worse than any monk," said Jack, with a sharpness that told Oliver he had little patience for that sort of behavior. "Besides, with that face, you'll never be beyond prayers." Then he snapped his mouth shut as if he couldn't believe he'd just said it.

It was the kind of comment that Oliver was used to, and he shouldn't really be surprised that even in the glow of a fire inside the Three Cripples, Jack would look at him and think it. But his face, however beautiful and graced by angels, had never done anything to save him, and, in fact, had got him into more trouble than it seemed to be worth.

"Anyway, your new hat, it ain't like your old cap," said Jack. "When you wear it, you'll look more like one of us, like Cromwell said."

Jack was just trying to change the subject, to be kind, perhaps. But it didn't matter. Oliver wanted to protest because whatever Cromwell had in mind for him, a new hat wasn't going to make any difference at all.

"Yes," he said to Jack anyway.

He felt Jack's thigh pressed against his. His mind was humming and his body felt slack, and the day had gone on too long, simply too long. He'd only vaguely heard the bells for nine o'clock, and though he'd often worked a harder day than this at the haberdashery, he still felt as if he'd been trampled by a string of clod-hoofed horses.

"Can I just—" He wasn't presuming on Jack's hospitality; Jack had already said he could stay. Cromwell had already said he could stay, even. But he wanted to leave the heaving throng, to turn his back on what, to Jack, must be only the young start of the evening. "I simply cannot—"

Jack shook his head. "Come along then. I'll come up with you, I'm supposed to—"

"Keep an eye on me," Oliver finished for him.

He'd not considered what it was like for Jack, that for all of Jack's posturing in the street, his roughness with Oliver, he was not, in fact, his own master. Even as he'd mocked Oliver for doing as he was bid at the haberdashery, Jack was doing as he was bid by Cromwell. But then, to Jack, belonging in a place that held so much of Fagin's history and Jack's own past was well worth the price.

"But have another drink first. It'll help you." Jack gestured to the girl, who brought two glasses of gin and a small pitcher of hot water and lumps of sugar in a bowl. "It'll help you sleep. Keep that worry from your eyes. I'll have some, too," Jack added as he put hot water in the gin.

Oliver looked at the glasses, which were almost clean this time, sparkling in the light from the fire, closed his eyes, and took a breath. He sipped the gin, everything unfocused and soft, and there was Jack, running his tongue along his lip, looking at Oliver with ladened eyes that bespoke of a contentment Oliver could barely begin to understand.

The doorway through to Jack's life led down to low streets and mean places. The way was slanted and steep, and Oliver felt himself slipping as though the path were slicked with ice.

One drink then, and now, and later, and the world would be edged in fog and nothing would matter very much anymore. At which point, he would be giving up his dream of that bookshop, but then, murderers didn't own bookshops. Then again, there was Jack's smile, soft, the sharpness of his features worn smooth by the warmth of the fire and the pots of beer he'd already drunk.

When they were done, Jack pulled the glasses to the edge of the table, not seeming to care if they dashed themselves to the floor. It was simply not Jack's job to worry about that, nor Oliver's. Jack pulled Oliver to standing, and Oliver followed him up the stairs that were suddenly too steep and too long, and Oliver felt as though he'd been at the Three Cripples forever, that now the dirt was beginning to soak into him. Jack tugged on Oliver's jacket and wouldn't let him pause along the way.

"With me, then, Nolly," Jack said without turning his head to check on Oliver's progress.

As they mounted the stairs and rose above the noise and clatter of the tavern, a cold dampness filled Oliver's mouth, and the smell of sewage from an uncleaned cesspit leaked through the cracks in the boards. Oliver felt the urge to turn and run, but there was nowhere else for him to go; he was a wanted man. It was this or the hangman's noose, so he must go where Jack made him go. There was nothing else except to do what Jack said.

Jack unlocked and opened the door, and left Oliver's side to walk across the dark room. Oliver could hear him fumbling for something along the mantelpiece.

"You can sleep next to the wall," said Jack, his voice coming out of the darkness, his face appearing in the soft, silvery glow of the candle as he lit it. The tallow sparked to life and began to emit a trace of burnt fat. "That way, I can beat off the rats if they come for you."

Oliver started in surprise because, of course, Jack must be joking. Then again, maybe he wasn't.

"Is there no water to wash with?" Oliver asked.

"No." Jack seemed unabashed as he took off his hat and jacket and tossed them on the clothespress. "There's a bathin' house in the Strand, but that's more for gentlemen. I could take you to the public bath in Smithfield; you can scrub the bed lice off you there for a penny."

Now Jack was laughing at him straight out, and Oliver wanted to lay into him much as he had Mr. McCready, only he didn't have a frying pan, and the rage ebbed as soon as it flared. He was just tired.

"Come on, then," said Jack.

Oliver watched Jack unbutton his blue waistcoat and sit on the chair to take off his boots, which he left in a clump on the floor. His trousers and stockings soon followed, leaving Jack naked except for his shirt. Then, as Jack slid back the blankets from the bare, flocked mattress, Oliver knew there was nothing for it but to do the same.

He sat on the edge of the bed, which, to his gin-softened senses, proved to be hard-edged and thin, and took off his boots, unlacing them with exaggerated care. He pulled off his jacket and, not seeing any pegs in the walls, stood up to lay it gingerly on top of Jack's clothes, with his hat balanced on top. Feeling exposed beneath Jack's watching eyes, he took off his trousers and stockings. He moved his hat to one side and made an ungainly pile. He blew out the candle and stood there, smelling the burnt smoke, then, barefooted, scuffed across the floor and found the bed. Taking care, he crawled over Jack's middle and tried to arrange himself comfortably against the wall.

In was dark, and the room was cold, and he shivered, realizing that Jack was the only warm spot anywhere. Their bare limbs touched, and they shimmied against each other as they attempted to find a comfortable position. Had he not been so drunk, Oliver knew he'd be more shocked than he was, only now, it didn't seem to matter.

"Back-to-back, then," said Jack, yawning.

This was how they'd slept when they were boys, back in the old den, back-to-back or tumbled beneath the blankets, knees banging against each other when Jack would turn into him with a cold nose and cold hands, burrowing into Oliver, as if searching in his sleep for some long-lost comfort he could not speak of when awake.

Oliver had forgotten for so long the feeling of another body pressed close, another beating heart nearby, another's warmth in the darkness. Now it came back to him with a slamming weight.

There was so much loneliness in the dark, and none of this was Jack's fault, and besides, Jack was there, and nobody else was. The nearness of Jack didn't remove his fear of being hanged, but it was muffling it to a low, dull roar. He turned toward the wall and pressed back till his shoulders met Jack's and their spines fused, hips low, pressed together. He made himself breathe and kept his eyes closed, willing sleep that never seemed to come.

The dark deepened, with church bells tolling, vibrating through the mist and the dank fog, slithering over the rooftops. Oliver huddled down with his arms across his chest, as though folded for some eternal rest. Which made his heart thud wildly, breath coming short, thinking of death after a short life where nothing pleasing ever lasted, and everything he'd ever cared about had gone or had pushed him away. And here he was, in this black place, on the edge of a pit that he was sure led straight to hell that burned with angry tongues of fire, and where he would forever and always be eternally alone.

The bed grew hard beneath him and the scratching of the rats grew loud and sharp in the ceiling. Oliver shifted away from the sound, rolling over, thinking that he might be half-asleep, praying that he was, rather than sobering up from too much gin.

Then he was startled as Jack turned also, curving his body into Oliver's, burrowing under his chin. Jack wasn't even properly awake, as he reached up to tuck his hands against Oliver's chest, offering himself up to be held.

"Nolly," he said, drowsy and low. The rest was indistinguishable, only a murmur of breath against Oliver's neck.

Oliver was warmer, suddenly, with Jack pressed up against him that way, heat soaking through Jack's shirt and into Oliver's skin. This was the way it had been between him and Jack back in the den, when the frost was on the windows and Fagin hadn't enough dross and goods to sell to buy firewood. In the dark chill of no firelight and barely even a rush of candlelight, Fagin's boys would burrow together amidst scraps of blanket and tags of wool, and always Oliver had stuck close to Jack and lain in the dark with him.

Only now, as Oliver opened up his arms and pulled Jack to him, only Jack was bigger. His shoulders were wider, hips demanding a space against Oliver's, his belly soft and warm. His thighs, where his shirt had ridden up, were ticklish with hair. His sex beneath the cotton of his shirt brushed against Oliver's, and his feet tangled with Oliver's. But Jack, in his sleepy need for closeness, made Oliver warm, like he used to do in the old days, so Oliver would say nothing of any of this to Jack. But then, he never had.

# 25

## PIES EATEN IN THE STREET AND
## A NIGHT SPENT IN NEWGATE

Morning brought light breaking through the window and a brisk wind that rattled the panes. Oliver's head thumped with a platoon of drums marching up and down inside his skull; he couldn't remember the last drink he'd had the night before. Only that Jack had been there, urging him on, ordering more and then still more, and all the while looking at Oliver with green eyes and a lazy smile that had tendered the message that everything would be all right if only Oliver would take one more drink, just one more.

As Oliver pulled the greasy wool blanket up to his ears, Jack woke up, the morning-hardness of his sex against Oliver's hip, his dark hair sprawled on the bare pillow. He was sleep-tumbled, almost gentled with it. He rubbed his eyes, then pushed his hand against Oliver's shoulder.

"Get me some coffee, you."

Feeling wide-eyed, Oliver blinked across the pillow at Jack and rubbed the back of his hand across his mouth, which tasted sour with the remains of the drink from the night before.

"As though I'd know where to go to get some," Oliver replied, with his head still on the pillow. Which was true; he'd hardly

339

know where to get coffee on his own. Not in this part of the City.

"Go to the kitchen. Light a fire, if someone hasn't already. Put water in a saucepan, add some coffee, an' heat it up."

This made Oliver remember where he was, and why he was there. It sparked through him, a cold that made him feel frozen even where Jack was touching him.

"I'm not doing that," said Oliver. His voice shook as he said it. "I'm not going down there. Alone."

Jack blinked his sleepy eyes and smirked, as though he'd meant it as a joke all along. He lifted his hand to scratch his head, the unbuttoned sleeve of his shirt falling back to his elbow. His night-scented sweat rushed from beneath his shirt, and Oliver inhaled, unsettled by other undefined urges such as his body wanted.

Instead, he sat up and pushed back the blanket, now grey in the frosty morning light, and crawled across Jack's bare legs to get out of bed. The contrast of the cold air and Jack's warm skin made him want to get back under the covers, but he made himself reach for his boots and look for his jacket. He pulled on his stockings and got dressed as quickly as he could. Then he sat on the bed and put on his boots, doing up the laces as he looked around the room for a washbasin that simply wasn't there.

Behind him, Jack was moving, getting out of bed. Out of the corner of his eyes, Oliver saw Jack's knees the length of his bare thighs, the curl of dark hair at his groin, and then he looked away. Jack went on, gathering up his trousers from the floor and going to the clothespress, as though there was nothing odd about them being half-naked together. He got dressed and pulled on his waistcoat, and then thumped down beside Oliver on the bed to lace up his boots. His hair was mashed to one side; he merely spat in his hand and settled it with his palm. As he pulled on his jacket and stood up, his eyes glittered at Oliver.

"Something on the street then? Pies?"

In spite of his thick, addled head, Oliver's stomach rumbled at the thought of pies, hot and peppery, with dense crusts and unidentifiable fillings. It didn't matter what was put in there. One bite would be enough to almost make him forget Mrs. Pierson's cooking. Almost. And he hoped Jack had money, for he had none. He'd not had his pay the day before, and his four pounds, two shillings, and sixpence were far away, locked in his chest at the haberdashery.

"Grab your coat an' hat, an' we'll scoot out before anyone wakes up an' sees us," said Jack. He didn't mention Cromwell's name, but Oliver knew who he was worried about.

Oliver doubted Cromwell would fancy Oliver wandering off without some sort of deal being settled between them. Still, Oliver needed fresh air, and did not want to worry about Cromwell. He did not think that anybody would recognize him the way he looked now, anyway, so he did what Jack said and followed him down the stairs, the cool air rushing up at them. But when they got down to the main room, Noah was waiting for them, jingling change in his pockets, looking bruised about the eyes, his lower lip puffy even as he smiled at them.

"Come along boys, all that drinkin' an' carousin' leaves an empty belly just waitin' to be filled."

When Oliver stopped to button his coat and place his top hat properly on his head, he looked at Noah askance. Yesterday, he'd pummeled Noah severely, and yet there Noah was, standing and waiting, as if they were all the best of friends.

As Jack put on his own hat, he brushed past Oliver to go out the door to the street, seemingly oblivious to Oliver's quandary.

Noah followed, shrugging. "Cromwell bade me to make amends, an' so here I am."

He didn't seem sincere in voice or manner, but Oliver didn't doubt that Cromwell had had words with Noah; he'd had words with Oliver as well and wanted things the way he wanted them. The Three Cripples was his domain, and he considered all within to be his.

Oliver nodded, not saying *yes* or *thank you,* as he did not want

Noah along on this particular morning when so much was a-tumble in his own head. But Jack smiled and tugged on Oliver's coat sleeve, and so the three of them went into the morning, into the damp and the wind.

The street was not yet thick with people, but the passage narrowed as they walked along down the dip into Field Lane, turning onto West Street toward the sounds and smells of Smithfield. Oliver had had little cause to venture near the place, not since Bill Sikes had dragged him through that wintry spring morning so long ago.

He could still feel the clasp of Bill's hand, strong fingers, hard along the edges with calluses, the whole of him smelling like dirt and oil. He'd never let go of Oliver's hand till they'd met up with a cart that had taken them the rest of the way, toward the house with the silver plate, toward the fullness of Oliver's destiny, though neither Bill nor Oliver had known it then.

To Bill, the venture had been a good opportunity for plenty of goods to fence, though Oliver had wondered, from time to time, why it was that Bill had picked that house, so far away, when there were acres of houses along the way that had been ripe for the taking. Maybe it had been part of Monks' plan all along, though that seemed a far stretch, even for Monks.

When the three of them came to the edge of Smithfield, Oliver's musings came to the point that they always did. He would never know the whole of Monks' plan; there was no one to ask, and most of his kin were happy to put the entire event behind them. His Aunt Rose, whenever he asked her, had gone into a swoon and had taken to her bed with salts and lavender water. Prayers had soon followed, making Oliver suspect she knew more than she'd ever told him. Which was frustrating; it was his story to know, wasn't it?

"What're you doin' there, Nolly, starin' off like that?"

Oliver looked up at the lines of oxen and sheep being assessed by the butchers in greasy aprons and battered hats. He could smell rotting animal fat and burnt fur, redolent even along the edge of the pens. And saw Jack scowling at him.

"I'm lollygagging," said Oliver. He could never explain it to himself either, how and why his mind would go off into the past.

"I've got sixpence," said Jack, rolling his hand in his pocket. "But I don't want no bath."

"Then don't get one," said Oliver, thinking that Jack could do with one. Only in Jack's world was being clean less important than other things. "Let's get something to eat or buy a pot of coffee."

Jack's eyebrows flew up, and Oliver thought perhaps Jack was surprised that Oliver had given in so easily. Then, with a nod, Jack began ambling along the edges of the market with Noah close at his heels, the two of them stepping along as though pleased, as though the air wasn't snapping with cold and the wind wasn't carrying the dank smell of muck and fresh manure and the sweat of animals marched too far too fast.

They headed for a row of temporary booths lined up along an old Roman wall, their thick canvas awnings bouncing in the damp wind. Oliver could see the hand-lettered signs announcing pies and hot drinks, so he followed close on Jack's heels. He let Noah pick three pies and pay for them, getting his change and handing one of the pies to Oliver.

That Jack had let Noah pay for the pies as opposed to stealing them was a marvel in and of itself, but perhaps this close to home, to the Three Cripples, where Jack was regularly seen, using those light fingers wasn't an option.

"Go ahead, Oliver, it's not made of cat or nothin'."

Noah smirked, and, to prove his words, Jack bit into the edge of the crust, holding the pie up to his mouth with both hands. His mouth smacked as he chewed, and Oliver did the same, more gingerly, nibbling at the crust and tasting the salt and grease more than any meat or potato. Still, while Jack smiled at him, it was a good enough moment for him to enjoy it, in spite of the growing throng of people in the market, and the smells cast about by the cold wind.

As Jack chewed, he wiped one hand on the side of his jacket, already darkened by grease, and Oliver tried doing likewise. But it was hard. He was used to cloth napkins and basins of water to wash in, both before and after eating. He wanted a table and cutlery and Mrs. Pierson in her wide, white apron, clucking over him if he ate too fast or not enough. But Mrs. Pierson probably hated him now, despised him; she had actually raised her voice to call for the constable. There'd be no going back to that now, to her kitchen and the warm fire reflecting off the clean black grate.

"Hey?" asked Jack, interrupting his thoughts.

Oliver started. Jack had come up so very close without him realizing it, his skin scented by the windy air, his hair perfumed with the night they'd spent together.

Oliver blinked, clearing his mind. It might be harder to walk away from that life than he realized.

"You want coffee?" asked Jack, tipping his head close to Oliver's and reaching out to touch Noah's shoulder, as though the three of them were sharing some type of secret rather than a perfectly ordinary conversation. "There's a cart over there; maybe he's got tarts, an' if you can go without a bath for a bit, we'll have both, tarts an' coffee."

Jack's stomach was in charge of all until filled, that was obvious to see. Noah, for his part, didn't seem to mind that Jack was suddenly determining how Noah's money was to be spent. Indeed, Noah didn't even seem to mind that Oliver benefited, even if the scuffle the day before had left Noah with a bruised face.

"Yes, that's fine," said Oliver. He could manage for one more day and find a way to wash later. And to figure out what he was going to do, now that he was a murderer.

When they went up to the cart, Noah only had enough for one tart and one large tin mug of coffee, which they shared between them, after Oliver made sure that Jack put enough sugar in. The tart he mostly left for Jack; after Mrs. Pierson's puddings, it tasted like plain paper. But it pleased Jack, who smacked his pastry-speckled mouth before wiping it with the back of his hand. Noah, Oliver noted, didn't partake, but was watching them both.

"Ready for it then, Nolly?" asked Noah.

"Ready for what?" asked Oliver, wanting to correct Noah that only Jack called him by that name.

"Why, for this."

A jumble of commotion started up behind Oliver—deep shouts coming from several men. When Oliver turned, he saw three constables coming toward them at a fast clip with batons raised. The crowd parted to let them through, and the shouts led the rough-jacketed men, the woman with the torn grey apron, the bottle washer, and the man who'd just sold them coffee—all of them—to turn and look at Oliver.

It was then that Oliver realized *he* was the constables' target.

Jack moved, tugging on Oliver's jacket to make him follow, but it was too late. Hard hands gripped Oliver, and something hit him on the back of the head with a stiff clonk. His new hat tumbled to the ground, and the sky, windblown and grey, dipped above him and sank below the roofline, over and over again.

Two of the constables had him fast with large, curled hands. The other one, the one who'd hit him with the club, stood in front of him and was saying something about *charges* and *assault* as Oliver's gaze flicked about as best it could, looking for Jack.

Jack was gone from sight, had dodged himself right into hiding. As he always did, as he *should* do. But Noah, smiling, with his hands in his pockets, remained standing by the brick-crumbled Roman wall. With a sinking heart, Oliver realized Noah must have planned this and turned Oliver in for the reward because the constables had come straight for him, right there next to the pie stand Noah had led them to.

The constables dragged Oliver off; there was a cart waiting

with two black horses pulling a black box with a black door with an iron grate over the window. They opened the door and shoved Oliver in and shut it with a clank.

He had barely enough time to settle himself on the bench before the cart lurched off, throwing him to the floor, making him scrabble on his hands and knees for balance. But he couldn't understand. What did they mean by mentioning only *charges* and *assault*? He'd assaulted Mr. McCready, yes, but he'd *murdered* him, so why wouldn't they have mentioned that?

The horses trotted at a brisk pace, rattling along the cobblestones, and Oliver could imagine that the dark cart made many —pedestrians and carriages alike—move quickly out of the way. He didn't have to guess their destination; it could only be Newgate. Even as the cart slowed, he had only to close his eyes to see in his mind's eye the dark, grey walls rising from the street, bold as iron against the moving throng of the people, devoid of any ornament save the jagged edges of the gate.

When the cart stopped, the back door was flung open, and he was hauled out, his feet banging against the iron steps. He had barely a moment to right himself and look across the crowd for Jack, though he knew better, he really did, than to expect that Jack would be anywhere near Newgate. Then he was drawn inside through the smaller door inside the larger gate to a courtyard he only barely remembered.

One of the constables held him, hard by, his baton jutting under Oliver's chin, while the other two talked in low voices to a man in a black coat. Oliver could hardly hear them above the roar of his heart as it thudded against his breastbone. He was going to hang by morning, just as Fagin had, and he wanted to faint upon the stones.

One of the constables nodded and broke away from his conversation with the man in the black coat. He came over to Oliver, eyes narrowed. Without a word, he nodded at the constable that held Oliver, and the two of them began walking toward a door on one side of the courtyard. They dragged him through the door and down a corridor lined with dripping grey stone. The corridor narrowed as the guards turned down a passage that led to a flight of steps that went down into the darkness. These were not the cells where Fagin had been kept. They were going underground; there would be no windows.

As they passed beneath the stone lintel, Oliver struggled, trying to catch his breath to protest. While he understood how he'd come to this, many a boy had rebelled against a harsher master and not been cast so low.

"No," he said. "*No.*"

The constables, with hard hands and impassive faces, gave his arms a yank.

"Come along with you, then, you young snake," said one. "The magistrate said one night's keeping before the trial, and that is what you shall have."

Oliver choked on his own indrawn breath, stumbling down the first step, and they held him up. The walls became darker with damp, the stone steps were slippery, and the way was lit by rough candles in iron sconces that reflected in narrow puddles of sour, stagnant water. He kept his eyes focused on the light till his eyes felt burned and hot so he could hold the memory of their light through the long night. Otherwise, he was not going to make it.

They came to the first barred cell door. One of the guards let Oliver go long enough to turn the iron key in the lock. He was pushed inside. Not hard, really, but with enough force to let him know there was no backing out. No slipping past the guards to run up the stairs and into the light. The door was shut and locked behind him before he could even turn around. He could see the profiles of the two guards through the long bars in the door, only half-lit by the single candle on a sconce on the wall in the corridor.

"You'll be right enough come morning," one of them said. Oliver could barely see his mouth move. "If the damp rot don't get to you first."

They rattled their keys and marched back the way they'd come, leaving Oliver with only the distant flickering of a single candle to keep the darkness away.

The cell was a solid, sealed tomb of blackened air, beyond which came noises that could have been metal on metal, or steps on stone, or the dark scatterings of rats' claws as they scurried through unseen tunnels. The cell was big enough to stand up in, long enough to lie down in, but narrow. Oliver could have reached out each arm and touched the walls with his flat palms, should he have wanted to come in contact with the seeping stone.

He stood at the door and looked through the bars. The candle in the iron sconce along the corridor wall had perhaps three hours in it. Maybe less. His hands circled the iron bars and held onto them; chips of rust came away on his skin. Something slid down his neck as it dripped from the ceiling. Filth clung to his shirt. The air, already dank, clotted in his throat. He willed the candle not to flicker. He would make it as long as the candle held. Beyond that, he could not promise himself anything.

Shaking, he made himself let go of the bars and turn around. In the corner was a long narrow board hung on chains from the wall. It was intended to serve as a bed, but there was no mattress on the wood, nor even straw. He could smell the tartness of mold, dimly see the greyish-white triangles of niter growing up in the corners.

He began to pace, feeling bits of dirt under his boots as he walked, sensing the slime on the walls but not touching it. The long ends of the cell were an almost comfortable six or seven paces apart, but the cell was only three or four paces across. His shoulder hitched up every time he had to turn so sharply to miss the niter in the corner.

The candle in the corridor continued to shiver as he paced on and off. When he heard a door being opened, Oliver raced to the bars and jammed his face against them to listen and watch, eyes wide. Two guards marched someone down the hall, past

Oliver's cell, and threw him into a cell some doors away. The iron door was slammed and locked, keys were rattled, and Oliver was no longer alone.

His new companion might have improved the condition of the dark, except for the keening sound that wavered with drunken tones almost right away. And the candle. As the guards went past it, the shadow of it dropped low and then grew larger. Oliver held his breath. The guards clanked up the stone steps. The light grew brighter. The keening waned for a bit. Oliver resumed his pacing, feeling his chest tighten, his breath shorten.

Beyond the stone, beyond the gate, somewhere in the open air, he could almost hear the bells tolling the hour. But the sound was too dim for him to be sure he'd caught all the bells. Was it afternoon? Or was it later? Maybe one o'clock, he guessed. Could he last until morning? No. He would not last the night at this rate; he would be dead by morning from the pressure of his heart bursting through his breastbone.

When he'd been young, much younger, though he felt so very old now and that time so far away, he'd hid from nights such as this with his hands over his face, crying in the corner. That cell's floor had been scattered with straw, and the stones paper-dry to the touch, but it was much the same as the cell he was in now. He, too, was much the same, and his impulse was the same, but if he sat down to howl, he would be soaked through come morning and gaol fever would come upon him. He'd heard of it happening. The air in a jail cell was so thick and poisonous a man could die of it in a day. Or a night.

That would not be him. He'd stand all night if he had to, but if he did that, he would be awake to see the candle's last flicker, which would come long before midnight. If he was asleep, he would not know it when the candle went out, would not know that the darkness was upon him with its smothering grip and silent scream. Yet he could not lay down.

His mind stuttered over this and he made himself continue pacing, continue thinking about how it had all gone wrong. He should have been more clever when he'd first run away. He should have left London. He could have gone to Aunt Rose and Uncle Harry to begin with, and why had he not thought of this? Killing your master was a sin, the worst kind, but perhaps Aunt Rose could have found it in her heart to forgive him. To hide him, at least for a time, till he could figure out where else to go.

But no. He'd gone to Jack, to the Three Cripples. Then Noah had turned him in, the honor of thieves be damned. Oliver wondered whether Jack had known. At the thought of it, his heart ached as though it had been pummeled with a fist. When Jack had taken him in, the next assumption was that Jack would have kept him safe. So Jack couldn't have known, or at least Oliver hoped that was true.

The night darkened. The light of the candle seemed to have dropped low at an alarming rate. Oliver tried to listen for more bells but could not hear anything. The soles of his feet burned inside his boots, but he could not bring himself to huddle in the corner or even to sit on the hard board of the bed. Perhaps if he sat in the middle of the floor. He lowered himself straight down, crossing his legs, wrapping his arms around his knees. The floor made him cold straight through, but his feet thanked him for the respite, just the same. He would stay in this position for a bit and then stand up. Then sit again. He might make it through the night. If the candle kept burning.

But then the candle went out, without warning or even a flicker to indicate that something was amiss. Perhaps a stray breath of foul, brackish air had done it in, or it had guttered itself silently to smoke. He did not know. Only that he was shoved into pitch-darkness as swift as death, and his breath jammed in his throat.

Even the keening from the distant cell had stopped, its occupant passed out, perhaps, or sleeping. Could Oliver sleep, then, now that it was dark? He could barely breathe, let alone unclench his body enough to relax even that much. Spots formed in front of his eyes, though he could not clearly see them and, at any second, now the heavy night had descended, the darkness would swallow him whole.

The back of his neck felt like a thick band of wire was wrapped around it; his thighs shook so hard it was all he could do to remain seated. But if he stood, his movement would be noticed by the dark, and something, *something* would grab him.

Now arrived the moment he'd been dreading, as waves and waves of panic foamed up from within. He shot to his feet, feeling the high-pitched sounds his throat was making, feeling the bands tighten around his chest and his legs, the cold film of ice across his flesh. He ran to the bars and held them. Jammed his head against them, let the jagged crusts of rust flake against him, cut into his face.

He could almost taste it on his tongue, the iron and the salt and the unwholesome funk of something leaching through the rocks above. He wanted to howl, wanted to bite, and shoved his fist in his mouth, which stopped the first urge and satisfied the second. He tasted his own blood, which pushed past his lips with an unsaintly speed.

The sudden fear that he would gnaw himself to the bone made him yank his fist away, but as he swallowed, he could taste his own salt, feel the jumpiness of his blood. His heart.

The man in the other cell gave a hard keen, and then Oliver heard the sounds of him turning over, quite clearly. Snoring quickly followed.

Then Oliver *knew* he was seeing things. Something flickered along the wall; he heard footsteps. The lights came closer, and the steady clip of boots on stone. There were voices, talking low, and the rattle of keys.

For a second, he thought it would be the guards and the hangman, or the ghost of Fagin. In an instant, Fagin would be there with his large mouth and crooked teeth, those dark eyes glittering in the candlelight. Making threats, demanding that Oliver accompany him to hell.

Oliver uncurled his palms from the bars and stepped back

from the door. Not that he could hide or run, but at the very least, Fagin would not be able to see Oliver's expression in the shadows.

Two figures stopped in front of his door; the light from a hand-held candle lantern shone through the bars. The first figure was a guard with a dull brass circle of keys. And with him, to Oliver's dazed surprise, was not Fagin's ghost, breaking through Oliver's darkness, bringing light with him, but Jack. It was *Jack*.

"Nolly," said Jack, looking unfamiliar in this place, though he was dressed the same as always, and in fact, looked as he had that very morning. The guard held the candle lantern, and Jack motioned for him to hold it higher. "You in there? Or have you gone missin'?"

By these words, Oliver knew Jack wanted to cheer him up, but Oliver did not deserve to be cheered. He hid his bloody fist behind his back and made himself take a step forward.

"What are you doing here?" he heard himself ask. His voice shook, and he flushed, thinking of Fagin in the cell the night before his hanging and how he'd gone mad.

"Ask you the same thing, I would, 'cept I was there. You've been a bold one, gettin' yourself collared on the street."

Oliver scowled. Jack was getting pleasure out of this, in an almost perverse way, watching Oliver squirm, trapped while he himself ran free.

"I didn't see you once they grabbed me."

"That's why they call me the Artful," said Jack, arching his neck.

"Then you've already had your reward, no doubt," said Oliver, his voice low. It came out more pathetic than he could stand, and he started to turn away when Jack stepped up to the bars. In the light of the candle lantern in the guard's hand, Jack's eyes sparkled, and he held Oliver with them.

"Nolly," he said, in a voice meant only for Oliver. "'T'warn't me. I never turned you in. But I came to you soon as I could."

"It was Noah, wasn't it," said Oliver, quickly. He should not have doubted Jack.

Jack nodded, his face darkening. Honor among thieves meant something to Jack, that was for certain, even if it meant nothing to Noah.

"Five minutes," said the guard.

Jack turned and handed the guard something.

"Did you just give him money?" Oliver asked, shocked.

He had not considered this, though, now that he thought of it, Uncle Brownlow must have paid the guard to let in a boy as young as Oliver to visit Fagin. Prayers had not calmed the Jew, nor had pleas freed him.

The guards standing by had been impervious to both, though the whole of it had left Oliver in tears and feeling weak at heart for days after. The guards had only cared about the money. So of course, that was how Jack had got in, though Oliver very much doubted that Jack would be getting down on his knees and asking Oliver to join him in a quiet word with the Lord anytime soon. The image of this almost made him smile, but then he thought better of it.

"How much?" he asked.

"Every penny," said Jack. "That's the last of it, just now."

Jack did not seem the sort of lad who hoarded his gold in the first place, so how he'd come by enough money for the guard, Oliver could not fathom. Perhaps he'd taken a collection at the Three Cripples, though that seemed as far-fetched as the idea that Jack took his earnings to the Bank of England.

"I'll repay you as soon as I am able," said Oliver. It was easier to concentrate on these mundane facts rather than the darkness behind his back and the hangman's noose waiting for him in the morning.

Jack did not remark upon this, though he nodded to indicate that he would go along with whatever Oliver wanted to do. Jack's eyes, in the uncertain light, seemed to say that it was nothing, that he did not expect anything back. Leaving Oliver, once more, confused as to the type of boy Jack was. He'd never really known, back in those days in Fagin's den. He realized he knew even less now.

"And hey?" Jack was looking at Oliver, wanting his attention, so Oliver came closer, enough so that he could see the shadow of Jack's lashes against his cheek. "You're not a murderer, after all."

"*What?*"

"He's alive, your old master. You clonked him pretty good, but he's alive. He's pressin' charges against you, of course, for assault an' runnin' away, an' you're in it deep, but you're not a murderer. You'll not hang."

Oliver tipped his head forward; his heart pounded. He could not imagine that Jack would lie about something such as that, whatever else he was, whatever else he might do.

Oliver felt something on his face, some damp, perhaps, falling from the ceiling, but as his fingers touched his cheek, he realized he was crying. Maybe the darkness hid this, maybe it did not. But the circle of the candle lantern's light that entered the cell made him feel perhaps it did not matter for this one night, and that Jack would not mock him. He certainly did not say anything as he watched Oliver and did not look away.

Then Jack surprised him, reaching through the bars as though the guard simply was not there, and cupped the side of Oliver's face. The warm skin of Jack's hand was rough against his cheek, but Oliver stayed motionless. And as for Jack, surely he could feel the dampness of Oliver's tears, but did not pull away.

"Nolly," said Jack, slowly. "The mornin' will come, by-and-bye."

Without regard to the guard standing there, Oliver turned his face to press it more firmly inside of Jack's palm, feeling the skin of it against his mouth. He was surprised that Jack did not take his hand away, not for a long, still time. His thumb moved across the edge of Oliver's jaw with careful strokes. His eyes were dark, and Oliver made himself look into them.

"Time," said the guard.

That was it. Jack was out of money, and the guard had better things to do. Jack drew his hand away and then jerked his chin upward, as if telling Oliver to rally himself, that the morning would be there soon, and, thank God, without the hangman's noose.

The guards motioned with the lantern and then took it and Jack away. When the darkness was full and the footsteps had faded, Oliver sat in the middle of the floor, folding his arms around his knees, waiting for his tears to slow. The floor was cold and soon he would have to stand, but Oliver's heart was warm and there was a candle lit inside of it.

## ❦ 26 ❦

# WHEREIN OLIVER APPEARS
# BEFORE THE MAGISTRATE

When Oliver had finally deigned to lie upon the wooden bed, his teeth had been chattering too hard for prayers, and his ears too sharply tuned to the sound of scurrying claws beyond the walls and the constant drip of water upon the stones. He'd fallen asleep in spite of that, but only realized this when he was woken up by the clanking of a key in the door to his cell.

Two guards came in, pounding and stomping, pausing only long enough to put metal cuffs around Oliver's wrists before dragging him out of the cell, up the stone steps, and down the long black passageway.

It was morning; he could tell by the bare grey light that eked its way along the stone-lined corridor as the guards dragged Oliver down another hallway and threw him into another cell, this one smaller than the one before.

While Oliver waited with his hat, which one of the guards had given back to him, he sat on the narrow bench against the wall in a wood-lined room with bars on the spotted windows. His hands were in shackles, and the movement around him had come to a halt. He'd been arrested, yes, but for a moment, as he awaited the magistrate, it was as if nothing had happened. He

357

was in another room, locked in, to be sure, but he was just waiting there. Waiting. They might not hang him, as Mr. McCready was still alive, but there were plenty of other options that awaited him, among them deportation or hard labor in a house of correction.

There was a snap of cold air. The door opened, and two guards stood there to take him into court. It hadn't been a long wait, though long enough for Oliver to lie to himself, for his body to get used to the wooden bench along the wall. For the weak grey sunlight to come in through the barred window in a place that reminded him, a little bit, of the cell that Fagin had spent his last night in. But this was not that place; it was a different room altogether.

"You, up," said one of the guards.

Oliver stood, his mouth dry. He walked toward them, and they grabbed him up under his arms as if he'd already made a motion to run. He wasn't running. There was nowhere to go.

The corridor leading to the courtroom was short, and as Oliver stepped into the room, the metal around his wrists clanking as he shook, he was struck at how this room resembled the last courtroom he'd been in when he was nine years old.

That room had been as cold and still as a meat pantry, grimed with soot along the ceiling and littered with scraps of paper and ash along the floor. This room was exactly like that one except that there were two high windows along the far wall instead of one. This situation, as well, was almost exactly like then except that while he was still an orphan, he was taller and could speak for himself, if given the chance.

The courtroom was packed with people who smelled of too much cologne, who had nothing better to do than to come to see the excitement and to entertain themselves with other people's miseries. He imagined their eyes reflected their rapt attention to the dissolution of the life of someone who they felt to be beneath them. The thought of it was making him shake again, so he made himself think of something else.

His eyes swept the room, and there sat Mr. McCready in the front row, a white bandage covering his forehead under his hat. He was pale and ill and furious, his eyes sparking dark. As he looked Oliver up and down and took in Oliver's shorn hair and disreputable coat, Mr. McCready's eyebrows went up, as they had often done when something had been amiss in the shop, and Mr. McCready had been obliged to step in and set things to rights. Only this time, he couldn't, not even if he wanted to.

Next to him, quite unexpectedly, sat Mr. Grimwig, his cane between his knees, his hands resting on it. He smiled at Oliver, that slanted ugly smile he used when he felt someone was watching. Why he'd come, Oliver had no idea, but it could not be to support Oliver.

Oliver turned away from the crowd and climbed up into the dock when told to. He held onto the wood railing and thought about being nine, and hungry and thirsty in front of a magistrate who did nothing but drink, and who assumed Oliver was a criminal before he'd even opened his mouth.

This magistrate did not drink, though he seemed of a kind with the glasses and beard, eyes stern as he reviewed the page before him. Or that's what Oliver assumed he was doing. He certainly was ignoring Oliver, just as he ignored the movement of the entire courtroom, and the chill of the air as it came through the room from some unchinked window or crack in the paneling.

Then the magistrate looked up and pounded on his desk with his wooden block. He rattled off his office, that the court was in session, and he wanted a verbal description of the offender in the dock before him.

Oliver's mouth fell open and the full weight of the moment slammed into him as though it were a runaway cart. He was under arrest. He was well and truly under arrest, and the shock of it was that he was *guilty*. For running away, for assaulting his master. All of it.

Uncle Brownlow would have been so disappointed; Fagin

would have been pleased. And, what's more, Mr. Grimwig had not been wrong, which would make him quite proud of himself so, at the very least, Oliver had not let *him* down.

The prosecutor, bewigged and black-robed, his sleeves pulled back to reveal lace cuffs, stood up and read the charges.

"Before us stands Oliver Twist, who is charged with assault and running away; he attacked his master without provocation. The court recommends deportation."

"If you please, under what auspices of the law do you recommend deportation and for how long?" The magistrate looked up at the prosecutor; he never looked at Oliver. He seemed serene.

"We recommend permanent deportation on the basis of the remarks which are to follow. In that Oliver Twist has not merely broken one law but two, and at the same time, demonstrated a wild disregard for person and property and proven himself to be a danger to his community."

"Continue."

"Two days ago, Oliver Twist ran away from McCready's Haberdashery, where he was occupied as an apprentice shop boy. That he ran away is a crime unto itself, for he signed an agreement with Mr. McCready to provide services until he was twenty-one. Oliver Twist has, in effect, stolen himself, and the charge is theft."

The magistrate nodded, and Oliver shivered. His fingers clenched tightly on the rail.

"On the same day, Oliver Twist got into an altercation with his master with regards to some trifle, and we attest that Oliver Twist willingly struck his master to the floor, opening his skull and leaving him to die in a pool of his own blood. All witnesses state that Mr. McCready treated his boys humanely and with compassion, so there was no reason for Oliver Twist to strike out."

"That's a lie!" The words came out before Oliver could stop them.

The magistrate looked at him. "You will be silent until given leave to speak, young Twist."

Something ripped through him; he looked down at his hands, linked by metal, gripping the railings, feeling the heat behind his eyes. Yes, he'd struck Mr. McCready, but it hadn't been because of a stray moment of ill temper.

"But he *murdered* an orphan." Oliver's voice broke on the last word, sounding shrill and young in the echoing space of the courtroom. He heard titters and the gabble of talk, and he flushed. "He left the orphan in the warehouse and he froze to death, and when I found him, Mr. McCready said that he—"

"Enough." The magistrate banged his block of wood. "There will be silence in this court. And if I hear one more word out of you, Oliver Twist, one more word that is not directed by me, I shall end these proceedings and have you deported directly. Is that understood?"

Oliver looked up at the magistrate and felt his cheeks grow hot. He should have known better. The world had never cared about small boys such as Martin, and it never would. There were too many of them; they were disposable and forgettable. There was no way to rescue any of them. What's more, the full weight of the law was behind Mr. McCready, and would stay there forever.

"Yes, sir," he said, his voice low, thick in his throat.

"Pray continue, Mr. Prosecutor."

"As I was saying, Mr. McCready was struck down with violence and left to die. A pursuit was activated, but Oliver Twist disappeared into the streets within moments. Mr. McCready, luckily, was tended to by his housekeeper and has recovered. To continue, the second charge is assault with attempted manslaughter. Either charge deserves deportation, which is what the prosecution recommends."

The magistrate wrote in his book and considered his notes for a moment. Then he cleaned his glasses with a soft cloth; he tapped the edge of his pen on the desk.

"Prosecutor, a question. How are these charges brought, and by whom?"

"Mr. McCready placed notices with the police, and in due course an informant came forth with information for a reward." The prosecutor nodded as he checked his handful of notes.

Oliver gripped the bars between his hands and made himself stay silent, even as wanted to shout to the entire courtroom what kind of man the informant was, and that whatever Noah Claypole had to say was either a lie or the truth for his own benefit.

"May we hear from the informant, please, Mr. Prosecutor?"

There was a pause. The magistrate looked at the prosecutor, and Oliver followed his gaze.

"The informant declines to testify; his written statement is asked to stand in his stead." The prosecutor was not just checking his notes, he was reading them. He looked up, his mouth a stiff line.

"What?" barked the magistrate. "But he received a fee, did he not?"

"Yes, he did, but he declines to testify. However, he's a known informant, so the information is good."

The magistrate appeared to think this over. "Very well. Proceed."

"The testimony is given, and statements from witnesses have been presented to the court. The crime itself is not in question, but Mr. McCready is here to testify, regardless."

The magistrate nodded, and Oliver turned his head to the courtroom behind him while the entire room shuffled to look at Mr. McCready.

Mr. McCready was in the front row, sitting at the end as though he'd been prepared for this moment. He nodded at the prosecutor, white-faced, his hands in his lap, and then he caught Oliver's eye. Oliver could see the disappointment and the fury there, and he looked away. Maybe deportation would be for the best; he deserved no better, at any rate.

Mr. McCready got up and walked to the front of the court-room. He mounted the dock adjacent to Oliver's. He stood straight and folded his hands; he was a model citizen in his black suit, white collar, and cravat. His boots were Sunday polished, hair slicked down, and his bandage was a white flag against his skin as he took off his hat and was sworn in. His eyes were like darts as he looked at the magistrate only.

"Mr. McCready, I understand that you would like to give a statement against the boy."

"Yes, sir, that is correct."

"You understand that anything you say will be captured in the records of the court."

"Yes, sir, I do."

"Then proceed." The magistrate waved his hand in Mr. McCready's direction.

Mr. McCready cleared his throat and began. Oliver made himself listen.

"My name is Evan McCready. I own a haberdashery at Number 116 Wardour Street. For the last fifteen years, I have devoted my life not merely to making a good living but to providing worthy boys the training in running a shop."

"Do all of your boys gain good employment?" the magistrate asked.

"All my boys, without exception, are now employed in respectable places around London. My most recent is now working for Harrods."

"You take them at fourteen, I understand, and let them go at twenty-one. Is this correct?"

"Yes, sir, that is correct."

"And yet, Oliver Twist, by my records, came in at seventeen years. Is this correct?"

"Yes, sir, that is correct."

"Can you explain this discrepancy?"

Mr. McCready paused, dipping his head to look at his hands. There was a flicker of memory across his face, and Oliver had to turn away. He knew what had happened that day, how kind Mr. McCready had been at Uncle Brownlow's funeral reception, and the intercession that Parson Greaves and Mr. Beauchamp had organized.

"Oliver Twist," began Mr. McCready, his voice a little rough. He cleared his throat and continued. "Oliver Twist is the adopted charge of a friend of an acquaintance of mine. When the friend, Mr. Brownlow, passed away early this winter, I learned of Oliver Twist's situation. He had no place to go. However, he was educated and a good candidate for this sort of training, for all he was almost too old to begin."

"And what did you do then?"

"I attended Mr. Brownlow's funeral reception. There I was introduced to Mr. Grimwig by mutual friends, and made my proposition to take in the boy."

"And who is Mr. Grimwig?" The magistrate looked at the prosecutor. "Do you know of this man?"

The prosecutor stepped up, waving his notes over the court-room to point at Mr. Grimwig, who preened and straightened up at the attention.

"Mr. Grimwig was a friend of Mr. Brownlow's and took on temporary responsibility for the boy at Mr. Brownlow's demise."

"Mr. Grimwig was concerned that Oliver should be able to make his way in the world," added Mr. McCready.

Oliver scoffed under his breath at that, catching Mr. Grimwig's eyes with his own. Mr. Grimwig smirked at Oliver and looked away. But Oliver didn't say anything. Couldn't, not when the energy of the court was focused on seeing him get his due.

"So you took the boy into your shop? Is that correct?"

"I did. We discussed the matter, and all agreed that this would be in his best interest. He was desirous of owning a book-shop one day, I believe."

"And when he is twenty-one, he comes into some money, is that correct?"

"Yes, when he is twenty-one, he comes into three-thousand pounds, which is now in an account with the Bank of England."

"Do you have any interest in this money?"

"No, sir, I do not." Mr. McCready seemed insulted by the very idea of the question. "My only concern is training the boys under my care. My shop garners me sufficient profit to make a good living and pay decent wages."

"And to what might you ascribe Oliver's turn of attitude, from the day you interviewed him and found him worthy, to the point at where he attacked you. With what was it?"

"A frying pan," said the prosecutor. The crowd made sounds of amusement and jostled in their seats.

"A frying pan," said the magistrate. He frowned at one and all, making the object serious once more.

"At first, he seemed to settle in." Mr. McCready looked over at Oliver, his eyes bleak, mouth in a straight line. Oliver was surprised by the sudden thickness in his chest. He *had* settled in; he'd liked working at Mr. McCready's. "He was quite—happy, as all my boys seem to be. They are well fed, trained, have time at liberty."

"Then what's the problem, do you suppose, Mr. McCready? Can you provide any demonstration of how it wasn't a suitable arrangement?"

"Oliver Twist was a good worker; however, he seemed somewhat daunted by the amount of physical labor involved, though he went at it with a good heart and seemed to want to do his best."

"And the problem?"

"There was a young man," said Mr. McCready. His jaw worked as he thought over his words, his eyes unfocused as he stared at the floor. Then he looked up, putting his shoulders back.

"There was a young man of Oliver's acquaintance, who, by his apparel and his voice, was from a low place. I could never ascertain his identity, but he kept coming to the shop. I warned

Oliver of the consequences of the association, but it did not stop. They were even seen together in the street, when Oliver was on an errand, making deliveries. I had to whip him for it, and still it did not stop. I believe Oliver was influenced by this boy to an unhealthy degree. When someone encouraged Oliver in his violence and sheltered Oliver when he ran away, I can only imagine that it was this same individual."

Oliver's heart felt cold in his chest. He'd not realized that Mr. McCready had been so impassioned to save him from what he saw as an acquaintanceship with someone of the streets. To have wanted so very badly to save Oliver from Jack, and not for any personal gain, but for Oliver's own sake—it was true kindness.

Well, it was too late for that, nor could Mr. McCready have ever saved Oliver from himself. As for Jack, well, everything that had happened since Jack's return to London, from that day to this, seemed a foregone conclusion.

Oliver made himself remain calm as he looked over the courtroom, keeping his gaze low. He looked at Mr. McCready in the dock and at Mr. Grimwig in his seat, cane steady between his knees. He even caught sight of Mrs. Acton, up in the side rows where other elegant ladies sat to watch the commotion and the human drama. But he didn't see Jack, and was glad, so very glad, that he did not. Oliver could not be saved, but that did not mean that he had to drag Jack down with him.

The magistrate sat up in his chair and raised his eyebrows. He settled his glasses once or twice on his nose as he contemplated Mr. McCready's words.

"You seem overly concerned by Oliver's association with this unknown individual."

"I admit to my own vanity in this, but I have never had in my charge a boy go astray to the degree where he could not be saved. And I—I would ask that the court would be lenient with Oliver Twist if I could ascertain the nature as to how this—this *ruffian*—managed to work his way into Oliver's association. So easily. So *disastrously*." Mr. McCready's voice shook as he said this, color dashing across his face.

"How do you know the person who sheltered Oliver is the same one who visited Oliver at your shop and was seen with him in the street? Do you have a description?"

"I had a glimpse of the back of his head, your worship. His clothes were rough, and his hair was dark, and the two young men were of a height. That is all I know." Mr. McCready paused, florid with restraint. "But Oliver could not have disappeared so easily, had he not known someone who would shelter him."

"But is it the *same* young man?"

"I believe so, your worship." Mr. McCready twisted his hat in his hands, rolling the brim around and around, then he stopped himself. "I believe so."

The magistrate turned to Oliver, holding up his hand to stay any comments from the prosecutor.

"Oliver Twist," he began. "This companion of yours seems to have caused you some trouble. But is it the same individual who sheltered you and took you in when you were wanted by the constabulary?"

Oliver's whole frame went absolutely still, a freezing-cold hand clutching at his heart.

"That a young man of good prospects is unduly influenced by someone from the lower orders is not a crime, Oliver.," said the magistrate with grave calmness. "But if this same companion sheltered him, after an assault such as you committed against your master, then that *is* a crime. Do you understand?"

During Mr. McCready's recitations, Oliver had been lulled almost into a stupor, his body working up a heat to keep him warm in this cold room, his brain spinning as though it was a wooden cog, grinding itself into dust. They wanted Jack. Wanted his name, wanted him cornered and brought to heel. Oliver knew his name, knew it fully, knew all of Jack's names and faces, and all the rest besides. Jack Dawkins. The Artful Dodger. The Dodger. *Jack*.

He stared with wide, dry eyes at the magistrate and could not speak.

"Oliver Twist, at Mr. McCready's urgings, and out of his passion to do right by you as a good Christian man, I might be inclined to do as he asks and decrease these charges to three months' hard labor. That is, if this young man can be proven to be the reason behind your decline into the gutter of society. Can you give me his name?"

The courtroom fell into a hush. There wasn't so much as the creak of a wooden seat or the rustle of a petticoat to be heard, though Oliver felt the wind in his ears.

"Oliver Twist, will you speak?"

Oliver kept himself from shaking his head; he needed to think. Jack might not be the most respectable of citizens, and the truth of it was he had taken Oliver in, not once, but twice.

But while the first encounter could not exactly be described as auspicious, Jack had done the best he could. He'd done his best the second time as well; he'd taken Oliver in even with his own head on the line, for surely he'd known that if Oliver was arrested, his association with Oliver, in return, would be questioned. And *still* he'd done it.

Uncle Brownlow would have said that a man never turned on a friend, never. Fagin, who no doubt had seen the inside of many a courtroom, would have said much the same thing, only differently. *Fagin's boys don't peach.* And while Fagin was a reprobate of the worst order, and the statement would have come out through rotting teeth and stringy fingers, the sentiment was identical. But while both men would agree on the tenets of loyalty, neither one of them was here to advise him on what his course of action should be. Perhaps that did not matter, for in the current moment, he was neither completely Uncle Brownlow's boy nor Fagin's boy. He was his own boy. Besides, he could never give them Jack.

"Oliver Twist, will you give this court the name of your companion and allow the law to lessen your sentence?"

Oliver took a breath as the courtroom fell to utter silence. He heard a board creak as someone shifted where they stood.

"I will not."

There was a roar in his ears, and then he realized it was the complexity of raised voices, the half shouts and exclamations that the magistrate's wooden gavel could not quite yet contain. The collection of sounds whirled up the ceiling and bounced off the walls. And still the magistrate pounded.

Through the din, Oliver could hear a single voice, rough-edged and slightly familiar, saying, "Sir, if I may speak before the court, if I may *speak*—"

The magistrate pounded his block, sending his pens to rattling until the crowd subsided, leaving Oliver feeling their reaction, their very voices, swamp through him. Of course, they wouldn't understand, no one of any decency would. He might have a hard time, himself, explaining it to Jack, would that they ever meet again.

"The court will come to order," said the magistrate in the first silence available to him. "And I have no other recourse but to—"

"Sir, if I may speak."

It was the same voice as before. Oliver scanned the courtroom, trying to figure out where it had come from. He saw a man rise and come forward, without permission. He carried his black top hat in his hands, and was washed and shaven, looking clean and awkward, but the expression around his eyes gave Oliver pause. With his hands clasped around his hat and the meek line of his shoulders, the dip of his head in the direction of the magistrate and prosecutor, all made him appear that his only desire was to be of use.

There was someone with him, a younger man, also newly cleaned, pious in a narrow white collar and black cravat, his cap in his hand. He had dark hair, and his head was bent down as they both walked forward. Then he lifted his head, and his green eyes glinted at Oliver.

Oliver's mouth fell open. *Jack.* Then he recognized the man: it was Cromwell, scrubbed and shaved and cleaned up to look respectable. But it was Jack who drew his eyes, Jack who had washed and combed his dark hair, and who now looked as sweet-faced as a choirboy.

"Who is this man?" asked the magistrate. He waved his block at the prosecutor. "Tell me who this man is, or I'll have him removed from my courtroom."

"I do not know, sir," said the prosecutor. He adjusted his wig, his black sleeves flapping. "But he appears to want to speak on behalf of—"

"On behalf of the young man, your worship," said Cromwell. "I am William Howard, come from the Holborn Society's Aid for Boys. We aim to assist young men out of a life of crime by givin' 'em them a good home, an'—"

"So you appear to appeal for the boy? His sentence is about to be passed, you realize."

"Yes, your worship, but I come to the court every so often, to listen and learn from the great wash of humanity." Here Cromwell stopped to throw a generous wave over the crowd, which had gone very silent, listening to the dramatic rise and fall of his voice. "And in this young man's case, I truly believe that his problem is more temper than temperament."

"So you believe he was pressed into the assault?"

"By his own passions, your worship," said Cromwell. Then he patted Jack on the shoulder of his velveteen jacket. "This here's Isaac White, late of the streets and current resident of my honest establishment. I cleaned him up, taught him some manners, an' he ain't a pickpocket no more. Are you, Isaac?"

The crowd was silent, enthralled. Even Oliver found himself leaning forward to hear Jack's reply. Of course, Jack and Cromwell believed none of what they were saying; it was all a joke to them. But it was so very well told, a lie to echo Mr. McCready's own tale, complete with the innocent Jack, who managed to look shy and bold at the same time, flashing a rosy curve of a smile, looking up from under his lashes at the magistrate.

"Yes, sir," said Jack, almost softly. "I would have died on the streets had it not been for the Society. Was about to go on a lark of stealin' an' that, when they found me."

"And how long have you been with them?"

"Only six weeks, your worship," said Jack. "But long enough to learn the difference between right an' wrong."

As the crowd broke into an excited rumble of talk, the magistrate considered the pair, and Oliver held his breath. Of course, a man as clever and learned as a magistrate would not be taken in by two men so obviously of the street, masquerading as both the saver and the saved. A quick run across London, as well, would easily prove that there was no such thing as the Holborn Society's Aid for Boys. But no one moved to do this.

"Can we beseech you, your worship," said Cromwell, raising his voice above the thrust of the din, "to consider the fate of this good English lad, led astray by his own passions, if he be sent into a country so far away? Where he will be surrounded by true convicts and dark natives with no sense of their own God? Wouldn't he be better off here? To be saved among his own where he can be of use to society? I can't save everyone in the world, but I can do my best in my own little corner of it. And this poor lad, just look at him. With a face like his, surely he deserves saving?"

The crowd turned, of a body, to look at Oliver, standing in the dock with the shackles hanging heavy around his wrists and the backside of his breeches stained with gaol mud. His hair was scraggled and black with soot, his face was grimy with sweat and ash, and he was no doubt jumping with lice, and still they stared as if at something they wanted for themselves. He felt himself flushing. There was a murmur from the seats, and a small cry from a despairing woman; Oliver ducked his head and stared at his hands, not risking a look at Jack.

He let the pull of emotion from the courtroom wash over him; he had no control at this point, only the magistrate did.

"Mr. McCready," said the magistrate. He had no need to bang his gavel; the crowd was absolutely silent, pitched forward in their seats, waiting on his next words.

"Yes, sir."

"An alternative to deportation has been brought before the court, and I, for one, am loath to be overly punitive. Discipline on English soil is always preferable in cases such as these. Yet, as the victim of this crime and, indeed, his master, would you countenance this? Or yet take him home yourself and deal with the matter in your own way?"

Before Oliver had a chance to consider whether or how he might handle going with the man he thought he'd killed, Mr. McCready shook his head and sliced through the air with his hand.

"I'd as soon nurse a snake to my bosom," he said. "But I have no objections to the Holborn Society's Aid for Boys, if they are willing to take him, and good luck to them, I say."

"Then I hereby remand Oliver Twist into the care of the Holborn Society's Aid for Boys." The magistrate banged his gavel and sorted the papers on his desk. "Mr. McCready, Mr. Howard, if you can come forward and sign for the boy, then I can close this matter and get on with my work."

Having not been otherwise bid, Oliver remained in the dock, waiting while one of the constables standing by fingered his keys and jingled them. There was talk in the crowd and Oliver could hardly believe the court system of London had fallen for a bit of velvet coat and grand speaking by a man who so obviously thought the lot of them to be fools. Oliver was a fool as well if he went with them, but where else was he to go? Mr. McCready didn't want him, and Oliver didn't want to be deported. There was no other solution.

The two men went up to the judge's bench and took pen and ink, bending over the prosecutor's table to sign a document that looked far too short to be recording all the events of the morning. Or maybe it was only in Oliver's head that the time in the courtroom seemed overwhelming, never-ending. The crowd rustled and stirred as if to voice their common displeasure that the next event wasn't already underway.

The constable came up and unlocked Oliver's handcuffs, neither harshly nor gently; he was just doing his job.

"Off you go, young'n," said the constable.

He seemed sensible, and the look in his eyes told Oliver that he might be among the few to see the truth behind Cromwell's lies. But it wasn't his job to say anything about it. Or maybe he knew Oliver wasn't truly evil. Or maybe Oliver was dizzy from the final judgment and reeling with being saved from deportation. Saved from months at sea, trapped in a little boat, to live the rest of his days on rocky soil far from home.

## 27

# OLD BRIDGES ARE BURNED AND NEW ONES UNWILLINGLY BUILT

The constable guided him to the doorway and waited with him while Oliver rubbed his wrists and looked about for Jack. He longed, suddenly, almost painfully, for Jack to be near.

Mr. Grimwig hobbled through the crowd. He was clacking his cane on the floorboards as he rudely made his way to Oliver, who couldn't imagine what they might have to say to each other should they pause to exchange greetings.

And yet, there Mr. Grimwig was, resplendent for his non-speaking appearance in court, hair oiled back, a black armband around the sleeve of his dark green coat, in a silk black waistcoat, with the shiny gold of his timepiece pinned to a scarlet ribbon. He was as he had always been, and Oliver felt startled to see him up close, as if it had been years since they'd seen each other instead of only weeks.

"Oliver Twist," said Mr. Grimwig, not bowing his head in greeting. Instead, he tilted his head back, looking at Oliver down his nose, showing everybody, anybody who was watching, exactly what he thought of his friend's ward.

"Mr. Grimwig, not a pleasure," said Oliver. And this in spite of who was watching; he was well past the point of giving a damn what anybody thought.

"I see you have, once again, swayed the entire English judicial system with your fine airs and cherubic looks, in spite of your shorn hair. You look like a dock worker, which is only fitting, given your background." Mr. Grimwig nodded at the throng of the courtroom as people moved into the newly emptied seats or moved past the two of them on their way outside for fresh, damp air.

"I didn't—" Oliver began, meaning to explain that it hadn't been his words that had released him from his fate; it had been Mr. McCready's. Then he saw that gentleman coming toward them, slowly, almost reluctantly, carrying something in his hands that Oliver couldn't quite see. "It was Mr. McCready—"

But Mr. Grimwig poked a sharp finger in the middle of Oliver's chest to get him to pay attention. Mr. Grimwig's brows lowered fiercely, and he was scowling, white-faced, angry.

"You ruin the life of everyone you come in contact with," said Grimwig through clenched teeth. "They are pulled in by your pretty face, your fine manners, then you plunge your dagger into their hearts, and afterward, they are never the same. You killed my best friend with your duplicity. You broke his heart, and you are well on your way to breaking the heart of Mr. McCready, though he is wise if he sticks to his word and never allows you to darken his door again."

Oliver backed away, though he was not surprised that Mr. Grimwig would speak the words aloud in so public a place.

"Because of this, everyone you have ever known will turn from you." Mr. Grimwig stopped, panting, short of breath, as though his passion had taken it from him. His eyes were wet and his face flushed; he pulled out a handkerchief from his waistcoat and patted his face with it.

Oliver felt as though he'd been slapped in front of dozens of people. But before he could make a reply, Mr. Grimwig turned away, stuffing his handkerchief back in its pocket, thumping his cane on the floorboards to make way for himself. Then he slipped into the crowd and was gone.

The constable took Oliver's arm to hustle him away, but Mr. McCready met them and, indeed, marched past them.

"With me, Twist," Mr. McCready said.

Oliver scrambled behind him, through the narrow stone corridor, out into the rainy morning. He saw Jack out of the corner of his eye, but could not stop. Cromwell was there with Jack. Perhaps they meant to jump Mr. McCready when no one was looking; something that Oliver already knew he had to be on the lookout for.

Mr. McCready was talking to a constable, standing there with a box in both hands. It was Oliver's box from the haberdashery, the one that contained his clothing and books and his money. Mr. McCready turned to Oliver and held it out.

"I didn't know where you'd be bound, but I thought I'd bring your belongings."

Mr. McCready's face was grave; Oliver felt that fist in his throat, a familiar hard ghost of regret. He'd done badly by this good man who, in spite of his treatment of the orphan, had only been doing what he thought to be right.

"About the orphan," Oliver began, meaning to explain, though he was never going to apologize.

Mr. McCready's expression darkened. "They're a penny a dozen, Oliver Twist, as you should well know, being one of them."

Mr. McCready shoved the box at Oliver roughly. Then, with a scowl, Mr. McCready tipped his hat at Oliver and plunged into the traffic on the wet street, slipping between a milk float and a band of street workers. Then he was gone.

A quick-stepping carriage hustled past Oliver; one of the wheels caught the largest edge of the box and snatched it out of Oliver's hands. The box dashed itself to the curb, snapping and cracking, splashing into the gutter of rainwater. Smashing to pieces.

Oliver reached into the gutter as his books, his mother's small portrait, the letters from his Aunt Rose, all of his belongings, swirled into the thick, gritty water. Someone came up behind him and slipped their arms about his waist. He had only a moment before he began to fight the hold, to see that it was Jack.

"Nolly, your hand is bleeding."

Oliver looked down at his hand, sliced along the thumb, and at the gutter where all of his belongings became unrecognizable and floated away on the narrow tide. Jack tugged out his handkerchief and pressed it against Oliver's hand before he let go of Oliver's waist and stepped away.

"Eh, then, Oliver," said Cromwell. He came up behind Oliver and clapped him on the shoulder. "You're one of us, then, my good lad."

Oliver was about to refute this; he'd already made up his mind about that. But Jack stood close by Oliver's side, touching the back of Oliver's hand with his own.

"I knew you was never goin' to turn me in," said Jack, leaning close. The brightness of his tone seemed to hide something else beneath the layers and the lies.

Oliver turned to look at him and opened his mouth to explain why he had not peached. But there was too much that he couldn't say, not in the street, not in front of Cromwell. And there was too much brightness in Jack's eyes. Oliver let his thoughts fall where they would.

Jack tipped back the brown cap on his head, looking much younger in it than Oliver ever could, and Oliver felt a bit of softness that he'd believed to have died.

"No, Jack," said Oliver. "Never you." He watched as one last piece, the corner of the box, perhaps, or the edge of a book, floated down the gutter. "Never you."

~

THE WALK TO THE THREE CRIPPLES WAS BRISK, GOING straight up Farringdon Street, bold, as if they'd not just come from Newgate Prison. It was uphill all the way.

As the street narrowed along Saffron Hill, the pavement begrimed beneath their feet in spite of the rain, Oliver felt himself being sucked into the darkness. The number of folk increased, and the pavement became crowded, rotting wood rising around him, the dank smells thick beneath the rain. He was soaked through and shaking by the time they came to the door of the tavern.

"Get him cleaned up, you," said Cromwell. His voice had dropped to its normal tones; gruff and certain. "We don't want 'im to stand out, but 'e shouldn't suffer neither, not with that pretty face."

He reached out as if to pat Oliver on the cheek, but Oliver jerked away. He was used to people, to Jack, saying he had a pretty face, but he did not care for the way Cromwell said it.

Jack, as if sensing this, opened the door to the Three Cripples and pulled Oliver inside. It was cold near the door, but Oliver could feel the heat of at least one coal fire, smell the familiar dust and the damp, as if he'd been away for ages and not merely a day or two.

"You hungry, Nolly?" asked Jack.

Oliver shook his head. He didn't think he could manage food; he had no idea how he would manage any of this.

Cromwell came in behind them. "Get 'im cleaned up, I said."

Jack scurried, taking Oliver with him along the bar, through the room, into the alcove that was Jack's. There was no fire. Oliver hesitated, but Jack tugged, and as Cromwell was muttering to someone in the main room, Oliver went and sat down in the seat next to where the fire was supposed to be and buried his face in his hands.

"Nolly?"

"Give me a moment," he said. "I shall be all right, in a moment."

But he would not be. Not in any way that he could think of. He'd committed a crime and had been given his day in court; his penance was this place and what it represented. He thought he'd left it behind, oh, so long ago. There had been years of a good and decent life between that day and this, so how was it he'd ended up right back here?

Oliver sighed with his whole body. As well, in the icy stillness of the room, he could smell his own sweat. His boots looked beyond repair, and he'd smeared mud right up his shirt bosom.

"Nolly?"

He took his face from his hands, and looked up at Jack, at the white collar over his green velvet lapels, and wondered where the red scarf was. Jack didn't move as Oliver's eyes searched his. He only stood there, blinking, a little pale, that brown cap still on, the mud from his boots tracked right across the floor.

"It's goin' to work out, Nolly, you'll see," said Jack. "You're with me, now, ain't you?"

Jack was content, so he thought Oliver should be, as well. To attempt to convince Jack otherwise would be wasted air.

"Yes," said Oliver. He made himself sit back a little bit; the seat was hard and cold beneath him, reminding him unduly of the bed in the prison cell. "But I still need a wash, and maybe after that, something to eat."

Jack nodded. "That's the spirit. Come on, up you get."

He reached down to haul Oliver to his feet; his hand upon Oliver was the only warm thing.

As they went into the main room, Oliver heard noises, a door slam, and footsteps. From down the corridor, near the stairs that went to the labyrinth below the tavern, Oliver heard a low cry. He followed Jack to see that Cromwell had Noah by the collar. Noah's nose was swollen and bleeding, and he looked sore about the mouth, as though Cromwell had just smacked him.

"Teach you to turn evidence in my place," Cromwell said, harsh. "Teach *you!*" Then he hit Noah again.

Noah cried out so piteously that Oliver started forward, only to be held by Jack's hand on his elbow. Though why he would want to help Noah in any case, he didn't know, except that he couldn't just stand by and watch.

"'E collected on you," said Cromwell, seeing Oliver there. "Collected the reward an' all, as 'e does, the slimy toad."

"The reward," said Oliver. So it had been Noah, though it didn't make him feel any better to be proven right.

"'E went straight down to Newgate when 'e found out about you, an' reported you, an' 'e collected the reward of five pounds. Pocketed the lot."

Which might be the problem. If Noah had split the reward with Cromwell, then he might not be hanging from Cromwell's fist looking like a drowned rat.

"Might 'ave cost me the use of you, besides, 'ad you been deported."

This stopped Oliver cold. "The use?"

"Of that pretty face," said Cromwell. He shook Noah to keep him still. "'Cause I own you now, owned you the second you walked through that door. But now, with the signature of the court to back me up? I own you for good and all."

Cromwell let Noah go to stumble against the yellow-stained plaster wall, nursing his nose with a snowy-white handkerchief that soon turned brick red.

"An' one step out of line? Out you go on a ship to sea."

"No," said Oliver. "You don't own me, the paper merely said—"

Cromwell surged toward him, pushing right past Jack to back Oliver against the wall, and slam the wall beside Oliver's head. Then he shoved Oliver's shoulders, hard, and moved close, pressing his body close, one thigh between Oliver's legs, his face only inches away.

"You're mine, an' I own you," said Cromwell as he raised a hand to stroke the side of Oliver's face. Cromwell was so close, his breath skittering across Oliver's cheek, that Oliver pulled back as far as he could, though Cromwell shook him, making

Oliver's head clonk against the wall. "There's a good many who'd pay to bend you over the edge of a bed, if I'd a mind to sell you that way. So you better do right by me. You hear?"

Cromwell let Oliver go, shoving back off of him, the ghost of the heat of his body shivering on Oliver's skin.

He stomped out of the room, leaving Oliver gasping; he did not doubt that Cromwell could do it, if he wanted to. Jack's eyes were wide in his face as he crossed to Oliver's side, touching his fingers to the edges of Oliver's jacket. And Noah, still bleeding, stared at Oliver as though this was his fault, and nothing but his bloody nose was amiss.

"He don't mean it," said Jack. "That's only him stampin' and yellin'. He don't mean it."

Oliver was about to argue the point that Cromwell was not the type to say what he didn't mean when suddenly Jack marched over to Noah, holding out his hand.

"Hand over a third, you," he said. "I know Cromwell's taken his bit, an' I want mine."

To Oliver's surprise, Noah lowered the handkerchief long enough to dig into his pocket for some coins, and whether the change was right or not, Jack took it and turned to Oliver with a small smile.

"I'll treat you right, Nolly. Though I don't think Noah's up to a wash this mornin'."

Or any morning. Oliver would sooner go with a shrieking devil than walk the streets with Noah Claypole. Though as he watched Noah snuffling into his handkerchief, seeing the low line of his shoulders, the blood spotted on his shirt, it was apparent that being Noah was its own punishment.

## 🦋 28 🦋

# JACK TEMPTS OLIVER WITH
# FOOD AND WITH DRINK

Jack took Oliver into the kitchen, which was a clattering
mess of unwashed pots and pans, and a rusty stove that
was sending smoke into the room. Every level surface was
covered with grease, and mouse-droppings littered the
windowsill, the corners of the room, along the wall.

A woman struggled at the dry stone sink to scrape dried
remains off platters, while another was cutting slices of bread
with a too-dull knife. In the middle of the room, a man hacked
away at a side of beef that was green round the edges and looked
to be more fat than meat. His cleaver whacked into the wooden
table with each slice as he scraped off rolls of flesh onto a sheet
of newspaper.

Ignoring this, Jack dragged Oliver between the table and the
stove, into the thick, sour air of the kitchen, and then out into
the crisp, wet air, along a narrow path between the frozen mud
to the pump at the end of the alley.

He held Oliver's hat and kept a lookout as Oliver sluiced his
face and neck in the icy-cold water. When he was finished and
there was nothing for him to dry his hands on, Jack pulled out
his shirttails and offered Oliver that.

Oliver used them and put his hat back on, but now he was

cold *and* wet and still not very clean, but he kept his mouth shut and followed Jack up the alley, through the foul kitchen, and back to the tavern.

At least the Three Cripples was a haven from the snow-flecked rain. Someone had lit a fire, so the alcove was relatively warm, although the constant dusty damp clogged Oliver's nose as he sat by the fire. He put his top hat on the table and watched the bustle of customers, the door swinging open and closed every five minutes, the movement bringing with it more air and cold, the push of damp bodies. But for all that activity that he watched for a good hour, he could see no sense to it, except that people came, drank, and left.

At one point, Jack went upstairs to change into his regular clothes, and when he came back down, Oliver felt a little better to see him resplendent in his bright blue waistcoat and jaunty hat. Then Jack brought them beer. Oliver took a sip of his and left the rest. It was too early in the day, though that didn't stop Jack from swallowing his share and half of Oliver's.

For all Oliver watched, he realized that the order and passage of the day was nothing that resembled the haberdashery. Well and truly nothing like it. The floor never got swept, the counters and tables went unwiped, dirty glasses and beer pots collected like litters of unwanted children at the end of the bar, and men spat on the floor wherever they would.

The girl behind the counter, Doreen or Polly or whatever her name was, slopped beer over her hands and licked them, and pushed back her stringy hair, and put her fingers in glasses, and on it went until Oliver felt as disturbed as a foreman inspecting a gang of drunk bricklayers in the street. It was easy to see that nothing was done with any eye to improving custom or making the place anything other than what it was: a local and disreputable but handy tavern, where the beer flowed and nobody cared about much of anything else.

"You all right, Nolly?" asked Jack. He stood up, finishing the beer, tipping his head back to catch the last drops. Then he lay his hand on Oliver's shoulder. "You're free now, remember? No more errands, no more gettin' yelled at for nothing, no more stupid job."

And that, right there, in Jack's unassuming statement about the world as Jack saw it, was the problem. Oliver could try to explain it, how the status of being an apprentice gave him a place in the world, put him several steps closer to his dream of owning a bookshop, but Jack would only look at him and frown and urge another drink on him.

For Jack, the dream was today, only this minute, this small circle of space encompassed by the Three Cripples. For Jack, tomorrow was an uncertain mess and not worth bothering about, certainly nothing worth planning for or working toward. For Jack, all of his tomorrows were a chance proposition at best anyway, so why not enjoy it while you had it? To explain it otherwise would be a waste of Oliver's breath.

Oliver remembered this feeling from the old days, of feeling lost, standing in Fagin's den with his cap in his hands, not knowing how or when or where the day would take him. Of Fagin, letting Oliver pick initials out of stolen handkerchiefs and praising him all the while. He'd not known where his tomorrows would find him then, either.

Strangely, he was right back there now, as he had been then, next to Jack, who tilted a smile at him, and who had a new smudge on his cheek. At least Jack was something familiar and solid in a world that kept shifting around him. Jack was the *only* thing—

"Nolly?"

"It's just that—" Oliver began, thinking at least, in part, to try to explain it. "What am I to do with myself?"

"You're usually deep in it by this time, ain't you?" Jack said, nodding. "All elbows and arseholes, workin' your heart out, sweatin' it that your master will be displeased by somethin'. But here?" Jack waved a hand over the company at the bar, the men at the table. "Here, there's nothin' you need to be doin' until we get sent on a job."

That was the problem. Not only was there nothing that needed doing, Jack obviously expected, now that Oliver had a prison record and no means of employment, that he would, naturally, operate in the world as Jack did.

Oliver wanted to say some comment to enforce the notion that whatever he would be doing, stealing wouldn't be one of them. Which to Jack would seem laughable because, of course, whatever else was there to do? Besides sleeping in and drinking beer for breakfast and thinking, as you looked at a black-shouldered group of men doing the same thing, that you were having a grand time. That this was the life.

Well, it wasn't. Besides, Oliver's stomach began to growl, a low, persistent feeling deep in his gut. He was already missing Mrs. Pierson's good cooking, the stately platters of buttered bread, not to mention the cleanliness of her kitchen.

"Come on, then, have some beer." The way Jack said it came out half annoyance, half warning. As if Jack wanted to point out that this was Oliver's life now, and he'd better get used to it. Besides, it suited Jack, so why didn't it suit Oliver?

"Nolly?"

It was disconcerting that he could feel soothed by the single utterance of a pet name, but he was.

"I need a purpose," said Oliver, shifting his shoulders, not thinking that Jack would understand.

"Cromwell'll give you a purpose, right enough," said Jack, as though this were a good thing. He even nodded as he said it with a little jerk of his head. He put his hat on the table as he finished the last of Oliver's beer.

"Not that kind," said Oliver.

He should start explaining, right at that moment, why he wasn't going to work for Cromwell, not ever. And why he should just button up his jacket and go out that door this very minute and march to Aunt Rose's and leave all of this behind him. But he felt stuck, and whether it was from indecisiveness or just plain exhaustion, he didn't know. He should leave. But he couldn't bring himself to do it.

"I merely need something to do," he said. "I cannot put it any plainer than that."

"Come get more beer with me, then, if you're so set on doin' somethin'. The day's better, when you've had beer."

Jack picked up the pint pots from the table and tugged Oliver's jacket sleeve with his fingers to make Oliver follow him as he made his way to the bar. Jack shouldered his way up to the front and snapped his fingers at Doreen, who snapped her fingers back and pretended she didn't see him there.

Determining that a beer would fill his stomach for the moment, Oliver followed Jack and stood close behind him, ignoring the startled looks he got, which Oliver wanted to believe was on account of his chopped hair and outdated jacket, but which he suspected was something else, as it always was.

Jack reached back through the throng and pulled Oliver up to the bar to stand next to him, pushing men aside, and why shouldn't he? He worked for Cromwell, who owned the tavern, so Jack could do as he pleased. Not that any of the men at the bar could have been aware of that fact. Still, Jack nodded at the girl and ordered two pots of beer and ignored the dark looks he was getting.

Doreen took his pennies and pushed over the beers, which slopped on the damp wooden surface, the pots slipping in the grease and liquor. Oliver made himself take one, fingers circling around the dingy metal edge, and then he drank from it. The beer wasn't bad; it smelled and tasted fresh at any rate, perhaps the freshest thing in the tavern, so Oliver concentrated on that, breathing in the hops and tasting the bite behind each swallow. He preferred gin—gin was sweeter when laced with sugar, but this early in the morning, not even noon yet, beer would give his stomach something to do and dull his mind a little.

After about five swallows, he still had half his beer left, but his brain started slipping apart as the beer tumbled into his empty stomach.

"Jack." Oliver raised his eyes to Jack, who was standing there, finishing his third beer of the day, wiping his hand on the back of his jacket sleeve, and looking at Oliver as though all of this was normal, all of this was good.

"I need something to eat."

He felt desperate, having not gone this long without food since he'd travelled from Hardingstone to London. Even when he was with Fagin, he'd never been this hungry, his stomach a hollowed-out shell. He thought back and realized he'd not eaten since the pies on the day he'd been arrested. Two days ago.

"Beer's what's to eat," said Jack, smacking his lips.

"No," said Oliver, feeling it hitting him, a swamp of hunger, his stomach grinding itself from the inside out, and waves and waves of dizziness.

Jack looked at him, brows drawn down in a dark line; Oliver felt the sweat popping up on his upper lip.

"You're as delicate as a miss an' twice as fussy," said Jack, frowning. "But then, you always was."

Oliver shook his head, turning away, thinking that he might go and sit in the alcove, amidst the filth and trampings of boots and the soot from the clogged fireplace, and lay his head in his arms and not get up again until his head stopped spinning. But Jack was there, pulling on his sleeve, cupping his hand around Oliver's wrist, startling Oliver at the gentle touch amidst the throng of men and the disaster that his life had become.

"I got a few pennies. How about we get you a pie?"

"No," said Oliver. "Just some bread. Some bread and butter." He had to blink hard against the heat in his eyes; any display would make him stand out even more, so he swallowed and tried to straighten his shoulders. "And coffee. From a stand. You know?"

Jack looked at him, and Oliver thought he could see the recognition there, flickering in Jack's eyes, and the memory of that day when Jack had roughed him up and then taken him to the coffee cart. Thereafter, Oliver had often thought of Jack eating bread and drinking coffee.

Jack went and grabbed his top hat and Oliver's hat from the table and ushered them out the front door into the rainy street. The pavement ran with water, and the refuse and strands of straw gathered in clumps along the edges of the gutter. It wasn't raining hard, but it was constant and icy, and had built up, sparkling around the edges of the buildings, women's bonnets, the scarred backs of horses in leather harness, on the hooves and beshatted hides of horned cows being driven to Smithfield along Saffron Hill.

The air was fresher outside, for which Oliver was grateful. Putting his hat on, he ducked his head down, his chin touching the black kerchief around his neck, the buttons cold beneath his fingers as he did them up.

"There's a cart down along here, I think," said Jack. He jingled his change in his pocket, Oliver's change purse having been traded or lost some time ago, it seemed.

Oliver followed close behind and tried not to stare at the cripple in the corner covered with a burlap sack and asleep under it, or maybe dead. Or the woman with the goat who was trying to sell milk under an awning that simply was too full of holes to keep out the rain.

He couldn't look at any of them because if he did, the reality of it would come to him too hard and much faster than he was ready for. This place, this street, these people, this was his home now, as if he'd been destined for it so many years ago. And while the man in the white waistcoat back at Hardingstone Workhouse had been in error, he hadn't been very far off the mark.

"Can we—" Oliver hurried to catch up and walk beside Jack, hogging the pavement, bumping into people, getting dirty looks. "Is there enough for extra sugar in that?" he asked.

They stopped at the cart, which was parked along a dripping brick wall. Its awning was solid cloth, at least, and they stood under the lip of it and warmed their hands over the brazier, breathing in the steam rising from the pot.

"Anything for you, petal," said Jack, smiling at him, teasing.

Oliver bumped his shoulder against Jack to get him to stop, but the coffee man looked at Oliver up and down the way people did, just the same.

"Two coffees," said Jack. "Sugar in his."

"Cheaper if you buy one big one; besides, I only got one mug at the moment."

Jack nodded and handed over three pennies, and then one penny more. He pointed at the sliced bread, slightly soggy around the edges, stacked in the narrow metal bucket next to the fire.

The man handed over a slice and prepared the coffee, putting in it, as Oliver could see, several large lumps of sugar. Jack gave the bread to Oliver, and, with motions of his hands, let him eat the whole thing. Oliver sighed as he chewed, his throat a little tight as the bread was old and there was no butter, but he ate it anyway, swallowing as fast as he could while watching Jack take the first sip of coffee.

"You like it with sugar," Jack noted, handing over the mug.

Oliver held it between his two hands, ducking his head down to suck the crumbs from his thumb, and glanced up to see Jack staring at him with round eyes. The coffee man was looking at him as well, curiously watching as if he'd never seen anyone lick crumbs from their skin. Oliver looked away and drank his coffee, gulping two hot swallows that sent the warmth fusing through him, racing to his stomach, warming him from the inside.

"Better than beer?" Jack asked, still watching him.

Oliver cast his eyes over the passersby, the stream of people along the muddy streets that simply never stopped moving. At the man pushing a handcart, the woman in the stained skirt with a heavy basket over her arm. The two boys leading a muddy pony. And then back at Jack, who was waiting for his answer; it was obvious that he wanted the answer to be yes.

"Yes," Oliver said. "It's better than beer."

"Not better than gin," Jack said. Now he smirked. "Gin with sugar. Or, with you, anything with sugar, eh?"

Jack patted Oliver's stomach with the flat of his palm, seeming to find this fact amusing.

"Yes," he said. "Anything with sugar."

Or anything served on a platter, on a clean white tablecloth, preceded by the niceties of hot water and soap, followed by a dry place to sit and read afterward, with no one stomping about, shouting. The whole day stretched ahead of him, a great, big, vast empty wasteland of filth and damp, and Jack was as happy as a spring thrush.

"Nolly?"

Oliver looked at him and handed over the rest of the coffee.

"I miss my books," he said. Although he'd only owned barely a dozen, in that box, now broken and dropped in the rain, it was the idea of them. That and the bookshop, which he was even further away from owning. Could he explain that to Jack, and would Jack ever understand? "Especially the one I'd only just bought, *The Arabian Nights*; I hadn't even had a chance to really read it."

Jack nodded, though his expression told Oliver that he didn't understand, not really. Jack's possessions amounted to, had always amounted to, what he had on him. Anything he needed he could trade for, or, yes, steal, and so the whole world was his wardrobe, his clothespress. His shelf of books.

"Let's go down to the river," said Jack, handing the mug back to the man. "That'll take your mind off it, then."

Jack started walking, and Oliver hurried to catch up, thinking how he'd walked with his thoughts and his grief the day of Uncle Brownlow's funeral, and how he'd met Jack in the snow. Now it was raining, his life was in ruins, and he was still with Jack.

The traffic, horses, carts, and people, thinned out a bit as they slipped and splashed down Field Lane, which was too narrow for many, and too dirty for most. Then they went along Farringdon, which spread out like a fat woman's skirts.

On the other side of Fleet Street, the throng picked up, out and about in the rain. These folk were women in cloaks and clean aprons carrying bundles, or men with shovels and warm scarves. Though they were not of the higher quality sort, as would be found on Wardour Street, they were somewhat nicer than those that skulked around the Three Cripples.

After a brisk walk downhill on slippery pavement, they arrived at Blackfriars Bridge, the humped and pale-grey stone arches reaching across the rushing brown river. Wooden pikes of wherries decked with clouds of sail rocked on the water, damp and draped in the rain. The tide pushed the wherries against the mud-clotted shoreline, and low birds flew over and ducked into the water, picking at trash and bits of refuse, wheeling and crying over their heads, and all of it surrounded by the smell of the water and the mud, and the steam of a pipe emptying thick red fluid into the river.

Jack raced up to the low stone wall that separated a portion of the street from the river and half flung himself over it, as a child might. His face was bright with excitement as he looked at the rushing water, the movement of the boats, the ferries being rowed back and forth, the rumble and clack of carts over the bridge, racing in the rain as though to get out of it. A gust of wind picked up, wet and drizzly, and smacked Oliver in the face.

"I missed this, when I was away," said Jack. Unexpectedly, it seemed, for he'd not yet talked about his time being deported except for a few wild stories and attempts to show Oliver his tattoos. "It was such a dry place there, I felt like I was a dried raisin half the time."

While Jack had been away, a convict, Oliver had been in the country, warm and drowsy in the summer, cozy and fire-lit in the winter. Studying at the table before it was cleared for meals, or in the little front parlor, where nobody ever went, and nobody minded if Oliver was in there, for he was considered a good boy and mindful of where he was. Well, he was no longer a good boy.

He looked at Jack, who didn't, and never could, understand that this was no life. Not for a young man who wanted to make something of himself. But for Jack? The river and the view was enough. This moment was enough.

Jack, leaning on his elbows on the stone wall, looked at Oliver.

"Tell you what. I'll pick some pockets an' get you somethin' to eat, a proper meal, would you like that?"

"What?" asked Oliver. "No."

Jack might understand Oliver's life, if Oliver could explain it clearly enough. Yet the real problem was that even if Jack did understand it, it wouldn't matter to him. Because here he was, talking of picking pockets as if it were a grand option, and fair game on a rainy morning.

"I'd rather go hungry," said Oliver, in an attempt to help Jack see where he stood on this.

Jack merely tipped back his head and laughed, rain on his face, on his teeth, bare hands cold in the air by the river, red with it, and he stood up and reached up to pat Oliver's face. Gently. Cold fingers against cold skin.

"I could do it," Jack said. "Get you a meal, as easy as anythin'."

Oliver half-wanted to tell him, *yes, go and get a fat wallet and buy me a slice of roast and steamed pudding,* but he held himself still until Jack took his hand away and shook his head.

"Or you could do it," said Jack, laughing with an open-mouthed smile. "You still owe me from the time I got you ham an' cheese at the market in Barnet."

"I'm not picking any pockets, not even for you."

Oliver felt fierce as he said it, but Jack moved his fingers across Oliver's face, sweeping away drops of rain. It was disquieting to think that Jack was the only familiar thing and that his touch was enough to calm Oliver as he stood there on the bank-side, with the rain coming down in sheets of mist.

"You'll get the hang of it, Nolly," said Jack. "By-and-bye."

The way he said it told Oliver that Jack didn't think it was a question of *if* Oliver would fit in at the Three Cripples. It was a question of *when*.

## ❧ 29 ❧

# A STRANGE AFTERNOON, WHICH IS A SEQUEL TO THE LAST CHAPTER

When they came back to the Three Cripples, the crowd had ebbed, and the fire was burned down to embers in the alcove. Jack planted Oliver along the bench, nearest the warmth, and poked up the fire, putting on bits of coal with his bare hands. Then he made Oliver take off his jacket and chafed his arms and hands and generally fussed over him, while Oliver let him and tried not to think.

Which was hard, because there was nothing else to do except stare out the doorway into the main room and watch the customers come and go, and listen to Polly and Doreen snapping and barking, and feel the wafts of cold air whenever someone opened the door. Eventually, he let his head fall on the scarred, dark table and rested his eyes, letting the coffee fade, letting the moment on the river fade, and letting everything become what it was now. This moment, and Oliver with nowhere to go, no one to be.

He dozed—he thought he had when he opened his eyes, for the fire seemed brighter and there was a lit candle on the mantelpiece, and Jack was standing over him, shaking him.

"Here," said Jack, pushing something at him.

The something was a pot of beer, crisp and golden, the only

395

thing the Three Cripples managed to keep clean and do well. Oliver took it and brought his lips to the edge, savoring the moment when the beer touched his mouth, and he swallowed, almost smacking his lips, looking up into Jack's eyes and seeing the little nod he gave.

"You're far too glum," said Jack. He sat across from Oliver and held up his own pot of beer in salute. "Far too glum for a man who ain't a murderer, an' who, in fact, was let off just this very day."

"Jack—" began Oliver. He didn't want to be cheered, in spite of Jack being near.

"We're goin' to play cards. I'll teach you my special hand where you can palm an ace or two up your sleeve, an' we're going to eat, an' I've ordered a chicken roasted, an' you, my good man, are goin' to learn to smoke."

"No," said Oliver. He put his beer down gently, not thumping it. "I don't want to smoke."

Jack smiled, his eyebrows going up. "Then everythin' else?" He waved his hand and snapped his fingers, not waiting for Oliver to agree or not. "Wench, wench, more ale!" he shouted, though neither Polly nor Doreen was likely to answer to that, and Oliver didn't even know if the Three Cripples actually served ale, though it was likely that they did.

At Jack's bidding, Oliver continued to drink, and the beer began soaking into him. But as Oliver watched Jack get up to get his pipe and cards, he realized he needed to think about what he was going to do.

There was a danger in staying where he was, with the memory of Fagin's stories about how glamorous and charming a life of crime could be. Though it wasn't just that Oliver remembered laughing at those very stories and being drawn in. More, it was what Cromwell wanted from him, which was the very thing that Fagin had wanted from him, though if Fagin were here, he'd be able to inform Cromwell fairly quickly about what a terribly useless criminal Oliver had been.

Perhaps, the problem wasn't that he wouldn't be a good criminal; the problem was that he *would* be. Or so it seemed because instead of turning up the collar of his coat and taking to the road this very instant, he was *still* here. Aunt Rose and Uncle Harry's was where he belonged; they would take him in, in spite of his brush with the law. Wouldn't they?

But Oliver was distracted by Jack coming back to the table and sliding into the bench across from him, shuffling the cards between his fingers, the begrimed edge of his shirt cuff falling back from his wrist.

"We're goin' to play whiskey poker," said Jack, splitting the deck and pushing it together.

"What about patience?" asked Oliver, his head swimming a little—beer on an empty stomach—thinking that he already knew the rules to that one, though he'd never practiced.

"'Tis for one person only," said Jack. "You're with me now, right, so we play this. An' when you're ready, we'll move on to whist."

While Jack explained how whiskey poker was played, Oliver paid attention, feeling his dull spirits fall away with the distraction. He noted the pairs and triples and colors, and how the backs of the cards were badly printed, the edges worn and stained. Oliver threw himself into the game, for, after all, what else was there for him to do?

As Jack won the first three hands, Oliver realized that the backs of the cards were more important than the fronts, and that Jack was cheating. But instead of saying anything about it, Oliver started keeping track of the backs of the cards too, and so his score went up.

He smiled as Jack puffed on his clay pipe, clenching it with agitation between his teeth, waiting for the moment that Jack looked up at him and understood that his cheating ways would not best Oliver Twist because Oliver Twist knew how to cheat *right back*. And when Jack finally noticed, indignation rolling over his face, Oliver threw back his head and laughed, right out loud.

Jack, after a moment, laughed as well, and seemed pleased at Oliver's cleverness.

It was a kind, almost harmless way to spend the afternoon as it turned into evening, drinking and playing cards, with no one telling Oliver to mind the shop or scrape the steps or carry in more coal because the orphan was dead now—and suddenly, the air seemed to cave in on him.

"Hey there, Nolly, you hungry?" Jack asked this quickly, as if he'd been paying attention all along. He touched the back of Oliver's hand.

"I have done the world a great wrong," said Oliver, wishing suddenly for some gin; it was much stronger than beer and it was what was wanted right now to match his mood, which seemed to be going up and down, quite without warning.

The smoky room was crowded, and he didn't want to go up to the bar to get some, nor did he want to ask Jack to do it for him. Instead, he swallowed the remains of beer in the metal tumbler and placed it on the tabletop. Waves and waves of a deep, searing pain that tasted as dark as regret rolled through him.

"I let that boy die, just as I let Dick die, and I'm a horrible person. You know that, Jack, don't you?"

"No," said Jack. His voice was low, and he seemed in earnest, though it was clear to Oliver that Jack didn't know who Dick was. "You're not a horrible person, don't you get that? Because if you were—on that day, you remember that day?"

Oliver shook his head; he had no idea what day Jack was talking about. There were so many things that had happened in the past, and Oliver had gone over them so many times in his head that he didn't want to do it now. But perhaps Jack had a different day in mind, a new one. Something better.

"Let me tell you the story. When we went out to Clerkenwell Green, you an' me an' Charley, to get some wipes. We took them off that old man, an' you went runnin' an' got arrested an' in court—they threw it all out an' you on the pavement. Do you remember that?"

Oliver remembered that long-ago courtroom with the magistrate and his drink; it had been much like the one that very morning. Uncle Brownlow had been there, somewhat tousled from the roughness in the street, and the bookseller, Mr. Beauchamp, coming in at the last minute. But Oliver's memory stopped there. He had fainted just as that had happened, and had woken up, days later, in Uncle Brownlow's townhouse.

"You were tossed on the street, poor wee mite that you were, an' who should come an' rescue you? Why, the old man, your Mr. Brownlow. He took you into that carriage as tenderly as if you were his own. He wouldn't have taken you in, not a man like that, if you were truly horrible."

Looking down at the tabletop, Oliver curled his hands around the tumbler of beer, now empty. He thought about the days that had followed, the kindness and then the cruelty and then the happy ending.

He looked up at Jack, not asking how Jack knew this story or whether it was true. Fagin probably had spies posted, and the word had gotten back to Jack, so that was how he knew.

"I ended up back here anyway," Oliver said. "With you."

Jack nodded and smiled, and yes, for Jack, this was a good thing. His smile reached Oliver, as though it were a physical touch, a good thing, bright against the dark memories that were rushing around inside of him.

"Somethin' to eat; the chicken should be here soon." Jack scanned the main room and nodded. "Here it comes."

But instead of being what Oliver had thought it might be, a piece of thigh or perhaps even a slice of breast, it truly was the whole thing, an entire chicken, seared on the skin, done on a roasting jack with grease dripping down its sides. It came steaming, with roasted potatoes cut up with roasted carrots, carried on a tin platter by the slatternly Doreen and slammed on the table. There were two little bowls, salt and pepper in each, and slices of buttered bread done up in paper, and as Jack paid the girl, Oliver's mouth started to water.

He didn't want to demand an explanation of where the money had come from, as he might have only days before; he wanted to eat and not ask questions and not worry, at least for at least a score of minutes, as to what his future might bring.

"Go on, then," said Jack. And then to the girl, "Go on, Doreen, an' get us some gin an' water, an' don't forget the sugar, mind."

He handed her some more money, then reached for the backbone of the chicken and tore the meat and skin from it with his bare hands. Huffing against the heat of the food, he laid the meat and skin on a tin plate and pushed it across the table at Oliver while it cooled.

Of course, in Mrs. Pierson's kitchen, there would be white china plates and snowy clean napkins and a knife and a fork so they could eat as civilized folk did. But not here; and for the moment, Oliver simply did not care. He took a piece of roasted carrot, all charred on one side, and bit into it, tasting the juices and the butter as his stomach jumped to attention.

Doreen brought the gin in two small metal tumblers, a pitcher of water, and a bowl of chunks of sugar. Oliver did up his own drink as the girl went away, using his fingers to put the sugar in, pouring in the hot water, not caring that he slopped it over when he took the first large swallow. It made his stomach warm in a way that the beer never did and took the bitterness out of the loss.

They ate the meal, he and Jack, in silence, next to the crackle of the fire, the hiss of water on the coals as snow melted from the chimney top, the rumble of feet and talk in the main room. When Oliver saw Jack favored the potatoes, their edges seared in grease, he stuck to the carrots, and Jack let him have first take at the curve of breast meat. Between them, they ate the roast chicken down to the bone, and everything else on the plate, finishing up with slices of bread and butter.

While Oliver licked his fingers, feeling the risk of it and the shimmy-slide into complete disreputableness, Jack signaled for more gin and water and stood up, stretching.

"I'm going to get more for my pipe," he said. "An' you, girl, clear this away."

The girl cleared away, and Oliver accepted the gin and water and sugar as the room swam, warm and easy around him. He made up a drink for Jack and drank half of his, his stomach warm and full, the glow of the fire soaking through him completely now, the din of the room falling away into a pleasant mumble and jumble of voices and sounds. He felt safe in his corner by the fire, with Jack returning, puffing on his clay pipe, holding it between his teeth, grinning.

"Scoot, then, you," said Jack, taking the place by the fire and making Oliver move over nearer to the wall whether he wanted to or not.

It didn't matter; Oliver moved and let Jack sit where he would, with Jack's shoulder brushing his. Jack's elbow jostled Oliver when Jack lifted his pipe for a pull on it, setting it down in a shallow dish on the table while he pulled the deck of cards from his jacket pocket and shuffled them between his hands.

"Another game?" asked Jack. "You know, we could move on to whist, or there's this new one, angels an' hearts, but then we'd need more players."

Oliver watched Jack's hands while he shuffled and cut the deck; it was the same deck from before, with badly stained and marked backs and the colors running as though the deck had been used in the rain.

"No," said Oliver, his voice sounding low, as though his head were sending some sort of message to him. He didn't want anyone else at their table to intrude, to draw Jack's attention away. He touched the back of Jack's hand as Jack spread the cards out in a fan in front of them on the table. "You play patience, and I'll watch."

"It's not very amusin' if you're only watchin'," said Jack, soft and careful. Barely teasing. But he did as Oliver asked and took up the cards to shuffle them once more, clicking them down on the tabletop, one-two-three, waiting for the aces to come up, and when they did, laying them in a row as though they were a band of black and red soldiers.

Every now and then, Jack would lift his pipe and draw from it, letting the smoke slide out through his mouth or his nose, as he pleased, and would then take a swig of the gin and sugar and water, and return to the cards, flipping them down as quick as he could, and then taking the pile up again to lay the cards down, one-two-three.

Oliver drank the rest of his gin and water and slumped on his elbows on the table, drawn into the rhythm of the cards, the rhythm of Jack's hands that moved as though no one, not even Oliver, was watching.

"Those cards are marked," said Oliver, leaning his cheek against Jack's arm to remind him he was there.

"Of course they are," said Jack smartly, as if they'd been discussing this all along. "But I'm ignorin' them; I aim to win without cheatin'."

"You'll never do that," said Oliver, making a scoffing sound in his throat. "Best to get a new deck, or, you being you," he said with a small laugh, "best to *steal* a new deck and play like a man, without the temptation to cheat."

Jack paused, curving a card against the table, pressing it down with his fingers.

"Always so righteous, Nolly, you are," he said. "What's wrong with cheatin' if you win?"

He looked over at Oliver, his eyes drowsy, half-lidded with drink, but affectionate, for all that.

"Because it's too easy, it's not a challenge. There's nothing honorable about cheating against yourself," said Oliver, looking right back, feeling that his voice was slurring a bit, and that maybe he wasn't making himself quite clear.

"You see—" he began, but stopped, in earnest to explain what he meant. How a man might make his way in the world, but that it had to be done right, with honor and goodness of heart. How was he to make Jack understand any of it when the deck he was using was stolen and marked?

"It's not right if it doesn't test your skill," he said, finishing up, locking the rest of his thoughts away.

Jack stopped and laid all the cards down on the table, his begrimed fingers splayed out, his head tipped toward Oliver, saying something so low that Oliver had to move in close to hear him.

"What, Jack?" he asked.

Jack took a breath.

"I'm glad you came," he said. "All those years ago."

"What?" asked Oliver, again. He knew he was muddled from drink, but he had no idea what Jack was talking about. "What do you mean, all those years ago?"

"In Barnet, when I met you, on the road from the funeral place you ran away from. Sowerman, or something. When you ran away, an' I met you there, in Barnet."

The memory of that day pushed up, right to the fore, and Oliver saw it clearly. The image of himself, on that cold and dusty step, his feet bleeding, his stomach collapsed with hunger, exhaustion weaving through him, in and out, no one in that village of a dozen taverns paying him much mind at all. Except for that boy, that strange boy, who crossed to and fro in front of Oliver before asking, *Hello, my covey, what's the row?*

And then, at that moment, had come from Jack a tumble of words, half of which Oliver had not the wits nor energy to understand, except that Jack had stolen for him a half loaf of bread and some ham. Then, in a tavern, he'd rightly purchased a pot of beer and had fed Oliver with the ease of one long accustomed to doing so and, more significantly, in a way that no one ever had.

Then Jack had taken him to the Three Cripples and Fagin's den, whereupon Oliver's life and destiny had ceased to be his own. But the fact remained that Jack had fed him, there in Barnet, and Jack had paid for all with money from his own pocket. As he had done so now, this very evening.

"Jack," said Oliver, letting the image of that time fade somewhat. "Whatever were you doing in Barnet, so far from home?"

It was a good long walk from Barnet to the Three Cripples, as Oliver now recalled, and he'd wondered this very thing, on and off, through the years.

"So far from home," he said again, looking up at Jack.

He saw Jack hesitate a moment, then put the clay pipe to his mouth as though about to draw from it. Then he smiled, the very smallest of smiles, as though Oliver was dragging something out of him in the most painful of ways and he loath to show it.

"Waiting for you, o' course," said Jack. "That's all I was doin', Nolly. Waiting' for you."

THE DAY SLIPPED FROM AFTERNOON INTO NIGHT, AND FINALLY, after one too many beers, Oliver's head sank to the table. He intended to let himself fall asleep there, it being the most sensible thing to do, until Jack drew Oliver to his feet.

They left the litter of pots and glasses on the table and wove their way among the crowd at the bar, stumbling as they went up the narrow stairs and along the passage. Jack's room was now familiar, though still dark with stale air, the stink of the half-burned tallow candle, old, damp ash in the fireplace, Jack's scent on unwashed sheets.

When the door was shut, Jack used the coals of his pipe to light the single candle on the mantelpiece, and Oliver saw again the red scarf on the headboard of Jack's bed, bright against the dark wood, making soft angles, as though Jack had recently arranged it with much care.

Oliver stared at it as Jack jerked his own jacket off, then Oliver's, making Oliver stumble on his feet, though he tried to remain upright. When Oliver's fingers tangled on his trouser buttons, Jack helped him with those and with his boot laces too, until his clothes were in a pile at his feet, and he was naked save for his shirt.

"Get your head on that pillow before you fall down," said Jack, mumbling. Rather drunk, it seemed, as was Oliver himself.

He let Jack push him to the mattress, his hand warm in the center of Oliver's back, and didn't pull away as Jack landed next to him, thumping his head on the single pillow next to Oliver's face. Between them they created a delicious warm tangle of limbs and linen.

"I kept it, you see," said Jack.

"So I see," said Oliver.

Unsure that he'd said it clearly enough, Oliver reached over his head, stroking the red scarf with his fingers. After which, his arm collapsed across Jack's neck as the room swam around him.

"Let me get that candle," said Jack, grunting. "Or it'll gutter."

He reached out as though he meant to push the hair back from Oliver's face, but his arm fell across Oliver's neck mid-gesture.

"Yes," said Oliver.

He closed his eyes, not caring that Jack didn't move again, nor, indeed, that behind his closed lids he could sense the candle flame dip and flicker, choking on its own dank wax, till at last, with a gasping click, it went out altogether, putting the room into darkness.

## ❦ 30 ❦

# AN EXPEDITION TO
# WHITECHAPEL

T he hard, gritty rain spat against the window, rattling the glass in the leading as a gale howled through the streets of London, dampening the air around Oliver's face. He awoke with a start and then was still.

The day before had been filled with drinks, which had been the proper way to celebrate Oliver's release from prison. The Three Cripples had been a tossed bowl of smoke; with warm bodies and coins clinking on the counter and golden beer flowing, it had been exactly the kind of time that Jack enjoyed. Bodies close along the bench, faces closer, stories spilled as the beer was swallowed.

Jack lay in the bed, round as a nested dove against him, and Oliver guessed Jack was still asleep. Jack tended to sleep when he slept, and be fully alert when he was awake. It was not Jack's way to be confused about what he should do, nor would he question whether or not he should do them. Only he, Oliver, was awake now, in the rain-grey morning, the room a damp tomb around him.

His head pounded a little as he sat up. The room was cast in a grey-brown light that came through the smear coating the window. The smell he'd thought was getting used to was more pervasive in the chill of the morning, with damp plaster, grease from the tavern below, and lines of mold along the corners of the walls, all weaving together into an unpalatable soup.

On the floor were clumps of mud from Jack's boots, the hump of their jackets, their hats. Spread across the end of the bed in a jagged line were Jack's trousers, which Oliver did not remember Jack taking off. And there was the red scarf that trailed along the headboard and across the single pillow, a river of scarlet.

Oliver could see hoarfrost on the nails along the roofline. Spring was coming, but it was butting heads with winter, rather like a spoiled child. He clenched and unclenched his hands; every part of him was tipped with cold now that he was out from under the blanket. His head ached as though it had been weighted with stones.

He looked down at Jack; sleeping with Jack was familiar from years ago. It was a simple, common thing, to sleep. But with Jack, it felt easier than perhaps it ought to have been, and allowed him to give into his desire for ease and comfort. And perhaps a bit more, that rippled beneath his skin, a spiraling low flame that made him want to pull Jack to him and hold him close. He did not know. What he did know from his experience in the old days was how to wake Jack up, which was gently.

"Jack," he said in a low voice. Then he put his hand on Jack's shoulder. "Jack."

"Eh?" said Jack, waking up quickly. "What you want?"

Oliver did not know what to say for a moment. Nor did Jack, who sat up on the edge of the bed, blinking against the cold, his back to Oliver, the blanket trailing off him.

"What you want is somethin' to eat. Don't you?" Jack turned to ask him this. "I've got fourpence; you can have it."

If this was a bribe to start Oliver thinking about food rather than the unformed future of his life, it was a good one.

"You're as hungry as I am," said Oliver. "So we'll split it."

"Pies, then," said Jack.

He rubbed his eyes, and Oliver got the sense that this was how it was going to be. Each morning would begin with late rising, any old time would do, followed by a scrabbling for funds for food. Still, being here with Jack was a sight better than waking in a dark Newgate cell, or being at the shipyard, waiting to set sail into the cold, wintry wind, or being already at sea, far away from everything he knew, everything he had been—

"Dreamin' again, are you?" Jack smacked Oliver's arm with the back of his hand, lightly, more to make contact than a reprimand, it seemed.

"Just thinking about—" Oliver stopped.

"Tell me," said Jack.

He lay on his side on the bed and curled his hips around Oliver's hips. The contact of Jack's skin beneath cloth settled around Oliver like a warm sea tide. Oliver let himself lean into it, into the physical contact that was not a blow, into the warmth and salt and musk, but only a little.

"I'd forgotten what it's like, being like this. At the haberdashery, the morning bell came at eight, breakfast was at nine, and on it went. But here?"

"We hang about an' loiter." Jack laughed, teeth flashing in his red mouth, shockingly bright. "An' then we steal!"

Horrified, Oliver moved off the bed, feeling Jack's palm in the middle of his back, pushing him, snorting the whole while.

"You can do whatever you like, Nolly," said Jack as Oliver searched for his jacket, standing barefooted in the middle of the room, his shirt hanging to his naked thighs. "Long as Cromwell ain't got somethin' else in mind for you, which he does, as he says."

"Where are my boots," said Oliver, ignoring Jack. He wasn't going to work for Cromwell, but if that was the case, what else could he do to earn his supper? "Jack, you put them—"

He turned as two thumps landed beside his feet. Jack was along the edge of the bed now, gesturing under it, still sleep-tousled, looking at Oliver in that way he had, as though Oliver was his best mate in the world. Which in a way he was, unless Noah was in the room, and then Jack beamed at Noah, his treasure, his history man, the one who knew almost as much about Fagin and his gang as Jack did.

But still. Oliver could not forget Jack's words as he'd reached through the bars of the jail. *Morning will come*, he'd said, in a way that told Oliver that he believed every word of what he was saying. *Morning will come.*

Well, morning had come and now, here he was.

Oliver espied his trousers on the floor near the table. He could hardly believe that he'd drunk enough to forgo the common niceties of putting one's clothes away before bedtime. Of prayers, those were long gone, of course, along with his inheritance, but that didn't mean that everything else had to be tossed aside, did it? No, it did not.

Oliver reached for his boots and dusted them, concentrating on dressing and not on the coldness of the room, or on Jack, who scurried out of bed and shoved his legs into his stockings as unconsciously as a child, hopping about, sparking Oliver a flash of his thighs, bumping into Oliver as if this whole thing were a lark. Which, to Jack, it was.

"Pies?" said Jack as he tucked in his shirt and laced up his boots. "I told you I've got fourpence, though I'll wager there's more coin left from last night." This said as if coin to spend magically appeared, and there would always be enough for more pies, more beer.

"Pies," said Oliver.

He dipped his chin down as he did up the buttons on his shirt. It wouldn't make any difference to point out the benefits of economy or budgets, or how prudent it would be to get a regular job with regular pay. Jack would scoff and laugh and ruffle Oliver's hair, which, in fact, he did now as he tossed Oliver his hat and coat.

Still tucking their shirts in and pulling on jackets, they trotted down the stairs and through the mostly empty tavern.

Jack poked Oliver with his elbow as they went out of the door. The street was wet with rain; the gutters ran with it, and they had to walk close to the walls of the buildings to avoid getting pushed off the pavement by the throngs of people.

"You wake up sour," Jack said, as they went along shoulder to shoulder, and it was evident by his expression that he didn't like it and wanted to fix it.

Oliver looked up and down the slanted street, at the plops of icy water that fell from the sagging eaves, then at the sky that refused to stop. He adjusted his hat and pulled his coat collar up, as he skirted around a pile of refuse, and then came back to walk next to Jack.

"I lost the life I wanted," Oliver said finally, not knowing how to explain it any better than that.

"Lost my life, once," said Jack. He tugged on Oliver's coat to get him to walk a little faster, and his unspoken message was clear: it was easier to keep warm if you kept moving.

"How?" Oliver could not imagine what Jack meant, or that he'd had any life worth the losing.

"You must know," said Jack. "When I got arrested an' transported, except when I got back, everythin' I knew was gone."

It was on Oliver's lips to retort that their respective situations were not the same at all when he realized that, for Jack, they were.

"But you know, I just kept my head down an' counted the days," said Jack, biting his bottom lip. "Knew I'd come home to London, one day."

"But I don't *want* to keep my head down," said Oliver. "I have a plan for my life, and I want to live it as I should."

"As a gentleman, you mean," said Jack, the corners of his mouth sneering.

"As a gentleman who owns a bookshop," said Oliver. His frustration was getting the better of him, making his voice sharp. "I can't spend the rest of my days drinking in a tavern and watching you play cards. I aim to leave London, and maybe you could come with me."

That he must leave London was a given; the pronouncement had sprung, unexpected, to his lips. But before Oliver could make his point by adding the benefits of this plan, Jack actually yawned in his face.

"Well, you can wish for that till you're blue, but you won't get what you want just by wantin' it. Besides, London is my home, an' I aim never to leave it again."

Jack didn't mean to sound harsh, he just wanted Oliver to stay with him. Such talk of Oliver wanting more from life than than the Three Cripples had to offer made Jack cross, that was easy to see. So Oliver touched his shoulder, and Jack shrugged, and the two of them walked down the slant of Saffron Hill to the corner of Field Lane to the pie shop.

It was busy as they approached it, the squat, square windows slightly dirty, making Oliver doubt the quality that they would find there. Suddenly he felt nervous, having been arrested when eating pies only days ago. But no one in the street was looking at him, so he wasn't standing out at all.

Then, once within smelling distance of something good, his stomach woke up and tore at him, reminding him he needed to eat. He missed Mrs. Pierson's cooking; he'd not had breakfast, and the warm smell of salt grease and hot pastry pulled at him.

Jack pushed his way in with self-assured shoulders, and Oliver followed close behind. They did not have to wait very long; the shop was the cash-and-carry type with no tables and only one counter, behind which stood two portly lads with white caps on their heads, serving pies as fast as they could. Their aprons were covered with flour and dark grease stains that would have had both Mrs. Bedwin and Mrs. Pierson shaking their heads and steering Oliver and Jack right back out into the street again.

"Four, then, you," he said to one of the lads as he held up his fingers.

FAGIN'S BOY

"Four?" asked Oliver to Jack's back.

"They're only a penny, an' I seen you put one away the other day; I know you can manage two."

Oliver sighed, watching Jack hand over the pennies. He was hungry, and the money would be well spent even if part of him, a large part, wanted to be saving against a day that saw them even hungrier than this.

"Four," said Jack, handing Oliver two pies wrapped in paper. "One for now, one for later at the tavern, with a pint of beer in front of the fire." He made it sound cozy, his mouth wrapping around the words as if they were already wrapping around the pie.

Oliver nodded, thinking that Jack took overly well to being in charge, or thinking that he was, but knew at the same time that he himself would rather not have to think. Nor to remind Jack that if they wanted a fire at the Three Cripples, they would more than likely have to build it themselves, after having cleaned out last night's ashes and blacked the grate. He did not imagine that Jack would want to hear any of that.

Oliver unwrapped the first pie and tested the corner with his fingertips. It was hot but not overly so, and he bit into the crust, tasted the meat and the gravy in one gorgeous mouthful, and let the crumbs flutter down his chin.

Jack was tucking in as well, making quick work of the hand-sized pie, then licking his fingers and wiping his chin with the heel of his hand. Oliver blinked at this and then remembered that in the old days, Jack could out-eat any of them, and was always first to toast and eat slices of cheese, or be the first at the frying pan full of sausages. Fagin had remarked at least once or twice that Jack was a growing boy and had usually followed this up with a cuff across the back of Jack's head, though that had never stopped Jack.

"C'mon, then," said Jack, jerking his head in the direction of the door.

He slid the paper-wrapped pie in his pocket to keep it warm,

413

and Oliver followed suit, trying not to think of the stains of grease they were leaving on their coats. As they stepped into the streets, the rain was letting up, but the wind, blowing over their heads, was getting colder, and Jack sniffed the air.

"Hope we don't get another blast," he said, and Oliver agreed. If more foul weather was on the way, they would be stuck indoors, where there was nothing to do but stare at the fire and smoke and play cards. Which might hold some charm for a day, but not for longer than that, no matter what Jack thought of it.

Jack stopped, even with the wind at his heels, and he looked at Oliver with his eyes big, something lingering there that Oliver couldn't quite understand.

"Let's not go back; I fancy some more walkin'. Will you come?" asked Jack.

Jack so seldom asked for anything. He would joke or boss or laugh, but never ask. So Oliver, with the connection of the night before still between them, licked his fingers and nodded.

He wiped his palms along the side of his coat, thinking that gesture would get a nod of approval from Jack, which it did. He could see that Jack liked it when Oliver attempted to fit in to Jack's world, and since Oliver wanted to be able to think of himself as a likeable boy, there was nothing more for him to do.

Jack started walking past the pie shop and down the lane, past Smithfield Market, where the smell of manure and old blood was strong in the icy air. The sounds of animals and of men shouting bounced off the brick walls as the lane narrowed before widening into the open area of the market. The wooden pens covered the area so thickly that it was hard even to walk around the edges of it, and Oliver kept bumping shoulders with leather-aproned men who smelled like blood.

The whole place had a dank, foul odor, and Oliver averted his eyes as they passed along the sheds where the necks of geese were being placed on worn stumps before having their heads chopped off. He was grateful that Jack didn't stop to linger but hurried on, past the narrow rivers of blood that ran in stone gutters, and the stink of animals, distraught and suffering, and the unimpassioned expressions of the men who slaughtered them.

Jack led Oliver around Smithfield, and then over to Cheapside to follow the narrow lanes of old buildings tumbling over each other, with the mud a constant, slippery carpet beneath their feet. As they went down Aldgate and Cornhill, Oliver felt he vaguely recognized where they were, only he didn't know how or why. They went along a brick-blackened lane that was even more a-tumble than any around Holborn with the refuse of humans, clumps of foul snow, chunks of bone and hoof.

He stuck close to Jack, breathing through his mouth; Jack took Oliver's arm, and Oliver didn't pull away.

"Is it much farther, Jack?" asked Oliver, hoping it wasn't but feeling indulgent, in spite of the spattering rain and wind.

"A little way, Nolly," said Jack, leading Oliver up the street and down a small lane till they passed the Church of St. Mark's, and went into another long, narrow passage.

The smell jumped up at Oliver. He knew this smell somehow. His head pounded and his stomach wanted to rebel, though he knew better than to empty its contents in the street when those contents were so hard to come by.

The rain began to splat down again, on his face, on the bricks, circles of rain smashing into the clumps of old snow, as big as the palm of his hand. Jack stopped and pulled Oliver back against a wall, opposite a building with a slate overhang that dripped into the street in long, sad grey plops.

The sun fought from behind the clouds for a moment, and sparks of stray light limned the bricks and wood of the building that now sagged like a craggy, dying thing. Sad beams of wood leaned against each other, and as Oliver watched, not understanding what he was watching, a brick slipped from the ledge of an upper-story window, crashing through a faltering lath to shatter on the damp paving stones, scattering shards of red into the street.

"What is it?" asked Oliver. "Why have we stopped; shall we go back?"

"This here was one of Fagin's old dens," said Jack, his voice rusty. He pointed at the wreck of a building with his fist.

Now it made sense that Jack would bring Oliver here and look as though he were listening for the sound of Fagin's voice. How mournful and lonesome it must have been for Jack to come back expecting to find some physical reminder of the past, only to find almost everything so changed as to not be recognizable.

"An' the last place I saw you, five years ago," said Jack unexpectedly.

His head hung low, almost brushing against Oliver's breastbone. When he looked up, his face was white, the skin tight around his eyes, making Oliver want to listen for Fagin's voice as well, in sympathy.

"Jack?" asked Oliver, dipping his head low to be a physical echo to Jack's frame, brushing his fingers on Jack's damp sleeve. "What do you mean, the last place?"

Surprising him, Jack stepped backward, moving away from Oliver to look up at the craggy remains of the building.

"I'd thought, you know," said Jack, somber, "that as I burned beneath that sun there, in Australia, carryin' water an' muckin' out stables or lookin' for stray cattle in the bush, that when I came back, everythin' would be as it was. As it always had been. Fagin in his fire pit, makin' sausages for one or two to feed ten, bringin' in bottles of gin, or screamin' at us to go out an' make more money. Countin' those coins of his, late, late into the night."

Jack's memories of that time so resembled Oliver's own, and he was about to say so when Jack looked up at Oliver as though he wanted to cry, only he couldn't remember how.

Oliver moved forward, somewhat alarmed by this show of deeper emotion of Jack's rising to the surface, as though the drink from the night before had made him transparent. Oliver, in return, knew that he was equally made vulnerable to the memory of Jack's confession, similar in sentiment: *You're the only person I know in London.*

But before Oliver could express how the revelation was causing something tender to shift within him, Jack moved away. He opened his mouth, struggling, it seemed, with what he wanted to say.

"We kept you here, days, weeks, even," said Jack, low, as if speaking to himself. "Feedin' you them books an' our stories about thieves—"

"In seclusion, like the dark room at the workhouse," said Oliver.

As memories sometimes did, this one came back to him in a rush, the dark single room where Oliver had passed so many hours alone that even the company of thieves and pickpockets and fences and their stories about the grandness of crime seemed preferable, even if only slightly.

"I laughed at those stories, Jack," Oliver said. "Right along with you." Though why he was comforting Jack for having applied this cruelty to him was almost beyond him. Indeed, he felt the heat of anger rising inside him that had, really, nowhere to go.

Jack stilled him with a look.

"I just wanted it to stay that way forever, an'—an' you an' me to be there forever," said Jack. "I kissed you good-bye, an' Nancy took you, an' the next thing you was left in a ditch with a bullet in you, left by Bill—" Jack choked off, sending Oliver rushing forward with his hands outstretched.

"But I was found, Jack," Oliver said.

He didn't remember Jack's kiss from that night, but he did remember being dragged into the street and going all those miles with Bill Sikes in the cold, damp air. He stood now, close to Jack in the street, and the devil be damned if anyone saw, if anyone in that street even cared to slow down enough to look at them. Him touching Jack, his fingers as red and raw with cold as any common street thug's.

"I was found by my own people, you know. That story ended well, at any rate."

Jack eyed him, looking young and wounded, bringing to the surface the memory of his tenderness and comfort when Oliver was in Newgate. Oliver wanted to comfort Jack in return, because none of this was Jack's fault. And he found his anger melting away, replaced by something tender in his breast.

"Shot with a bullet an' I warn't there to protect you," said Jack, mumbling, looking away, eyelashes damp in the cold.

"You *weren't* there, so how could you protect—and why weren't you there?" Oliver asked. The small distraction felt safer than the feelings building up from the telling of Jack's story.

"Got arrested, you know that," said Jack glumly. "For takin' a tuppenny-ha'penny snuffbox."

"But didn't you once tell me—" Oliver stopped, realizing just then how astounding this fact was. "Yes, it was back in Barnet when we'd just met that you told me you were Fagin's particular *pet* and *protégé*. With all those skills—you? Arrested?"

"I—well." Jack stopped to tip back his hat and scratch the back of his head, then replaced his hat with a jerk. "Fine, I'll tell you. I knew you wasn't dead, but then Nancy had a fit one night, an' Fagin tells me that in spite of everythin' he'd done that you'd never broken to his teachin', that they was goin' to bring you back, that he had a plan. I knew it weren't right."

"Then why didn't you stop it?" Oliver asked this, though Jack, being only slightly older than Oliver at the time, wouldn't have been able to do anything.

"It was because—my mind was thick with the thought of you, 'cause I didn't want you back, but I *did*. Well, with one thing an' another, the very next day I was arrested an' sent to Australia soon after. Had a trial an' everythin'."

Oliver thought of that time, so confusing with its kaleidoscope images shifting in his head. One thing was startlingly clear: Jack had let himself be so distracted by Oliver's fate that he'd got himself arrested and deported.

Oliver ought to have been amused by Jack's fallibility, but he wasn't. He didn't laugh, not at Jack, because while everything else in his life had flung itself around like a mad bull and trampled every dream, Jack had been, and was, the only unchanging thing.

"You were well out of it," said Jack. "An' when I came back, I knew I had to look for you—I knew you would never come lookin' for me."

Jack's gaze flicked along the street as though seeking a place between the then times and the now. With Oliver standing absolutely still in front of him, he seemed to gain strength, and finally, Jack's hand tightened around Oliver's, as though Oliver was *Jack's* anchor in a storm. This feeling was new after having clung to Jack all those years ago and during the past few days; it made him feel strong, oddly, perhaps for the first time in his life.

"I do have a scar from the bullet," Oliver said, wanting Jack to look at him without that sad expression in his eyes. "From where they took it out. I healed after that, and well, so you've no need to—"

"A scar's like a tattoo, ain't it?" said Jack, taking this idea up, brightening, stepping away from his somber declaration about looking for Oliver. "Like the one I got; a woman at the docks did it for me, afore I left—"

Knowing from the newspaper that criminals convicted for transport were kept locked up, with no access to women, before they sailed, Oliver doubted this version of the tale more than any other.

But he didn't chide Jack; it would ruin the story, and besides, he might be ready to see Jack's tattoo now. Especially now, in this moment, when he realized his scar was, as Jack said, one of life's marks and something Oliver could trade with Jack to get a glimpse of the alleged tattoo. At which point, Oliver would no doubt become acquainted with the many more stories behind it, which made him smile.

"Jack," said Oliver, gently, because he wanted to go back to the Three Cripples with its modicum of warmth and dryness. Only he didn't want Jack to feel bad for having dragged him here to this place, with its dark and fear-stained memories.

"I missed you," said Jack, simply, looking at Oliver's hand curling around his own. "An' I was so—well, you was the only one prosperin' after I came back. I left an' I came back an' there was no one left but you. No one to tell my story to but you."

"I know your story," said Oliver, soothing, as he pulled Jack away from the ruined building and up the street, back to the Three Cripples. "And besides, Noah knows your stories as well."

"Yes," said Jack, straightening up. "He tells 'em good, he does, all vibrant like. Except—"

"Except?"

Oliver let Jack pause them in the middle of the lane as it slanted uphill toward the main thoroughfare, thinking that if Noah were to have told some story improperly or had made Jack any less than the most important player, Oliver would have more words with him and use his own fists for punctuation.

"Except he warn't one of Fagin's boys, not truly. Not like you an' me."

Giving Jack a tug, trying not to be pleased at Jack's easy dismissal of Noah's charms, Oliver began walking up the lane, toward the street that would take them back to the Three Crip-ples. Jack came with him, easy, melting into the direction that Oliver was headed.

"Why is that?" asked Oliver, turning his head away as they passed a dead hog in the street.

"Because he peached on you, an' collected his winnings after. Something you never did, even when you could."

As they walked, side by side, through the muck of Whitechapel, Oliver didn't point out that if Noah wasn't one of Fagin's boys, Oliver was even less of one. Neither would it do to point out that Oliver's lack of peaching had much less to do with Fagin's precepts than it had to do with Jack himself and the memory of Jack's hands through the bars of a Newgate jail cell, telling Oliver that morning would come. Jack was a shared blanket on cold nights, a touch to his head, somehow gentle even amidst all of Jack's street hardness. He'd been the recipient of all these gestures and words from Jack when he'd had needed them most.

That Jack cared for him was obvious, in a way that went beyond common affection. Oliver could not refute his own feelings in return, as jumbled as they were, because who should want the companionship of a street thief? Well, he did.

Jack's declarations were like a balm that filled the empty places within him, even if some might express disdain, even if it might get them arrested. But somber explanations of morality or grim reminders of legality had no place in how bestirred he felt, so Oliver said nothing of it out loud, and together they walked back, eating their second serving of pies as they went, rather than saving them.

They went along Aldgate Street, thick with shops that looked busy and prosperous and a step above Field Lane. Mid-slope, they passed a bookshop beneath a swinging, rain-dripping sign that said Grey's Books.

The shop wasn't much like the one that Oliver hoped to one day own; the canvas awning kept off the rain but only barely, and the door frame and the window casing were badly in need of paint. But, for all that, the window had a shelf pushed right up against it, with the spines, dusted clean, turned out toward the street for easy viewing.

Oliver stopped in spite of himself, causing Jack to tumble over his heels as Oliver pressed his face up against the smudged glass.

The gold- and silver-gilt titles tumbled together in a row, and he read them, silently, thinking of the times with Uncle Brownlow when he had only to express a desire for a certain title, and the book was his.

"What's this then, Nolly? You want to go in?" Jack spat in his hand and was pushing back his forelock in preparation, quite ready, it seemed, to indulge Oliver in this particular fancy.

"No," said Oliver. He dragged his eyes away from the books to look at Jack, feeling the sharp contrast of it. If he stayed with Jack, in Jack's world, he would never own a bookshop. "There's no point in it, is there?"

"There is, if you want one," said Jack. It was easy to see that he didn't quite grasp the siren's song that books had, especially ones that Oliver had not read before, but he was attempting, in his way, to be kind. "We could just—"

"No," said Oliver.

He shook his head, understanding exactly where Jack's thoughts were running. Jack was imagining that they could sashay into the bookshop, tuck a book or two into their jackets, and be off as if nothing had happened. For one thing, their jackets weren't big enough to hide any book, and for another, well, it was inconceivable that Oliver would stoop so low as to steal a book, of all things.

Jack nodded as if he gleaned what Oliver's rebuttal entailed, even if he might not quite understand the why of it. His eyes scanned the street, flicking over the row of books that glimmered behind the mud-spotted window. Then he gave Oliver's sleeve a tug.

"Look there," he said, pointing at the window.

"At what?" Oliver didn't relish continuing to long for books he couldn't have, nor for all that they represented.

But Jack was insistent. "No, not them. Look. Us."

Jack pointed at the glass, and, after a moment's confusion, Oliver's eyes refocused and he could see what Jack was pointing at. In the window, in a streaked reflection made gloomy by the rain, were two young men.

One young man Oliver recognized directly as being Jack, the reflection of Jack, with his shabby top hat and his bright blue waistcoat and those coattails that banged against the backs of his knees. His spit-shaped hair reflected like black ink; his grin was a crooked, white slash; his eyes were two bright spots. That was Jack, a part of the streets he constantly roamed, a child of them once, with the stamp of grit and sly ease that never seemed to leave him, and appeared clear, even in his reflection.

The other reflection was of himself—it could be of no other. The reflection of the shinier and newer top hat in the glass matched Jack's in height, and the silver-buttoned jacket seemed at once like a bright bird's wing, hanging from the shoulders of an entirely different person than himself.

The sleeves of his jacket were too long and uneven, the trousers he wore hung badly, crumpled with mud, damp along the hems, the whole of his outfit reflected the filth that he'd been living in. He could not bear to look more closely at the reflection of his face; he did not want to see what it would tell him. He was so changed he might not be able to recognize himself.

"C'mon, then," said Jack, his voice low, as if disappointed Oliver was not pleased at how much his reflection matched Jack's.

He tugged on Oliver's sleeve, and so, bookless and feeling disjointed, Oliver followed where he was led. They went up Aldgate and Cheapside, past the smells and sounds of Smithfield Market, up Field Lane to the door of the Three Cripples, where custom had picked up and the doorway to the Three Cripples was as popular as a town square on market day.

# 31

# CONTAINS THE PARTICULARS OF JACK'S STORY, AND ADDITIONALLY, THE ONE ABOUT NOAH AND NANCY

A s Oliver opened the door and stepped into the Three Cripples, he saw that at a table in the middle of the room, Noah was sitting with a pot of beer in his hands, with men gathered around. It appeared he was telling a story, waving his mug in the air. Then Jack, right behind, saw him as well, and went straight over to Noah's table.

Oliver followed him, trying to hold his breath as he passed through the press of men, and some women, whose woolen coats and tattered, dragging shawls were stained with grease, and with the rain, smelled like old fish or untanned hides or whatever else it was they worked with.

He thought he heard someone say, *Bet his backside is as sweet as his face*. Making Oliver flush and again doubt his decision to come to the Three Cripples and Cromwell be damned.

When he got to the table, Jack was already sitting next to Noah and had a pint pot of beer in his hand, his short pipe between his teeth that he was just lighting. The circle of smoke from the pipe smelled as though it had come from an unseen fire in some deep wood, and Oliver made a gesture to catch Jack's attention.

Jack looked up, and the circle of men around the table parted to let Oliver through.

"So then I says," said Noah, continuing on, all but ignoring Oliver as he took a swig from his pot of beer. "Then I says, 'Whatcha carryin' around so many 'andkerchiefs for, Mr. Leaming?' Turns out, 'e was a fence, a sloppy one, not one of you lot, an' all the while 'im a shop owner, carryin' on sellin' 'ardware for 'arnesses in the front an' havin' illicit dealings in the back!"

"You are a card, an' a canny one," one of the men said, laughing. "Did you get the reward, then?"

"Indeed," said Noah, patting his breast pocket. He took a slug of beer in his mouth, cheeks puffing out, beer sliding from between his lips and down the side of his mouth. "This'll keep me till spring, I wager."

"Till you lose it on the ponies again!" The man barked this out, his laugh spreading beer on the air in a fine mist. "You never could stay away."

Noah dismissed this with a jerk of his chin and leaned back in his chair.

"There you are, Nolly." He held out his pot. "Be a lad an' bring me some more beer, eh?"

There was a moment of silence as the men around the table drifted away, and Oliver looked at Noah and Noah looked steadily back. The bruises on his face that Cromwell had left had barely begun to fade, but Noah seemed oblivious of them, only daring Oliver to disobey him.

Jack gave a shrug and pushed some coins over to Oliver. Oliver took them, thinking to buy himself and Jack a beer, as well, and, besides, it would be rude to refuse such a simple request.

But before he could walk away, Jack stood up and cuffed the side of Noah's head.

"I told you once, only I calls him Nolly," Jack said, squinting through a puff of smoke, his voice even. "Don't make me tell you again."

He sat back as if nothing had been said, and the sounds from the tavern, the clink of glass, the frantic lilt of someone talking, filled in the space around them. All the while Noah sat there, his mouth open, as if astonished Jack had dared to lay a hand upon him. But Jack merely shook his head and put his pipe back between his teeth.

Jack looked up at Oliver, who nodded, turning to get the beer, feeling well content that Jack did not currently seem to be pleased by Noah as much as he had been. Oliver shouldn't have been gladdened by that, but he was. As well, Jack's pet name for him was precious to him, and to Jack, also, to go by Jack's defense of it.

Oliver went up to the bar and shouldered his way through, pushing over the coins and asking for three pots of beer. Then he returned to the table, carrying the pots. How had his life taken such a direction that he was carrying beer for Noah and Jack? Only a month ago he could not have imagined it, yet here he was. Still, he wouldn't do this again, at least not for Noah.

Jack was appreciative upon getting his beer, swallowing half of it at one go before Oliver had even sat down next to him. Noah stared into his beer, frowning, as if drawn into the dapple of foam on the surface. Oliver wondered why they weren't in Jack's alcove instead of halfway to the middle of the floor, with the draft from the door at their necks and too far away from the single fire for it to do any good.

"It's ages till spring comes," Jack said, companionably, to no one in particular. As the door opened again and sent a squall of damp air to settle around them, Jack shuddered and drew up his shoulders.

"I wish I was a lizard," said Jack. He smirked as he said this, for now he had Noah's attention. "Like one of them lizards, down below, an' I could spread myself on a stone till my blood boiled. Then I'd be warm. But a lizard can hardly be a thief, can he? No fingers an' thumbs." Jack laughed, open-mouthed, at his own cleverness.

"You don't need fingers an' thumbs if you've got a gang of boys, workin' for you. Did you ever think, while you was away, of startin' your own gang, then, Jack?" Noah asked this directly to Jack as if Oliver wasn't even there.

With another swallow of his beer, Jack nodded with a jerk of his head.

"Certainly I could do it, certainly. Start off with a small boy or two, make myself known to the fences as dependable to my acquaintances of a particular circle."

"Except," said Noah, with that small curved smile that Oliver remembered when Noah would badger Oliver at Mr. Sowerberry's beyond Oliver's ability to resist the temptation to kill him. "Except, sad to say, you would no doubt run across your very own little Oliver, who, as you recollect, upset a very decently balanced apple cart."

When Oliver started in his chair, Noah turned to him, *tut tutting*.

"Oh, don't make a face, that pious little face, all your worryin' and prayin', an' never you mind. It's Fagin who told me who messed up that job, that pickpocketing job—"

The words struck Oliver like a blow. He rose in his seat, intending to smack Noah directly across his pasty, smug face, but Jack stopped him with a hand on his arm and made him sit back down.

"If only you'd have stuck by my side, Nolly," said Jack, leaning forward earnestly, attempting, it seemed, to make a circle of conversation between the three of them. "If only you had, then all would have been well. You could have been a workin' member of the gang an' brought in loads with that face of yours."

Oliver couldn't understand why Jack was talking to him like this. Then he heard Noah chuckle under his breath and realized why. It was the stories; Jack loved stories, and Noah had been telling this one, so to be of a kind, Jack told his in return. That was all there was to it; he had no reason to be jealous of Noah.

"You know I'm no pickpocket," said Oliver, covering up his disquiet at the idea.

"That you are not, my friend, that you are not. Your face gives you away, dirty or clean." Jack saluted Oliver with the pot of beer, sloshing some over the rim.

"Well," said Oliver slowly, considering, wanting to steer the conversation away from crime and pickpocketing. "I do want a bath, it is true, after our jaunt to Whitechapel this morning." He looked at Jack to remind him of what he'd said during that walk, how he'd said it. And, truth be told, he wanted to let Noah know how things stood between him and Jack.

"What?" asked Noah, sitting up as if suddenly interested that Oliver was actually at the same table with him. "Whitechapel, whatever did you go down there for?"

"Oh," said Jack. "It's a long story, a sad tale; you've no interest in it, I'm sure."

"Just a stroll in the fresh air," said Oliver, finally drinking from his beer at last. It was cool in his mouth but slightly bitter, as though it were the dregs of the barrel.

"In this weather?" Noah shook his head. "C'mon, tell us. What were you about, then? C'mon, Jack."

Jack sat up in his chair, pulling the pot of beer to him with the curve of his hand, ready to give Noah what he wanted. But what they'd shared in that dank street, those confessions given and taken, was something that Oliver wanted to keep for his own. The memory of the morning belonged to him and Jack. Was Jack really going to share it with Noah?

Just as Jack opened his mouth to speak, Oliver caught his eye, a frantic pounding in his heart. There was no way, really, that Oliver could impart his meaning without actually saying the words aloud, but he did not want Noah to know anything about them. The whole world could know, and Oliver wouldn't care. But Noah knowing? He could not bear that.

"Well, then, since you insist," said Jack in that cavalier way, tipping his head back to assay his audience and determine what type of story they truly wanted. "It was old times for me an' Nolly, takin' a walk, you see, into the wintry wind." He took a drink of beer and smacked his lips. "We walked to one of Fagin's old dens—"

"Is it one I'd know?" asked Noah. His eyes were wide and searching, as if desperate to find out whether he'd missed something good.

"Don't know," said Jack, shaking his head. "At any rate, this was an old den. We kept Nolly there, weeks an' weeks it was—"

Noah snorted out a laugh, because, of course, he couldn't help himself, not at the idea of Oliver being held captive against his will. The sound of his jagged breath made Oliver want to smack him all over again. And perhaps Jack as well, who would not stop *talking* about it.

"We worked weeks to try an' make a good hand out of him, somethin' Fagin could use. But he's so—I mean, look at him." Jack took his pipe and waved it at Oliver, then took a good strong draw from it, letting the smoke flow out in tides from his nostrils. "Too pretty for words, an' while that might be useful, it goes *through*, gentlemen. It goes *through*, all the way to the bone."

"What does?" asked Noah.

Oliver, frankly, wanted to know as well, in spite of his irritation at Jack's reference to that dark time. Because while his face was often a cause for discussion, his features didn't go down to the bone, not in the normal sense.

"Piety," said Jack, pounding the table with the pot of beer. "Piety, goodness, cleanliness, all of it. This is a boy who, when he says his prayers, he means 'em! There was no turnin' him, and Fagin nearly tore his hair out, havin' made such a bad judge of things."

Noah considered this, his mouth twisting as though he were crestfallen that the story wasn't a better one.

As Jack gave Oliver a small wink, Oliver realized Jack had done it on purpose. That, in fact, Jack had never planned to tell Noah anything that mattered, anything about what had happened that morning. Noah had gone and cut himself out of Jack's confidence when he'd peached on Oliver for the reward.

Oliver considered whether it might be a pleasant thing to get drunk enough that evening to tell Noah exactly what Jack thought of him, and whether he'd laugh in Noah's face while he did it.

"That's not the truth of it, though," said Noah. He grabbed the skirts of a passing barmaid and gave her backside a pat. "Three more, my lovely, an' haste with it!"

"Truth of what?" Jack asked. He tapped his pipe and laid it sideways on the table.

"Of what Fagin wanted."

"He wanted Nolly to steal, that's what he wanted." Jack nodded at his own truth, and for him, there was nothing more than that. "But Nolly's a terrible pickpocket, ain't you, Nolly?"

Oliver nodded, but he sensed Noah was intent upon telling a different kind of story. It was in the way he sat, leaning forward, tapping his finger to his nose. His eyes were narrow, and when they looked at Oliver, they flickered with hate. Noah had something new for Jack; the story of Oliver and Jack in the streets looking at one of Fagin's old dens had brought it out.

"I know why Fagin was 'anged," Noah said.

"Because someone peached," Jack said, swallowing, trying not to look at Oliver and failing.

Of course, the identity of the person who had peached was what Jack wanted to know, what he always wanted to know. But no one he knew could tell it, so he would not be able to resist Noah's story.

What Oliver had delivered up to Jack, when threatened, had been scatterings, and nothing to satisfy. Back at the townhouse, long ago it seemed, when anyone would talk of it at home, like when the parson came and his elders had discussed it, Oliver was sent out of the room. It was after the prayers and the tea that they would discuss it, and Oliver was sent out for a walk, to fetch a book, or for a slice of cake in the kitchen. Anything. He'd lingered when he could to get the rest of it, but the story had always come in snatches, and he could never know the whole of it.

"Ah," said Noah with the exact smile he'd had back at the undertaker's, gloating and rude and triumphant. "But I knows how, an' I knows by who."

The beer foam on Noah's mouth was drying to a crust, and he took another swig and belched. Oliver pretended he hadn't; bad manners were rife at the Three Cripples, and there was nothing he could do about it.

"How could you possibly?" asked Oliver. If Noah got his way, he'd string this story on until it was thin and weak, and Jack, poor Jack, would get no sustenance from it. That or Jack would be drawn in so hard there would be no separating him from Noah from that point onward in spite of the fact that he'd peached on Oliver for money.

"Because I was there, Work'us. I was *there*."

The name stung, but Oliver made himself not react to it, though everything—his limbs, his hands, his heart—made him want to launch himself across the table and make Noah shut up. But at the same time, Jack was enthralled, and so the story must be told.

"How?" asked Oliver. He knew he sounded disdainful, and he was. Noah tended to say a great many things, and all to a bounded and specific effect, whether true or not. "How? Tell us that, then. Otherwise, it's just a story, and I think Jack has better things to do. And I do as well." Though what, Oliver couldn't imagine.

"Be still, then, an' listen," said Noah. "The day after I gets to London, I 'ooks up with Fagin 'imself. 'E sends me to the courts to watch Jack get sent abroad for that snuffbox—"

"I know this part," said Jack. He had a small, secret smile, but he was looking down at the tabletop rather than at Noah or Oliver, and Oliver knew why. It was because this story was in the court rolls, and a part of written history for evermore. That was the meat of it; there was no denying that Jack felt it the pinnacle of his career.

"—with Jack demanding his privileges an' talking back to the magistrate, insisting 'e'd an appointment with a gentleman in the City—"

"An' don't forget," said Jack, "that my attorney was breakfastin' with the Vice President of the House of Commons."

"There isn't a Vice President of anything in the 'Ouse of Commons," said Oliver, blinking, mocking Noah's rough speech.

He felt left behind in their joy and ridicule of the whole situation. But there was bad weather outside and bad company within, and no real retreat from any of it. The only thing he could manage was to derail any part of the story that put Fagin in less than a heroic light in Jack's eyes. For Jack's sake.

"Yes, yes," said Noah. "But that's not it. When I saw Fagin, I told him this, an' 'e told me that 'e'd lost his very best 'an' brightest."

"Who's that, then?" asked Jack, though Oliver suspected he already knew.

"You, Dodger," said Noah, looking fairly pleased with himself. "'E says to me, 'e says, *Is there one of you that could touch 'im or come near 'im on any scent?* And then the other fellow says, *Not one, not one.*"

"Who said *that?*" Jack's mouth hung open. "Was it Fagin?"

"Fagin said the first bit, an' the other, well, I don't know 'is name, properly, but 'e 'ad 'is 'ands in his pockets an' laughed a great deal of the time."

"Charley," said Jack; his voice was low and reverential, as though reflecting upon some private inner memory.

Oliver had known Charley, a brash young man who found humor everywhere, and who laughed even when there wasn't anything to laugh at. Oliver sensed Jack had adored him, in his way; it was Charley who had taken the hand-off of the handkerchief on that day so long ago.

"They said that," asked Jack. "Fagin an' Charley said that?"

"As I live an' breathe." Noah took a large swallow of his beer, finishing it down to the dregs. When he came up for air, he looked at Jack, his mouth wet, and he wiped it with the back of his sleeve. "There's more though."

"More?" asked Jack in a way so expectant, so hopeful, that it gave Oliver a twinge, remembering wanting more, and how painful it might be if Jack were not to receive it. "How ever so?"

"When you was taken," said Noah. "Though you were 'is best 'and, you were not present, an' not one to take up the job of dodging a certain female by the name of Nancy."

This stopped Jack, but he only considered it for a moment before he asked, "He had you follow *Nancy*? Why?"

Oliver had heard something about this; he knew where the story was going. Nancy had met with Uncle Brownlow and Aunt Rose late one night, but he'd never had the full of it, what was said or why they'd let her go back to her old life. Aunt Rose tended to cry into her handkerchief whenever Oliver had asked her about it, so he'd stopped asking long ago.

"Because Fagin suspected she was up to somethin', an' she was, oh, definitely. Tryin' to get word to that Brownlow fellow about where Oliver was an' 'ow to get to 'im. Somethin' about that whole conversation set Fagin off, an' 'e told Bill, an' then Bill—"

"But how do *you* know this?" Oliver found himself asking, knowing that Noah was leaving something out. He berated himself for being drawn in, but perhaps, at last, it was time to know the full of it.

"Because, you daft, pious workhouse boy, I told you. Fagin sent me to follow 'er, which I did. I stood there on the steps of London Bridge an' 'eard everything Brownlow and Nancy said. When I went back to tell Fagin, 'e 'ad me tell it again to Bill. Which I did. I know all of this because I was *there*."

Noah turned to look at Jack now, only at Jack, because of course, it was for Jack that he was telling anything at all.

"I 'eard Nancy tell of 'aving drugged Bill Sikes so she could get out an' meet with 'em. She met with your old Aunt Rose, Oliver, not once but twice, gave 'em Fagin's name, an' Monks, an' told of whereby Fagin would get Oliver to be a thief an' Monks would pay 'im. It 'ad to do with your inheritance, Work'us."

"The inheritance I won't be getting," said Oliver, hearing the severity of his own tone through clenched teeth.

On the heels of that, he was shocked at finding out that Aunt Rose, delicate, fragile Aunt Rose, had actually walked London's streets in the middle of the night to meet with a whore beneath the shadow of London Bridge. He could hardly believe it, yet the location of that meeting, one of the elements of that time that no one had been willing to tell him, could hardly be denied. Noah's details were too specific, and in the end, it made sense. Aunt Rose, or anyone, would have been more willing to tell him the facts of that meeting had they not been so squalid.

"Fagin wanted to make a good profit off Oliver, you see," said Noah to Jack, ignoring Oliver's gloomy statement. "For Monks' sake, but it was Nancy who did you all in, don't you get that?"

"How's that?" Jack's face tightened. "What do you mean, *Nancy* did us all in?" Jack's voice rose. There was a stir as the nearer patrons of the tavern turned to look at them, and a small momentary island of silence surrounded them.

Noah looked around and handed out glares, until the noise grew again, and then leaned forward, as if he were telling the most important of secrets.

"She gave a description of the dens where Fagin could be found, a description of Monks. She cried after she did it, but she did it anyway. She told 'em about Bill, the man she wouldn't leave, but who she 'ad drugged, mind you, to peach on all of Fagin's lot, includin' him. Bill was in a terrible way when 'e found out, gnashin' his teeth and spoutin' off about poundin' people's 'eads into the ground. Which—"

Noah paused as he arched his head and pulled on his lapels because, of course, this was the moment, his moment, his and Jack's. Oliver wanted to get up and walk away from the table.

He'd not heard the entire story before, had only gotten brief sketches of borrowed conversations he was never supposed to have overheard, and now, when he could hear the whole of it, he didn't want to. Besides, he already knew how it had ended.

"Which he did, Nancy's 'ead, that is." Noah smacked his lips around the juiciness of this revelation. "Killed 'er in their rooms according to the records an' the newspapers. He beat her with 'is pistol an' left her to bleed on the floor. Then 'e ran from the coppers, an' anyway, the game was up for Fagin an' all, what with Nancy 'aving told Brownlow, who, it seems, went straight to the law with it."

The thought of Nancy with her blood soaking into the floorboards made Oliver feel cold inside. Nancy had been a stout, friendly girl, untidy about her person and confused enough by life to consider staying with Bill Sikes her best option. But in her way, she had been kind to Oliver, and for that, she hadn't deserved to die, not that way, not *any* way, and surely, she would not have—

Suddenly, Jack reached up across the table to grab Noah by the lapels, one in each fist. And never mind the pot of beer upset to spill musty suds across the table to spatter into Oliver's lap, never mind the people looking at them again.

"She *never* would," said Jack, baring his teeth, almost growling at Noah. "She never would give up Bill, an' you don't know anythin' about it!"

"She did," said Noah, baring his teeth right back. "I was *there*, I tell you, an' I 'eard what she said. She told about Fagin an' the dens, an' about Bill—"

"She didn't!"

"She *did!*"

Jack was shifting his weight, standing up, resetting his hands on Noah's jacket, coming around the table, as if ready to slam Noah to the ground and give him a sound thrashing, something that Oliver knew Noah deserved for telling the story in this way. Making Nancy out to be the culprit for the loss of Fagin's gang and ruining Jack's last memory of her was the cruelest thing he had ever done.

"Jack," said Oliver, standing up, putting his body right next to Jack's. "Come away, then. The story is old; Noah's brain is addled by drink. You have the right of it, I'm sure, for Nancy would never—"

He had his hands on Jack's arm, but he had to stop because he didn't know what Nancy had said or whether she'd loved Bill enough to avoid talking about him. She *might* have said something about Fagin, that dark, far-ago night. But, if Noah had misinterpreted the meeting on the bridge somehow, Fagin would have seen that as a betrayal.

Feeling within his rights to wreak revenge, Fagin might have twisted the story even further upon telling it to Bill. Who then would have turned into the best weapon Fagin had to take down Nancy. But this was all supposition on Oliver's part, and certainly nothing he wanted to share with Jack.

Jack shook off Oliver's hands, twitching away, straightening his neckerchief as Noah got up and backed away from the table.

"She never would, now, would she, Nolly!" Jack shouted loudly, and he didn't seem to care how many heads in the Three Cripples turned to stare. "And you, Mr. Bolter, should know better than to say such things!"

Jack actually shook his fist at Noah, his breast heaving, watching Noah with narrowed eyes as Noah adjusted his lapels and took up his hat, as if he'd meant to leave all along. Leaving Oliver standing there, with Jack next to him, shaking, so angry at what he considered to be lies.

Oliver imagined Noah had saved this particular story for when he wanted to draw Jack in the most. Which it had, except to the exact opposite effect, much to Oliver's secret pleasure.

And—yes, there was something else. On the night before Fagin was hanged, deep in his madness, he'd muttered about someone named Bolter, and how it was he, and not Nancy, who should have his throat cut, sawed off, in fact, because, as Fagin had said, Bolter was *somehow the cause of all this*. Bolter, who was actually Noah Claypole.

But to tell Jack the whole truth of Noah's complicity in the downfall of Fagin's gang would mean that he'd have to include the part where Fagin had gone quite mad before his execution, something Oliver never intended to do. And, if Jack found out this more severe truth, he'd follow right after Noah and end up with blood on his hands, clapped in irons, and on his way to Newgate before the day was over.

No. Oliver couldn't do it. Not to Jack. Not now. Besides, Noah had just dug his own grave; he didn't need any assistance from Oliver.

# 32

# AFTER WHITECHAPEL

They moved from the table in the middle of the room to the small alcove. Oliver stood by, holding his hat and Jack's as Jack shoved and threatened for the current occupants to leave, which they did, muttering and stomping off. Oliver didn't care how rude Jack was, but he couldn't stand being in the middle of the room with all eyes upon them, watching and listening. Especially after Jack's display of temper. So the alcove was much better.

Much better, that is, than being at a table in the center of the main room, but that did not mean it was better than his old life, not by half. Since he could remember, things had gone from bad to worse, and even when they'd been better, as during those dear, gentle years in the country with Aunt Rose and Uncle Harry, they'd got bad again, in the end. His own attempts at setting his life to rights had led him back here, to this very spot, at the Three Cripples. With Jack.

Jack, who, even if he'd come from quality people, would always be what he was, a child of the streets. Nothing would ever change him, so even if Oliver's world whirled around him like a sandstorm—

Raising his hand to order them something to eat and drink,

Jack took his cards out of his pocket, shuffling them between the fingers of one hand. He took his hat from Oliver and lay it on the table, pushing his dark hair back from his face, distractedly staring at nothing. Oliver looked at Jack, seeing the spark of candlelight reflecting off the silver buttons of Jack's blue waistcoat, seeing the flash in his green eyes.

When Doreen brought them some food, Oliver eyed the tin plate of slices of beef that looked none too fresh, and the boiled eggs, which had a tinge of green around the yellow yolks. He stuck to the beer, taking huge swallows and, it being fairly fresh beer, he drank the rest of the pot.

With the arrival of the food, Jack became his usual self, relaxed, scanning the crowd, keeping an eye out, taking a drink from the pot of beer when it was brought to him. Perhaps he was expecting that Oliver would ask him to teach him a new card game in spite of Oliver's rather emphatic declaration that he did not want to spend his life this way. So why was he continuing to do that very thing?

But now that the afternoon was becoming evening, what Jack had said to Oliver earlier kept coming back to him. Jack, who so rarely spoke about how he felt about anything, and never about himself. It was as if Jack had given Oliver something that was only Jack's to give.

*You was the only one I knew in London...I knew I had to look for you—I knew that you would never come lookin' for me.*

No one had ever said anything like that to him. No one had ever looked at Oliver the way Jack did, as though he meant something, that he mattered to Jack. But Jack's expression now, the furrow between his brows when all he was about was a drink and some cards and his pipe, as usual—perhaps it was that Jack feared he'd said too much.

Jack looked at him, flipping three cards face up in front of Oliver, as if inviting him to play a game. In spite of heartfelt comments that anyone might regret the impulse of, Jack was now the very figure of equanimity. As if ignoring the fact that

Oliver was staring at him, Jack drew from the pipe and laid it aside. And in that moment, in the quietness of Jack's eyes, Oliver saw a place there that was for him and him alone. It made something stir inside of him, a sense of having found something that he'd not known was lost. That Jack truly cared for him and that he, in return, truly cared for Jack.

"What you frownin' at, then, Nolly?" Jack asked, tapping the edges of the cards against the table.

"Nothing," said Oliver, ignoring the galloping of his heart as it tried to race ahead of the lie and at the quickly unraveling control of his own arms and limbs. "The beer—it always goes to my head."

"You always could suffer the gin better," said Jack. "Shall I get you one?"

"No, I just want to—I need to put my head down."

And this not merely because the room was becoming dim and booming around him, but also because he couldn't gather his thoughts, was unable to collect them into a tidy bundle that would indicate to him what he should do.

What he *wanted* to do was to reach out and touch Jack and wipe away the last traces of Noah's story, and in their place, leave his own scent behind. To follow the curves of Jack's face with his fingers, as his eyes were now doing. And untangle the sparks in his belly that were spreading up his spine and down the backs of his thighs.

"I just need to lie down," he said. "Can we just go up—go upstairs?"

As Jack's eyebrows flew up, Oliver felt his face flush, and he had a heated, desperate wish to take it back. Jack was going to mock him, tip back his head and laugh—

But Jack didn't. Instead, he half-blinked at Oliver with lazy eyes, and stood, taking up the cards and the clay pipe, still smoking, in the cup of his hand.

"C'mon, then, you," said Jack.

He gently pushed Oliver before him on the bench, pulling

Oliver to a stand, as though he were a young child who needed a gentle hand to the back to guide him through a dark place. Oliver let him, feeling the heat of Jack's hand through layers of wool jacket and muslin shirt that seemed, now, quite thin.

Though some faraway part of him heeded caution, Oliver led the way through the crowded tavern, and Jack followed close behind, up the stairs, and down the narrow brown hallway, gloomy in the dim afternoon light. Their footsteps echoed on the worn floorboards, and Oliver waited, leaning against the doorjamb as Jack took out his key and undid the useless lock, the metal jaws of the key scraping loudly against the rusty tumblers.

Jack walked into the dark room, with Oliver close on his heels. Jack went over to the mantelpiece, a dim, narrow line along the wall above the dark maw of the cold, empty fireplace. He didn't light the candle but stood there a moment, drawing the last mouthfuls of smoke in preparation for dampening the ashes in the pipe to put it in the bowl on the mantelpiece. Oliver closed the door, leaning back against it.

"There should be a fire in that grate," he said.

"I'll get coal," said Jack, though he made no move to go past Oliver or to open the door or anything.

Oliver knew his teeth were chattering, as if he was cold, but he wasn't. His breath felt tight in his throat, as if he were scared, but he wasn't. It was as if his whole body knew he was alone with Jack. Alone in a room with Jack, as if this were a new thing, one that he'd never done before.

He had not anticipated his hands feeling so empty, his arms wanting something to hold, his belly feeling hollow, full of sparks, or his groin tightening, as if it wanted particular action, and it wanted it now. Or that Jack would be looking at him with the expression of someone who is seeing the Rapture for the first time, eyes wide and expectant. Unless he was mistaken, and Jack truly believed that Oliver wanted to rest simply because his head was thick with beer. Oliver blinked, quite unable to explain in words what he wanted, either to himself or to Jack.

From somewhere deep within him came an impulse, from a place so still and untrammeled by grief or sorrow or doubt. A strong, deep place in his heart that still believed in blue skies and that all would be well. A place that had enough strength to weather any storm. If Jack didn't want Oliver, if he hadn't meant what he'd said before, hadn't intended Oliver to feel the way he was feeling—then he could simply push Oliver away and continue smoking his pipe. The risk would be all Oliver's.

There was a tiny pause as Jack drew on his pipe, and before he could do anything else, Oliver walked over to him and kissed the smoke from Jack's mouth. Pausing with his lips over Jack's, sensitive and shivering, he drew the smoke in, tasting it on Jack's breath, and the beer. And thought of that long ago day when they'd met, when everything had changed, and nothing that had happened since had been able to stand in the way of this moment.

"Oh," said Jack, holding his pipe to one side, not pulling away. "If that's what you're about, then—"

It didn't matter that Jack was pretending with his casual words, pretending not to be nervous. Oliver was warm through, his hands on Jack, warm, tugging on Jack's coat and touching the skin of his throat. The room was dim; Oliver could barely see; the only light was the spark from Jack's pipe.

"Here," Oliver said, holding the pipe to Jack's mouth.

Jack took it and drew in a breath, holding the smoke till Oliver kissed him again and tasted the smoke. Then he took the pipe and, in the darkness, put it in the bowl on the mantelpiece. The wooden ledge was narrow, but the pipe would be safe there till morning or later in the evening or whenever Jack might look for it again. But now Jack was pulling off his coat, and Oliver heard it land with a thump on the floorboards.

He didn't remark on Jack's slovenly habits, because it didn't matter. His own jacket fell to the floor also, and the night would hide the scatter of boots and stockings and the loose collar of Oliver's shirt that Jack unbuttoned with slow and careful hands.

Then Jack put his hands on Oliver's neck, pushing the collar away and down, untying the kerchief around Oliver's neck, putting his mouth on the curve of Oliver's jaw, sending a shiver through him.

Many a hero in the books he'd read had kissed his princess, but the descriptions had never indicated that a kiss would set his whole body shivering. No written word had ever described it quite like this, a raw enfolding, a consuming mouth, the smell of sweat and salt. The jerky breath, the sparks wherever Jack's mouth alighted.

But whether it was love, as written of in the books he'd read, or something brought on by the drink, his body pushed into Jack's hands, which stroked his hair and pulled at his trouser buttons and seemed to be everywhere all at once. Jack did not say words of love nor even really speak, though Oliver was sure he would not have been able to hear him over the thudding of his own heart, the effect of the beer seemingly burned away by the heat of his skin and the sear left behind in the trail of Jack's fingers.

"Will you, then, Jack?" Oliver asked, not quite clear what he was asking or why.

Jack answered him, just the same, by undoing his own trousers and then Olivier's, and pushing Oliver on the bed, tipping him back, suddenly, to land against the hard, flocked mattress.

It was an uncomfortable bed at best, but when Jack was on him, his thighs straddling Oliver's thighs, his hands stroking the bareness of Oliver's ribs where his shirt rode high, he forgot about the bed, for Jack was hard and soft against him all at once, the dust and the salt from his skin so close as Jack shucked his shirt, trailing the long tails of it across Oliver's face as he pushed it aside.

Jack would be cold that way, all on his own, his chest bare in the night, so Oliver struggled to put his hands on the folds of his shirt to pull it free from his trousers, arching his back. Jack helped him for a moment, then pressed Oliver's hand to his crotch, where the hardness of Jack's sex was outlined as an iron brand. He moved Oliver's hand on him, over the trousers, then pulled Oliver's hand inside, and Oliver touched Jack where the skin was soft and shockingly hot.

"Come along, then, Nolly," said Jack, when Oliver's hand jerked away. "Just a little bit. It won't hurt you none, an' then I'll show you how nice it can be. Right?"

How Jack had his wits about him enough to speak, Oliver didn't know; he couldn't imagine being sane enough to articulate a sequence of events, the end to which Oliver didn't know, had never known. But Jack knew, and he leaned low and kissed Oliver on his temples, brushing softly as he kissed Oliver's eyelids and his nose and then his mouth, a little rough and tasting sour from the beer, but sending shocks through Oliver's body that felt like small, sharp flickers of lightning.

When Jack pressed even lower, their chests touching, Jack's bare one to his shirted one, Oliver's arm was trapped between him, and only his hand could move. So he did, curling his fingers around Jack's hard sex, his palm dampened by Jack's pleasure, the hair of Jack's private hair scratching against Oliver's wrist.

When he moved his fingers and did it again, Jack made low sounds in his throat that Oliver had never heard anyone make before. Anxious pleas and some unspoken pain vibrated into Oliver's ear, simmering all the way down to his belly. Desire flared, hot as flame, as Jack thrust into his hand, pushing faster than Oliver could keep up with, and finally, his hips against Oliver's, he shoved one time so hard it almost hurt, as he pulsed into Oliver's hand, leaving hot dampness behind.

Jack flung himself backward on the mattress, sideways, almost knocking Oliver off, and before Oliver could get up from the bed, shocked, eyes wide, Jack reached for him, pulling Oliver alongside him, hips hot together, saying, "Come here, come here."

Laying hands upon him, Jack pushed down Oliver's open

trousers, and took Oliver, now hard as a poker, against his belly. The sin of it clanged inside of his head as the pleasure of it, of Jack's hand, moving up and down, overrode sense like a thundering horse until sin was only a vague notion.

Squirming against Jack, Oliver felt the wildness of his body, out of control, as Jack stroked him up and down, chastity vanishing as his whole body clenched. Sweat and heat raced up his spine, and he spent into Jack's hand, curling forward with a violent spell of heat that left him panting into Jack's shoulder, sweat freezing along his almost-bare hips, the small of his back.

"There, then, petal," said Jack, whispering into the crown of his hair, kissing his temple. "You belong to me now, as ever you was."

Oliver could only nod, struggling to breathe, thinking to straighten his trousers and tug his shirt into place as Jack reached behind him to drag the thin woolen blanket up over them. Letting the scratchy edge be tucked under his chin as Jack refused to let him go, wrapping his arms around Oliver's shoulders and pulling him close till they were both on the bed, squarely, the pillow beneath Jack's head, and Jack himself for Oliver's pillow.

"Sleep now," said Jack, his voice mumbling off in the darkness.

As Oliver obeyed, part of his brain thought of Jack's shirt and how he would be cold without it. But Oliver could not move his arm, as it was across Jack's belly, rising slow and deep in sleep, where Jack already was. Oliver's eyelids flickered to the blue sky in his mind, now moving low into a slow, darkening nigh, where there was peace and stillness and a river inside of him that overflowed and seeped gently across thirsty green banks. Oliver closed his eyes and let himself follow Jack.

## 33

# TREATS OF A BATHHOUSE IN SMITHFIELD, WHEREIN OLIVER CONSIDERS HIS FUTURE

When Oliver woke up, he stared at the brown-splotched ceiling, thinking for a moment of the places on his body that Jack had touched, his mouth that Jack had kissed, the stroke of a hand, gently, along his neck, and, with more urgency, on the flesh between his legs. His skin, all over, seemed to hum, a silvery-toned hum that bespoke of the spill of his seed, his scent mixing with Jack's, like salt from the sea. An ancient holy sea he'd been taught should never be spent in pleasure; it was a sin to do so, a waste of a man's capacity, and a crime. What he and Jack had done—

He sat up, jerking the blanket back, feeling the hot wave climbing up his chest, his face. He was almost vibrating with it, the shock of realizing it, the memory of Jack's hands, and the length of Jack's body next to him, the warmth and the closeness, the intimacy—he didn't know whether he was hot with shame—and he should be, he really should be because he was no longer a virgin—or whether he was hot with something else. Because the sense of quiet deep within him was good; it settled him, as a long walk down a summer's country lane might have done. Had done, in the past, when he was young and the world a green and blue and innocent place.

His skin was itchy and ached for clean water to wash with. But was he going to wash away the sin of it, wash away what had been between him and Jack? He couldn't, even if he was confused as to how he might talk to Jack, now that they'd had relations.

But the memory of their tryst flickered all around, quite clearly, as if it were happening that very moment. That impulse to close his eyes to all propriety and let the sweep of affection tumble him into bed with Jack, their bodies curled around each other, that sense of belonging, he could deny none of this. And would not, not with the memory of Jack's hands upon him and Jack's mouth upon his.

Jack had touched him as no one ever had before and kissed him and said, in a low, husked voice, *You belong to me now, as ever you was.* There was still the unsettled future, choices to be made where roads diverged. But with the streets of London before him, now that he had Jack at his side, the world seemed wide open.

Not that Jack was anything lawful or even good, and perhaps not even steady. Jack was a sprite, a child of the streets, pulling Oliver to him as the sky pulled toward the blue. That was enough for Oliver, though he did not know what Jack's thoughts were of the night before.

Jack propped himself up on his elbow, hair mashed on one side, eyes sparking. He looked up at Oliver as though trying not to smirk.

"Been wallowin' in the grief of sin, have you?" Jack asked.

What they'd done was indeed a sin, not only in the eyes of the church but in the eyes of the law. But when he looked down at Jack, bare except for his trousers beneath the woolen blanket, with the dirt around his neck, his naked chest, the dark tuft of hair below his collarbone, and the smudgy marks of kisses around his mouth that Oliver had left there, he knew it didn't matter. If Mr. McCready could walk the street a free man after the willful neglect that had killed Martin—well, Oliver's passion for Jack was the lesser evil. Oliver felt he might struggle with this, but not that morning, not with Jack looking at him that way.

"I'm not as shocked as you think I am," said Oliver, letting his mind have its way with his mouth even though he *was* shocked, a little. Certainly enough.

Jack's eyebrows flew up, and he pushed his thumb in the corner of his eye, perhaps to disguise his delight at this news or perhaps just to wake up faster. Oliver rubbed the back of his neck, struggling not to scratch the various places that seemed to want it, all over, under the blanket, and everywhere, places that should not be scratched.

"Do you want a bath?" asked Jack, in a perfectly ordinary way, as if he were merely asking it, the way he always did, with no shame or recrimination, either for himself or for Oliver.

"Yes, but—" Oliver paused, considering how to point out a very obvious fact in a kindly way, without snapping. "There's no water, Jack."

"Got pennies," said Jack, yawning, showing his red mouth. "There's a bathhouse on the Strand, but that's more for old, fat gentlemen, so you might try the one that's just up from Smithfield Market."

"Where's that, then?" asked Oliver.

It seemed that Jack understood Oliver might need a moment alone to work through overthrowing seventeen years of Sunday school teachings, and for that, he was grateful.

"Down Peter Street, or somethin' like it. Can't miss it."

Falling back against the pillow, Jack tugged on the blanket so he could wrap it around him, giving Oliver a small push with his foot to get him going so that Jack could have the bed to himself. Oliver stood up, straightening his shirt, buttoning up his trousers.

"I'll come back," he said to Jack, his fingers shaking a little as he did up the buttons, flattening the tabs with the heel of his hand. Getting dressed, focusing on that instead of on Jack's assessing eyes.

"I know," said Jack. "I'll see you after."

THE BATHHOUSE WAS INDEED ALONG PETER STREET, DOWN A side lane, in a low, two-story building, cobbled together from a collection of houses around a lopsided court. Oliver could see steam coming from slightly opened upper windows, and the growth of mold on the frames of the doors, the slimy, dark moss on the cobblestones, the slick of mud and damp that covered every surface.

The air smelled slightly of soap and ash, and, at every moment, he expected somebody might recognize him on his own and point out that he was heading into a common bathhouse, a place where only the lower orders went. But here he was, and he needed a bath, so there was nothing for it but to carry on.

In spite of the chill of the pennies in his pocket that Jack had given him, and the fact that his head felt muzzy, he was distracted by Jack's scent in the collar of his shirt, the tender feel of his skin beneath his waistband. He wanted to keep that scent upon him, but in he went to be met by a lady in a bottle-green skirt. Her apron was more grey than white; she seemed to be covered with a layer of damp as well. Her smile missed teeth, but she was pleasant enough and took Oliver's pennies with an open fist.

"Tuppence for first water, and hot, thank you, sir. For another penny we can brush and set your clothes to rights."

Naturally, the woman wouldn't concern herself with *why* his clothes looked as they did, with the stains of Newgate prison still on him. With Jack's scent pushed through the cloth, along with the sea-tang of what they'd shared between them.

"Yes," said Oliver, swallowing as his nervousness ate at him. "Thank you, miss."

"We'll send a lad by, once you're in," she replied, taking the additional coin from Oliver.

If he kept going as he was, spending money as soon as he'd acquired it, he'd be more like Jack, who had no sense of thrift or savings and would spend it all as soon as it came in like the criminal he was, living day to day.

A lad, dressed in a thin shirt and trousers in deference to the steamy heat, led Oliver down the wooden passage. When he stopped, he pushed his arm through a long flap of canvas that served as a door to a small room with a single window. In the middle of the water-stained wooden floor was a straight-edged tin tub full of water, and a bowl of soft soap on a tall stool, with a thin towel draped over one of the stool's rungs. Some unseen breeze chased through a gap in the windowpanes.

"Is this the best you have?" asked Oliver, with some dismay.

"No refunds, mister," said the lad. "But the water is new."

The lad trailed his fingers across the surface of the water, as if to demonstrate this fact. A bit of steam rose around them. Oliver's skin began to itch, and he started pulling at the buttons at his neck.

"Thank you, then," he said.

The lad pulled back the curtain on the fogged window and then left the room. The barred glass let in light, and this made Oliver feel a little better. He got undressed, lay his clothes on the rungs of the stool, and climbed in the tub, trying not to look at the bruises on his legs or the state of himself.

His body had been through enough; it didn't need to be examined for faults and flaws. But there were marks there. Marks from Mr. McCready's switch, from the handling of the constables, from the bricks of the jail cell, from Cromwell's hands. The bullet scar from where Giles had shot him that Jack had yet to see. From the lumps of Jack's mattress.

From Jack, any marks bespoke only tenderness, but otherwise, marks of harshness were all over him, from everywhere he'd been. The question was, where was he going?

Settling into the water, he sighed. It wasn't hot enough, and the metal of the tub was cold where it touched his skin, but at least it was a bath. As he reached for the soap, he could hear, through the thin walls, other people splashing around. Bathing was not only the next thing to godliness, it was also civilized. But if he could hear them, then they could hear *him*, and perhaps were speculating why he was taking a bath first thing in the morning, and not in the evening in preparation for going to church the next day.

He rubbed soap on his face, and then through his hair, standing up for a moment to get it all over his skin, even though he was loath to wash away Jack's scent. Then he sank back into the water to soak.

When he returned to the Three Cripples, he wanted to tell Jack about soap and hot water and how good it felt, but he doubted Jack would believe him, preferring, it seemed, to live with the lice on his skin, the nits in his linen. How easy it was to think of going back directly to the Three Cripples with the intention of talking Jack into taking a bath, despite the fact that the Three Cripples and all that it entailed should be the very *last* destination in his time on the earth.

With a quick knock, the lad came in through the canvas curtain and took Oliver's clothes from the chair, sparing Oliver only the briefest of glances. As he left, the curtain swayed damply in the breeze, giving Oliver a quick view of the narrow brown passage, letting in the smells and the damp and other people's perfume, or lack of it. Oliver closed his eyes.

He would bathe and get dressed in his disreputable clothes and go back to Jack at the Three Cripples. After that, he didn't know what he'd do. Cromwell seemed to think that Oliver belonged to him now and felt he had the papers to prove it. Oliver knew he could go to Aunt Rose, and that she would shelter him if he asked her to. But now that he was a person of low quality, with his criminal record that included not one but two visits to the dock, he knew that Aunt Rose didn't deserve that kind of trouble.

Besides, he couldn't leave Jack, who, in spite of his rough ways, was a tender anchor against a world that constantly shifted beneath Oliver's feet. He could still feel Jack's hand on his face, reaching through the grate on the cell door to comfort him, tender in spite of the grit of the rusting bars, gentle in spite of who Jack was, where he had come from. He could still feel Jack's kisses and his hands, hot on Oliver's skin, but silk-soft in contrast to the rough wool of the blanket.

Oliver's face grew flushed; he felt as though he might be boiling inside despite the cooling water, his skin sparking, currents racing to his groin, even in this disreputable place. Jack had been there then, and Jack was here now, and there didn't seem to be any way of getting away from that. Unless Oliver determined that what had happened between them the night before was never to happen again. Which he *should* do, if he had any sense.

"You done, mister?" asked the lad from beyond the canvas.

Oliver sighed. He could hear other people splashing and muttering, making the whole affair as intimate as if he were bathing in the same room with them. He sank low into the water and pretended the back of his neck was comfortable against the rim of the tub, and that the water was much hotter, the soap softer, less gritty against his skin.

"In a moment," he said. "Just give me another moment."

He scrubbed the length of his forearm with his hand, and let it fall below the surface of the water. He closed his eyes against the round, silver drops on his skin, on the rim of the tub. Unless he could convince himself not to go back to the Three Cripples, he was well and truly lost. But the truth of it was, the night before, with Jack, had been the sweetest sin, so in being lost, he had been found.

~

AFTER GETTING OUT OF THE TUB, DRYING WITH THE THIN
towel, and getting dressed, he headed back to the Three Cripples, for there was no other direction he wanted to take. He
followed the lane to West Street, where the wind whisked across
his hair, still damp against his neck, making him cold.

Water ran in the center of the street, ripples of the
runoff of grey and melting snow splattering his trouser legs
with damp and mud, with feckless drops from the over-
hanging rooflines making their way down his neck. Then, to
make matters worse, as he turned the corner into Field
Lane, he ran, literally, into Noah Claypole, who had, it
seemed, also been making his way up toward the Three
Cripples.

"'Ang about, Work'us, where's your manners?" demanded
Noah, his shoulders pushing forward beneath the narrow cloth
of his jacket.

"As to that, where are yours?" Oliver demanded in return.

Noah raised his fists, as if he were about to give Oliver a good
walloping, and why not? They were in the street, *sans* Jack, and,
more importantly, without that particular audience, Noah could
do whatever he pleased, as he always had. But then, so could
Oliver.

Then Noah stopped, fists unfolding as his fingers spread out.
He leaned forward to sniff along Oliver's neck.

"What you been about, then, Work'us?"

"I *am* allowed out-of-doors, Noah," said Oliver with some
tartness. He pulled back from Noah. "I'm not a prisoner,
however much you'd rather I was. I've just had a bath, if you
must know."

There was a look in Noah's eyes, a narrow, calculating gleam
that struck Oliver as it had in the old days. He was looking at
Oliver as if he knew exactly what Oliver was thinking and
feeling.

"Thought you smelled like a posy," said Noah. "But what I can't imagine is why for?"

"That's none of your affair," said Oliver.

He started to attempt to sidle by Noah when, out of the corner of his eyes, at the top of the street, just where it began to slope down from Saffron Hill, he saw Jack. He had his top hat on and his jacket buttoned over his waistcoat, and he'd not yet seen Oliver. But there he was, resplendent and confident, hands in pockets, whistling, and Oliver knew, right then, with a fierce and protective stab in his belly, that there was no getting away from what was between them, from how he felt about Jack.

"Eh?" said Noah, and Oliver whirled back to face him.

"Stop following me," he said, turning on his heel to march up the lane to meet Jack halfway, at least. Naturally, Noah was quick to follow him, annoyingly close, as if with the intent of being as intrusive as possible.

Just then, Jack reached them, breathless, his hat far back on his head. He looked at Oliver, his face bright with pleasure that Oliver had, indeed, returned, warring with some hesitation that Oliver knew to be caution. What he and Jack had shared the night before was *not* meant for common consumption.

And yet, there they were, with Noah as their first audience, witness to the furtive glance Jack gave him, to the flush that colored Oliver's cheeks because he didn't know whether to reach out and touch Jack on the sleeve, at least, to reassure him. The tense line of Jack's jaw, the stiffness of his shoulders, stopped Oliver; he wanted to explain his own confusion while at the same time resolving Jack's. That is, if Jack *was* confused, which perhaps he wasn't. But the flash of his green eyes in the crisp air of the street brought back the warmth of the night before, so perhaps, regardless of what Jack was feeling about that, his current irritation might not be about Oliver at *all*.

Feeling warm from Noah's attention, Oliver turned to look at him, dragging his attention away from Jack with some reluctance. Noah was looking at Oliver and then at Jack, his gaze flicking between them, as though they were the newest curiosity since the lions had been brought to the Tower. Oliver froze as Noah's eyebrows shot so far up into his hairline that they disappeared, and his mouth had fallen open.

"'Ave you an' Jack—" Noah stopped, and Oliver attempted to tighten his face so that Noah could not see there the memories of the night before.

But with that and Jack's slight cough, it seemed too late to hide anything. And evidently, Noah did not need Oliver's face to find out their secrets. He pulled at the buttons on Oliver's collar, which popped open, sending several buttons to bounce in the street. Noah's eyes were on his neck, and Oliver knew what he was seeing there, the marks from Jack's mouth, which still hummed with Jack's soft whispers.

"Bloody sodomite," said Noah, giving Oliver a shove.

Anger sparked in Noah's eyes. Oliver knew Noah was furious not only because of the crime, and indeed, in *spite* of it, but because of the fact that no matter how many clever stories Noah had told Jack, this was the one story only Oliver could tell.

"I can smell it on you, Work'us, as 'ard as you tried to wash it off, an' I can see it on your face." Noah almost snarled this. "You're better off goin' back to the workhouse; you're not one of Fagin's lads, an' you never were!"

"I'm more of one than you," said Oliver, feeling the heat of it in his breast, forgetting that he'd ever denied it before. "For I never peached on one of my own."

It was almost in slow motion that Noah clenched his fists to demonstrate to Oliver exactly what he thought of it all, but Oliver, faster by seconds, punched him in the nose and smiled while he did it. Noah staggered back, clutching his face, blood streaking down his chin.

"What's goin' on, then?" Jack asked, jumping forward to clap a hand on each of their shoulders as if they were all the best of friends. "Why ain't you two gettin' along?"

"You know why," said Noah. "Besides, 'e 'it me!" said Noah, his astonishment muffled beneath his hands.

"What? Nolly?" Jack shook his head as if he'd not just seen Oliver do that very thing, though it was plain to anyone that Noah was the only one bleeding. "Why, he's as delicate as a petal an' wouldn't hurt a child."

Oliver could not help but smirk at this, evil gladness racing through him. It was one thing to best Noah, he'd done it before and would do it again. But to have Jack take his side was worth giving up all the hot baths in London. Worth the sweet confusion that sprang up between them as they looked at each other.

"You'll regret this, Jack," said Noah, licking his lips and wiping his nose with the back of his hand. "You just see if you will."

But before Jack could say anything to placate Noah, as he might have done, Noah stormed off down Field Lane to where it led out to Holborn, banging through icy puddles as if he might melt them with his fury.

"Eh?" asked Jack, turning to Oliver, reaching out briefly to touch a mud-splattered lapel. "He knows, then?"

"For all he's a fool, yes, he does."

Oliver did not jerk back from Jack's hand, his eyes flicking to Jack's, feeling a quail of nerves and foolishness and the terrible intimacy of it, the memory of the curves of Jack's body, the taste of his mouth, his scent up *close*.

Then he saw the worry in Jack's eyes and stopped the train of thought with a twitch that seemed to run through his whole body.

"He's a fool, but he's very astute," said Oliver. "I'm not very good at lying to avoid him finding out more than he already knows."

"Never you mind, Nolly," said Jack, stroking Oliver's neck. "It'll work itself out, by-and-bye."

Jack leaned in, his cold nose beneath Oliver's ear, where his hair was still damp.

"Besides, you smell lovely, an' how can I be cross about it all when you smell like you do?"

"Soap and hot water, Jack, is all it is," said Oliver, shivering with the faint touch of Jack's skin on his but not moving away. Rather, he leaned into it, right there in the street.

"You were comin' back," said Jack finally, pulling himself upright, as if he might rescue them from being a spectacle on the street, though it was far too late for that.

"I told you I would," said Oliver.

Jack shook his head. "Not with that look on your face, the one you had this mornin'. It was like a storm come over them blue eyes of yours."

The thoughts from the bathhouse came back to Oliver then, as did a flurry of nerves. "I do need to leave London, Jack, as I told you," he said. "I don't know as to where, but—"

"You know I can't come with you," said Jack. "Besides, you don't need to leave ever so quickly, do you? Stay with me awhile, won't you, an' I'll help you get a kit together, an' some brass so you won't be starvin' on the streets like the poor, wee mite that you are."

Jack's casual answer sounded as though he believed he would, in time, be able to convince Oliver to stay. Besides, Oliver had never been able to resist how he felt inside when someone offered to feed him, and he did not resist it now. Not when Jack was looking at him as he was, with a flash in his green eyes, sharp as a mirror.

To Jack, anything anybody thought, any rules written by man or God, mattered very little. He wanted Oliver to stay, and that was all there was to it.

The thought of leaving in the face of that desire was not impossible, for it was quite true that many had looked upon Oliver as an object to be gained or even, simply, as though he were something good to eat. Oliver was used to leaving others' faux desire behind, ignoring it, pretending it wasn't there. But that became impossible when true desire was accompanied by

Jack's smirk that half bespoke confidence and half whispered to that place inside of Oliver only Jack could reach. If Oliver left, it would not be right away, for he had no plan to speak of, no direction in which to head. There was London, and there was Jack, and there was the rain and the wind whistling down the lane where they stood, within eyeshot of the Three Cripples.

Jack smiled. "No long faces," he said, stroking his thumb along Oliver's jaw.

Oliver nodded and resigned himself to having his heart broken by a street thief.

## ❧ 34 ❧

## WHICH CONTAINS THE
## SUBSTANCE OF A PLEASANT
## INTERLUDE

I n that moment, silent and sweet, Oliver cast his eyes down the mud-drenched lane, where Noah had so recently gone. Jack did likewise, then looked at the throng by the door of the Three Cripples, as if he couldn't bear to charge his way through it. He tipped his head back, hand on the crown of his hat.

"Say, Nolly," said Jack, interrupting the thread of Oliver's thoughts. "I've got an errand to run. Will you wait here, or come along?"

It wasn't quite as sudden as a smack to the face, but this was the moment Oliver feared would come. Jack was going out to pick pockets; Jack was a thief, and not all the angels in heaven could change him from that. It might suit Oliver better if they could, but what other employment could Jack gain? Oliver could not imagine him clerking in an office or even chasing bullocks in a field. So he wouldn't ask what Jack was doing nor implore him not to go. It wouldn't change anything, anyway.

"I'll wait for you at the Three Cripples," Oliver said, taking a side step up the lane. "But not forever, so hurry back."

Jack's whole face cinched up in a smile, one that reached his eyes. He touched Oliver's face with his fingers.

"That's somethin' old Fagin might have said." Jack was laughing at Oliver outright. Oliver tried not to return the smile but failed, and wondered why he tried, when Jack's smile was so good to see.

"Well, then," Oliver said, clearing his throat. He knew the words, remembered Fagin saying them, but couldn't dig up the charming oiliness of Fagin's voice to do it justice. "Hurry on, then," he said, just the same.

With a wave and a smile, Jack turned to go, and was soon swallowed up by the crowd on this rainy day, leaving Oliver on the slanted, damp paving stones, to be looked at by rough men who shouldered past him, bumping into him because they could. Or because they wanted to get close. And they stared; people did, but without Jack as his shield, or even Noah's annoying presence, Oliver felt naked and bare to the soul.

Gritting his teeth, Oliver tightened his neckerchief as he walked up the street and shouldered his way in amongst the men standing around the doorway of the Three Cripples. There were women too, with slatternly hair and singed aprons and too much toilet water applied about their person. All made way for him with knowing and saucy smiles.

When he was inside, he looked through the smoky haze of the coal fire at the crowd drinking their money away, thinking of what Mr. Grimwig might say. Or how he would pound his cane and state, for anyone to hear, that this was Oliver's lot. To live amongst the unwashed, to shelter in such a place, to consort with thieves.

Oliver hurried up the stairs, and when he got to the door to their room, he opened it; the lock gave way at the slightest push. The room that he and Jack now shared, bright in the morning light, was littered with clumps of mud. The bed was unmade, the mattress grimy and stained. Cobwebs sparkled in the window, and soot streaked across the old brickwork that surrounded the unlit fireplace.

Perhaps Mr. Grimwig was right. Oliver lived as he deserved

to live, with thieves, in fetid, small quarters. But at least he had Jack. He had that, though for how long, Oliver didn't know.

He needed to leave London, only he didn't want to leave without Jack. Which meant staying. Which also meant, as he waited for Jack, that he needed something to do. Or at least until Jack talked him into joining him on the streets, or Cromwell made good his threats to make use of Oliver. Until then, he needed to keep busy.

He took off his jacket and laid it on the back of the chair and put his hat on the table. Then he began to make use of his idle hands. He pulled the blankets from the bed and hung them on the string over the narrow mantelpiece to air. He leaned the mattress up against the wall, found a scrap of cloth to dust the slats, and turned the mattress to the other side before putting it back in place. Not that it made much difference; the stains on both sides made it look as though someone had died upon it.

When he tried to open the window, it was jammed shut. Looking closely at it, Oliver knew he'd need a lever of some sort, not to mention hot water and soap and perhaps an army of maids to make any real difference in that room.

In the flurry of dust created by his attempts at cleaning, Oliver opened the door and went back down the narrow corridor and down the stairs. Skirting the crowd as best he could, he went past the bar and through the side door that led to the kitchen. No one stopped him because, of course, he was known as belonging to Jack.

The kitchen wasn't as busy as the last time he'd been through it, though there was the same slovenly woman stirring something on the stove while completely ignoring that there was ash from the flames getting into the pot. The same man from before, with his red-and-brown stained apron, was using his cleaver to cut the last bits of scraggly meat from bone and putting it with bare and unwashed fingers into a large wooden bowl. There were dried leavings on the long, thick table, a pile of bread that had been scorched, a lump of something that had flies all over it and smelled, and, wrapped in torn blue paper, an old, well-scraped cone of sugar.

The fireplace needed cleaning worse than the one upstairs did. The grime on the walls was thick, and there was something splashed darkly on the windows. Tar, perhaps, or old wax, he wasn't sure. He couldn't believe he'd actually eaten food prepared in this room. But he wasn't going to do anything about the kitchen; he only needed to keep his hands busy until Jack returned.

He poked around the kitchen for a bucket, but neither the man nor the woman turned around to ask him what he was doing or what he wanted. After looking around one more time, Oliver found the bucket but decided against attempting to find soap in a kitchen like that, and forwent getting water from the pump, which would likely be found outside in the alley. Instead, he found a stiff wire brush and went over to the fireplace and filled the bucket with a few handfuls of coal, along with a few chips of wood, to help the fire start. When he slunk through the main room, he kept his head low and used rusty tongs to grab bits of live coal from the fireplace in the alcove and put them in the bucket as well.

Back up in the room, he tried scouring the hardened ash on the grate with the stiff brush, but while he managed to clean the fireplace a little, his efforts mostly resulted in coal dust flying up all around. In spite of this, at last he could place the coal and the wood chips in the grate, and light them with the embers. Soon, the chill of the room eased, and most of the smoke went up the flue.

He straightened the bed, put the blanket and pillow in order, and dusted the windowsill and the mantel with the scrap of cloth he'd used on the bed slats. Then, on his hands and knees, he went over the whole of the floor, pushing clumps of mud and layers of dust between the seams of the floorboards, where no doubt they would fall unnoticed onto the shoulders of the customers in the main room below.

He knew he wasn't cut out for a life of this type of grimy work, but there was something about putting things in order that filled him up as much as a good meal did. In spite of this, once the fire was lit, and the room done, there was nothing much for him to do.

He sat cross-legged in front of the fire and held his hands out to the glowing coals. His palms were dirty, and the knees of his trousers were black with coal and street grime. No doubt his face and the back of his neck reflected the same state in spite of his recent bath. And he wondered when Jack would return. And wondered, after that, what they would do, he and Jack, together. Or apart. He did not know.

WHEN THE BELLS OF ST. ANDREW'S CHURCH WERE STRIKING the hour of two o'clock with long, slow tolls, Oliver realized that he'd fallen to dozing in front of the fire. The coals needed building up, and the ash shoveled away, or the fire would die out altogether. As he stood up, rubbing the back of his neck, he wondered where Jack had got to, and whether maybe he should have gone with Jack instead of staying behind. What if Jack, while pinching another twopenny snuffbox, got himself arrested again? And how was Oliver really going to manage being with a common thief?

He made himself shake this off as he straightened his clothes and went down to the main room. It was still thronged with people, the air thick with damp because the door to the tavern was closed against the rainy weather. He saw that one of the fires had been built up, small flames flickering and jumping as the rain came down the flue, the wind whistling through the grate.

There was Jack, coming through the front door with a sack in his hand and a bottle under his arm. He was almost soaked through. Oliver went to him, trying his best to ignore the looks he got with his jacket off, the buttons broken from his collar, and his neckerchief tied only loosely, leaving his breastbone exposed.

"Jack," said Oliver, and then, on an impulse that found his body quite unable to resist, he cupped his hand around the crook of Jack's elbow. "Come, then. We should eat, and I built a fire in the room, although the chimney is no doubt still choked with soot, and the fire smokes."

"You built a fire?" asked Jack, letting himself be turned away from looking at the men who now piled in the alcove that Jack considered his.

"Yes," said Oliver. He nodded and tugged on Jack's arm. "I built it for the both of us. I'm sure it's died down by now, but I can build it up again."

"Maybe," said Jack in a way that seemed to indicate he was wondering which fire, exactly, that Oliver was talking about, which made Oliver's face feel warm. Either way, he shook off Oliver's hand and settled his damp jacket with a tug. He held out the sack, which was mud-stained and ragged along the edges. "I got you somethin'; was going to share it with Noah, but never mind him, anyway. Here."

He handed the sack to Oliver, finally looking him in the eye; though his brow was furrowed, at least he was attempting to forget about Noah.

"What is it?" asked Oliver, his voice coming out as a young child's on its birthday. He hefted the sack in his hands; it bulged with corners and points and was heavy as a small anvil.

"Upstairs," said Jack. "I honestly thought you weren't goin' to be here when I got back."

Though the statement seemed to beg for reassurance from Oliver that he would *always* be there when Jack got back, Oliver could not, in truth, respond to it. All the while he struggled to say no when he wanted to say yes simply befuddled him. Instead, he focused on the tickle of excitement that Jack was here, home at last, and let himself be led up the narrow stairs and down the brown hallway to Jack's room. There, indeed, the fireplace was smoking, as the fire had died out and there wasn't enough heat to take the smoke up the flue. Jack made Oliver sit on the bed and arranged the sack on Oliver's lap.

"Only for you, mind," said Jack.

There was a light in his eyes, as if, once in the room, alone with Oliver, he could let it show. He handed the bottle to Oliver as well, though Oliver's hands were already occupied with the sack.

"Very well," said Oliver, trying for some sternness to keep his voice even. It didn't quite work, so he concentrated on Jack's gift instead. He balanced the bundle on his lap with one hand, and with the other, he shook the contents of the bottle and looked at the cork, which was sealed with brown wax.

"It's brandy," said Jack.

Oliver had never had brandy before and wondered at the cost of it before belatedly realizing that, of course, Jack would not have *purchased* the bottle at a shop. But he pushed this thought away, as it would be rudeness in the face of Jack's kindness.

"Thank you," Oliver said.

"An' there's more," said Jack.

He reached into the sack, shifting the weight of it on Oliver's lap, and pulled out a still-warm pie, large enough for a family of four, that had a lovely baked crust and smelled like onions.

"Rabbit pie," said Jack. "Definitely not cat." He put the pie on the bed near the pillow and sat down next to Oliver, taking off his hat and laying it aside. "Go on, then."

When Oliver pulled three books out of the sack, he was astounded. They were used books, with the edges a little battered, but still fine, the faded gilt on the covers promising that the pages had been well-thumbed because the stories were good. One title, *The Castle of Otranto*, he thought he'd seen in the townhouse; the other title, *The Last of the Mohicans*, was entirely new to him. The last book was a worn copy of *The Arabian Nights*, exactly resembling the copy he used to own, back when his life, which while this troubled, lacked the confused memory of Jack kissing him.

As Oliver held the books in his lap, he moved his fingers along the edges. He should feel worse about it that these were stolen, though he was thinking more about how he'd missed out on the pleasure of browsing among the titles with Jack at his side. Indeed, his chest ached with the pleasure of it, that Jack had thought to acquire these for him. Then he looked at Jack.

"You didn't *steal* them," he said. It was more of a statement than a question, because while it might be defendable, in certain circumstances, to steal a bottle of brandy and a rabbit pie, it was an entirely different action to steal books from a bookshop.

"'Course I did," said Jack stoutly. "However else would I get them for you?"

Oliver knew he should push the books aside and admonish Jack that although stealing to survive was one thing, but for pleasure? Most assuredly not. But there was his own bright expectation at Jack's expression, his pleasure at the books, to contend with, much improved from his encounter with Noah. And then there were the books themselves, inviting him with covers and edges and titles.

"I've never read this one, *The Last of the Mohicans*, it says," said Oliver. "Have you?"

"Do you take me for foolish?" asked Jack, drawing back. "I have more important things to do."

"And this other one, I think I saw it on Uncle Brownlow's shelf, but I was never allowed to read it, because it would addle my head."

"Which one's that, then?"

Jack moved closer, tipping his chin down until it rested on Oliver's shoulder, as if wanting to share in the moment where Oliver stroked the book with reverent fingers. Oliver traced the title, his skin prickling a bit with delight at the warm feel of Jack's breath on his neck.

"*The Arabian Nights*," he said, reading aloud. His fingers

itched to shove everything from the bed so he could begin reading *The Arabian Nights* without delay. "Really, Jack, wherever did you get them?"

"Nolly," said Jack, taking off his jacket and tossing it on the floor near the bed. "You don't want to know, trust me. But I'll get more coal for the fire, an' when I come back, we can eat, an' then—"

Jack paused. He stood up, looking down at Oliver, and brushed the dust and grit from hands on his trousers and reached for the bottle to uncork it. Taking a swig straight from the bottle, he swallowed some brandy and closed his eyes for a minute.

"Do you want me to read to you, Jack?" asked Oliver.

He felt a shiver that was akin to comfort at the thought of it. The boys at the haberdashery had never allowed that reading was good or pleasurable. Any time spent in the room with them as they lolled on the beds when he tried to read was constantly interrupted by their idle chatter.

Jack's eyes flew open, and there, yes, was the glitter of desire. For after Noah and his cruel words about Nancy, Jack needed a new story as much as Oliver needed the book to tell it from.

"Here," said Oliver.

He scooted back on the bed till his back was against the low headboard. He crossed his legs; that his boots were still on didn't matter. The blanket was filthy already, and besides, a book awaited him.

But Jack took a moment to undo the laces for him and to pull off Oliver's boots and throw them aside. Oliver didn't let himself make a comment about this, since that was how Jack was with his own clothes. And, as well, Jack was now undoing Oliver's neckerchief and pushing his collar open, taking a small moment to place a feathery kiss on Oliver's temple. The hairs on Oliver's neck stood up, making him want to tip his neck aside for more of the same, but he took a deep breath and didn't move and waited till Jack sat back, smiling at him.

Jack took off his own boots and kerchief, and his blue waist-coat besides, while Oliver thumbed through the pages, noting the slightly worn edges, the thumb stains from a cup of tea, perhaps, or a splash of something else. The book had been well read and well loved, but he didn't let himself think about how the original owner might miss it. It was Oliver's now.

"C'mon," said Jack. He lay down next to Oliver and arranged himself, using the whole of the pillow. He pulled the pie onto his stomach, wedging the bottle of brandy between them. "Don't hold back; if you're goin' to read, then read."

There was enough light to see by streaming in through the grit-dappled windows. Oliver opened *The Arabian Nights* and turned to the first chapter, and tracing his finger down the page to settle it, began to read about Scheherazade and her stories about the jinn and magic lamps and mystical, faraway places.

At first, his voice was shaky and rough. But then, between bites of pie that Jack handed to him, and mouthfuls of brandy, supplied to Oliver's mouth by Jack with care so as not to splash on the pages, it smoothed out to the tones that Aunt Rose would praise when he would stand in the parlor on a Sunday and read stories from the Bible.

As Oliver read, the words enchanted him with images of desert hills dappled with glowing stones and deep caves of secrets and adventure, and turbaned Moors sitting on fine wool rugs with the frankincense-scented smoke from gold-bound lamps settling on their shoulders. From there, the tale continued, and all the while, Jack ate most of the pie and half the brandy, continuing to feed Oliver and giving him swallows from the bottle, as he remembered. Then, with a satisfied sigh, Jack sank even lower, and curled on his side, his head resting on Oliver's belly, an idle hand draped across Oliver's thigh.

Eventually, Jack began to breathe through his open mouth and fell asleep. The sight of him, the relaxed slope of his shoulders, the contented curl of him on the bed, made Oliver's eyes droop and want to close. And that, added to the effects of the brandy and the last of the rabbit pie, made him want to put the book down and curl up next to Jack. So he did.

He put the bottle on the floor, as there was still some brandy left, and put the pie on the floor next to the bottle. Reaching out, he curved his arm around Jack's shoulders and pulled him close, putting his head down on the pillow, pulling the blanket over them both.

He did not let himself think it was the middle of the day and that most of the world was at work, being useful, being industrious. Besides, none of that mattered. He was here, with Jack, on a rainy afternoon, lazy and adrift with thoughts of a faraway land contained within the worn binding of a stolen book.

## ❧ 35 ❧

# AN UNPROPITIOUS
# INTERRUPTION BY CROMWELL
# AND THE RESULTS THEREOF

When Oliver woke, Jack was already sitting up, shirt half-jumbled around his waist. He was taking a long swallow of the brandy, and when he offered the bottle to Oliver, Oliver at first shook his head. It was bad enough to sleep away the day, but to drink it away as well? But then, they'd already done that. What of it? So he held out his hand and took the bottle and, indeed, finished it off. Jack took it from him and then put it on the floor with a clunk.

There was shouting at the door, and the wooden panels shuddered under the banging. Jack got up, pulling his shirt straight, checking the buttons on his trousers as he went to get the door. As the door opened, Oliver thought the better of them admitting they were within, but it was too late. Cromwell stood there, broad shoulders filling the doorway, looking rough and dressed for the weather.

"I'm 'ere, as you see," he said, smiling with his teeth. "An' now you're goin' to work for me."

"I told you," said Oliver. The blanket scratched across his arms, bringing back sleep-dappled memories of Jack, half-awake, petting Oliver's hair as he might a cat. There had been softness and, again, pleasure from Jack's hands to spread on the sheet,

473

made even more welcome by the brandy in his head. But now the brandy chased itself unpleasantly in his stomach. "I'm no thief."

"An' he ain't," said Jack. He found his boots on the floor and put them on, as if to regard some semblance of modesty, though Oliver suspected it was merely because it was chilly. Or, even more likely, because there was nothing Jack could do about Cromwell, and it made him nervous. "He can do other things, scholarly things. Or—"

"I'll 'ave him stealin'," said Cromwell. He didn't come closer, but then, he didn't have to. "Hell, I'll 'ave you *both* up on charges of sodomy. That's still an 'anging offense, ain't it?"

In spite of his attitude, that of carelessly buttoning up his waistcoat, arranging his clothes, as if Cromwell was of no account, Jack's face went chalk white.

"Or maybe it's castration an' deportation, I can never remember which."

Cromwell bent to pick up Jack's jacket and handed it to him. Jack took it with a snap, his hands shaking.

"Make up your mind, then, Cromwell," said Oliver evenly, with a calmness he didn't feel, because he was uncertain as to whether or not they had committed actual sodomy.

Certainly, either of those punishments would suit the crime they had, between them, committed. But whether their crime was worse than the fact that Noah had run straight to Cromwell with the news of what was between Oliver and Jack, he didn't know. What he couldn't bear was to see the way Jack, normally a bright spark no matter how gloomy the weather, was standing. Cringing, really, his shoulders drawn, as Cromwell watched him finish dressing.

"An' you mind your mouth, orphan," Cromwell snapped. He made a fist and pointed his thumb at Oliver, shaking it at him as if it was meant to be a threat. "I'll come up with somethin' you're good at, you see if I will. A lad as pretty as you, there's all kinds of ways you can be useful to me. An' if you don't, why—"

"Cromwell," said Jack. "I'll talk to him, like I said I would. I will, if only—"

"See that you do." With a jerk of his head, Cromwell left the room, leaving a trail of his smoky sweat behind and slamming the door after him.

In the silence, Jack picked his hat up from the floor and ran his fingers along the brim. He wouldn't look at Oliver.

"What did you mean, like you said you would?" Oliver tugged on his shirt, his fingers becoming tangled with the red woolen scarf, which had fallen down upon the mattress.

"Get dressed, Nolly," said Jack. "Just get dressed. I only said that I'd talk to you, not that I'd make you."

"Make me what? Steal?"

"Well, yes," said Jack, looking at Oliver now, though hesitating to hold Oliver's gaze for long. He came over to the bed and sat on the blanket, making it harder for Oliver to move away since Jack was sitting on one of Oliver's sleeves now as well. "What else could you do but what I do?"

"I've told you," said Oliver, muffled, as he tugged hard enough to pull the sleeve away from Jack.

He did up the buttons on his collar, his fingers noting the missing ones, and sighed. It was happening already; Jack's world was taking him in, and there seemed nothing that Oliver could do about it. But it wasn't Jack's fault, for all his expression said that he was aware that Oliver would be resistant. To Jack, this was the world, and if Oliver was with him, then why wouldn't he want to be a part of it?

Jack pulled Oliver's trousers from beneath the bed, along with one of his stockings. Oliver put his feet over the edge of the bed to pull them on, then put his bare feet on the floor, rolling and unrolling the stocking between his hands.

"I'm not meant to be a thief," Oliver said finally, to the stocking, his hands, the floor. Anywhere than to Jack, who would be very disappointed to find out that this was so.

"It'll just be a few times," said Jack. "To satisfy Cromwell, then you'll have some brass an' you can be off."

"I can be off anyway," said Oliver. "I walked seventy miles from Hardingstone to London with only a penny in my pocket, as you'll recall. I imagine I can do the like again." He felt cold and there was a chill in his throat. He and Jack had come, once again, to this particular crossroads, and for no man but Jack would Oliver even deign to discuss it. "But I can't stay in London, there's nothing here for me now."

Jack moved as if to get away, scrabbling around on the floor to find Oliver's other stocking.

"Besides," said Oliver, taking the stocking. "Stealing's a crime and a sin."

"Other things're a crime an' a sin, but that don't seem to bother you none." Jack came up to Oliver and tossed his hat on the bed. He stood close to Oliver's knees until Oliver looked up at him. "A crime an' a sin," said Jack again, his green eyes hard.

"But you and I, we're not hurting anybody," said Oliver, somewhat shocked that Jack, like Cromwell, would think to use the intimacy between them to convince him. "And we're not taking anything from anybody."

"But rich people deserve to be taken," said Jack, earnest, as though glad of the change of subject, gesturing to the window as if to indicate the wide world beyond it. "They deserve it!"

"Just because someone is rich doesn't mean they deserve to be stolen from." Oliver didn't bring up Uncle Brownlow because this wouldn't convince Jack in the slightest.

"Well, some, yes, like your old gentleman," said Jack, surprising Oliver with this insight. "But what I mean is those rotters who walk around with their noses in the air an' won't trouble themselves to toss a penny to a beggar, them's who I mean."

Oliver couldn't speak, for he was one of those. Not rich as a king, no, but not willing to give a beggar a penny, not willing to pay the street sweepers, not willing to hand out even a crust of bread.

"Ain't there a one?" asked Jack now, insistent. "One among them rich folk, so rich an' mean that they might deserve to have something lifted? Cromwell never goes to the same place twice, but it would teach 'em. Surely you could come up with someone to give him."

Unwillingly, as he got up from the bed to get his boots from where they were by the door, Oliver thought of Mrs. Acton. Of her fine gowns and grasping arms. Of the tea set, all over silver. And of her cruelty to him. She could have taken his rejection with much more grace, seeing as there were plenty of young men in London who could dream of being in her lush parlor and, later, lolling in her bed among her perfumed sheets.

"Well, then?" Jack urged Oliver to sit back on the bed, while he knelt at Oliver's feet and put his boots on him and did his laces, looking up into Oliver's face with bright, hopeful eyes. "You see? You've thought of someone, haven't you?"

Oliver shook his head, but it wasn't to disagree with Jack. More, it was his surprise Jack had seen, so easily, the wicked thoughts in Oliver's head. Mrs. Acton didn't deserve to be stolen from any more than Uncle Brownlow had, or even any more than Mr. McCready, because while Mrs. Acton had been cruel, cruelty wasn't the same as being dishonest.

Oliver reached out to touch Jack's face but withdrew the tender gesture at the last moment.

"He won't want to stop at one victim," said Oliver. "I had the whole of London to deliver to; I know a good many places with silver plate and more besides."

"That you do," said Jack, as he stood up, trying not to smile and failing.

It was in the flash of his eyes, the snap of his smile as to how pleased he was by this turn of events. Oliver didn't have the heart to say, once again, that he was leaving London as soon as he was able. Because in Jack's mind, his desire for Oliver to stay would be more than enough to make it happen.

Jack pulled on his coat as he reached for his hat. With a quick grace, he took up Oliver's coat and hat as well.

"I'm ready," he said.

Of course, Jack was ready; Jack was ready to steal day and night, and Oliver knew that, had always known it. Jack would never stop, and for Oliver to expect him to was madness.

~

WHEN THEY WENT DOWN TO THE MAIN ROOM WITH THE intention of having a pint or two of beer in their alcove, Cromwell appeared, as he always seemed to do, and gestured for them to follow him back to his room beneath the arched ceiling with its smoky beams.

"Don't you forget, pretty one," said Cromwell, snarling, "that castration is just a-waitin' for you, the second you think to cross me."

Oliver felt a rush of fear slithering through him at the thought of it. He looked at Jack as Jack looked at him, wary. Of course, Jack knew Oliver would never peach, but he seemed uncertain whether Oliver could protect him from the surgeon's knife or another trip across the ocean, or indeed, whether Oliver would cut and run, right then and there, leaving Jack to his own fate.

Knowing he could make a decision for this moment only, Oliver nodded and walked down the passageway beneath a ceiling that lowered, the white plaster shading darker with soot, Cromwell close on his heels. Once in the small room, Cromwell gestured Oliver should sit across from him; for Jack, there was no chair. Cromwell pushed a scrap of paper and a stub of lead across the table.

"You only need give me one name, from all of your deliveries that Jack said you was on," said Cromwell. "Just write down an address for us to go to. Of course, you'll come with us, but we just need a lookout, is all."

If Oliver had known Cromwell better, he'd say that his tone was coy. And besides, with a man like that, like Cromwell, and like Jack, there was always a lie behind a deceptive truth. Oliver tried to think of a way to say no with a gentleman's grace, although he wasn't sure why he was trying to be polite to a thief.

"You're going to give me that address," said Cromwell, as level and assured as if he'd been speaking to a willing accomplice. "And then you me an' Jack, we're goin' on an inside job, a little bit of breakin' and takin', if you see what I mean. You could be the lookout for 'im, an angel, like."

From where he stood by the wall, Jack looked at Oliver. The expression in his eyes was guarded, dark hair falling over his forehead as he looked away, forced, it seemed, to keep silent. Oliver felt an ache in his heart at the sweetness there that only he could see. This was no way to live, but Jack didn't know any better. Didn't want to know any better.

"C'mon, Nolly," said Jack in the silence, as if it was up to him to make this happen. He pulled himself upright against the wall, shoulders back as he put his hat on and tipped his head back to settle the hat on his head.

"Safe as houses," Jack said, looking at Oliver directly. "All you have to do is stand watch, an' if the peelers come, you whistle. So say yes; you'll be bored witless else." He reached out to hand Oliver his coat and hat. "Say you will. Then, when we come back, you can read to me some more."

Out of the corner of his eye, Oliver could see Cromwell's eyebrows go up, but Jack was only looking at Oliver, so Oliver shut his mouth into a firm line. He felt less panicked than he ought to have, given that this was a line over which he could only cross once. But then he nodded. Being the lookout for a crime wasn't actually a crime. Was it?

"I'm only giving you one name," said Oliver sternly as he looked at Cromwell, knowing his pride had lied to him that he might have been able to give some other answer. "And it will be someone who might deserve it because I can't stand by and watch you take from someone good."

Oliver took the paper and stub of lead and wrote Mrs. Acton's address in careful script. He ignored the fact that if anyone were to acquire this particular piece of paper with Oliver's handwriting, it would lead directly to Oliver, and there would be no stopping the hanging that had long been foretold for him.

But as Oliver pushed the piece of paper across the table, trepidation becoming thick in his heart, Cromwell just laughed and ordered some beer and food for them.

"It's on me, fellows, so eat 'earty."

Cromwell waved to someone in the passageway, and a man came and whispered in Cromwell's ear, taking the paper and going back down the hall without a word or even a glance in Oliver's direction.

Doreen came with a platter laden with pots of beer and a plate of cuts of cold meat and slices of bread and cheese.

"Come then, Jack, that's a dour face you've got on," said Cromwell with a gesture at the table. "'Ave some beer to take it away."

There was no place for Jack to sit, making him a tense accomplice to the meeting that had mainly been between Oliver and Cromwell. But he took up a pot of beer and drank, as if this were any other evening and their intended activity merely the normal course of things.

"My friend there has gone to scout out the 'ouse," said Cromwell, "because I like to know where I'm goin', as you may as well know. Besides, I ain't the type to sit on a job, unlike some. I like to get in, grab, an' then get out. It's fast, an' that's safe, an' just you remember that." He pointed at Oliver with his beer pot in his hand, sloshing the suds over his knuckles. "So drink up."

Oliver drank some of his beer and took a piece of bread to eat, knowing that the beer on an empty stomach would make him dizzy and short-tempered. The afternoon's sleep he and Jack had shared, though, had left him wide awake even with the light along the corridor from the main room was dimming in angles and shadows along the floor.

They waited more till the beer was drunk, and Jack, propped up along the wall, looked as though he were about to fall asleep. Oliver's legs had gone numb from sitting so still for so long, and his thoughts moved slowly through a beer-induced haze. Cromwell dozed while looking into the dregs of his beer. Then, there was a motion along the passageway, and Cromwell stood up.

"Drink, drink!" Cromwell said.

He clapped Oliver on the back and made a gesture that Jack and Oliver should follow him. Which they did, clattering down the narrow corridor and through the busy tavern into the damp, chilly night. There was a mist coming down, laced with bitter fog, but it wasn't snowing, wasn't anywhere near as cold as it had been.

If spring was coming, which it was, then whatever Oliver earned on this job, he'd take with him when he left the City. This would be his only job and he would tell no one. He'd make sure Jack wouldn't tell anyone either. Cromwell wouldn't tell anyone, so that was that.

THEY TREKKED THROUGH THE DANK STREETS, WHICH WERE dark and almost devoid of traffic. They skirted any lamps, staying to the shadows, keeping to the walls of the Old City, ducking beneath curved and crumbling archways while the water dripped down on them. At first, while his heart hammered, Oliver considered they might be going the wrong way toward the river. But as they went uphill, and he recognized Grey's Inn Gardens, he realized they were going north.

When they crossed Little James Street, he knew they were

headed in the right direction, though, truly, it was the wrong direction, and when they got to Doughty Street and slipped into the back alley, he knew, deep down inside, that he couldn't go through with it.

"I've changed my mind," said Oliver. "We can't rob this house."

Whether it was Mrs. Acton's house or another, this fine, graceful building in this pleasant neighborhood of terraced dwellings was not meant to be stolen from. But his second thoughts, however delayed, were smashed when Cromwell grabbed his jacket and pushed him against the damp wall.

"You chose this bitch for a reason, slammed down the address like a tinker's plug." Cromwell's breath smelled like onions. "You know the inside, you know your way around—"

"I'm not going in," said Oliver, hissing. "I'm not."

"You will," said Cromwell. His face was only inches from Oliver's, glittering with rain. "You *will* come in with us. You'll show us the right stairs that'll take us directly to the silver. Unless you want to stand 'ere in the street an' wait for the peelers to find you."

Cromwell's additional threat, that of turning them both over to the courts for sodomy, went unspoken. Oliver's mouth fell open; he tasted the rain on his lips as he looked over at Jack. Jack merely shrugged because, of course, none of this was under his control.

"So you will come in," said Cromwell. He grabbed Oliver by the lapels and pulled him even closer. "You will, as it will be better for Jack if you do. Safer for 'im if 'e knows what to contend with when 'e goes in there, which he will if you're with 'im."

Oliver felt the heat in his face. It was as if Cromwell knew what was in his head, his heart. Knew the key, then, the hook, to get him to do what was wanted, was to use Jack as leverage. Fagin had never used Jack against him, but then, it might not have worked back then, anyway. Oliver struggled in Cromwell's grasp, his shirt rucked, his neck exposed to the rain, but it was a flutter of movement only, a protest meant to make a point that Cromwell would never understand.

"We have to go in through the kitchen area," said Oliver, finally. "The stairs to the ground floor are to the left. She has three, no, four servants. As for what you want, it's on the sideboard on the ground floor."

The articles, the object of their crime, silver and polished and valuable, were always out to show how stylish Mrs. Acton was.

"Showy," said Cromwell. He let Oliver go, and pulled a narrow, leather-bound case from an inside pocket of his coat.

When they went skulking down the stairs to the kitchen area, Cromwell took some spiked tools from the case and went to work on the lock on the narrow door. The door opened with a click, and Cromwell and Jack slipped inside, leaving Oliver in the dank area, alone for a moment, with the rain coming down and the full darkness like a cloak overhead.

He couldn't imagine that a constable would come around the block. Then again, Oliver didn't know; he had never before paid attention to the patterns the law made as they went about their rounds. But in that second, he could see it. If you watched the constables on their beat, you could figure out where they weren't likely to go and then go there, to that dark place beneath a constable's vision. And that was the way Jack saw things.

But he, Oliver, didn't want to see it that way, nor live a life full of thoughts of evasion and trickery, didn't want to be skulking about when nice people, law-abiding citizens, walked in the light of broad thoroughfares and took the omnibus and paid their fares and purchased goods at a store, and were regular. Ordinary.

Except his heart was beating like a drum against his breastbone as he waited in the dark, his eyes widening to every sound, hearing the hum and clatter of the traffic from a nearby street, feeling it in his stomach. He was helping while Jack robbed someone, and giving in to Cromwell's threats, and all to punish a woman who had done badly by Oliver. While it was a crooked justice, it was justice. And it was a far cry from the time he'd watched Jack and Charley rob Uncle Brownlow of a very fine silk handkerchief; this time, he knew what they were doing, and he was *helping* them do it.

Just then, Cromwell reached through the open door and grabbed Oliver by his rain-spattered lapels and yanked him in so hard that his teeth clicked together. The wickedness of it tasted like copper on his tongue, and his whole body was tight, the blood humming in his veins as he trod softly through the dark, warm kitchen and up the wooden stairs behind Cromwell. Jack was already at the landing, a hemp sack in his hand, standing there, quite calmly, it seemed, in the darkness, as if he were on an everyday errand.

Oliver's whole body started at the shock of it, at the sight of *his* Jack, functioning in the law-breaking world that he knew best, in his element, calmly unrolling a sack.

Jack looked up as Oliver came up the stairs, showing a flash of white smile, ready to steal. And though no words came forth, and Oliver's heart was bursting in his chest, it wasn't right to see Jack like this; there should always be a curtain, however shadowed, between Oliver and Jack's world. But that was gone, permanently gone, and when Cromwell gave Oliver a shove, Oliver went, leading the way to the main parlor where the silver was.

It didn't take them long to load up their sacks. The silver plates and the enormous teapot glinted in the gaslights from the street before they were jammed into the bag, with wads of linen handkerchiefs and some points of lace stuffed between each item to keep them from clanging together. Oliver's mouth went dry as he took the silver creamer, now washed and clean, and put it in the sack.

Now there was no backing out of the fact that he was complicit, because he himself had assisted in the theft. He could have stood by, complaining and praying as he was wont to do, and had done in the past, but no. He was standing beside Cromwell, watching Jack, who opened the drawer to find the silver teaspoons and little butter knives, also silver. And the round, copper-gilt butter plate with its cunning curved lid and dozens of other items, all in pure silver.

Oliver had never seen Jack like this before, so calm, self-possessed, fingers nimble, so steady and so sure. And he wasn't sure that he should feel proud, but he did, even though what Jack was doing was so wrong.

Jack was concentrating, a somber expression in place as all the silver things went in the sack, and a few in Cromwell's pockets besides. When Cromwell flicked Oliver on the back of the neck, Oliver was jolted out of the spell, like a blind man coming to sight.

"Time to go, dreamer," hissed Cromwell. "I knew you'd never be as bad at this as Jack always claimed."

Whether or not Oliver should be insulted, he didn't know. Nor did he have time to contemplate the matter, as there was a rustle of feet from upstairs.

Jack hauled him by his collar to race down the stairs to the kitchen, across the flagstone floor, and out the door. Cromwell took a moment to lock the door behind him, which, as Oliver could see, would give the mistress of the house, and the peelers, if they were called, some confusion as to what had happened. Nothing had been knocked over or broken or damaged. It was only by the light of the morning, or by a dozen candles, if someone was awake enough to light them, that the Acton household would discover all that was missing.

Oliver's heart raced, as though with pleasure from one of Jack's kisses. His mouth open, he tasted the rain as he ran after Cromwell and Jack. Cromwell suddenly stopped, making both Jack and Oliver jostle on his heels as they neared the corner of the block. Oliver could hear footsteps, the steady tread of a constable on his beat.

As Oliver rubbed his mouth with the back of his hand, Cromwell stopped and handed him the hemp sack, inside of which the bits of silver dully clanged.

"'Ere, you, look sharp."

Cromwell's hands were on him, turning him back the way they'd come. When Oliver looked over his shoulder, Jack was already walking in the other direction, away from Oliver, as calm as could be.

"No, don't look, don't look at him. Just walk it, walk it through. If someone stops you, say you're on an errand for your gran or whatnot. With that face, well, they won't even think of stoppin' you."

Oliver's hands were shaking so badly, and blurred darkness began to swallow Jack, whose footsteps were fading away in the dark. Oliver dropped the sack at Cromwell's feet, making the silver jump and clang, accompanied by the high sound of crystal breaking.

"I can't carry it," said Oliver, dancing back as Cromwell reached out to throttle him. "I *can't*."

He couldn't explain it, not even if he tried, not with his very breath leaving him, his heart clenching at the thought of it, the truth of it. If Jack had remained at his side, he would have been able to do it, but without him, it was impossible.

Without a word, Cromwell picked up the sack and gave Oliver a shove toward the gas lamps in the other direction from Jack. Then he disappeared into the darkness, taking the hemp sack with him.

Oliver was already walking, his heart pounding. He'd assisted in stealing goods from Mrs. Acton's house. He'd objected, but he'd still done it. Cromwell was taking the stolen silver in another direction, and Oliver was the last person anyone would suspect, so he was going to get away with it. The thudding against his breastbone was so hard he thought his chest would break open, rend him into bits right there on the street. And still he kept walking.

His thoughts of Jack, walking along the darker streets of London somewhere, wove in and out of his head as he walked past Little James Street until he got to the paving stones of King's Road. He was about to head downhill until he got to the Three Cripples, but just as he was about to turn left, he felt someone touch his shoulder from behind.

When he turned, it was a constable with a bull's-eye lantern. He was dressed in impeccable blue wool and a shiny black top hat. He was sturdy and tall and looked down at Oliver, holding his lamp high to spread the light better.

"Why are you going down that way, young fellow? It gets dark down there, not a very nice place, you see."

Oliver was having the same feeling as when Jack and Charley had stolen the handkerchief that day, so long ago. Oliver had been trembling and shaking when Uncle Brownlow had turned and shouted *stop, thief,* and Oliver had been the only boy in sight. But then, there was Jack, in Oliver's mind's eye, heading down another street, hands empty, innocent as a rose.

"I'm on my way to see my grandmother," he said, his voice coming out a bit higher than he thought it should as he told the lie. "To pay her a visit, with her being so ill and all. The cholera, Mother says. Her house is right there."

Oliver pointed to a row of houses, several of which had a light in the window. The constable might know whether or not an elderly woman lived in any of them, but it was something.

"I'm going just there," Oliver said. "Not much farther. Grandmother expects me, and then Mother wants me back directly, you see."

It wasn't just the lie that had his pulse racing, it was the easy way that the lie was taken as truth, and this in spite of the fact he'd beaten Noah any time he'd called Oliver's dead mother's reputation into question. Oliver hoped she would forgive him. Fagin had always said that Oliver's face would be his fortune, and now, yes, he was right. After years of hearing, here, now, was proof. Beneath his skin, something lurched, something dark and slippery, coming up to the surface, tasting bitter, but oh, how easily it was sliding through his veins.

"I must be going, sir," he said. "Grandmother is waiting for me."

"I see," said the constable. He waved his lamp at the paving stones. "Well, mind how you go, it gets uneven along here. Going downhill."

There was something in the way he said it that made Oliver watch as the constable walked off, and he realized he was right. That Oliver was going downhill, in more ways than one. That his first step onto the London road, back, oh, so many years ago, when he'd run away from Sowerberry's shop full of black coffins, had been downhill.

It occurred to him he might have been better off taking Gamfield's offer of being a climbing boy. At least then he would have found honest work. His face would have been permanently stained with coal dust, no one would have thought he was pretty, and he could have slunk into his life without being pulled this way and that. Gamfield would have beaten him, to be sure, but that would have been it. In that life, at least, there would not have been this horrible crossroads constantly demanding which way he would go.

But now, he'd ended up this way, doing *this*. That he'd gotten away with it this time was obvious. That he could again, also, yes, he could. And could keep doing it.

He kept walking, thinking these dark and unpalatable thoughts, his feet taking him directly to the Three Cripples, where the lights shone through the dirty windows and the door opened to present Jack to him., Jack in his shirt and unbuttoned blue waistcoat, the sleeves rolled up on his arms. Smiling, pipe between his teeth, smoke swirling away in the cold air.

Oliver's conundrum was still there, but Jack was also there, real and alive, and bursting with joy that sparked out of his eyes like warm lights on a cold river.

"Shall we eat somethin'?" asked Jack.

With a flourish, he made some men move from their spot in the alcove where the fire gleamed and vibrated with heat, and Oliver let himself be seated on the bench by the wall. Jack sat there next to him, a warm barrier between Oliver and the rest of the room.

Oliver had committed a crime. He'd committed a very serious crime, and no one was chasing him. He was going to get away with it. He was a criminal. Again. Yet. *Still.*

"We'll wait, an' Cromwell will bring us our share," said Jack.

He waved to one of the girls to bring some beer, and though Oliver felt he couldn't manage a single swallow, when the dented pot was handed to him, he drank half of it down with one gulp. With a shaking hand, he wiped his mouth with the back of his coat sleeve and looked at Jack, who smiled back at Oliver, green eyes glinting, mouth moist with beer, as though he'd not a care in the world.

"You did well, Nolly," said Jack. "I knew you'd do good once you got goin'. Told Cromwell it was the better idea than tryin' to make you walk the streets, sellin' yourself."

"You spoke to him about me, about this." Oliver wished he were more surprised that Jack would have ideas about who and what Oliver should be.

"I did, but only in passin'," said Jack. He took a long draw on his pipe. The smoke oozed out of the clay stem, draping Jack, ashes lighting on the rim. "Told him you was too fancy for rough work but that you were an educated man, an' we can always use one of them."

"I won't do it again, Jack." Oliver looked at the rough crowd, boots stomping on the floor, the drink spilling, the smell from the cesspits rising through the movement of bodies. It was appalling to think of the rest of his life being made up of what he saw before him. "I don't want to live like this."

"Yes, you do," said Jack as he reached out to touch Oliver's cheek where it was flushed with the heat from the room. Then Jack puffed on his pipe for a moment, spilling out smoke that traced its way across his skin. "Think of it this way. Mrs. Acton can afford more of what was taken. As well, no one was hurt, so why are you bothered about it?"

"It's still wrong."

Oliver's heart was beating hard now; he wanted Jack to understand just how wrong it was, but Jack never would. To Jack, that was how the world went, and Oliver had just better go along with it because this was his world now. Which was what was tearing at him; it was not the one he wanted. He wanted a good place, with clean streets and decent people; a tidy bookshop in a tree-dappled court, and books to read.

On that long-ago day, in front of the bookshop where Uncle Brownlow browsed, and just before the chasing had started, and the rest of it, there had been a moment. A deep, still moment where Oliver had seen into the windows of the bookshop, and had realized how it could be. How he wanted it to be.

He opened his mouth to protest all of it, Jack's ideas of how it should be and Oliver's place in it, when Jack pulled the pipe away from his mouth. He dipped his head and put his hand on Oliver's arm.

"I know it's not the dream that you've had in that pretty head of yours, Nolly," said Jack, in a very low voice.

Jack's face was close, the breath of smoke a bitter taste on Oliver's tongue.

"We'll steal books, you see. I'll teach you how. An' we'll collect a whole great many, an' then find some old, empty place, an' we'll take it over. We'll paint a sign over the door, *Nolly's Books*, an' you'll have your place. An' when I'm not workin' the streets, I'll come payin' a call, an' tease you from your work. It'll be fine, Nolly, you'll see."

The breath in Oliver's throat choked him with the utter loss of it. He would never be able to explain to Jack that a good bookshop, the *right* kind of bookshop, wasn't full of stolen books, wasn't situated in some disused place that no one wanted. It must be a new place, and well cared for and freshly painted

490

and full of books that Oliver had picked out with particular care. It should be a place that people wanted to come to, not some dark, back-alley room that smelled, where the roof leaked, and all those mean conditions that Jack considered normal were present.

Oliver's impulse to bury his face in his hands was stayed by the look in Jack's eyes, the open, almost soft expression on his face. To Jack, the picture that he painted was the very idea of coming up in the world.

"It'll happen, by-and-bye," said Jack.

Jack lifted his hand to trace a line on Oliver's forehead, quite gently, then pulled out his deck of cards and began flicking them through his fingers, as if everything were settled between them.

"I need to leave London, Jack," said Oliver. He tried to say it to that place inside of Jack where he imagined someone good and decent existed. "Come with me."

"No," said Jack. He sat back, breaking the hope in Oliver's heart. "You're far too somber for someone who's just had a great success. Doreen!"

Jack half stood and waved to a girl, one who was not Doreen, but who nodded at Jack and stomped away to get them more beer.

"Gin and water," said Oliver, thinking that Jack wouldn't hear him.

But Jack stood up and shouted, "Gin and water!" across the room, making several heads turn to look at them till Oliver tugged on his jacket and made him sit down again.

They weren't going to discuss it. Oliver needed to leave London, but Jack wouldn't go. It would kill Oliver if he stayed, but it would break his heart to leave. So, in light of this, he lingered at the crossroads deep within him.

OLIVER WAS ON HIS SECOND GIN AND WATER, WITH ENOUGH sugar to make it as sweet as tea and enough gin to make the room seem warm and pleasant. Cromwell came into the alcove, his shoulders filling the doorway and blocking some of the movement and din behind him.

"A fine evenin', gentlemen," Cromwell grunted at them as he sat down across from them without being asked. He loosened his grease-spotted neckerchief and took Jack's beer and swallowed it all without taking a breath. "Though I ought to give your friend 'ere the back of my 'and for droppin' the bag in the street like that an' leavin' me to carry it, I've got your take, less my cut, of course."

"Of course," said Jack, nodding.

There was not even a twitch across Jack's forehead to show that he was the least bit interested in why Cromwell had carried the sack of silver rather than Oliver. Instead, he concentrated on the table before him, clenching his pipe between his teeth as he swept the cards together, piling them into a stack. The edges of the four and two of clubs stuck out from the edges of the other cards, as they always did, slightly larger than the rest.

"There's a fiver between the two of you," said Cromwell.

He pushed a folded paper bill across the table at them, covering the bill with his grimy fingers until Jack took it up beneath his palm, as if it were a code passing between them.

"There's more of that, if your friend 'ere can come through." Cromwell jerked his head in Oliver's direction. "If 'e can stand to make a list of the other places 'e delivered, what sort of makeup they 'ad."

Oliver's whole body stiffened, fighting against the laxness created by the gin. He looked at Jack. Jack gave a shake of his head and took a draw on his pipe.

"He won't say yes," said Jack. "But then, he won't say no, either. Will you, Nolly?"

After a shocked moment, Oliver realized he was thinking of it. That it was in him to give Cromwell Mr. McCready's address.

492

To tell him where the money from the till was kept until the end of the week, when Mr. McCready would take it to the bank. Where Mrs. Pierson kept the money she got from selling grease. Even to the chests in the attic where the boys slept and where they kept their pay packets. The silver knives and forks in the drawer. The old Bible, which might be worth something to somebody.

"Perhaps," said Oliver, even though he knew he could never give out the addresses of people who didn't deserve it. Stealing from Mrs. Acton had been one thing, but he couldn't do that to Mrs. Pierson. He didn't want to become that kind of man, regardless of how satisfying it had been to teach Mrs. Acton a lesson.

Cromwell seemed unaware of Oliver's internal duplicity, and was mollified by Oliver's reply. He nodded as he got up and winked at Oliver before he turned and walked back out into the main room. His broad form was swallowed up by the press of bodies, the churn of brown coats and boots, the splash of beer, dull sounds from far away.

"I won't do it," said Oliver. He spoke to the table, trying not to raise his voice. Jack couldn't help who he was, but Oliver *could* help the direction his own life would take.

"I know," said Jack. The back of his hand knocked against Oliver's, pushing the five-pound note into Oliver's palm. "Take the money, keep it safe. We'll use it to buy books so you won't fret so about the sin of stealin' 'em. I don't want you lookin' at me like the world has ended; you'll get your pretty face frozen lookin' like that."

Oliver took the bill, folded the thin paper, and tucked it in his trouser pocket, tilting his head as Jack touched Oliver's cheek with the back of his hand.

"Now," said Jack, taking the last swallow of his beer. "Drink up your gin, and we can rejoin to upstairs."

Of course, Jack meant *adjourn* or *repair* or something like it, but Oliver didn't have the spirit to correct him. But he got up, just the same, slugging back the last mouthful of gin and sugar before following where Jack led.

Oliver's heart raced, but in a way that was more pleasant than painful as they went through the main room and up the stairs and down the narrow corridor to their room. It was gloomy and dark with no fire in the grate, but Oliver didn't need to see as Jack briskly tipped him on the bed and pushed back his shirt collar, undid the buttons.

The weight of Jack's body was on top of him, between his thighs, pressing him into the flocked mattress, with Jack's hands busy pulling his shirt out of his trousers and petting Oliver's ribs. It felt good, as gentle as soft fur, leaving shivers running through him, and he tipped his head back to let the warmth of Jack's hands, Jack's breath on his neck, soak into him. Nothing else mattered but that touch upon his skin.

"So," said Jack. He shifted to nip at Oliver's ear, and Oliver opened his mouth, waiting to feel Jack's mouth, waiting for the kiss. "If you had a list, like what Cromwell wants—"

With a snap, Oliver sat up, his head clonking Jack's chin. He shoved Jack in the chest with both hands, sending Jack tumbling from him. He heard Jack land on the floor, the scrabble of his boot heels as he picked himself up, then stood next to the bed, a grey shadow in the darkness.

"What was *that* for?"

"I already told you I won't do it, Jack. I'm not like that." Oliver's chest heaved, and his body ached with the absence of Jack. But he couldn't help that; he needed to make Jack understand how it was to be. "You say that Noah was never one of Fagin's boys, well, neither was I."

"But you—you helped out with the house tonight, an' you did a fine job."

Jack's body bent down, his knees creating a dipped weight on the bed, and Oliver could see the grey outline of him now that his eyes had adjusted to the darkness of the room. He felt Jack plant a hand on either side of him, crawling up along his body to plant a kiss on his thigh, his hip, his neck, wherever it might land.

"You hurt me to the quick, you do, sayin' you weren't one of Fagin's lads." The tone of the words was joking because Jack liked to joke, but beneath it, there was a frail shake.

Oliver reached up to take Jack's face in his hands. He kissed Jack somewhere near his mouth, and when he found his cheek, he moved his lips across skin, tasting salt and dust and the smoke from Jack's pipe. Then he pulled Jack full on top of him, enjoying the weight, the safety of Jack's body on his in the dark, Jack's legs tangled with his. The red scarf was somewhere in the blankets, tickling his neck.

"Well," Oliver said, more gently now with the pleasure of having Jack so near, of it just being the two of them in the dark, the gin holding sway, the darkness rich with the scent of Jack. "Cromwell is such a *common* thief, you see."

"Common?" Jack asked in a tone that said he wanted more of the story.

He peeled off his coat, arching above Oliver to toss it to one side. Oliver could hear him and feel him pulling his shirt out of his trousers to float loosely about them. Jack tugged Oliver's shirt over his head so he could press his mouth to Oliver's chest. Oliver let him, his skin twitching with the promise of Jack's touch.

"Common, I said," said Oliver. "A housebreaker is so terribly common nowadays, you know."

Jack grunted his confusion, rising to kiss Oliver, nipping at his mouth.

"What I mean to say," said Oliver against Jack's lips, telling the story he knew Jack wanted to hear. "That is, if we're going to be thieves, we should be highwaymen. Like Jack Sheppard."

"Who?" Jack stopped, the cloth of his shirt pressing against Oliver's bare ribs.

"I'm sure there's a book of stories about him; I'm sure you'll find one or two to steal." Oliver knew he was saying all of this to placate Jack. But it was working, so he continued with it.

"Jack Sheppard, the notorious highwayman. He robbed from the rich and gave to the poor, and ended up in Newgate. From which he *escaped*." Oliver put the emphasis on the last to make the tale a better one. "And when he was recaptured, they hanged him, and before he went, he tipped his hat to the ladies and blew kisses at the babies." The last part wasn't true; when they hanged you at Newgate, your hat was already gone. "We'll wear masks when we go out, and I'll ride a grey mare, and you a pitch-black stallion. Will that suit?"

This seemed to satisfy Jack.

"Trust you," he said, squirming so he could reach down for the buttons on Oliver's trousers. "Trust you to come up with somethin' high class like that. You an' me, highwaymen. I know how to ride a little; mayhap we could kidnap a ridin' master an' have him teach us better."

Back in Chertsey, when Oliver had been living with Aunt Rose and Uncle Harry, Oliver had ridden the pony that pulled the trap. It hadn't liked it at first, having been trained to pull rather than carry. But Oliver had softened the pony's temper with lumps of sugar and sweet carrot tops, and the two of them had spent many a sunny afternoon galloping along the fields of golden rye and under the shade of the edge of the forest, Oliver's elbows ungainly, falling off half the time. So he already knew how to ride, after a fashion, but Jack seemed to like the kidnapping part of the story; Oliver kissed him and sighed as Jack stroked his hardening sex.

"That bullet wound," said Jack, sounding a little breathless. "You were goin' to show me."

"Only when you tell me the truth about how you got your tattoo, which I have yet to see."

Oliver caught his breath as Jack's hand swept up along the inside of his thigh, the friction of wool between his skin and Jack's hand.

"It's right here," said Jack, not able to point to anything in the near dark. "I did it myself with a bit of flint when I landed in Australia."

Oliver laughed, a scoffing sound in the back of his throat. The story might often be told, but the truth of it never known, it seemed, and yet, what did it matter? Jack probably had never had a tattoo to begin with.

At the sound of Oliver's laughter, Jack jumped up and went to the mantelpiece, where he lit the candle with a single flick of a match. The smell of tallow burning in the cold, still air was strong as it floated over to Oliver. Jack came and pulled Oliver to a sitting position, standing between Oliver's knees, looking down at him.

In the yellow light and the shadows that loomed across the floor, Oliver took Jack's hand and pulled it to his left arm. He stroked Jack's fingers along the slightly ridged scar, just above the crook of his elbow. There, Jack's fingers rested while he looked at Oliver. Jack couldn't possibly know that the bullet wound was not something Oliver, readily or otherwise, ever showed to anyone. Or maybe he did, as he drew his thumb with some reverence across it.

"So," said Jack in a voice he might have used in church, were he ever to attend a service. "This is what you got that night. When Bill left you to die."

"He did carry me," said Oliver, remembering the light from the house that dimmed and shook as Bill's rough coat rubbed against his cold-numbed cheek. "As far as he could, and then he left me."

"What?" Jack had not heard this part of the story, not that Oliver had had any occasion to tell it, and his fingers tightened around Oliver's elbow. "Left you? Bleedin' and dyin' like you was?"

"He carried me as far as he could." Oliver repeated this with some insistence, thinking of Bill's voice, hoarse with panic as Crackit ran on ahead. With the dogs close behind, Bill had shouted *Damnation, how the boy bleeds!* But even in the midst of saving his own neck, Bill had not been without some consideration to a fellow thief, even an unwilling one, than to leave him in the direct path of the local law and angry citizenry.

No, Bill had wrapped something around Oliver's arm, painfully tight to slow the bleeding, and picked him up and carried him till his own sense of preservation had caused him to place Oliver in a low, damp ditch. Then, growling *Wolves take your throats* at the party pursuing him, Bill had finally abandoned him. That Oliver couldn't remember anything after that, not even crawling through the wet grass to the nearest door, didn't matter. He'd been saved, and Bill's charity had helped him, so he was grateful for it.

But he couldn't tell Jack this, not now, not when his heart was hammering, and he felt warm down the back of his neck, and his arms felt cold except for the spot where Jack was touching him, which was as hot as an iron brand from a blacksmith's forge.

"Never mind." His voice was uneven. He stood up. "It's healed now, as is, I imagine, the tattoo you've spoken of so often."

Jack let go of him and pulled his shirt over his head, letting it land with a thump on the floor. His chest was pale in the candlelight, with that slight, dark tuft of hair along the center. He didn't seem shy as he looked at Oliver, but hesitant as he looked down at himself, along his arms, his belly, his chest, where there was no tattoo nor any sign that there had ever been one.

The whole of it had been a lie, a merry chase of facts to suit the conversation, to entertain or distract, whatever was called for. The fact that Jack never once had felt chastened by any remorse nor bent to any man's scruples other than his own except for this lie, this bold, colorful lie—well, Oliver couldn't find fault in him. Instead, he stroked Jack's pale, bare, unadorned arms and smiled. Feeling glad with Jack and this one single truth between them.

"It's a beautiful tattoo, Jack; I think it suits you," said Oliver.

"Now, considering that there's no fire in the grate, I'm going to come down with the fever if I stand here in practically a state of nature."

"I'll warm you," said Jack in a reverential tone, threaded with relief, it seemed, because Oliver wasn't cross with him.

Jack moved forward, bending over Oliver till Oliver was flat on the bed, thighs spread, the pillow askew, the blanket rucked to reveal the rough ticking of the flocked mattress.

Jack pressed the weight of his body down, holding Oliver in place, kissing his mouth, sliding down to kiss his neck as he reached with his hand between Oliver's legs. He stroked Oliver roughly, the wool of Oliver's trousers between Jack's hand and Oliver's hard sex. The threads dragged as Jack's hand moved, pulling Oliver's hardness out to the chill air, making the thrum of energy building hotly along Oliver's spine sear right up into his brain. And all at once, Jack surged up and put his mouth on the scar, sucking on it, and licking the edges with his tongue. Oliver felt his whole body tighten before he spilled his seed into Jack's hand.

OLIVER DREAMED ABOUT FIVE-POUND NOTES, AND FLICKERING through that was the memory of what had happened. The bet between Uncle Brownlow and Mr. Grimwig that Oliver, with a new suit of clothes, a pile of books, and a five-pound note, would not return from his errand.

*It is a standing and very favorite joke for Mr. Brownlow to rally him on his old prophecy concerning Oliver, and to remind him of the night on which they sat, with the watch between them, waiting his return; but which Mr. Grimwig contends he was right in the main; and, in proof thereof, remarks that Oliver did not come back, after all: which always calls forth a laugh on his side and increases his good humor.*

## ❦ 36 ❧

# A DEBT OF FIVE POUNDS IS PAID

T he bells were tolling early, and they were loud enough to wake Oliver up with a start, the dream still skimming in his head. He sat up in the bed, his head ringing with the gin from the night before. He could taste Jack in his mouth, the salt and the smoke, and took a deep breath. There was something he had to do; it had come to him in his dreams: he needed to do this before he lost his nerve and before he could move forward.

As quietly as he could, he slid out of bed and got dressed. He needed to be gone before Jack found out what he was going to do; Jack would be furious in any case. He laced up his boots. Then, unable to find his own jacket, he borrowed Jack's, and Jack's top hat besides, and slipped out of the room.

He paused at the bar to down a tot of gin, and with that simmering in his veins, once out of the Three Cripples, the fresh air was like a slap in the face. It was not quite dawn, and the air was damp, smelling of manure, and old straw, and the flecks of acrid coal spilling down from above. But there was no snow, only the quiet glimmer of recent rain on the pavement, early candles from inside of windows, reflecting on the glass.

Oliver walked on, taking care to breathe calmly, and not run even when he came down the slope to the Strand. From there, he hurried, before the gin wore off and it became too late to say what he needed to say. He hurried, following the curve of the Thames along wide streets and skirting through neighborhoods where the lanes were narrow and quiet.

The sun was coming up behind a veil of clouds, and church bells were again ringing by the time he reached King's Road and turned onto Old Church Street. As bold as any delivery boy, he banged the knocker of the front door of the townhouse now owned by Mr. Grimwig, and waited in Jack's jacket, which did not quite fit, with the back of his neck bare and cold. When no one came, he banged again, and then again after that; surely someone would have heard him.

And indeed, the parlor maid opened the door. She was not as spruce as she might be, but given the hour and that it was only Oliver, no one would remark upon it.

"Can I help you—why, Master Oliver, whatever are you doing here?"

"I've come to see Mr. Grimwig. Can you roust him?" It came out more of a question than the demand he'd intended, leaving Oliver to wonder if he wouldn't be able to say what he'd come to say.

The maid hesitated, looking over her shoulder, and perhaps hearing something from within, opened the door a little wider.

"You'd best come off the street, young master, and I'll fetch him."

That she hadn't turned him away was a miracle in and of itself. That she'd called him *young master*, well, it had been ages since anyone had called him that or treated him with deference. It wasn't entirely comfortable, even as it was familiar.

Once in the front hall, the maid stepped away, leaving Oliver's eyes to track the familiar cleanliness of the hallway, the low shine of the black-and-white entryway, the spotless wooden floor of the parlor, the fine, thick white tablecloth on the table near the fireplace upon which sat a neat assembly of newspapers, perhaps only a day or so old, for Mr. Grimwig to read when he so desired it.

Before Oliver had a chance to step into the small front library, Mr. Grimwig appeared from his bedroom on the ground floor. He'd been too aged to climb stairs for some time now, and so that back bedroom was his. He'd not changed locations, it seemed, nor his habit of wearing a floor-length flannel dressing gown for most of the morning, and a nightcap of sheer white until it suited him to take it off.

As was his custom, he carried his cane, and marched on Oliver with the boldness of a much younger, more able man. When he was within one foot, he stopped.

"You will tell me your business, and being quick about it, then be upon your way, and never mind that you've disturbed an entire household." Mr. Grimwig's face was mottled and red, his eyes blazing. "Come on, out with it. Or has a life of crime abused your brain to where you can no longer speak?"

"I've come to give you this," said Oliver. He pulled the five-pound note from his pocket. "Here's your five pounds." He wanted to spit a curse and shove the fine, crinkled paper down Mr. Grimwig's throat, but he only held it out, his hand shaking.

Mr. Grimwig reached for the five pounds, his amply cuffed dressing gown falling back from his wrist. But then he stopped.

"What five pounds?" asked Mr. Grimwig.

Oliver stared at him, feeling the backs of his eyes grow hot.

"This five pounds, old man. The five pounds I was to take to the booksellers, only I was grabbed on the street and the money and the books were taken from me. *This* five pounds."

Oliver held out the bill and flicked it in the air.

"The five pounds of which you *never ceased reminding me*, day in and day out, for *years*." Oliver's voice rose to a pitch that echoed against the ceiling. "I might now be a thief, as you said I always was, but I'll be damned if I'll be charged with taking money from a much beloved guardian. So here, take it and mark it in your ledger, and never mention it to me again."

"What do you mean, you're a thief?"

Mr. Grimwig took a step back, and Oliver could see the parlormaid and the butler lingering in the hallway near the back steps.

"I've taken to thieving. I've thrown my lot in with a den of thieves, and my future income is subject to ill-gotten gains, such as this money." Oliver felt his jaw tighten as the effects of the gin began wearing away. But he'd come this far so he might as well finish it. "You were right all along, and I just thought you'd like to know it. I've lost my inheritance, thanks to you; you've probably already spent it, so what does it matter?"

The room began to tip slowly up and down, the light from the candle the maid had lit reflecting from the highly polished floor and striking the backs of his eyes.

Mr. Grimwig took a breath, his eyes narrow, and as he straightened his back, he brought a change to the room, as though a wind had swept through it.

"I've done no such thing," said Mr. Grimwig, sneering, haughty. "There have been no charges pressed against you, and so your inheritance remains intact. The money is in my care until you are twenty-one, but I, unlike you, am an honest man, and it will still be there until that day, as it ever has been."

As angry as Oliver had ever seen him, Mr. Grimwig now had righteous indignation on his own behalf. Everything he'd ever thought of Oliver had been proven true, from the first moment they'd met till this moment in Mr. Grimwig's front hallway, and yet he was stating that the money that Oliver intended for his future bookshop was still intact, still available. Oliver felt his knees give way, and he reached out to the nearest table, knocking over the candle, which snuffed itself out on the polished tile.

"What do you mean?" Oliver's voice came out in a gasp, and everything was tilting and grey before his eyes.

"It is just as I have said. I've explained it to you, did you not hear?" Mr. Grimwig waved his cane in Oliver's direction.

"Now, you're drunk, and you need to leave before I call the constable."

"Call him, then," said Oliver, snarling. "I'll be gone before he gets here."

In Mr. Grimwig's eyes was the first light of fear at the unaccustomed sight of Oliver's anger, full out and plain on his face.

"I'm leaving," Oliver said, reaching for the door knob. His fingers failed, and he was forced to clutch at the doorjamb. The five-pound note fluttered to the floor.

"And take that with you." Mr. Grimwig pointed to the note with the tip of his cane.

Oliver grabbed the foot of the cane and swung it back, intending to strike with it, but Mr. Grimwig cringed backward, throwing up his hands.

In all of Oliver's imaginings about what he might say to Mr. Grimwig were the chance offered him, he'd never thought that Mr. Grimwig would be afraid of him. If Oliver so much as twitched, Mr. Grimwig would collapse to the floor before the cane even hit him, and this, above all things, stopped him.

He thought to put the cane on the table, to lay it between them like a fallen sword, but Mr. Grimwig snatched it back from him, and grasping the long end of it, smacked Oliver with it, hard, against his shoulder. Although the blow stung, it was a far lighter blow than it ought to have been, and certainly lighter than many a blow Mr. Grimwig had delivered in the past.

Oliver stepped back and picked up the five-pound note, as he might need it to get where he was going, out of London and out of Cromwell's reach. He shoved it in his pocket, all the while aware of Mr. Grimwig's gaze and the wide-eyed stares of the servants, several more of whom had crept up from the kitchen.

"You will not darken my door ever again," said Mr. Grimwig, his jaw tight, voice shaking. "Until you are twenty-one, and even then, send someone in your stead, for I do not wish to see your face *ever* again."

Oliver turned to go and caught his reflection in the gold-gilt looking glass that hung in the front hall. It had been one he seldom used, and the odd feeling of looking into it now must have been what made the image there so unfamiliar.

The reflection showed a young man with shorn hair in a worn top hat and a gentleman's coat and tails, cut back to fit a smaller frame. The shirt, it was obvious to see, was of old muslin, and was much stained with dribbles of beer and circles of grease, as might be seen on some careless person who didn't know the use of a knife and fork, let alone a napkin. As for the face, it was streaked with soot and long marks of unwashed sweat. The only way he recognized it as being himself was because he was the only person standing in front of the mirror, and the eyes, though glittering, were still his own, and as blue as ever they had been.

Oliver's whole body felt tight; not only did he more resemble Jack Dawkins than himself, the encounter he'd imagined, with the feeling of justice, hadn't happened. Mr. Grimwig was not impressed by Oliver's attempted return of the five pounds and was even more morally indignant at Oliver's presence than he'd ever been when they'd lived under the same roof.

Shoulders sinking, his errand for naught, Oliver opened the door, the cool feel of the brass knob familiar beneath his hand, and slipped out into the silvery morning's rain.

## 37

## AND LAST: JACK AND OLIVER

He struggled as far as the corner, where winter-bare trees clustered in a triangle of muddy earth, then sank to his knees to vomit in the gutter. The smell of gin, the sour taste of it in his mouth, made him feel faint, and he had to push away from the mess on the stones before he fell into it.

The most he was able to manage was to sit on the edge of the pavement with his feet in the gutter, head resting on his knees, and his arms wrapped around. Jack's top hat fell at his feet and got knocked by a passing cart, and Oliver made himself grab it up before someone took it.

He stared at Jack's hat, twirling it, running his fingers along the begrimed brim, tracing the satin lining, worn raw to the felt in many places, and the corner of a torn-off ace of hearts jammed into the satin. It was one of Jack's trick cards, aimed at cheating, or at denouncing a cheater, whatever was called for. And all the while, a light rain fell, until Oliver was soaked through to the skin. He couldn't get any wetter or have sunk any lower.

Sighing, he made himself put the hat on and got to his feet, staggering a bit until he could catch his breath and determine the direction he needed to go. What he needed, more than a precipitous arrival at the Three Cripples, that is, before Jack awoke, was to make sense of what Mr. Grimwig had said. The inheritance from his father was intact, as long as he didn't become a criminal. And thanks to Mr. McCready's sense of duty, Oliver was not that.

Well, he was, but not charged; there was nothing on his record to implicate him; he was a free man. And when he turned twenty-one, he would be a rather well-off man, with enough funds to start that bookshop. One day.

In the meantime, he needed to get out of London before Cromwell's influence, and Jack's, the worse of the two, headed him in a direction from which there would be no return.

The thought of his inheritance stayed with him as he started on the long and weary way back to the Three Cripples, while the wind whisked light rain into his face and bits of paper across the tips of his boots. Oliver pulled up the collar of Jack's jacket; the wool lapels and silk lining smelled like Jack, and it made his heart jump.

He settled Jack's top hat firmly on his head, paused on the pavement to wait for two ladies and their maid, a hackney cab, and finally a sad-looking sandwich man to go by, and then stepped onto the cobblestones.

His shoulder throbbed as he hurried up the Strand, away from the river, away from the brisk morning activity of good, honest shopkeepers, and up Holborn Hill. Into streets where the buildings hung close, and the air pushed even closer. The sky was filled with rain now, as if the clouds had lowered and become a river's current upon the stones, flowing with as much force as if to wash everything to sea. Rain glittered on the windows and on roofs and on chimneys, unlit by coal or comfort.

By the time he got back to the Three Cripples, he was soaked through. The main room was full with the morning crowd, early risers intent on taking their breakfast in beer and spirits.

The Three Cripples was, as it ever had been, a place for the drained and ragged souls of the City to come and drink and deal and swindle with no questions asked. The whole of the area, filthy and muddy and dank, was always going to be that way, and none of Oliver's observations or protestations, albeit unspoken for the most part, would make any difference whatsoever.

He was at the bottom of the stairs when Jack came down them, thumping on the narrow treads. Noah was at his side as if nothing were amiss between them. Jack had on Oliver's jacket, swirling Oliver's fairly new hat in his hands, and when he saw Oliver there, he frowned, as though he was cross that Oliver had gone anyplace without telling him.

"Where have you been, eh?" Jack's voice was hard, but he kept it low as he reached the bottom of the stairs.

"You look ridiculous in my jacket," said Oliver, feeling cheerful in spite of Noah's presence.

"Give me that money," said Jack, brushing this aside. "We're goin' to buy breakfast, us an' Noah."

"Cromwell wants to see you," said Noah, his lips curling as if he were well satisfied with this announcement. "Sent me to bring you."

"But we can have breakfast first," said Jack. He held out his hand, and Oliver gave him the crumpled five-pound note, the movement making his shoulder ache.

"That money was for—" he began, but then looked at Jack, and shook his head. Jack's promise about the money being set aside to buy books for the bookshop didn't matter now. Any money between them was stolen money, and that was no way to start a new life, so it was best spent.

"Never mind," said Oliver, as he looked away from Jack to hide his flare of irritation that they were going anywhere with Noah. "I wouldn't mind something to eat."

"Then breakfast it is. Noah, are you game?"

They moved through the men at the bar and stepped out into the street where the air was damp and fresh, and Oliver took his first deep breath of the morning. The gin was well wearing off now. He had a headache, and he had his answer from

Mr. Grimwig: Oliver was a ne'er-do-well of the first water and would always be considered so, especially after today. Yet, Mr. Grimwig had not hit him as hard as he might, and had let him keep the five pounds and told him—

*Come back when you're twenty-one.*

It struck him anew how few years away that was, and the freedom the money would one day bring him.

Noah pulled ahead in the rainy street, skipping like a fool to avoid the puddles, which was an impossible goal. Jack lingered, his hand on Oliver's arm.

"Nolly?" asked Jack. "What is it? You look so cross."

Oliver looked at Jack, whose eyes were sweet, with damp specks across his cheeks, his oily hair hanging low over one eyebrow.

"Why are we going to breakfast with him?" Oliver asked, deciding to say something about it. He walked on, almost dragging Jack, whose hand was pulling at him as though he wanted to stop. "He peached on me, so why are we going anywhere with him?"

Jack stopped Oliver with a hard tug on his sleeve. Rain spattered on the canvas awning overhead, and there was a foul smell drifting out from a nearby gutter.

"He's the only one from the old days who knew Fagin," said Jack, all in a rush, as if he'd expected this objection. "The only one, once you leave, since you said you were goin', so what's it to you? 'Tis only one breakfast, after all."

Oliver felt this as a direct threat. That with Oliver gone, Jack would soon resort to his basest instinct and sink into the low seepage of company that was Noah Claypole, a reckless direction from whence he would never return.

But indeed, though Jack's mouth quirked up, defiant, there was a sad flicker to his eyes as he tried to look away from Oliver and couldn't. Though Jack wouldn't say it, Oliver's intention to leave was hurting him.

Oliver had to go, but instead of saying it again now, he only shook his head and started walking, pulling Jack with him, wanting only that they could carry on as if he wasn't leaving. And that Noah would go away, though neither of those was going to happen.

Jack seemed to know there was something else going on, that something had happened to Oliver in the short time he'd been away. He hung close to Oliver all the way to the nearest tavern, and when Noah stepped inside to get a table for them, Jack hung back, his hand on Oliver's arm, and regarded Oliver, his eyes wide, looking earnest and young.

"Nolly," he said, using his most convincing tone. "When you left this mornin', without me, I might add, you looked like your nearest an' dearest had expired. An' now, well, you look like you've got angels singin' in your head."

"I went to see Mr. Grimwig," said Oliver, ducking his head close to Jack's. "And my inheritance, three thousand pounds, it's still mine. That is, when I turn twenty-one."

Before Jack could do anything more than make a noise of surprise, Noah came out to get them.

"Come on, you louts, there's a table waitin' for us," he said in that bossy way he had.

The Cheshire Cheese was an old pub of dark wood, creaking floors, and coal smoke that had soaked into everything within its walls. It was crowded, as well, making them walk single file to a side room where they were seated at a table with high-backed bench seats that were nailed to the floor. The good part was that the table was directly next to a brightly burning coal fire; the heat came at them in delicious waves as they sat down.

Noah and Jack put their hats rudely on the table, and Oliver followed suit, for what did it matter now? Noah ordered coffee and bread and ham, and never counted the cost because, of course, he wouldn't be the one paying for it.

When the coffee was brought to them with their food, Noah picked up a bit of ham with the tip of his knife to bring it to his mouth, watching Oliver the whole while. Oliver took a large swallow of coffee, milky and smooth, from the cup, and licked his lips.

"You made your dear friend quite anxious, goin' off like that, Work'us," said Noah, between bites. "'E was in quite a state, sure you wasn't comin' back."

"It's all right now," said Jack, slurping hot coffee from his saucer. "He went to see Mr. Grimwig."

"Who's 'e?" asked Noah, paying more attention to the sliced ham on his plate than the details of the conversation.

"None of your damned business," said Oliver. He felt the words explode from his mouth before he could stop them.

"Mr. Grimwig's that friend of his guardian angel, the one who passed away," said Jack, more gently than Oliver had ever heard him. "Why did you go to see him?"

"To return something, only he didn't want it." Oliver put the cup of coffee down; the ham and bread were as unappetizing as dust. He now had more to live for and wasn't interested in the kind of life that stolen pennies could buy.

"The fact of the matter is," said Oliver. "I plan to leave London as soon as I am able. After I get my things."

He couldn't bring himself to look at Jack because, by things, he meant the books, all three of them, that Jack had given to him. Those were his, stolen or not. That Jack had already expressed a firm dislike of leaving London he knew; he couldn't look at Jack's face and see Jack's mouth saying the words again, denying Oliver the gift of his presence, so he didn't ask it.

"He can do exactly as he likes, now that he's got his inheritance," said Jack, into the bleak bit of silence that had fallen on the table. "It's three thousand pounds, an' all."

"Three thousand *pounds*?" asked Noah with a squawk as half-chewed food fell out of his open mouth. "A workhouse orphan like you?"

Feeling a flare of annoyance that Jack would be so free with Oliver's information, he made himself think instead on his surprise that Noah didn't know the story. But then, even if he'd been in Fagin's employ, Fagin was hardly likely to let Noah in on the arrangement Fagin had had with Monks.

"I *do* have family," Oliver said, taking some small satisfaction from that, in telling that to Noah, a mere charity boy, after all these years. "They are the Flemings, along the coast in Lyme Regis, I think, or near there. And my father did leave me money, though it's in the bank till I'm twenty-one, and I intend to—"

He stopped. It didn't matter what he intended to do. Noah wouldn't care, and Jack wasn't going with him. Oliver would leave London on his own and come back when the time came to get his inheritance. Until then, he would have to find work, honest work, maybe as a clerk in a shop, for which he had skills, in spite of having no reference from Mr. McCready.

"Well, excuse *me*, Work'us, I 'ad no idea I was dinin' with royalty."

Noah got up from the table, sending the pile of bread scattering across the tabletop. The competition was both won and lost, as it ever existed between him and Noah, and not likely to change.

When Noah was gone, and the table settled, Oliver could feel Jack staring at him.

"You goin', ain't you," said Jack. "No matter what I says."

"I can't stay, Jack, you know that. London has let me down time and again, in spite of my best intentions."

Jack looked at the table, his fingers along the edge, seeming a little lost without his pipe and cards.

"Well," said Jack, a shaky warble in the word. "If you've a mind to go, then best get it over with, before—"

Before what would never be known because Jack stood up, scattering the plates and calling for the young miss to give them their tab so he could pay her. Oliver watched as change was counted out from the five-pound note Jack gave her, and he thought about the money in the bank and how different it was from any money in Jack's pocket, which got spent as soon as it touched Jack's fingers.

Without saying anything more, he and Jack left the tavern and strode up the street beneath a sky that was peeling clouds away from the rain, and went into the Three Cripples. Something clutched hard at Oliver's throat as he climbed the stairs, Jack at his heels.

Once in the room, he pulled off Jack's jacket and top hat and lay them on the bed, hoping Jack would do the same to him without him having to ask for it. Then he pulled the books Jack had stolen for him from the mantelpiece. They were dusty with ash, as if they'd not been touched in a decade, and this alone told him he was about to do the right thing. For no book should be treated so; they should have their spines dusted and placed on their edges rather than their sides, and they should have their pages kept warm and dry—

"Here's your jacket, then," said Jack.

Jack was holding it out, and when Oliver turned to look at him, Jack's eyes were as they had been that first day, the day of Uncle Brownlow's funeral. They were flinty, difficult eyes, and contained an expression to match. They seemed to indicate that Jack didn't think much of Oliver and would soon be moving on.

It seemed a long time since Jack had first come calling, looking for Fagin's gang, and finding only Oliver.

"Thank you," said Oliver, taking the coat and hat. He tried to swallow against the thickness in his throat, but he couldn't even manage that.

"Don't waste any of your fine airs an' graces on me," said Jack. His mouth was white as he said it, and his whole body was stiff.

Oliver took the red scarf from the bed and wrapped it around the books that Jack had stolen for him, feeling defiant while Jack watched. Then he put on his own coat and hat, feeling the dampness from where the rain had soaked through, smelling Jack's scent, the smoke from his pipe, the oil from his hair. He felt as though he was choking, but there was nothing for it but to go out the door and down the stairs, with Jack clattering behind him.

The main room was full of men drinking at the bar, their bodies close and damp, creating that smell that he knew he would not miss. Not that, nor the clutter, nor the brown paint, nor any of it.

Oliver would miss Jack, even as he turned to look at Jack, and knew, deep in his heart, that Jack did not want to hear any sentiments that Oliver might care to express. Jack's expression told him that Jack wanted a quick good-bye, and that Jack would be moving on, if you please.

Oliver paused, just the same, at the door to the alcove, wanting to say something in spite of Jack. But then he saw Cromwell, with Noah at his side, coming in the front door. Noah must have told Cromwell something, for his face was dark with fury, his shoulders bunched together, and when Cromwell spotted Oliver, his hands became fists.

Oliver skirted down the passageway that led to the kitchen, thinking to go out that way. He went into the kitchen, sensing that Jack was still following him. The kitchen was empty of people but was full of dishes crusted with food and unscrubbed pots and the smell of spoiled food, old grease. There was also the din of the main room bouncing against the walls.

From behind him, he felt a pair of large hands on his neck, then his head was dashed into the doorjamb of the alcove. He lost hold of the bundle in his hands as he tried to push off the wall, but his head was spinning, and his feet couldn't quite manage to move the way he wanted them.

"That's enough. You need to learn when you've been bested," said Cromwell, somewhere behind him, ringing low, in the way of a solemn bell. "An' Jack, pick that up. You're needed as well."

With black spots filling his sight, Oliver couldn't understand who Cromwell was talking to. It couldn't be him with Cromwell's hands on his shoulders. He struggled, and Cromwell hit him again and slammed him against the wall. Sharp arcs of pain lashed through his shoulder, and he could barely stay upright as Cromwell shoved him again and finally let him go.

Oliver was unsteady as he stood in the middle of the kitchen. No one would come even if Oliver shouted; he was at Cromwell's mercy. And, of course, Noah was there, smirking from his place by the door that led to the courtyard and the alley behind the Three Cripples. That he'd come directly to Cromwell with Oliver's news about his inheritance was obvious; he probably thought he was going to get a cut of whatever Cromwell might manage to take, though he'd be wrong.

"You won't be so pretty, Work'us, when Cromwell's done with you."

That was Noah, all about revenge and satisfaction that Oliver had been, once again, brought so low. That didn't matter; where was Jack?

Jack was at the door to the main room, closing it behind him, coming into the kitchen slowly and carefully, as though he'd just been scolded for being too loud indoors. He carried Oliver's books under one arm, with the red scarf trailing down his leg to the floor.

His hat was askew, and when he looked at Oliver, his expression was blank, and Oliver couldn't tell whether Jack was in on this or merely surprised by it. Either way, he was blocking the only other exit, and Oliver didn't know which pained him worse, Cromwell's blows or Jack's potential betrayal.

"What do you want?" asked Oliver, trying for boldness even though he felt faint, as though he couldn't get enough air.

"You 'ave an inheritance, I 'ear, my dear boy." Cromwell came close, his broad shoulders rising tall, his boots making hard sounds on the stone floor. "An' I want it, so 'and it over."

Oliver backed away, even though he knew it was the wrong thing to do; it would just make Cromwell come at him with even more cruelty.

"I don't have it till I'm twenty-one."

"Then I keeps you locked up till then, eh?" Cromwell took off his jacket and rolled his sleeves above his forearms, until the muscles threatened to break through the thin cotton. "A good return on my investment, I'd say. A few pounds a year to keep you on an' a three thousand return? I don't 'ave to be good at numbers to know I'll come out ahead. So which is it to be, 'and it over now or later?"

"It's in the Bank of England," said Oliver. He grit his teeth as he saw Cromwell's fists bunching up. "I can't acquire it, and you can't mean to imprison me till then, someone will—"

"Someone will miss you?" Cromwell's smile was full of teeth, and he snapped at Oliver. "No one will. You've been dismissed from your position, an' no one cares where you are. Or where you'll end up."

One of his fists smashed into Oliver's face, and Oliver staggered from the blow, tasting blood, barely able to keep his feet.

"You're only an orphan that nobody loves anyway, ain't you, Oliver?"

With another grin, Cromwell grabbed Oliver by the collar of his jacket and hit him hard enough to send Oliver tumbling to the floor. But Cromwell's grasp was solid, and he hit Oliver again; Oliver hung from his fist, blinking, blood seeping between his teeth.

When Cromwell pulled back his fist again, Jack suddenly flung the bundle of books and scarf aside and launched himself at Cromwell, hitting and kicking, but Cromwell swung back enough to smack Jack across the face, sending him flying, his head landing with a thunk against the wall.

"*No*," roared Oliver. No one, not even a hulking criminal such as Cromwell, had the right to hurt Jack. The awful rage, so long kept chained inside him like an animal, escaped.

Oliver shifted his weight as Cromwell stepped back. There was enough movement for Oliver to wriggle free, grabbing up the first heavy thing his hands could find.

This should have been a cast-iron frying pan, but it wasn't. It was the cleaver, still stained with old blood and bits of dried meat, and Oliver hesitated only a moment as he hefted it in his hands and swung the sharp edge at Cromwell's shoulder. He felt the blade sink in, felt sick and glad at the same time, and watched the bright slash of crimson stain through the cotton of Cromwell's shirt.

Oliver pulled the blade out, hefted the handle, and swung it again as Cromwell lifted his arm. The cleaver sank into Cromwell's ribs, hard enough that Oliver could feel it hitting bone, could hear bone breaking. Breathing hard, Cromwell staggered, and Oliver hit him again, this time in the leg, the blade going in heavily, sinking to the bone. Cromwell's trousers gaped open as they became stained dark red, and, without a sound, Cromwell crumpled to the floor.

Stepping back, Oliver flicked the cleaver in his hand, holding it away so that none of the blood would drip on him. There was a tiny spot on the cuff of his shirtsleeve, but that was all. No one would have visible cause to stop him when he ran.

Feeling the energy spilling through him, he advanced on Noah, swinging the cleaver in front of him. Blood spattered from the cleaver onto the floor.

"You'll not say a word of this to anyone," said Oliver, in a clear, level voice that did not quite sound like his own.

"What?" Noah's voice was high, and he pressed himself back against the door to the alley, his eyes wide as he took in the lake of blood that was spreading across the stone floor around Cromwell's fallen body.

"I said, you'll not say a word of this to anyone, or I'll give you a reason to regret it." His voice was low, as though coming from a deep place inside, and now that he'd stopped moving, he felt cold all over.

He laid the cleaver down, where it sat, bloody and precarious, on the top of a pile of dishes. When Noah moved back, Oliver kept one eye on him while he went over to Jack, whose eyes were open and blinking. When Oliver pulled him, Jack sat up and then got to his feet, rubbing his jaw one moment and the back of his head the next.

"What did you do?" Jack was taking in the body on the floor, which was barely moving, though there were low, jagged sounds coming from it.

Oliver shook his head. His heart was pounding now, and all the strength he'd had when he'd hit Cromwell had left him. He felt dizzy, and his breath felt sharp in his throat, as though he were going to faint.

He wanted to say something that the heroes in books always did, about having just vanquished his foe, but he couldn't even begin to form the words. So he merely pointed at the cleaver and at Cromwell, who was making small, twitching motions with his fingers.

Oliver was going to try to talk. He truly was. He was going to explain it to Jack, so that Jack didn't think he was a killer by nature.

"No matter what," said Oliver, his throat catching over the words. "I couldn't let him hurt you, couldn't *let* him—"

"Never mind it now," said Jack.

He took Oliver's hand and rubbed some of the quickly drying blood on his own hands, making it look like old paint or rust from an iron gate, nothing that would alarm anyone. Then he tucked Oliver's arm under his own. The blow to the head had left him pale, but he bent to grab his hat, and Oliver's hat, and the books, and the red scarf, and took Oliver by the elbow.

"You," Jack said to Noah, in that tone he used when all was not as he thought it should be, such as when there were people in his alcove, or that Oliver needed fresh air and it wasn't happening fast enough.

Noah moved to the side so they could use the door. His face was paper white, and he was shaking all over, but somehow resolute, he said, "Whether 'e lives or dies, you'll be a wanted man, you know that, don't you, Work'us?"

"And you'll be there to collect the reward, won't you, Noah."

Oliver realized he was lifting his hand to reach for the cleaver so he could use it on Noah because he'd be damned if some charity boy was going to terrorize him into giving himself up.

Jack grabbed Oliver's arm and made him lower it and started walking. Jack reached for the door knob. The knob was old and rusty, and Jack had to tug it a few times to get it to open. The doorjamb splintered apart, letting the rain in, and the freshet of wind, which, coming from the alley, smelled none too fresh.

Jack stepped out into the small, muddy courtyard and slammed the door behind him. Then he looked at Oliver as if to ask him the way.

"I need to cross the river," said Oliver, his mind still barely able to think clearly enough to consider it. "I need to leave London."

It was a strange conversation to be having as the rain spattered against the cobblestones, and the dank smell of mud and of cesspits rose around them in the sheltered yard. But he let Jack lead him to the pump at the end of the alley, where Oliver took off his jacket and washed his face and hands under the thin, icy stream while Jack pumped the handle.

When Oliver put his jacket back on, he was shivering all over, his teeth chattering, unable to stop, until Jack came up to him, close enough that Oliver could feel his warm breath against his cheek.

"Let's get you out of here," Jack said, tugging on Oliver's sleeve to get Oliver to continue down the alley, down backstreets that Oliver had never known existed before that moment.

The way was tricky and narrow and dark, with glimpses of the river between the gaps in the buildings, but Jack knew where he was headed, and he took Oliver with him, all the way keeping Oliver close to him, till they came to the narrow grey stones of Whitefriars Stairs.

"This way." Jack pointed to the last bit of dripping, brick-lined alley, a thin path between the buildings. Then Jack moved on, with Oliver behind, following the narrow passage between the warehouses along the wharf until they got to Blackfriars Bridge.

They stopped on the north side of the bridge. The river

moved beneath the great grey-stone arches, swelling with the rain and the movement of ships and skiffs, tumbling against its own banks, threatening to spill over into the streets of the City. Oliver remembered that day of his release from Newgate when Jack, with his rain-kissed face, had smiled at him, and, for a moment, the world had seemed a good place.

The world was no longer a good place, but as water dripped down his neck and beneath his shirt, he looked at Jack. And for a long moment, next to the roar of the river, Jack looked at him.

Those green eyes were serious, and they wanted to know, without any words at all, whether or not Oliver was going to be all right. Perhaps Jack thought it wouldn't have done for him to have asked this aloud, but he asked it all the same. Oliver lifted his hand and touched Jack's neck. Just once, then let his hand fall away.

"You don't have to follow me, you know," said Oliver, frustration cracking in his voice; he hated having to explain his decision over and over again only to have Jack tell him no. He had to make it clear that he couldn't stay. "I'm leaving London."

"I'm goin' with you," said Jack. There was a bright flush on his face, which Oliver could interpret as trepidation or merely the cold air by the river.

"But I've asked and asked, and every time you said no to me." Oliver felt the heat of anger as he said this, unable to believe what Jack was saying. "You said you weren't coming with me because London was your home."

"It ain't home," said Jack simply. "Not to me. Not if you're not in it."

This caught Oliver's heart and all the air in his lungs until he could barely breathe. But as he opened his mouth to remark upon Jack's statement, or at the very least, confirm it, Jack tipped back his head, giving it a jerk to straighten his low top hat.

There was a small light in his eyes, some shy, uncertain thing, and Oliver knew he could say what he wanted, in his heart, about how it would gladden his life if Jack were to come with him, all the way to find his mother's people. Yet at the same time, Jack was not one for soft, sweet words or poetry.

"Do you mean it?" asked Oliver.

"'Course I do," said Jack, as if this were the most obvious thing, and Oliver was merely being stupid not to have seen it long ago.

Feeling undone by this, Oliver looked at the river and scrubbed his eyes with the back of his hand, telling himself it was the sharpness of the wind that pricked at him and not the dangerous secret that he and Jack carried between them. Or the fact that, at least for a while, while on the road to a destiny he did not quite understand, he would not be alone.

"Is that all right with you, then, Nolly?" Jack asked in a perfectly clear voice, as if nothing were amiss or strange about their plan to walk out of London and into the unknown without so much as a backward glance.

Oliver made himself nod, swallowing as he did so, and then looked at Jack, who was looking at him with that jaunty hat atop his head and the cut-back gentleman's tails, that bright blue waistcoat, all parts of Jack that resonated in Oliver's head, and in his heart.

And in Jack's eyes, green and sharp against the grey weather, Oliver, just for a flickering second, saw himself as Jack saw him, someone worth being with, someone worth caring for. Then Jack smiled, as he did, with bright teeth and sparking eyes, and so Oliver nodded. The smile was Jack's message to him.

"We'll go together, you and I," Oliver said, keeping his voice steady. "All the way to the sea."

"Have you ever seen it?" asked Jack, pulling on his lapels, tipping his head back. "I lived on it for months, you know, bein' hextricated an' come back again, an' then next to it for years an' years, so I could show you."

"I'd like that," said Oliver. "I'd like that very much."

He looked at Jack's mouth, at the bruise forming from

Cromwell's smack, at Jack's hands, grimy from the streets, and thought of what books had said about the sea, and of drawings he'd seen of the houses ringed around a cove of blue water. They might not ever find his mother's people, but at least he'd be out of London, where nothing good had ever lasted, and Jack would be with him.

Oliver stepped onto the bridge, watching Jack out of the corner of his eyes, then Jack tugged on his coat sleeve to stop him. Frowning, Oliver watched as Jack put the books on the damp stone of the bridge, as books ought not to be treated that way, but perhaps Jack didn't know that. Oliver opened his mouth to tell him, but when Jack took up the scarf from the books and furled it on the air, a bright red sail in the grey, rain-dappled sky, he stopped.

Jack took the scarf and stepped close to hook it around Oliver, tucking the soft wool deep into the space between the coat's collar and Oliver's neck. Then Jack looped it, in the jaunty way that he did, in the way that had no sense of fashion, but felt, indeed, incredibly warm.

"I reckon you can have it back, then," said Jack.

Oliver did not quite know what to say to that. The scarf was worn from wear and dirty from Jack's hands, and yet Oliver felt warm, not just against the chill air over the river, but against the lonely places inside of him.

"Thank you," he said, not quite trusting his voice to say anything more than that. To cover the flush on his face, he bent to pick up the books, tucking them comfortably beneath his arm, and straightened up to look at Jack.

Jack nodded, jerking his hat aright on his head, and smoothed his lapels one more time, not saying anything. Then he turned to Oliver and tugged on his jacket and fell into pace beside him.

Side by side, they crossed the strong stone bridge, with the traffic flowing past them and the river flowing under them, the rain coming down, a grey curtain, till they could see the City of

London no more, and the damp, paved street stretched out in front of them.

~

WOULD YOU LIKE TO READ MORE ABOUT THE ROMANCE between Oliver and Jack? Pick up *At Lodgings in Lyme* today! (https://readerlinks.com/l/2237535)

~

WOULD YOU LIKE TO READ A COWBOY ROMANCE? CHECK OUT *The Foreman and the Drifter*, the first book in my Farthingdale Ranch series. (https://readerlinks.com/l/1703675)

~

WOULD YOU LIKE TO READ MORE ABOUT THE BACKGROUND OF how I wrote *Fagin's Boy*? I have liner notes! Click here. (https://claims.prolificworks.com/free/Tp8ukUDP )

# JACKIE'S NEWSLETTER

Would you like to sign up for my newsletter?

Subscribers are alway the first to hear about my new books. You'll get behind the scenes information, sales and cover reveal updates, and giveaways.

As my gift for signing up, you will receive two short stories, one sweet, and one steamy!

It's completely free to sign up and you will never be spammed by me; you can opt out easily at any time.

To sign up, visit the following URL:

https://www.subscribepage.com/JackieNorthNewsletter

facebook.com/jackienorthMM
twitter.com/JackieNorthMM
pinterest.com/jackienorthauthor
bookbub.com/profile/jackie-north
amazon.com/author/jackienorth
goodreads.com/Jackie_North
instagram.com/jackienorth_author

# AUTHOR'S NOTES ABOUT THE STORY

Long ago, I once saw a movie called *Oliver!* (1969), and fell in love with the character of Oliver Twist. I also fell in love with the lad who seemed to care a great deal for Oliver, and that was the Artful Dodger (also known as Jack Dawkins).

To say this movie affected me for years is an understatement. The book you have just read, as well as the others in this series, are a testament to my devotion to Oliver and Jack. So much so that in April 2006, I began to toy with the idea of writing about the affection I saw between these two characters.

In 2009, or thereabouts, I read a book called *Mr. Timothy* by Louis Bayard, which is a sequel to *A Christmas Carol* by Charles Dickens. It's a fun read, fast paced, interesting, full of great details, but what I loved about it was how it took another look at the relationship between Tiny Tim (the titular character all grown up) and Ebenezer Scrooge.

I was inspired to imagine that Mr. Bayard had just given me full blow permission to write my book and revisit the relationship between Oliver and Jack. However, according to my records, it was not until October, 2011, that I seriously started writing *Fagin's Boy*.

Around the same time was when I first actually read all of

*Oliver Twist* by Charles Dickens, and discovered the horrible truth that in addition to Nancy and Bill Sykes being killed, Fagin himself did not live past the pages of the book. In many movie versions, including *Oliver!* (1969), Fagin supposedly lives. And, not only that, with great poetic license, Jack and Fagin are back together on the streets, living their lives.

In truth, Jack is deported midway through the book, and is never seen nor heard from again. Imagine my horror and my shock! Something had to be done, and I was going to be the one to do it, to correct this insalubrious error on Dickens' part.

Around 2012, I read a snippet in Time Magazine about the rise of m/m romance. This gave me permission to go full-bore on the romance between Oliver and Jack. I wrote the story and finished it; it was around 100,000 words.

With some amazing feedback from beta readers, I began to reshape the story. And again, refining it as best I could.

Today the story is around 170,000 words because I had a lot to say about those two lads. I wanted them to be together, I wanted them to be happy.

Welp.

While Oliver and Jack are relatively happy, *Fagin's Boy* ends on a cliffhanger and the ideas I wanted to write about in *Fagin's Boy* turned out to need their own story, and thus, there are five more books after this one.

I hope you have enjoyed the journey thus far.

# A LETTER FROM JACKIE

Hello, Reader!

Thank you for reading *Fagin's Boy,* the first book in my Oliver & Jack series.

If you enjoyed the book, I would love it if you would let your friends know so they can experience the romance between Oliver and Jack.

If you leave a review, I'd love to read it! You can send the URL to: Jackienorthauthor@gmail.com

*Jackie*

facebook.com/jackienorthMM
twitter.com/JackieNorthMM
instagram.com/jackienorth_author
pinterest.com/jackienorthauthor
bookbub.com/profile/jackie-north
amazon.com/author/jackienorth
goodreads.com/Jackie_North

# ABOUT THE AUTHOR

Jackie North has written since grade school and spent years absorbing mainstream romances. Her dream was to write full time and put her English degree to good use.

As fate would have it, she discovered m/m romance and decided that men falling in love with other men was exactly what she wanted to write about.

Her characters are a bit flawed and broken. Some find themselves on the edge of society, and others are lost. All of them deserve a happily ever after, and she makes sure they get it!

She likes long walks on the beach, the smell of lavender and rainstorms, and enjoys sleeping in on snowy mornings.

In her heart, there is peace to be found everywhere, but since in the real world this isn't always true, Jackie writes for love.

*Connect with Jackie:*

https://www.jackienorth.com/
jackie@jackienorth.com

facebook.com/jackienorthMM

twitter.com/JackieNorthMM

pinterest.com/jackienorthauthor

bookbub.com/profile/jackie-north

amazon.com/author/jackienorth

goodreads.com/Jackie_North

instagram.com/jackienorth_author

Printed in Great Britain
by Amazon

56494722R20310